More From Meta Mad Books!

Translations:

From Swann's Side (1913)
Volume One of *In Search of Lost Tim*
Newly Translated into English
by Marcel Proust
9781763641723

Siddhartha: An Indian Poem (1922)
by Hermann Hesse
Translated by David R. Smith
9781763726260

Steppenwolf
By Herman Hesse
Translated by David R. Smith
9781763726253

I was in Great Perplexity:
New Translations of my Favorite Kafka Stories
Translated by David R. Smith
9781763641716

Original Fiction:

River: A Dark Romance in the Kishotenketsu Style
Mia Sandalwood
9781763512160

The Book Depository:
Tales from the Children of the Egg, 2nd Ed.
David Apricot
9781763641709

John Free and Intervention X: The Bodhisattva Wars
by David Apricot
9781763622913

Saint Susan is a prequel to *The Campbell Club* (2024). *Saint Susan* is set in the years 1978 to 1981, when Robbie is a teenager, while *The Campbell Club* takes place in the years 1985 to 1989, when he attempts university. You can read either book first.

The Campbell Club:
An Historical Romance, 1985
David R. Smith
9781763726277

SAINT SUSAN

Mesa My Heart

KICKSHAW

David R. Smith
Meta Mad Books

ISBN: 978-1-7638539-5-9
Cover artwork by the author.
5 x 8 inches
Typeset in California FB 10pt.

Second Edition. (Parts 3, 6, and 8 have been largely re-written).

This book is a work of fiction. Any resemblance by characters to actual persons, living or dead, is purely coincidental.

No "AI" was used in the writing of this book. I wrote every word.

For my sister, who did not get to go

SAINT SUSAN

Mesa My Heart

David R. Smith

There once was a Saint named Susan,
Who found her true self through confusion,
But when love came too near
She held it too dear—
And drove a nail into love's false illusion

A Novel of Forbidden Love. And Cafeteria Food.

The Parts of the Chicken

PART ONE — *The Long-Distance Prat Fall*......................2

PART TWO — *California Reaming*......................62

PART THREE — *Long Showers*......................143

PART FOUR — *A Conspiracy of Ground Meat*..........163

PART FIVE — *Inner Astronauts*......................182

PART SIX — *Mr. Chunkie and the Dragon's Den*........197

PART SEVEN — *Night of the Living Chick*..................207

PART EIGHT — *Death by Hand Job*......................242

PART NINE — *The Piano Murder Mystery*..................257

PART TEN — *Kumbh Mela Mayhem*......................286

PART ELEVEN — *Rope-a-dope at the Senior Prom* 298

PART TWELVE, SAINT SUSAN — *(Backstory)*.......334

FINALE — *'A Very Memorable Yearbook'*..................340

PART ONE — The Long-Distance Prat Fall

There once was a fine young black filly
Who thought science-fiction was silly
But when she got made
By an alien's blade
Her bum was left feeling quite chilly

I had completely forgotten my father's face. My mother held out the phone—it was a wall phone in the kitchen with a cord like a long tan umbilicus—and asked me to talk to him. The year was 1978 and I was a teenager. I was 15.

"Hello? Dad?"

"Hey son, how are you?"

"I'm good. I was just watching *Star Trek*. How are you?"

"Just fine. It's nice to hear your voice. I'm sorry it's been so long. Am I interrupting your dinner?"

"No, it's OK."

"Which episode is it, the *Star Trek*?"

"What? Oh, the one where Spock is, you know, kind of getting a hard-on."

He laughed. "Ah yes. The *Pon farr*. Well, I suppose it happens to us all.... Listen, your mom and I were talking. There's an opportunity that has come up. I was wondering if you would like to go to school out here."

"You mean, like, move out there?"

"Yeah. There's a prep school up in the foothills near where I live, a private school. It's called Kickshaw. It's a boy's school. I've got more money these days, so this is something I could do for you. I was wondering if you'd like to go."

"Gee Dad, that sounds amazing. I don't know. Is this a limited time offer?"

He laughed. "Well, probably, we have to apply and do the paperwork, and all that. I know this is all a bit sudden. But you don't have to worry. It's mostly, you know, how much money you have. That's how this world of ours works. So we can probably get you in."

"What, are you rich? You trying to say you're rich?"

He laughed again. "No, son, not at all. I just sell real estate. But the market here in Santa Barbara has really heated up."

"Well. That's cool." I didn't know what to think about all this. As I said, it had been a long time and I couldn't quite remember my dad. There were no pictures of him in my mother's house, perhaps for obvious reasons, and actually in those days we had fewer photos. Photography cost money and was a thing you saved for a special event. We had a lot of Polaroids somewhere, of course. But my mom hid those.

For lack of images I imagined my father being a bit like James T. Kirk; dark haired, well-built, perhaps a bit less athletic than Kirk but still a dynamic character, an action figure. A leader. My last understanding, formed years before, was that he was working as an auto mechanic. I remembered in a very child-like disconnected way visiting him at work, with my mother holding my hand, we went into a Volkswagen showroom. And we found him in the immaculately clean mechanics bay in the back, and he gave me a bent, burned-out steel engine valve as a souvenir.

"I think your mom's OK with it," he was saying. "With you coming out here. No pressure. Just talk to her, OK? Talk to her and then she can let me know what you both decide."

My mother and father divorced when I was quite young, and she remarried soon after to an electrical engineer, Sam Harmon was his name. He was gray on the sides, like a battleship painted gray, and physically quite a strong specimen of *homo economicus*; I noticed his arms the most. They were short farm-boy arms with thick forearms that had absorbed a farmer's tan, like Popeye, from the Florida sun, and his stubby fingers dangled on the end of the arms next to solid thumbs. His barrel-like chest reminded me a little bit of

Tregonsee the Rigellian from the *Lensman* series. Sam, my mother said, had worked on farms in Kansas when he was growing up. Or maybe it was Iowa. He loved beefsteak and my mother despaired of keeping him in hibachi charcoal; it was part of the regular ritual to burn the sweet, fattened flesh over hot coals. Yahweh certainly would have been satisfied by the smell of that pyre. Beefsteak with butter on it. Corn on the cob. Coleslaw cold from the fridge. Sam worked for Lockheed, he wore a white vinyl pocket protector over the white shirt pockets of his white work shirts, and he sometimes wore a black suit. His Oxford shoes were always beautifully shined, black and polished, like black stone, perhaps even onyx, but I never saw him doing that work; he must have had it done by a shine. I was going to say, "shine boy," which is what we said then. So, yes, his shoes were gloriously shined, I could even imagine in my mind's eye the shine working those shoes with spit and polish. I wouldn't mind shining shoes, personally. I think honest work is honest work. But anyway, I'm getting off track.

Soon after they married, we moved to Florida for his job. He left in the mornings for work, and returned tired in the evenings to a big tumbler of booze. It was always the same drink, Vodka and Seven Up. My mother would mix it for him over ice. The tumbler was as big as a tub. I don't think they were Tupperware, although we had a lot of Tupperware in the kitchen in those days.

I did not use those tumblers, obviously they were too big but they were also not mine, I had my own cups, also of the same green plastic, for my juice and my milk. Apparently he, Sam, helped keep the rockets that seemed to regularly launch from pads out at Cape Kennedy, from falling down. I gradually understood more about his job over time but never the reality of it. And it didn't matter to me. I could easily invent a story about what he did without too much effort, if that were required.

I had two younger siblings who were fathered by Sam: Jackie and Sam Junior. I was probably ten years older than Jackie. They were small and kept my mother continually on the run.

So that was our household, and my mother, who was a stay-at-home mom (as we say today, but then it was just an ordinary mom) was very protective of us. When my dog, Kwai-Chang, was killed by a Copperhead snake, she did not tell me about it. What happened was, this dog, he was a Beagle, the dog was in the habit of digging its way under the back yard fence.

There was nothing past that fence but hardwood hammock, a dense wooded area that was mostly shaded due to the thick undergrowth. In years to come, that whole area was cleared and houses built out (as I discovered later when I visited my childhood home, that woodland fun zone was completely gone 20 years later). But at this point in time, it was "undeveloped" by which we mean, "nature not yet ransacked for profit." I remember playing out there and the joy of cutting a path with a machete through thick mazes of native blackberry, sucking my cuts from the thorns. It was great fun and my play friends and I would tromp around looking for old, abandoned orange groves filled with dirty acid fruit, or build a plank bridge over a stinking drainage ditch full of crawfish and African violets.

The dog did not go on these sorties, which come to think of it may have been my fault and the reason the dog was always trying to get out. But at that age I was only concerned about myself and not the feelings or needs of others.

One day Kwai-Chang dug himself out and disappeared for several hours. I came home from school to find him not in the house as per usual; he knew my routine, and would be waiting. But today, no. Looking in the backyard, I saw nothing, but then I heard a weak whining sound. Walking to the fence line, I saw Kwai-Chang was laying in the escape hole he had dug, but his head was oriented in, not out. He was trying to pull himself into the yard. His body was covered in blood.

I ran into the house and cried, "Mom! Come quickly! Hurry!" and she rushed out and we wrapped the dog in an old blanket and my mother drove the big green Ford Galaxie 500 to the vet. That car was huge. I don't think people today understand the concept of a V-8 engine. It was like something Darth Vader would have driven. The thing looked like a World War I tank. I thought at first Kwai-Chang had been shot with a shotgun, as he had little marks on him that looked like maybe from birdshot; but no, those were the bite marks of a Copperhead. The dog was taken into the office proper and I sat stoically in the waiting room as my mom, carrying the old blanket now bloodied, disappeared with the vet. After a while she returned and explained that Kwai-Chang "needed to stay at the vet to get well." And I did not hear more about him. A few days passed and it seemed that he wasn't coming home.

"Mom, how is Kwai-Chang?" I looked at her face but she did not look back.

"He's still getting better, son," she said. She was looking away, focusing on her sewing. I didn't understand why.

"But mom, can we go and see him?"

This seemed to fracture her resolve. She looked at me and spoke very softly. "Robbie, Kwai-Chang died."

"What?"

"He died a few minutes after we took him into the vet's office."

"But why didn't you tell me? I didn't get to see him." I started crying then.

"I'm sorry, Robbie."

After that my mother was unwilling to let me go into the woods, but I did it anyway. I just didn't tell her. Occasionally I would come home with a tick bite, the little fucker embedded in my neck or on the crown of my head, and she would tweezer it off. (So, obviously, she knew what I was up to). But she didn't say anything and just made a huge fuss about the tick. She had a morbid fear about things like that. She was convinced ticks spread terrible diseases, just like the mosquitoes she obsessed over when they landed on Sam Junior, and maybe that was true; but none of those fears were going to stop me from my fun with a machete.

There are a few more things that are worth reporting about my life in Florida before I left for Kickshaw. These stories will have some bearing on what happened later.

First of all, because my stepfather was white collar, because he was well-to-do (at least to a certain extent, for example, we had a sailboat), because we lived in an expensive subdivision where there were only white people, I had very little interaction with African Americans. My play friends called them niggers or bogeymen, because they were ignorant evangelical clowns with Klansmen fathers, but I didn't have those bad habits of language; I was a Californian (that's how I thought about it).

That is to say, at age 15 I thought Californians were more enlightened beings. Perhaps they are, or were. Hate had no place in my vocabulary then, or even now. Nevertheless, there were very few Black people in the immediate vicinity. Even Middle School did not do much to expose me to the wider world outside our White Meat Colonel Sanders Chicken enclave.

It was not until my last year in Florida, my 9th grade in high school, at Titusville High, that I shared a classroom with Black kids. That was a change.

What I'm saying is, what I thought about race was a moot point—my high and mighty attitude about being an enlightened and noble Californian among Klansmen was not being tested. Certainly ours was a clearly demarcated white neighborhood; it was not for them. The place was called Hickory Hills; that was the name of the subdivision. It stood alone and isolated down a length of highway, perhaps ten miles out from Titusville, and I have validated it, there were actual hickory tree species in that part of Florida. So the name was not completely fanciful. Still, they cut every-thing down to build the houses. There were no hickory trees that I can remember. Anyway, going back to the Black people, my time of testing had not yet arrived and was per-haps only to occur by chance.

We lived on a street called Mahogany Lane. Now, Ma-hogany Lane (ironically enough) was where the first Black family moved in. It was my mother who made this joke. "There are no Mahogany trees, but now there sure are Ma-hogany neighbors." That happened in the year before my Dad's phone call.

I have to go back a bit and explain that I inherited a paper route from the next-door neighbor's son. He was consider-ably older than I was—I think he was 17—and was moving out, had a car—I believe a Camaro—and he was moving on to parts unknown—it was not like me to inquire—and so the offer of a paper route came to me. Perhaps my mother organized this. At any rate, I started delivering papers. I did this on a bicycle, and wore a double-sided canvas paperboy carrier that was loaded thick with papers.

This business of delivering papers is worth going into be-cause of the pure, unadulterated joy at the execution of the throw: I would first fold and band the papers with green rubber bands, the ink staining my palms and fingertips, and then pack my bag up, front and back, and put it on. If it was a rainy morning, there would be an additional step to put the papers into plastic bags. I then mounted my bike after stuffing additional papers into a basket that spanned the front tire on either side, and rode around the neighborhood, in the dark, under stars or moon, or silent cloud. As I ap-proached a house that needed a paper I drew one from the canvas carrier, and launched it in the direction of the house with a single flowing circular motion. The paper projectile explosively gained velocity from the unfolding of my arm; it exited my hand with a satisfying snap. It then flew through the air with grace and aplomb, I felt, and eventually im-pacted on the target destination—a front door, a driveway, or perhaps a chosen step. This throwing technique was actually quite similar to the way a cricket ball is bowled; there was a lot of wrist in it. I know, however, that this comparison to cricket will do no good for an American. Throwing a football might come close, but I don't think so. At any rate, it was magical and the best part of the whole paper delivery experience. I loved to throw papers. From my vantage point, my "POV," I watched the papers exit my hand and leave my great circle (the circle surrounding my body, which I could feel); the paper then began to spin on its axis, like a planet, and with some time and practice, I could get it to land anywhere I wanted it to land.

Later I understood this was Zen; the exact analog experience to the archery in *Zen and the Art of Archery* by Eugen Herrigel. I did not consciously link this action with *Zen and the Art of Archery*, however, even though I later owned the book. It was only at Kickshaw, when this was applied to the frisbee, that I connected these things. And indeed, this skill was probably why I became friends with Christian. But that story must wait.

So, I was a paperboy. As most people know, the way the business works, or at least how it worked in the old days, was that you got a bill that you had to pay for the papers, and then you had to go around and "collect" that month's cost in cash from your customers; and finally whatever was left after whatever fees and charges for late papers or missed papers, and so on—the company rip-off, they took whatever they could—then what was left was your profit. For an adult, with one or two paper routes, it was hardly food money.

But for me, this job was wildly lucrative. I made something like fifty dollars a month—an astounding sum for a 14-year-old in those days. Sure, I worked seven days a week and had to get up at 5 AM, *but I had money*. Not my family, me personally. It changed everything about my social standing. My play friends were stunned when I was able to buy a new ten-speed bike, but I told everyone I was saving for a telescope. That much was true; I fancied myself as a bit of a future scientist; perhaps an astronomer. I certainly loved natural history. The money made me feel good, too, just for its own sake.

Now, I can complete the story I started in regard to the Johnsons. Yes, the Black family there on Mahogany Lane were the Johnsons. "The negros," my stepfather said, "have wormed their way in." He said this when he thought I was not within earshot. But I heard him alright.

And then the Johnsons signed up for the paper. I saw that the order had come through on my morning paperwork, the sheet on top of the bundle, and spent a moment looking at the address, just to be sure. It did not occur to me that I would blackball them, as I had with the Hendersons, whose son was a bully. It was my route, after all. But I was no bigot, like Sam. That was for sure. I would have delivered to space aliens even. So of course the Black people could be part of my route.

And so I started delivering to them. I was very conscientious; I wanted my service to them to be without flaw. Not a drop of rain on that paper, not a loss in the bushes, or under a car, ever. Always on the doorway, always easy to find.

But when it came time to collect, I didn't do that. An ordinary person would have wanted their money. But the fact is I was scared. It was a stupid ridiculous fear, the kind a child has. I just didn't collect from them. I would see their ticket on the collection book, and pass it by, as if it were unreal. And I walked right past their house when I was collecting, keeping my face turned away, as if to avoid the possibility of seeing a human being within the house. I avoided that house like a plague in the daytime. It was fine in the early hours of morning, when I was alone with my Zen and my paper folding and my Zen throwing technique using the great circle of my body, in the keen morning air, stars still in the sky, the sun still thinking whether it was reasonable to rise. But during the day, when someone might have been up and around in the big red house—yes, it was actually painted red, like in the Jimi Hendrix song—no. No way.

This irrational fear was not, however, entirely without cause. The reason was this: young Reggie Johnson, who was perhaps 16 or 17, very tall, very dark skinned (one of those African Americans who looks a bit like a Zulu as portrayed by natives in the 1964 film with Michael Caine, which I had seen on television), this young man came to the door. It was during a flurry of activity, a time of neighborhood connection, which seems to me was rare. It was Halloween. I was in charge of giving out candy after returning from my own Halloween walkabout. It was late, and most of the kids, indeed all of the younger neighborhood kids, had already come through. My younger siblings were already in bed. It was quiet and my assumption was my duties were completed, and I had just begun the all-important process of sorting the loot from my plastic jack-'o-lantern bucket—when the doorbell rang. It was Reggie Johnson, although at that moment I did not know that. "Shaka!" I cried.

It was indeed the case that Reggie had arrayed himself in a costume reminiscent of the murderous Zulu king, complete with spear and lion skin cape (this may be a false memory, but to be sure, he was very striking in appearance) and he shouted, "Trick or Treat!" as he held out the biggest Halloween candy bag I had ever seen. It was a white pillowcase, and it was three-quarters full at least with candy. This was far more than I had collected, and far more than anyone else I had seen all that night. I do not think I could have even hefted the bag, which he carried lightly and at his ease.

I put a miniature Snickers into his bag, ejecting it from my hand with a rapid flick of my fingers, and he was gone almost instantly, darting into the blackness of the night without a sound. His athleticism, height, and general demeanor in that costume were terrifying.

This irrational fear of the Johnsons continued for some period of time. It was like a weight I carried around, and I didn't tell anyone. Not my mom, and certainly not Sam.

But I was not fated to avoid contact with the Johnsons forever. It is in the nature of karma that what goes around comes around. And my test was about to begin. It happened one day when I was collecting. I was walking past the big red house, keeping my eyes turned away, when I heard a man's voice.

"Hey there, boy! Hey there!"

I turned and saw an older black man, perhaps he was fifty, gesturing towards me. He was wearing a suit and tie over his broad chest and wide belly, as if he was just home from work. The bottom of his crumpled suit pants rested on his black shined shoes. And indeed it was closer to the dinner hour, so his arrival made sense. I had foolishly crossed by his big red house at the wrong time. He came out of his doorway and accosted me. I stood there, frozen with terror. "Yes? Hello?"

"You there, son. Are you our paperboy?" His voice was thick with the South, like an Alabama rain had soaked his ancestors.

"Yes," I said.

"Well I am glad to know it. Come over here."

I had no choice then; I had to walk up towards the house. I came forward, and he held out his big hand. We shook hands, and his hand was warm and very large, like a man who could palm a basketball easily. "I am Clarence Johnson."

"Robert Gray. You can call me Robbie."

"Robbie. Thank you." He was smiling now. "I wanted to tell you how happy I am with the paper. It always arrives very early. I like that. I get up early. And when it rains, it is always wrapped in plastic and safe on my porch."

"Yes, sir," I said.

"But I had a question."

"Sir?" Now I knew I was in for it.

"I notice you don't come and collect."

"No sir," I said. I looked down at the concrete driveway and didn't say anything.

"But why not, son?"

Then, suddenly, I realized the first beginnings of my genius, which was to spin a story, to spin a tale worthy of the great Ulysses. I would lie my way out of this. But I did not quite see it that way as a bad thing, but as Salvation. I was not lying; I was saving my ass.

"Well, sir, you see, to my knowledge you are the first black family in the neighborhood. That is an occasion. And I wanted you to feel welcome. I wanted you to feel, perhaps, that you had a friend here. But, I am very shy, sir, as you can see. I was too shy to say anything."

He looked at me with a peculiar gaze, as if he did not quite swallow my bullshit story. But then, all of a sudden, it seemed he had accepted it. His face changed. "Well, I'll be." He shook his head again. "I'll be. Lord." He then turned and called out to his wife. "Gladis, come on out here." And then an older black woman, who had a tremendous girth, like a beach ball on stilts, with thick legs and small feet that seemed completely incapable of supporting such a massive weight, came forward. She peered at me from behind her husband, and turned her head to see around him, and then smiled as if she were looking at a small puppy. "Why Clarence, who have you got there?"

"This is our paper boy. Robbie is his name."

"Oh? So that is a mystery solved."

"But listen, this boy has not been asking for collection. He says he is giving us a paper gratis."

"Gratis?" she said. "Gratis?" It seemed possible she did not know the meaning of this word. Either that or the concept was so distant from her experience that she did not immediately recognize the word's meaning.

I piped up then, holding strongly to my lie. "Yes Ma'am. Welcome to the neighborhood."

"Well, isn't that something," she said. "I don't know what to say."

"This boy is a wonder," said the man. "But son, I cannot take your charity. Even though it is good will and most Christian. I must pay you for your services. Come."

"But, it is all right sir," I said, vaguely.

"No, no. Absolutely not. Come with me." And he gestured for me to follow him. That gesture was irreconcilable to my previous way of being. Nothing could be done but to go with him.

We went into the Big Red House (as I thought of it), which it turned out was not so dissimilar in plan from Sam's and my mother's house, that is, not so dissimilar to my own. It was very well appointed but there were some differences. The house was clearly larger. There was a stair running up where we had none. But otherwise the plan seemed similar. The smells in the house were also very different: there was a smell I later understood was okra, and other components of Southern and Cajun cooking, such as oregano, chillies, the sweet smell of grits and bacon and biscuits. I had never eaten any of those things and had no idea what the smells signified at that time; but they were not necessarily unpleasant.

"You ain't from Florida, are you, son?" said the man, looking over his shoulder.

"No sir, I'm from California."

"California? You hear that, Gladis? The boy is from California."

"Well, that's wonderful," the old woman said.

"Just let me get my wallet," Clarence was saying. "Alright now. How many months am I behind?"

"Uh, I'm not sure, let me see..." I consulted my ticket book. "Well, sir. I make it six months, sir."

"Six months? Oh my lord! You about put me in the poor house."

I did not say anything, for I was by this point somewhat overcome by it all.

"Well, no need to worry," he said, looking at my face. "No need to worry. Here you are, son. And here also is a little

bonus." He put a bill in my hand, it was a bill I was unfamil-
iar with, Benjamin Franklin was on the front.

"One hundred? But sir, I can't break this."

He laughed then. "You don't worry, little Robbie. Just
consider me covered for a while on my bill. Now we are all
caught up. Do you agree?"

"Well yes. Yes sir. Sir, of course."

He laughed again. "Good. Alright then, Robbie. Please
give my regards to your parents. They have raised a splendid
boy. One who knows how to say Sir and Ma'am. I like that.
I like that very much."

"Thank you, sir. Thank you."

I fled.

***

One of the things that came out of the money I raised
though my paper route was the opportunity to go book
shopping. And, yes, even to buy books, not just look at
them. For me, this was a delight, a kind of almost sexual—
but no, it was pure. Clean and wholesome. I never went and
gawked at the porn mags often piled in a back section if it
was a used bookstore. I had a serious intent, almost a religious feeling, about my reading. My interest in books
seemed to have something to do with the strong connections I felt through them. The people who wrote the
books—they were not present; in fact, many were not even
alive. But somehow they still spoke. Often, I can say, they
spoke much more clearly than any of the human beings I
had around me at the time.

My mother was very circumspect about those purchases.
It was not that she opposed reading—in fact, she was very
pleased I took an interest in learning. But, perhaps out of a
sense of thrift, or some internal sense of propriety and cor-
rectness, she believed the public library should have everything I needed. "There's no need to spend money, Robbie,"
she would say. "Save your money."

"For what, Mom?"

"For a rainy day. Save it for a rainy day." She always talked about saving for this much-vaunted rainy day. I guess I had no idea what that meant. "I'm sure the library can keep you busy with books to read." And of course, she was not entirely wrong, we went on many a Saturday. But the library did not necessarily give me everything I wanted. It was curated, and of course, this was Central Florida in the 1970s. Not exactly a fountain of exotic knowledge or a bounty of wisdom, in my way of thinking. For that I had to go further afield.

In those days—this was long before the streaming media madness that has engulfed us today—it was possible to know secret knowledge, to participate in secret, even clandestine knowledge—of certain books, of certain forbidden movies, and icons of popular culture. It was a time when the counterculture of the 1960s had infiltrated and percolated amongst the detritus, and produced a layer, almost a geological layer, thin, but provocative, of mysterious art, music, and thought. I was only vaguely aware of this crust in the beginning; but with time I became a prospector, a fossicker.

In my world, particles from this thin layer could eventually be seen in everything I was attracted to, like gold dust in the bottom of the pan, although at the time I did not know that. I was attracted to the East, to things mystical, to History, and Natural History fell into this category.

There was a book—oddly enough it was a book Sam had brought into the house as part of the marriage—a Natural History book. On the inside of the front cover was a spiral design, with the center being something like two billion years in the past; and the spiral wrapped around and showed the geological ages of the earth as then understood, step by step, and gave the names: Pre-Cambrian, Cambrian, Ordovician, Devonian, and so on. Millions of years were represented and fell into uneven periods of a few centimeters, collapsing and telescoping time. Small animals and plants were represented, fossils and strange creatures and things no one could imagine, but they tried.

Inside the book itself was the total summary of the understanding of Natural History as of 1934; that is, before the theory of plate tectonics. But very much after Darwin. At that time the generally accepted theory of earth science was Gradualism. The idea that a great flood filled the Mediterranean sea in a few days (which we know today is what actually occurred not once but repeatedly) would have been completely untenable due to the similarity of such a theory to that in the Bible. But for myself, it mattered not that the book was old or some of the theories presented had been superseded. What mattered was that I learnt how coral atolls form, and I learnt of the existence of giant clams, clams big enough to trap and drown a foolish, unsuspecting diver; and mysterious islands in the glowing South Seas; and I learnt of fossils and dinosaurs and ancient worlds when the earth was covered by ocean; slimy amphibians crawling onto land; and then later, when all the land was consolidated into one great continent, and so on.

These great vistas of time and space were to me a kind of mental and spiritual oasis in the past. I could go there any time I wanted to escape the abject stupidity and crudity of my current surroundings.

Besides science in this form, the geological, I was also treated to the wonders of the electrical, chemical, and biological worlds: vast empires of human knowledge and understanding, encompassing hundreds, if not thousands of lives of study and experimentation. These came to me through several channels. My mother, who maintained we should not spend money, and mainly wore clothing she made herself, nevertheless was not stingy at Christmas, and I got chemistry sets, electronic breadboards for constructing crystal radios and other gimmicks, plastic airplane kits to construct, rock tumblers, and all manner of science-oriented stuff. It seemed that Sam was probably behind some of this, because my mother would not have necessarily known about all of it. But on the other hand, the toy stores in those days were jam-packed with such things. It was an age different from this one, an age before the internet or computers or smartphones, in which we still had faith in doing, and the need to explore and find out for oneself, an age when individual opinion was discounted or not really valued at all. No one cared what I thought, or what my parents thought, even. What people cared about was Authority, such as the Bible or Darwin (depending on your persuasion). Or they cared about what the President said, or what they heard in church, or what was on the TV. There were only a few stations, so of course everybody watched the same programs. It was like a common language. Walter Cronkite. That was our truth. The idea that just anyone could express an opinion and have that somehow rise to the top—that would have been absurd. We wanted facts or faith. No one at that time would ever have preferred to express their own dull, idiotic opinions, or count that vomit as meaningful. Sure, we had the editorial pages. But those were more for comic relief.

Yes, facts, exploration. Knowledge, the great search for knowledge; or else the stolid faith in the eternal truths of the Good Book. Of course, in my case, it was the search. I thought the Good Book was drivel.

The great magical engines for some of this searching and exploration came in the form of catalogs for ordering chemical, biological, and general scientific supply: *Edmund Scientific*, is the one I remember best. I used to pore over this catalog, daydreaming for hours about Fresnel lenses and little pickled pigs and microscopes.

The climax of this exploration, at least for me, was the desire to buy a telescope. I fantasized about this purchase for a long time, and I may have already mentioned, taking on the paper route was originally motivated by the promise of sufficient funds to get one.

I put a lot of time into choosing a brand by reading *Sky and Telescope*. But then, when I shared my decision with Sam, he said my choice was questionable and pointed me in a different direction. I was not interested, but he then said if I bought the telescope design he favored (it was a very traditional Newtonian optics design from a particular company) then he would pay half of the cost; and so I reluctantly acceded to his requirement.

The telescope was ordered. Days passed, then weeks. Finally the great day arrived. Two massive crates, each one seemingly heavier than I was, arrived by truck.

The joy that I had constructing and erecting my telescope in the back yard was beyond description. It was suddenly possible to see and experience for myself a few of the things that were in the hallowed pages of the science books. Not everything was fully available; of course, Saturn, for example, was a smudge, and Jupiter a round blob with tiny flyspeck moons. But much of what was in the books came from time-lapse photography; I understood that concept of collecting more and more light. I had only the pure and continuous light of the distant objects in the sky, which I could catch in my own mirror and magnify with my own lens in real time. But it was glorious to do so because of the raw immediacy. The moon, in particular, was so bright and awe-inspiring a sight that my mind immediately seemed to expand. It changed me.

But my joy was punctuated by something that happened soon after. I was talking about the moon with Sam, and I expressed the idea that the moon does not rotate on its axis. "You see, Sam," (I always called my stepfather by his first name, not as Dad or anything) "the moon doesn't revolve. It can't. The face of the moon is always towards us."

But Sam shook his head. "No, that's not how it works."

"What?" I said.

"The moon definitely revolves around the earth. It has to."

"But it always faces us! It can't be rotating!"

"Yes, Robbie. It just rotates at the same speed as it re-volves. It's just an appearance."

"But that doesn't make any sense! Why would it do that?" I was beside myself at this point. But then Sam did some-thing that he probably shouldn't, which was to insist on winning the argument. He didn't explain the crucial fact as to why this happens (which is that planets are not homo-geneous, the weight inside a planet is not evenly distrib-uted, and so one side has slightly more mass and eventually is pulled to face the same side all the time, the heavier side, as its rotation gradually slows down). We kept going back and forth about it until I was in tears, and finally under-stood. It was only years later that I learned about the rea-son. But at the time, it was painful. My childish, joyful un-derstanding of the natural world was giving way to a less poetic reality, one in which the facts of life are sometimes not what they appear, and the truth not at all easy to obtain.

***

After my experience with the Johnsons at the Big Red House, my general sense of dread about black people pop-ping out of the dark carrying large white sacks did not di-minish, but the immediate pressure of collecting was off—Mr. Johnson had essentially paid me forever in one go. I did not have to be seen there again any time soon. But such are the ways of the world—what I later would attribute to karma, to the great turning wheel of Samsara—such are the ways of fortune that I was not done by a long shot with the Johnsons.

What happened was that Clarence's granddaughter, Ce-cilia, came to live with her grandparents for some unspeci-fied reason, and soon started going to my school. She would get on the school bus one stop before mine. I remember her first day, it was mid-week, when the principal came to my class. He had a private word with the teacher, Mrs. Evans, who seemed surprised by what she heard, but recovered quickly, took a deep breath, and pasted on a large smile. The principal then called Cecilia in from the hallway and in came this small girl. She stood at the front of the class almost as if for inspection, her eyes downcast under big coke-bottle glasses, hands held together at her waist. Her pale blue knee-length dress was like something a child would wear, but I could see that she was no child; she was blossoming into a woman. Everyone could see that, I think. She was wearing a bra, for one thing. Her small feet were encased in round-toed black leather shoes with petite white socks. Her hair was in cornrows, and it curved around her head and hung down in the back in a way that seemed fantastic, like a sculpture. "Class, this is Cecilia Johnson. She just moved here from Chicago. That's in the state of Illinois; in case you are wondering. Please make Cecilia welcome."

Cecilia then went to find a desk—there were a few empties in back—and the homeroom continued. At lunchtime she sat by herself. I saw this, but the thought to go over and join her or say hello never entered my mind. It was only the next day, when she got on the bus one stop before me—yes, on Mahogany Lane, my street—that I put two and two together and realized this Cecilia Johnson was one of *the* Johnsons, was somehow a relation of Gladis and Clarence and Shaka Zulu.

I did not intend to sit next to her on the bus, it was not planned, it was something that just happened. I sat down and she glanced at me, a little tentative, and I smiled and said "Hi."

"Hi," she said in a small voice.

That was all we said to each other on that bus ride, but I continued to make eye contact with her occasionally in our homeroom class that day. She did not seem to be in any of my other classes except Science.

At lunch, I had the temerity to sit at the same table. I came out of the cafeteria carrying my tray—I bought lunch that day—and was hoping Cecilia was not in sight so I did not have to do anything. But, no, sure enough, she was sitting alone and in a seat that faced towards me, and when she saw my face, her eyes lit up, and I knew I was caught by social etiquette and had to go over. We said hello and I said I knew her father, because I was the paperboy.

"Oh, yes, Grandpa said he knew the paper boy on the street. Grandpa loves to get up early. He said you were very polite."

"Yeah, I see him sometimes when I'm on my route." Of course, I was lying about this. I never saw anyone on my route, which was a big part of what I liked about it. I was too busy with the joy of tossing papers to think about people.

"Do you like science?" she said.

"Oh yeah, definitely. I'm probably going to be a scientist some day. My stepdad, he's an engineer, he works for Lockheed Martin."

"Does he do the rockets?"

"Oh definitely. They are doing some work for the Apollo Missions..." And on and on. I spun a glowing story about his critical involvement, about which I had no real idea, but the invented details seemed to flow easily enough. When I mentioned that Sam had recently given me his slide rule, after purchasing his first Texas Instruments electronic calculator, her eyes widened.

"You have a slide rule? A real one?"

"Sure."

"Do you know how to use it?"

"Well, not for certain. But I'm sure I can figure it out."

"Maybe we can look at it on the bus, you know, together."

Soon the lunch bell rang, and I regrettably had to discard the remains of my half-eaten sloppy joe dreck into the garbage can and suck down what was left of my milk through the thin plastic straw as the lunchroom emptied out.

Sam's slide rule was of good size, at least 8 inches long, too big to fit in my shirt pocket, and it came in a brown leather case. The case was well-worn, as if the contents had

seen frequent use. I did not bring the slide rule immediately
the next day; I waited for Friday. Friday was a bit different
because my mother was gone in the morning when I left for
school. She took the younger children to school by car on
that day to facilitate whatever she was doing, maybe shopping. But I knew on Friday that she would not be there to
see me off. So it was a good day to pack the slide rule, an
action which for some reason that I could not pinpoint, perhaps a vague fear or premonition of potential danger, I
knew I should not tell my mother about. At least, not yet.

I got on the bus and Cecilia was there. As I had imagined
and hoped. She was sitting towards the back. "Hi Robbie,"
she said. She was smiling.

"Hi Cecilia, look what I brought." I pulled out the precious instrument and she let out a little 'ah' of delight.

"May I hold it?"

"Sure." I handed it over with a flourish.

She took the slide rule out and laid the case on her lap.
Examining it closely, she considered. "Hm, yes, I see. So, say
we want to multiply 2.3 by 3.4. Then, we put the 1 on the C
scale on 2.3 on the D scale, and then we set the cursor on
3.4...and then the answer is on the C scale—7.8 and a
smidge...I'd say 7.82. And there you go. 78.2."

"How so?"

"Well, it doesn't calculate the decimal point, does it?"

"Yeah, I see." I didn't really, I had to think about it a bit
later. "You seem to understand this really well, you really
don't have one?"

"No, but I've read about it."

"So you read books?"

She laughed. "Please don't tell anyone."

I laughed then, too. "OK, it will be our secret."

The bus rolled on, but things had changed in my world
from that point forward. I was in love with a girl. I did not
consciously know that yet. It took some days or perhaps
even a week for me to figure it out. To be honest, it was a
bit like the Copernican Revolution in miniature: everything

before then had been about me; I was the Sun, and people like my mom and Sam were planets, like Venus and Jupiter. Sam Jr and his sister were minor planets, or perhaps asteroids, and the school was another galaxy. But they all went around me. Now, however, the center of the universe shifted. Cecilia rapidly became the center of my small universe. Everything else became small and insignificant.

My mother, who was very observant, and as I have said, very protective, was probably the first person to notice a change in me. One day she said, "Robbie, what has come over you? You aren't watching much TV. I think you missed *Star Trek* again. And what about *Kung Fu*? There was a new episode last night."

I didn't respond immediately. I was not sure how to explain the situation to my mother and probably unwilling to delve too deeply into the sources of my own sudden ridiculous happiness. Everything seemed better to me: food tasted better, I was more willing to do things to help out around the house, like take out the trash, and even up to and including helping with my younger sister and brother. My mother physically stopped short when I offered to play with Sam Jr out in the backyard. I was also strangely interested in going to school and could not wait for the bus. Formerly my mother had struggled to find ways to get me out of the house, and connect me with play friends, as none seemed to materialize from school. For example, she organized for me to join the Boy Scouts—an absurdity, in my mind, but yes, I did enjoy collecting the merit badges and yes I did love the woodland skills, sharpening axes, making fires, and so on. I studied the book filled with the descriptions of badges cover to cover.

But as far as play friends, yes, there were one or two to be had in the troop. Kids my age. And I think they liked me more than I liked them. In fact, when I left for Kickshaw, it was these same boys from Scouts who set up a going-away party for me. But none of them were particularly interested in reading, and none seemed to be scientific or have a literary bent, or even to have read the Christian Bible, something I did at age 10. (Spoiler, I thought it was nonsense.) Not to talk about something esoteric like the *Tao Te Ching*. The main interest of these Florida boys, even the ones who were not retards, seemed to be escaping out into the woods to make a fort, or dig a trap, or wrap a handful of pine needles in toilet paper and then set it alight, inhaling the smoke. Something that I thought too absurd to actually try, although I watched and feigned interest. OK, maybe I took a puff just to satisfy myself it was madness. After all, it was not even dried banana peels, which I had read about, but just ordinary dry pine needles. What was the point of that?

When we went to Boy Scout camp, the primary source of enjoyment turned out to be swimming in leech infested water and splashing pee wildly into dirty urinals, or else reading *Mad Magazine* late into the night (actually I loved *Mad Magazine* but my mother would not allow me to buy them), or else playing War with two combined poker decks, until one of the more rowdy campers decided to convert the game into 52 Pickup and the cards went flying.

But Cecilia was entirely different. It was not that she was a girl, although that was true; but she seemed to have an inner life; that was what attracted me to her. 'She was smart,' I suppose is how I would have said it then, although in truth this was saying nothing at all.

The fact that Cecilia was of a different race did not actually occur to me for some time. I mean the idea of "race." I know that sounds absurd or hard to believe, and in fact I'm sure everyone reading this assumes this narrative is some sort of meditation on race relations: "a white boy falls in love with a black girl, complications ensue." But that is not the case. That was not the essence of the matter and not the story I am trying to tell. The story was actually that Cecilia was like me, and it was the first time in my whole life that I met anyone who was even vaguely like me, on the inside I mean. Cecilia was "black" only by accident; it was a fluke. That was how I conceptualized things. Her outside appearance was of no immediate interest to me, although as I came to perceive her femininity, her natural beauty, got accustomed to her scent from the intimacy of being in greater proximity to her, breathed the same air that had been inside her young lungs, and gradually perceived her form, her whole being, dreamed about her, even—then yes, eventually I saw her as a girl and understood I loved her as one, without quite understanding what a girl was. But all that took time. Initially it was about the joy of true friendship.

For example, when we were in science class, Mr. Stevens, the teacher, who we always called old Dent Head because of the divot in his cranium—it was about the size of a golf ball, and for all I knew had been caused by such an impact—Dent Head would ask a question and then there would be a show of hands; and it was often my hand in the air, but just as often it was Cecilia's. Initially she was a bit subdued, but it only took a week or two for that to change.

One thing that I have to explain is that Cecilia sat wherever she liked in science class. This was 1978, and the Brevard County Public School System had not been integrated for very long. It's true that technically integration came about due to a Federal lawsuit in 1964, but the horrible truth was that, up until my 9th grade year, the white kids had sat on one side of classrooms and the black kids sat on the other. But Cecilia didn't care about that. She sat next to me, often, or if I was busy with the remedial seniors, who liked to sit at a table together at the back and leverage my superior knowledge (i.e., cheat off my answers), Cecilia would then sit towards the front.

I was so happy to have someone in my life who I could talk to. For example, Cecilia didn't think it strange that I liked to go to the library, or that I avoided the school library sometimes in favor of the grown-up, city library, that had 'real' books. When I told her that using some of my paper boy money I had subscribed to *Scientific American*, she was envious. "Wow. I wish I could do that."

I considered buying a subscription as a gift, and writing in the Johnsons address, but something held me back—perhaps the idea of having to explain myself to Clarence.

I don't remember when I told Cecilia about my telescope, but I do remember clearly trying to figure out how to explain to my mother that I wanted Cecilia to come over so that we could do astronomy together. I mulled it over for days. Finally I decided the most direct way was probably the easiest.

"Mom, I want to have a friend come over and we can do astronomy. Is that OK?"

"Sure, Robbie, that sounds like a great idea. Who is it?"

"Her name is Cecilia. She lives down the street a bit."

"Cecilia?"

I could see my mother was trying to work out who that was. She sort of laughed and said, "You don't mean, from down the street?"

"Yes, Mom. Cecilia Johnson."

My mother instinctively crossed her arms, which I understood was an automated defensive action to something she heard that cannot be right, and then she said, "So this is a girl who goes to your school?"

"Yes," I said. "She's in my science class, Mom. Why is this a problem?"

"Oh, no problem, Robbie...I guess I should meet her mother."

"Why is that necessary?"

"Well, I just think she would want to know where her daughter is going. That's pretty normal, Robbie. You don't understand how moms operate."

"OK," I said. "Well, she's not got a mom, as far as I know, she lives with the Johnsons. Those are her grandparents. She's only been here in Florida for a few weeks."

"Oh." She seemed to be digesting this. "So you've been over to the Johnsons? You know them?"

"No, Mom. Not really. I just collect there sometimes." I didn't want to tell her the whole story, about me lying and saying I was the Welcome Wagon for the neighborhood, how happy we were to see black people, or about the hundred-dollar bill. I still had it, actually; I had not spent it. So my idea was none of that would come out.

But my mother had a way of working things out and she also had the help of spying Sam Jr., who was young enough and curious enough to have gone through my things. "Robbie has a 100-dollar bill, Mom!"

"What, Sam?"

"Robbie has money in his drawer."

"Yes, he has a paper route."

"Well, I saw a one-hundred-dollar bill."

My mother laughed. "That seems unlikely, Sam."

I looked hard at Sam Jr., and considered hitting him. "Shut up, Sam, you little pig!"

"Robbie, stop that," my mom said.

I quickly rushed out of the house, leaving the TV on, hoping things would blow over, but no, sure enough, my mother must have gone and inspected the contents of my top dresser drawer. I had a shoe box in it with my collection ring of subscriptions, little orange tickets I punched with a special tool, and a manilla envelope with money in it.

My mother did not say anything to me immediately. I thought perhaps things had blown over. But presumably she discussed it with Sam *Pere*, my step-father (not his little fat-fucker offspring) and they concluded my mother should get to the bottom of it.

Meanwhile my desire to have Cecilia come over in order to share the wonders of astronomy was in a sort of limbo. It was a painful mental state for me, having asked and got no definitive answer, and I felt some considerable tension, and a sense of foreboding. The days dragged on, and I did not think I could go on much longer without bursting at the seams. "Mom, I still want to have Cecilia come over for astronomy."

"I know son, I haven't spoken with the Johnsons yet."

"But why not?"

"Robbie, I will do things in my own good time." She was quite cross with me. "Now I need you to explain to me where you got all that money."

"What?"

"I looked in your drawer and Sam Jr. was right, there's a 100-dollar bill in there."

"Well, what of it? I'm earning a lot of money collecting."

"Are you sure that's all that's going on?"

I had no idea what was in my mother's head. I asked her to drop it, but I could see her little mind kept whirring, like a thinking machine working through possibilities. So I pressed on the gas. "Look Mom, I really like Cecilia. I think I'd like to date her. I've decided I want her to be my girlfriend. Is that going to be a problem for you? Or maybe for Sam?"

My mother's eyes widened and her mouth opened just a bit. "But—but—Robbie—!"

"I see. Now I am starting to understand how things are."

"No, no, not at all," she sputtered.

I put on the full court press, now, because I could see I was winning. "Mom. Are you a bigot? Is Sam some kind of a bigot? Maybe that's why you have not done what you said?"

"Robbie!" My mother slumped a bit. "You're making this so hard!" She burst out crying, then, and I began to feel guilty, because maybe I was pushing her too hard and for the wrong reasons. After all, I knew that I liked Cecilia, but we hadn't even kissed or anything. It wasn't like Romeo and Juliet. I just wanted to show her my telescope. And, also, obviously, I was trying to shore up my lie. My big fat lie that followed me like Fat Albert.

To her credit, my mother rallied very quickly. In a matter of half an hour, her face had changed, and I suddenly realized (perhaps to my horror) that I might have to actually go through with it and ask Cecilia to be my girlfriend (whatever that actually meant—I had no idea). All I wanted was to see her, to be with her, but most importantly to show her my telescope, to do astronomy together on a beautiful night with the moon in the sky and a planet or two looking on at us, astronomy in the backyard with this cool girl in cornrows and big coke bottle glasses who read books and knew how to work a slide rule. I had no idea what she, Cecilia, wanted, nor did I care. As for my mother, well, I knew her all too well. She would have continued ferreting out my secrets until she learned the whole truth, and I would never live it down. It had been necessary to go full ballistic missile on her. I had gone several levels up to atomics, like in *Dune*, blasting away the shield wall. And her response, her retaliatory strike, was like nothing I had ever experienced before.

The first salvo was a call to Sam *Pere*, who was at work. I was more or less afraid of Sam. After all, he was a grown man. He also had adult children from a previous marriage; he was a bit older. Those adult children were completely mysterious; I never met them, ever, and he never spoke of them. This mystery was compounded by my complete inability to see what my mother must have seen in Sam: I thought he was an ogre. I've explained about the drinking. So, yes, I was anxious about what he would do or say. I was not present, but from the hysterical nature of my mother's voice seeping in from the other room through the thin melamine veneer of the particle board door, I knew it was blistering, and that Sam was being excoriated. Something had passed between them, perhaps when I was not in ear shot, perhaps about the Johnsons, and that had to be handled as the top-most problem if any progress was to be made on my issue. After that call she came out of her room and into the kitchen and put the kettle on the front electric burner of the stove. As the water whistled, she addressed me.

"Robbie, go and get some better clothes on," she said. "And comb your hair. I want you presentable."

"But Mom—"

"Go and do what I say." She went about making tea and sat at the Formica counter and drank it mechanically while sitting erect on a bar stool, like one of Asimov's robots. She then went to get herself dressed. She put on her best dress—not one that she had made, but one she had purchased from Sears. Her hand-made dresses were all nice, I would say, they were always clean and fresh, and I loved to hug her in them because they felt so good, and her soft body was inside of them, but they were not ironed, they were what she was comfortable in at home, but I suspect, in her mind, they were too practical, too dish and vacuum cleaner, for her current purposes. Too utilitarian and maid. She wanted to look church. Church and, if possible, educated. She also put on jewelry, which was rare. She liked pearls but we did not have money for that. One day we visited Sea-World in Orlando. And among other things, they had pearls for sale, all kinds really, but she bought herself a strand of freshwater pearls. I knew I was in for serious trouble when I came out of my room with my hair combed to see her wearing her hair up and those pearls around her neck. Was it possible she was wearing makeup? God, yes, she was. I was stunned. Makeup was saved for the really big things. It would have taken a serious event, like a Church Social, to get those pearls out of the jewelry box and onto her neck. But to get makeup onto her face!

She made me get into the car, our Galaxie 500, I've talked about that car, green and gruesome, the cat killer—yes, my mother accidently ran over our cat with it, the cat had crawled up to sleep on the front left tire—the thing belonged in a novel by Stephen King. (I did not read those because they just seemed too scary and mom also concurred Stephen King was not for me. But yet we had one of his cars.) And so, we entered the tank and slowly drove down the street. It was like moving in slow motion. The Big Red House was only a few hundred yards, but she drove anyway. She pulled into the driveway and parked, and we got out. I made to go with her, but my mother waved me off. "Stay here, Robbie."

She approached the door and knocked. The door opened. It was Clarence, Mr. Johnson. I could not quite make out what was said. He was wearing the mask that black people wear when speaking with white people. But he looked past her and saw me, and then suddenly smiled, and the mask seemed to slip off to some extent. Then Clarence continued to speak to my mother, and then Gladis, Mrs. Johnson, appeared behind her husband, and looked around him, as if she were looking at a strange atmospheric phenomenon, and then she too smiled, and my mother was admitted into their home. The door closed.

My mother, who I did not consider brave, and who was not a large woman, actually rather petite, stood only about 5'1". But she was quite unflappable when push came to shove. In those moments her face took on the resolve of a person who is absolutely convinced they are in the right, like a martyr or a schizophrenic. And now she had gone in alone to the Big Red House. I wondered if Shaka Zulu was in there, or even Cecilia.

It seemed that I was not to be party to what was said. Time passed, and it must have been for some little while, because I remember it was long enough for me to become bored. But suddenly the door opened, and my mother emerged. She was radiant, perhaps with relief. Behind her came Mrs. Johnson, and then Mr. Johnson, and finally Cecilia herself.

I mainly had eyes for Cecilia. Truth to be told, she was rather grim, even stone-faced. She just looked at the ground. My mother then beckoned to me and I came forward. I said, "Hello, Mr. Johnson, sir, Mrs. Johnson."

"Hello there, Robbie," said Mr. Johnson.

"Look Cecilia, Robbie is here," said Mrs. Johnson.

But Cecilia said nothing.

"Robbie," My mother said. "Cecilia will be coming over tonight for dinner. You can do astronomy until 9 p.m. You will then walk her home afterwards."

"Yes Ma'am," I said.

That evening, Cecilia appeared at our front door. ...

There are a few stories from this time period that I must relate before we get to that night. The first is about a boy from the neighborhood. In any neighborhood there are always boys, and they play. I think that is a universal. Hickory Hills was no exception.

One of the boys was named Henry Maitland. He went to my school. He was a stout little fellow with sandy blond hair and a pimply face that still had a lot of baby fat in it. "I'm from Alabama," he told me in his finest Southern accent. "Where you from?"

"Me?" I said, "Oh, I'm from Florida. But we lived in California. That's where my Dad is."

"So you're from a broken home?"

I did not know what that meant exactly, so I lied. "No, I don't think so. My dad just works there. I see him pretty regularly. He flies into Orlando all the time."

"My Daddy works selling cars," Henry said. "My older brother works down there, too. They fix cars. We moved from Montgomery a few years back."

I knew his house well in my own way; it was towards the tail end of my route and so of course all my perceptions were early morning perceptions. But the house was one of those where there are a lot of cars, the front yard was more or less a parking lot with motor oil dripping and leaving stains where grass should have been. I would say hello to Henry on my collections sometimes, and he got on the same school bus, so I knew him that way, too.

One day Henry invited me over and we had a play in his yard and looked at the cars and then went in the backyard, where there were lots of odd bits of machinery and rusting iron tools, and things like that. Eventually we went into the house when it began to get hot. "Let's get a drink." Henry's mother probably had gone out, I don't remember anyone else in the house.

We went and sat in the living room and probably watched some TV. At some point he said, "Hey, take a look at these!" He produced a number of underwear catalogs that were hidden carefully under a stack of other magazines in piles on the coffee table, they contained pictures of women in their bras and underpants. Underwear models. We studied these intently, each with our own catalog, and Henry began rubbing himself. When I realized what he was doing, I considered joining him, but I became uncomfortable about it and said it was time for me to get going.

After that I started making fun of Henry, calling him *Hedda*, which was short for "Hedda head." We believed this to mean the head (glans) of a cock. I don't know where this idea came from, except that Henry's face was pink and his cheeks puffy. I suspect the terminology was of my own coinage. Anyway, Henry didn't much like this.

"Hedda, hedda, hedda!" I would chant when we were on the school grounds and I saw him. We would sometimes tousle and he would vent his frustration on me about it. But I seemed to take a sort of enjoyment from taunting him. I was being cruel, and I knew teasing him was wrong, but for whatever reason, perhaps because there were no apparent consequences, I kept doing it.

Now, after things had progressed with Cecilia, and we were often seen together on the school bus, Henry was of course aware of us. I was now a bit older, and so was he, and his face had not improved much, I would say. We had both grown in the way kids do, somewhat unevenly, and our bodies were passing through puberty, which is a transitional stage and leaves the body not especially coordinated. I was not talking to him much but it did not matter, we were all just kids going to Titusville High School and riding the school bus to get there. I remember bumping into him on the bus and he said something indistinct, but it was not friendly. Still, I had ignored him.

But one day after school I was out and about in the neighborhood and Henry and some other kids were in one of the vacant lots down towards the end of Mahogany Road. It was a few hundred yards and then there was one of the ubiquitous Floridian drainage ditches, and then roads with no name and a lot of sand. Sand and antlions by the millions, and of course ants to feed the antlions, big red ones that stung when they bit you and smaller black ones that just existed as alien colonial organisms in the way ants do. This was the no-man's land, the Wasteland, which was Hickory Hills development yet-to-be. We used it as a playground, basically, it was mostly open and if there was a fence, well, that was nothing to us. We would just pass on over or under or around or do the necessary.

So I saw Henry and a few of the other boys from the neighborhood, and they were all gathered around in a tight knot looking together at a magazine that Henry had. It was open in a way one does not usually hold a magazine, and they were all laughing and pointing as Henry clowned and made faces. I wandered up on my bike and stopped, and got off to see what was so interesting.

"Hey Robbie, come take a look," said one of the boys.

"Yeah," said Henry. "Take a look at all this cunny!"

I came over and looked. They had found a pornographic magazine, or perhaps Henry had procured one somehow, not *Playboy* or *Penthouse*, but something considerably rougher and more grotesque. It might have been *Club*, because the women all had exposed butt holes, and it was understood by us, though some means that I cannot explain, that *Club* was the magazine best known for that type of thing; but I did not get a look at the cover.

The boys were flipping through the pages and then Henry opened up a spread, but in this case it was a montage of different women, all splayed open wide at the thighs. "Alright, which one is your favorite?" said Henry to one of the other boys. That boy pointed at the woman who was more or less in the center of the montage. Her breasts were bigger and she was abundant with whatever had caused the editor of the magazine to place her in the center of the spread; and so as Henry went round and demanded from each boy his favorite, they all pointed at her. But when it came my turn, I didn't do that.

"Robbie? Your turn."

"My favorite?" I paused and considered. "Well, I guess I like that one."

I didn't like the extreme nature of the magazine. It made me distinctly uncomfortable because the women, I thought, were showing too much and it was gross. They looked like animals or perhaps aliens, but with sex plastered onto them in a way that was not even erotic, at least from my point of view. My eroticism was very soft at that age, a boob or a down blouse was a big deal that I would think about for days. So instead of pointing at the big breasted woman in the middle, who had the editor's eye, I pointed at a subsidiary woman in the surrounding montage, one who was performing the function of magazine filler, and this lesser model was wearing a shirt. Yes, her dark pendulous breasts were still exposed, and her crotch was wide open with the anus visible under another gaping open hole ringed by kinky hair, but I somehow felt she was less offensive than the others because she was at least partially dressed. She was also, perhaps in my mind a minor detail, a black woman, the only black woman in the spread. For some reason this appealed to me, perhaps because she was different.

I had sneaked a look at African women many times in *National Geographic*, and their naturalness and exotic tribal scarification seemed beautiful, even as their naked breasts were pleasing in a gently forbidden way. *National Geographic* was something even my mother would allow; and yet there were beautiful and exotic breasts to be had there. I considered a subscription, but thought it might be too much of a risk of discovery.

So I was being different from the other boys, but I didn't care. My response was driven by my inherent modesty, something that was also connected to my (possibly excessive) politeness.

But Henry immediately jumped on this detail of skin rather than the fact this was the only woman who had on a stitch of clothing, in an utterly disgusting magazine. "He must be a weirdo to like that one's hairy cunt. Or is it because she's a nigger? Robbie loves niggers, y'all!"

The other boys all laughed nervously. They knew what Henry was getting at.

I, on the other hand, did not immediately get it. "What?" I said. "What's your problem, Hedda?"

But Henry was flushed now with triumph. "You're a nigger lover, aren't you, Robbie! You got yourself a nigger! I've seen you two on the bus! Nigger lover, nigger lover!"

"Hedda!" I shouted. "You lousy piece of shit!" I pushed towards him, then, and impulsively punched him full in the face with a left. I am left-handed. I don't think I hit him very hard, but perhaps by chance the blow landed on his nose, which immediately began to bleed. I think Henry was a bit surprised by the ferocity of my attack. He had been laughing but was now faced with violence instead of just words. I had struck him; something that I had never done before basically to anyone in my whole life, except Sam Jr., and that was only arm punches when he was being an idiot. But now, I was consumed with anger, and perhaps hate, which seemed to inure me from pain, and I wanted only to hit

Henry again and again. We then traded punches back and forth, prancing and stumbling in the sand, a bit like dancers, but I had the height advantage and the rage on my side. I kept hitting him flush in the face, and each time I hit him, his head kind of popped backwards, but I must have not been hitting very hard because he kept coming; my blows were mostly ineffectual. Eventually he stopped, though, I think because he looked at the blood on his shirt, noticed it, and that sent him crying. I think he suddenly realized he would have to explain himself to—mother, father—someone in that decrepit house with all the cars and the boat.

Meanwhile the other boys made a rough circle around us where they laughed, watched, and taunted us both. "Fight! Fight! Fight!" they kept yelling. But when Henry started crying, then they backed off a bit. They knew it was done, and they moved on and started throwing sand at each other and clowned, having enjoyed the entertainment. It was a big joke to them, but I was far from satisfied. I wanted to continue to beat Henry senseless. I was like Spock in that episode where he strangles Kirk, I wanted to kill Henry. But Henry was done for that day.

"Robbie's the winner!" Shouted one of the boys, laughing and cavorting, having already moved to mount his bike, as he knew the blood was a signal that parents would soon be involved. "Hedda go home!" shouted another boy, who also knew it was time to bail.

Henry roared at me then, crying, a low roar of sorrow that his shirt had been bloodied, and he started to run off. I suddenly felt a little sorry for Hedda. Just a little. He got about fifty yards and then slowed, stopped, and finally turned around and came back. He was almost furtive. I thought maybe he wanted to keep fighting, but no, he needed to recover his precious porn mag full of cunt holes, which lay sprawled open on the sand, looking for all the world like a piece of trash, which it may well originally have been. We often found bits and pieces of magazines, cigarettes, condom wrappers, all kinds of detritus out in the Wasteland, and it was finders keepers out there.

Henry picked it up and pointed at me and shouted. "Nigger lover! He loves a Nigger! I seen them on the bus smooching! I'm telling my dad!" And then he ran off, one hand cradling his nose, and the other clutching the precious magazine.

After that we weren't friends anymore. And it is a true fact that eventually they did cancel their newspaper subscription.

***

This was not the only incident where something happened because of my friendship with Cecilia. However, I don't want to go through all of that because in truth, I was not a knight in armor defending human rights or fighting racial discrimination. I just liked a girl. But because I was soft, because I was smart and sometimes coached the remedial seniors in science, and wore glasses, and was usually last in the athletic contests, like the run we did in P.E. around the school grounds —for all those reasons I was seen as a weakling. It did not help that I took an interest in a girl who was black.

Greg Vitali was a sallow-faced kid with dark hair and a high BMI, not formidable in the physical sense of being muscular, but formidable in the sense of being over-large for a kid his age. He was always laughing in the hallway as he tore into kids smaller and weaker than himself. He was lazy; his homework was always half-completed or not completed at all. But for all that, he was clever. For example, he had found a way to avoid detention for being late for the bell: he would casually come in late, and then say he had been in the bathroom. "I have diverticulosis! I must use the toilet often! You cannot expect me to soil myself?" He would say this to Dent Head in front of everyone and then inevitably the old teacher would shake his head and point at an empty desk. And so he never wound up in detention. Dent Head would point, and then Vitali would turn away, out of Dent Head's sight, and grin his big grin, as if he had won a prize at the Indian River County Fair. His side-kick was Obie Blackmore, a small, deformed kid with round wire-rimmed glasses and a broad wide face. Blackmore's mouth hung open a lot with his tongue hanging out, like a dog, so we sometimes called him dogface. But his deformity was a withered arm. His left arm didn't work very well; the hand looked like a claw. The two of them, Vitali and Black- more, did things like shit in the boys bathroom in such a way that their turds plopped onto the concrete bathroom floor, completely missing the toilet bowl, and then they ran out laughing. They stood outside and complained about the terrible stink, having destroyed any possibility that others could use that toilet for the rest of the day.

I actually met Blackmore much earlier, back in 7th grade. I went into the school library one day and was doing my thing—some sort of research into eutrophication, in prepa- ration for the science fair—and Blackmore was there and for whatever reason—perhaps we were alone—we started talking.

I said, "What are you working on, Obie?" and he said, "Oh, just doing some research."

"You doing the science fair, too?"

He laughed. "Oh, no, nothing like that. This is more like, what I do for fun."

"Well, that's cool. What are you reading?"

"Oh, I like to read about war stuff. Adolf Hitler, you know? Nazi stuff. Did you know they burnt people in ov- ens? They gassed them and then they burned them."

"That's not cool, man."

"No." Obie laughed. "No, that's not cool at all."

We chatted for a while and I kept talking about science, mainly astronomy. I said I wanted to be a scientist of some kind.

"Do you think you'll be a chemist?"

"Oh, maybe, or maybe a zoologist. I like animals. But right now I'm really into astronomy."

"I think a chemist would be a good job. You could make Zyklon B. Have you heard of that?"

"No, I don't think so."

"It's nerve gas. Good for killing jewwwwws," he said, like he was telling a ghost story and jews were what haunted the house. His flipper-hand flapped up in the air as he mouthed the word.

"I don't know, Obie. That's, you know, a bit over the top. But what about you? What do you think you'll be when you grow up?"

"Oh, I already know."

"Really?" I was a little surprised that Obie had definite career plans.

"Oh yeah, for sure. I got it all figured out. I'm going to be a Demonologist."

"What's a Demonologist?"

"That's a person who studies demons."

"Is that a thing?" I said.

"My dad says it is. He's an Evangelical preacher. So he would know."

"I did not know that."

"Yeah, demons. We see a lot of them at church. They make people thrash around and roll on the ground. And then my dad makes them leave."

"That's, well, that's probably kind of scary."

"Oh, by no means. It's cool. Actually very cool." Obie's eyes lit up. "My dad, he casts them out, you see."

"But how do you study that? I mean, to learn."

"Well, there's books."

"Really?"

"Oh, yeah. For sure. See, take a look."

And I kid you not, he showed me the book he was reading from the school library, his "research," and it was a book of demons. It had color illustrations. The demons all had names. This particular book was not the only one of its kind on the shelves. In fact, I was so amazed that I asked him to show me. He pointed out a section near where we were sitting. It seemed that, at least in Florida, "demonology" was a thing.

So Blackmore was not necessarily pulling my leg, and his ambition of one day becoming a "Demonologist" may have come to pass. I never did find out.

But later I suspected his career goals had changed, because by 9th grade he had become a punk. Or at least, a sort of grubby proto-punk. He liked to wear black, and his hair was shaved or cropped roughly into a mohawk, not a wildly big one, but the intention was clear. His ghostly pale skin complimented the black tee shirts and pants, always dirty, and he was now talking endlessly of guns. Adolf Hitler, Jews, and guns. He'd be in science class and Dent Head had his back turned and he'd gesture like he was going to shoot a rifle at him, or maybe a machine gun, and start making sound effects: "Bah, Bah, Bah, Bah, Bah!" or "jew-wwwwww!"

Vitali did not seem to share his friend's obsessions, exactly, as far as I was aware, he dressed in a normal way, but his general demeanor was just as menacing. And I found out at some point they were after Cecilia and me. It happened like this: sometimes kids would laugh for no obvious reason, and I would see them talking to each other as they looked in my direction, especially when I was with Cecilia. I didn't know what it was about. Then one day a kid dropped a note on my desk. It said: "ROBBIE (heart) NIG-GER" in crude crayon. The letters were roughly drawn, like those of a child or a retard, and capitalized and black and hyphenated with that small red heart. I looked over and saw Greg and Obie laughing.

This was after my fight with Henry in the wasteland, and I was not brave, I had no desire to fight, but it just made me go nuts to think this was about Cecilia, they were demeaning her. I considered my options. Yes, I could go to the Principal's office and complain, and cry like a baby, but I wasn't ready to do that yet.

As I have mentioned, some of the seniors were in my science class. That's because they had neglected to get the necessary credits to graduate; they had to pass Dent Head's General Science class for that. Everyone else in class was a freshman, but there were a few seniors. Three of them, Charlie, Tommy, and Gerry, to be exact. Charlie was from New Jersey and his accent was very strongly of the northern end, the New York end, where mall becomes maul and Jersey becomes Joisy. And Tommy was just straight-up New York, maybe Brooklyn or even the Bronx. Gerry I will speak of in a moment. These guys became my friends because I seemed to know the answers and I let them cheat off me. I didn't care. I enjoyed the attention. And as a result, I got to hear them talk about cars and girls and music.

"You into any bands, Robbie?" Tommy would say.

"No. But I'd like to be," I said.

"Good." Tommy had let his black hair grow out and he was perpetually wearing the tee shirt of some rock band, the merch from a concert.

Charlie was much the same, but he was of Italian extraction. His face was covered in acne and he was quite large and strong, by the looks of him. "You need to get some wheels, man. Car stereo. Then you can do the jam."

"Yeah," said Tommy. "You need wheels for sure. And then you can get the Zeppelin."

"What's Zeppelin?" I said.

"What's Zeppelin, he says!" laughed Charlie.

"Led Zeppelin, Robbie. That's the greatest rock band in the world." This from Gerry, who almost never spoke.

"Damn right," said Tommy.

And Charlie would nod his head. "Oh yeah, baby. The Zep. Gotta have it. And then he would sing, 'I got the juice, the juice running down my leg!'"

"Squeeze-my-lemons!" sang Tommy.

And they'd laugh.

"Settle down back there," said Dent Head. "Settle down!"

"You gotta check it out, man."

***

These guys were good to me in their way and I had a real sense of affection towards them; they were just so dumb. I had no idea where they would end up. But the camaraderie, the acceptance, felt so good. I had no older siblings. Of course, I knew they were in some sense using me. But it did not bother me in the least. One of the best things was, Charlie often told stories of his experiences with girls. "This one time, Robbie, I was at the drive in, we were in my car, and this girl, she let me play with her titties. And I was squeezing her nipple, you know, and a little milk shot out!"

"Hit you in the eye, did it?" laughed Tommy.

"Oh she was such a sweet piece," said Charlie. "What a great pair of titties." He looked at me, then. "So, Robbie, you interested in any girls?" And then he kind of glanced over at Cecilia, and nodded in her direction. When he did this his eyebrows raised. "Eh? Eh?"

I hedged, and became bashful. "Yeah, yeah, I guess."

"It's all right man. I seen you with that cute little black girl. You should work on that."

"Yeah, I like her," I said. "She's really smart, you know."

The guys looked at each other. "Oh, yeah, no doubt."

"She wears a bra, man," said Tommy. "She's got titties for sure. Hey, don't take it hard. That's cool that you are into a black chick, Robbie. You're so progressive, my little dude. I like that. You're a smart little dude. There's plenty of hot black chicks back in New York City, man. You would dig it."

"Chocolate city! Let's all go to Chocolate City!" said Charlie.

"Marrrry Jaaaaane!"

They laughed and laughed. I had no idea what all that was about but it was good that they were supportive.

So that was how things were, and then Vitali and Blackmore started their little campaign of terror. It wasn't just the notes. I could get past that, but then Vitali and Blackmore escalated to hanging around outside the girl's bathroom. When Cecilia went in, they waited and as she came out, they threw some sort of dust on her head. I think it was ground up fiberglass.

I found Cecilia crying as I was walking to class. "Robbie, they threw something on my head! It's in my eyes!"

I walked with her to the nurse's office.

That day I was really down. In science I didn't say anything, didn't raise my hand when Dent Head called out. A lot of his questions went unanswered and he finally started asking the guys instead (which they took notice of pretty quick). And then the guys noticed Cecilia was absent as well; she had been sent home for the day.

Charlie was the first to say something. "What's going on, little buddy?"

I kept my voice low. "It's that fucker Vitali. You know that guy over there? And then that Obie Blackmore."

"You mean the idiots who shit on the floor in the Southside bathroom?"

"Yeah. That's the guys."

"What did they do now?"

"Vitali did something to Cecilia. Dumped something on her head."

Tommy was listening. "The old itching powder trick?"

"I don't know, man. It's not cool. She had to go home."

"That's fucked up," said Charlie.

"Yeah that's fucked up. Those guys suck."

But now my creative impulses took over. I started to imagine the guys giving Vitali and Blackmore a beat down. "And you know what else, Tommy? They said Led Zeppelin sucks. Did you guys know that? They're not into Zeppelin. I think that Blackmore kid is into punk."

"Punk?" said Tommy. "What the hell?"

"They said Led Zeppelin sucks," I repeated.

"Who said Led Zeppelin sucks?" said Charlie.

"That guy Greg," I said, pointing. "He and Obie. They said Led Zeppelin sucks, man. They hate Zeppelin."

"Those fuckers," said Charlie. "Fine. I guess they're gonna be on my shitlist. Oh yeah, man. They got something coming to them."

Gerry had sat and listened to this, and was nodding his head. The bell rang, and I was getting up, but Gerry held me back for a minute and waited for the kids and Dent Head to file out. Gerry watched them leave, and then spoke in a very soft voice. "Robbie, what happened to Cecilia?"

"She had to go home, I think. I took her to the nurse. She had that shit they threw on her in her eyes."

Gerry gave me a rather intense look. He kind of rocked back and forth. He was never one to say much. "OK, thanks for telling me."

It did not take very long for word to get around within the senior class that Vitali was a problem. He was in CTE (Career and Technical Ed), that was his elective, and one day they were working on a brick wall as part of the training. Somehow a heavy cinder block fell from a scaffolding about ten feet high, and it hit Vitali in the shoulder, narrowly missing his head. He ended up being rushed to the hospital with a broken scapula. They said he screamed like a baby. No one was particularly sorry to hear about it.

With his collaborator in crime gone, Blackmore started acting out even more (if that was possible), and his fascination with guns eventually became a focus of attention and then concern. It took a surprisingly long time for that to happen, at least in my view; because I knew Obie was completely insane. One day the local police showed up at the school. There was some sort of altercation, and Blackmore was dragged away kicking and screaming about Hitler and Jews and niggers. It seemed that he had been found with a loaded handgun; it was just a .22, almost a cap pistol, but all the same, the Principal had to act. I never saw him again. I assume he was expelled.

It was Gerry, they said, who let drop the cinder block on Greg Vitali that day in CTE. "It was a accident!" he told the Principal at the time. He was believed, and nothing came of the deed, other than my relief when Greg Vitali stopped going to Titusville High. They said he had opted for another school. But I think he understood his welcome had run out.[1]

***

Now, this is probably where we can go back to the night when Cecilia came over for backyard astronomy. It was about 5 p.m., but Sam was not home from work yet. I heard a knock on the front door and rushed over to open it. It was Cecilia.

"Hi Robbie," she said.

"Hi." I was a little flustered. I thought Cecilia looked beautiful. Of course, she could have been wearing a burlap sack and I would have wanted to compliment her on it. And yet, I didn't say anything nice to her at all. I suddenly felt

---

[1] *But many years later, I learned Gerry was probably Gerold Brown, the son of a woman who had once lived up in Tallahassee. The story, which was in the papers at the time and garnered a lot of attention in the news, even overseas, was of a black woman, a student, who was raped by four white men. Her name was Billie Jean Brown, and she was beaten and raped and left for dead. But she survived, and the men involved were charged, although the all-white jury did not find them guilty. Billie Jean fled the panhandle and went south, and later married and had a family. And based on my research, Gerry, who always passed for white, but had a broad nose and straightened hair, was probably her son. - DRS*

shy. Everything I had imagined for so long was suddenly real. Those moments in life are usually alienating. "Come on in. Mom—" I yelled. "Cecilia is here!"

"Yes, I know, Robbie," she called out. "Hi Cecilia, sorry, I'm just in the kitchen."

"Hi, Mrs. Harmon. I brought you something from my grandma."

"Oh, wonderful, bring it in dear."

Cecilia had a plate of some kind and my mother made cooing sounds when she put it on the counter. "Dinner is in about ten minutes, OK? We're just waiting for Sam. You two go out on the deck and sit by the pool."

"Alright, Mom," I said.

"You have a pool?" said Cecilia.

"Sure," I said. "Come see." The in-ground concrete pool was a fairly recent addition to the backyard, and Sam said it improved the value of the house considerably. But it seemed to work mainly as a frog trap—an abundance of frogs always seemed to be falling into the chlorinated water, and as they had no means of escape and nowhere to sit, they eventually all seemed to die. I did not know frogs died in a swimming pool—but they did, and it was my job to clean them out. But when we went into the backyard, by chance a frog had got himself into the pool and was splashing about. Normally they came out only at night. This frog must have been a bit of an oddball.

Cecilia saw it. "Look, Robbie!" She pointed. "There's a frog! He's pretty big!"

"They fall in all the time. They die in there and I have to clean them out."

"I think we can save him. Let's see if we can get him out."

"Sure. OK." I got the pool hook down from the wall and put the net attachment onto the long rod in place of the brush. I fished around in the pool.

"Keep going, keep going, you've got him!"

"He's in."

Cecilia motioned for me to hold the net up towards her, and then she reached in and gently took the frog in her hands. "I think he's alright."

"They don't usually last too long in the pool," I said.

"Why do you think that is?"

"Well, probably they just drown. That's my theory."

"OK, well why would that be?"

"I think they get tired like anyone would. Of swimming. There's no ledge on the pool for them to climb up onto. That's my theory, and I'm sticking to it!"

Cecilia looked at the pool. "Very good theory I would say. My theory is the chlorine bleaches them. Yeah. Seems like the pool design could be improved a bit. You know, to be more ecological."

"Hmm...maybe I could make something they could use as a ladder." My imagination started to click over, and I began to visualize a frog escape mechanism. "You know, it would be really cool if they could get out. Like a frog ladder or something."

"Yeah. You know, Robbie, you could probably do something for the science fair about that."

"Wow! You're right. That would be really cool." I was suddenly totally stoked. "But wait a minute, what do you want to do with our little friend?"

"I don't suppose I could keep him?" She smiled so sweetly. She was still holding the frog with one hand, and now gently petting it with the other.

"It's fine by me."

But my mother was less excited about the idea of Cecilia transporting a live frog back to the Big Red House and having to explain it came from our place. "I doubt your grandparents would be too excited about it, Cecilia."

"Yeah, I guess," she said, looking down at her momentary pet. We looked at each other. It was a dilemma. But my mother offered the most reasonable solution, even if it was the least romantic. "I think you probably need to let it go," she said. "Besides, Robbie's step-father has come home now, so dinner is very soon. Better get washed up!"

"Come on Cecilia, I'll show you a good place to release him." We went back outside and I showed her back to the fence line. It was wetter back there. Cecilia set the frog down gently in the muck by a moldering grapefruit tree. We watched the frog for a while.

"Don't be sad, Cecilia. You saved him from a fate worse than death; he would have eventually sunk to the bottom and then been fished out and tossed into the garbage bin. This way he's got a new lease on life."

"You're right, Robbie. What's that hole under the fence?" Cecilia was pointing at the hole Kwai-Chang had once dug to escape. It had been a long time. Somehow the hole seemed very small.

"Oh, that's where my dog died. He got bit by a Water Moccasin or a Copperhead. He crawled all the way back. I found him there."

"I'm sorry, Robbie. That's kind of sad."

"Yeah, old Kwai-Chang. He was a good dog."

"Kwai-Chang? You mean like on *Kung Fu*?"

I laughed. "Yeah. That's probably my favorite show, next to *Star Trek*."

"Wow, I like those shows too. My granddad lets me watch *Kung Fu* sometimes. Not always."

"Yeah." I was feeling a bit wistful about my dog and wasn't paying much attention to Cecilia.

"Robbie, I do need to talk to you about something—"

But just then my mom called out. "Come on you two. Get washed up."

So we went inside.

Dinner was a lot like Sunday Dinner, which was the only day of the week we did anything special food-wise: my mother had roasted a chicken. We sat around the table, the whole family. Sam sat at the head of the rectangular oak ta-

ble and presided over the meal like a king in a small kingdom. His green tumbler was set beside his plate. My mother
took the trouble to put a tablecloth on the table, and the
pale crème linen was smooth so I knew it had been ironed.
On the other hand, she had not got out the silver that was
reserved for times like Christmas Eve and Easter. My
mother sat at the other end of the table with Sam Jr. at her
left, and then Jackie, who was smiling and wearing a little
dress, and to my mother's right was Cecilia, and then myself, and finally Sam at the other end.

"Let's have a quick prayer, then" said Sam, and he then
started our usual prayer from special occasions, which we
intoned:

> *"Come Lord Jesus, our Guest to be*
> *And bless these gifts bestowed by Thee."*

My mother closed her eyes for this prayer, but no one else
did.

"All right," said Sam. "Who's hungry! Pass that chicken,
this way, would you Robbie? Yes, serve our guest first."

"Oh, I don't eat meat, Mr. Harmon. Thank-you though. I
will have some of those peas, please, and the mashed pota-
toes."

"Don't eat chicken?" Sam said. "Hm. That's very odd."

"Perhaps she doesn't like the taste," said my mother.

"No, ma'am, I don't eat meat generally. It's not good for
the planet."

Sam scoffed. "Well, suit yourself. Please pass the rolls,
would you Jacqueline?"

"Yes, Dad."

My mother was trying to think of things to say, and she
lighted on the obvious thing, which was astronomy. "So Cecilia, I understand you like star-gazing?"

"Yes ma'am. But mostly because I am interested in math. Maybe Robbie and I can learn about the motions of the planets."

"We should be able to see Venus and Jupiter tonight," I said excitedly.

Sam let out a little laugh, though. "It seems unlikely your people would be intellectually able to understand planetary motion. I had to explain to Robbie about the moon's rotation and even he couldn't get it. It took him forever."

This remark was not exactly appreciated from where I was sitting. But I didn't say anything. My mother tried to change the subject and for some reason, she mentioned my father. My real father.

"Cecilia, Robbie's father, who lives in California, has offered to pay for Robbie to go to private school. Isn't that amazing?"

"You mean a Catholic school?"

"No," said my mother. "I think Kickshaw is more of a prep school, isn't that right, Robbie?" By now I had the brochures and other materials that they had sent. We had also done some of the application paperwork. There was even a reading list for the summer.

"It's a prep school," I said. "But I haven't decided to go yet. It's a long ways away, you know."

But Cecilia smiled. "I think you should do it, Robbie."

"So you think so, too?" said my mother. "I have been encouraging him to do it."

"It will help you get into college, Robbie. Maybe a good one for science, like Cal Tech."

My mother was gratified at having an ally. "Are you planning to go to college, too, Cecilia?"

Sam, taking a drink from his vodka tub, snorted. "It's not so easy to get into college," he said. "I never went. But women are not going to be welcome in the sciences especially. Sorry dear, it's true. It's a man's world."

Cecilia did not answer my mother's question, but I think my mother was conscious of the sensitivity of this subject to me. She was quick to gloss over Sam's *non sequitur*.

"So what happened with the frog?" she said. "Sam, they caught a frog that was in the pool."

"Yeah," I was looking at my mother. "Cecilia let it go. We're thinking it would be a cool science fair project to make a sort of life raft or a ladder, a frog ladder, so the frogs that fall into the pool can escape."

"That's ridiculous!" said Sam. He seemed to have made good progress into his tub. I thought how nice it would be if he drowned in it.

"Oh? Is that so." said my mother. "And why is that?"

"No one cares about frogs falling into swimming pools," he said. "Robbie would be laughed out of the science fair."

Cecilia then set her fork down abruptly. "Mrs. Harmon, is there a bathroom I might use?"

"Yes dear, it's just down that hallway."

"Thank-you, excuse me."

After she had gone I was considering saying something rude to Sam, but my mother gave me a look. Basically, she said through mental telepathy, 'just relax, dinner will be over soon.' But it was very hard for me not to explode. Instead I said, "I'm done, Mom, may I be excused?"

"Of course, Robbie. Why don't you go on out and get the telescope set up? I'll tell Cecilia when she comes back that you are outside."

I moved the telescope out into the backyard and started getting things ready. I put in a wide field lens for starters. I was thinking we'd look at the moon. I heard the screen door open and I thought it was Cecilia, my back was to the door, and I said, "Sorry about that, my step-father is such a—"

But it wasn't Cecilia, it was Sam Jr. "Mom said I could look, too!" he said.

"I don't think so, you little rat!" and I punched him in the arm.

"Ouch!" he cried.

"Stop making so much noise." I was really not in the mood for little Sam *Fils*. He was shaped exactly like his father—I did not see anything of my mother in him. "Go play on the swing!"

He was crying a little, whining. Luckily Cecilia came out at that moment and he stopped. He stared at her for a minute and then went over to the swing set. But it was getting dark and he was not interested in swinging. He came back and sat nearby on the ground and swatted the occasional mosquito. I completely forgot him instantly.

"Cecilia," I beckoned. "Come see."

Her eyes did indeed light up when she saw the telescope. "Oh my, it's a reflector."

"It's an 8-inch mirror."

"That's pretty good sized."

She was standing next to me now, quite close, and I felt her human presence in the way two animals are aware of each other when they are in proximity: by some pheromonal interaction. It was quite dark by now in the yard and I had the back porch light off.

"I wanted to get a Schmidt-Cassegrain, but Sam insisted on a Newtonian design. But it's still pretty good. Check this out!" I pointed the telescope at the moon, which was low in the sky and a waning crescent, like a smiling mouth on its side. "Here, Cecilia." I wanted to reach out to her and touch her, and I felt shy about doing that, but she came directly over and gently brushed against me. Her face was near mine and she took off her glasses so she could see. "I have to refocus this, Robbie, without my glasses I'm blind as a bat."

"Sure," I said, "turn this here."

"Oh, that's incredible!" she said. "Wow."

"Yeah, isn't that something!"

"That's so cool that you have a nice instrument like this."

"I had to save a long time. You know about the paper route."

"Yeah, that's so cool you have a job at this age."

The horror dinner had started to fade from my mind by now, and little Sam *Fils* had reluctantly gone inside, probably he was afraid of the dark. It had suddenly come on and the stars were now intense in the Florida sky. Cecilia and I were now alone together, and I think we both noticed this.

"Robbie, I need to tell you something."

"Oh?" I was smiling, thinking how she was going to agree to be my girlfriend. In my mind, this was what was negotiated when my mother went into the Big Red House: Cecilia would be mine. I didn't know, of course, what being boyfriend and girlfriend even entailed, my understanding of love and relationship was drawn entirely from the limited and thoroughly censored comic book conceptions presented on network television, in programs such as *The Love Boat* and *Love, American Style*, which ran in re-runs on the single UHF station, channel 47.

"Robbie, do you know Jeffery Felton?"

"I think so," I said. Jeffery was a black boy. We actually had met in seventh grade P.E. when we were playing dodgeball and he hit me hard with a ball and I fell, and then later he asked if I was OK. I said yes, I was fine. But from then on, I knew him. I thought of him as having a nice, well-developed frame, like a black *Conan*. His eyelashes naturally curled up, I noticed. Jeffery did not seem to be into science; so he was not that interesting to me except as another example of how all black people seemed to be physically superior to myself. (He was not an extreme case, like Shaka, but he was impressive). On our bus ride Jeffery got on towards the end in a very crappy part of town. Yes, a lot of the kids called it Niggertown, although I did not. But when we both got to 9th grade, then I lost track of him completely. We didn't have any of the same classes, and he was very sports-oriented. I was the opposite. I thought sports were stupid. So we just didn't have much in common. Possibly, there was also the dawning realization that we were different. It was high school now and everyone was sorting things out.

"Robbie, Jeffery is my boyfriend. I have a boyfriend now."

"You do?" I had not been really listening to her; in my mind a completely different conversation was still going on, one that was figuratively, but also perhaps literally, in the stars. But now I was, in a sense, pulled back down to the ground. "You mean, you and Jeffery."

"Yes."

"But. I don't understand."

"Jeffery is really nice. He plays sports a lot. He's talking about playing football."

"Yeah. But how is that.... How is that what you want?"

She laughed then. "Well, that's just how girls are. Don't feel bad, we can be friends. We'll always be friends."

I felt like sitting down but unfortunately I had not provided chairs, and so I had to steady myself by leaning against the telescope tube, which then caused it to swing violently off its axis. "Oh crap," I said.

"Let's keep looking," she said. "Or do you not want to?"

"No, I want to. I want to."

Unfortunately at that moment Sam *Fils* emerged from the screen door. "Mom says I can look too!"

"You little turd!" I shouted. I hit him, perhaps a little harder than I should have, and he ran off crying. I suddenly perceived things were falling apart in my life. It was like a cold shower.

In a few minutes Sam *Pere* came to the screen. "Robbie, can I talk to you please?"

I went in.

"I think you should call it a night with Cecilia. You can't go around hitting your little brother."

"He doesn't belong out there! We're older kids!"

"No. I'm not going to say it again."

I was pretty torqued; I can tell you. "You drunken bastard! You're not my father! You don't get to order me around!"

Sam's reaction was rather swift. He hit me square in the chin with his fist. I suddenly found myself on the floor. The pain was not that great, but my jaw felt suddenly heavy. It was more the surprise of being punched that startled me and sent me into a state of shock. Sam had hit me; that had never happened before. I started crying. He walked away, leaving me on the floor in the hallway with my back to the wall, cradling my chin.

Meanwhile, my mother, seeing things were out of control, and it was family time, had apparently ushered Cecilia out. I heard their muffled voices. After a few minutes I slowly got up off the floor of the hallway and went outside; but she was gone. "Where's Cecilia?"

My mother did not immediately respond. "Come inside, Robbie," she said.

"No, I don't want to."

I was rubbing my jaw. "Sam hit me."

"I know Robbie. But you mouthed off."

"Where's Cecilia?"

"I sent her home, Robbie."

"But I was supposed to walk her home! That was the arrangement!"

"Come inside."

I was beside myself at that point, because in my mind everything had been planned out so carefully and rehearsed: Cecilia and I would do backyard astronomy and wonder at the night sky and my incredible 8-inch reflector telescope; I would show her amazing things; and then I would walk her home, and when we got to the Big Red house, I would ask her to be my girlfriend, formally, as it were, and then we would kiss. I would then give her the present I had prepared, the slide rule. I had it carefully wrapped in paper with ribbon tied into a bow. It was all so clear in my head, and I had so convinced myself of what was going to happen, it was almost as if it had happened already. It was past. But now the entire thing was gone. That's when it occurred to me that my mother had sent Cecilia home by herself. Not just without me.

"So you sent Cecilia home. No one to walk her? Is that it?"

"Yes Robbie. It's just a few blocks."

"But you made a big deal out of me needing to walk her. Isn't that so?"

"Well, I said you would. But I didn't say you had to."

"That is a stinking lie. You definitely said I was going to walk her home."

"Robbie, do not take that tone."

"I can see how it is. She's just a nigger, isn't she? You don't care about her at all! Her safety means nothing to you!"

"Robbie, what has come over you? That is not a word I want to hear coming out of your mouth!"

"Oh, don't try to lie to me. I know all about Sam and what he says when he's drunk. Farm boy racist bigot from Iowa." I was completely coming apart now, there was no stopping it.

"Robbie, you need to go to your room now!"

"No. I'm fed up with this place. You, Sam, those dirty little piglets you brought into the world from that hog, I'm done with all of you. Filthy drunken swine."

My mother had stopped talking. I think she realized I was out of control and all that was coming was more damage, but she did not have the missing piece—the fact that Cecilia was not going to be my girlfriend. Had she known that, maybe things would have taken a different turn. But she didn't learn about that until it was too late. "Robbie, I think we need to send you out to your Dad's."

"That's what I want, too," I said. "I'm sick of you. All of you. Fuck this place. Fuck it!"

She shook her head now and turned away in the darkness. "I'm calling your father tomorrow."

***

It was three weeks later, and I had graduated from 9th grade. Old Dent Head had written a glowing recommendation for Kickshaw, and I found my grades were pretty good. I had already sent off the application. But it was now the summer, and I was very keen to get out of Florida. A summer in California! With my father, my very own father, the real one, not this thick-necked pig standing with my mother and sniffing the air in the terminal as she cringed and gripped her hands.

My mother looked around her, anywhere but at me, and her eyes were red. Probably she had cried that morning, but I didn't care. The last few weeks had been very quiet, because everyone knew things were changing. There was no point in expending energy.

But Sam Jr. did what he normally did: he filled in my mother on my business, repeating some of what happened that night. So now she knew the truth, she understood why I was so upset. That knowledge changed everything for her, but nothing for me.

"Robbie, can we talk?" We were in the kitchen, the same room and in basically the same positions, as when my father had called a few months before.

"I don't want to, Mom."

"But Sam Jr. told me a little about what happened. Cecilia."

I hated the idea she knew anything about what had happened, so telling me she knew only enraged me further. "It's my business! It's too late now, Mom. I said goodbye to Cecilia yesterday." I didn't tell her I had almost tearfully given the girl with the coke bottle glasses Sam's slide rule. It was the last day of school and I sat with her on the bus like always. But it was different.

The slide rule felt heavy in my hand.

"This is for you, Cecilia."

"But Robbie, I don't know."

"Please. Just accept it. It's what I want."

"That's really nice. It's cool. I'm glad you're going to California. Maybe someday I'll get out of Florida too."

"Yeah," I said. "Someday." It's a true fact that I never saw Cecilia again. I don't even have a photograph, and over the years her face has faded from my mind like in that song *Katie's Been Gone* by *The Band*. Probably there's a yearbook somewhere, but I don't think it would show me what I want to see.

My mother continued to try to work her own angles for a while. "I thought you could stay for the summer. I don't want you to go. Robbie, listen. You can go a few weeks before school. How about that idea?"

"That's not what you said before. Remember? Words matter, Mom. You told me to go—said it was best." I was really being an asshole, but it turned out that was my forte.

"Robbie, listen. You are my first-born son."

"So?"

"I love you more. I love you more than the other children."

This hurt me, which I'm sure was the opposite of the intended effect, because I was convinced parents all loved their children equally. Learning that idea was an illusion was not a lesson I wanted in that moment; it was like the moon had stopped rotating the way I had believed it should. "That's crazy," I said. "There must be something wrong with you. You should love all the kids the same."

"No, Robbie. It doesn't work like that. You don't understand love yet. It's really hard for me that you are leaving, and especially in this way, the way things are. I'm your mother. Whatever happens, I will always be your mother. Please stay. For the summer. Things will improve."

"No. I want to be with Dad. I can't wait to get out of here."

And then Sam had the bright idea we should all go to the airport as a family and they would see me off. Of course, that just drove the stake in deeper, and I had no chance for a private discussion or any kind of last hour rapprochement with my mother. No reprieve of execution. I was beginning to realize this was all real; that I had to actually go through with it and leave. But I ended up insisting they leave me alone at the gate. "I don't want you here! Go! I hate you!"

"But Robbie, please," my mother said. Yes, I could see she was crying now. People were looking, which would have embarrassed her. But she openly cried.

"No." I said. "No more. This is it." I didn't even look at Sam or Sam Junior, or little Jackie. She was crying too. I didn't say goodbye to any of them.

"I don't plan to ever come back to Florida, Mom. I'm done. You'll never see me again," and I turned my back.

I was a bit of a drama queen, obviously. But I would do the long-distance prat fall and eventually take my medicine.

PART TWO — California Reaming

A boy from Lorenzo was rude,
And claimed that his sister was nude,
With the barnyard door open,
And not a word spoken,
And the cow thought it all very crude.

The big jet engines gunned, pushing me back in my upright seat like four invisible paws. That curious sensation of leaving the ground swept through my bowels. California, I knew, was six hours away and hyphenated with a half-hour layover in Houston. I'd never flown alone before, so I didn't know which of the many emotions I was feeling to allow myself. Certainly I was not supposed to cry, but it was there, ready. I felt like an escaped prisoner.

A young stewardess, nametag Shelly, kept one eye on me. Her uniform bunched in interesting places. I was shy with her and full of fantasy, like a wimpy teenaged Walter Mitty obsessed with fan fiction, which was in fact largely who I was then, and I looked out the window at sad blue and pearly, iridescent cotton white when I wasn't eyeing Shelly's eye-level blue skirt and her taut nylons descending into tiny black shoes. If she leaned over there was more to be seen; nothing outrageous, like a patch sewn onto her ass that said, 'Bite Me,' but just her natural flesh, her smooth femoris and the flat of the back of a knee coated in nylon. I contemplated this, because nylons were not something I understood; it seemed they went all the way up? But then what was the point of that? Surely they should end at the thigh, like a sock.

There was a stain on her skirt, just a small stain; but I put life into it by telling myself a story about it. How it got there, what it signified. Perhaps the pilot had invited her into the cockpit and spilled his—but no. That outfit was no doubt made, I thought, through a rigorous process of industrial design, to show off and uplift what it contained: a bag of mostly water in a prim era fascinated by airplane sex, by Star Wars aliens and reckless faceless fembots.

Deep azure butt pads. These curiously flat utilitarian cushions were like the ones on the Disney ride *Spaceship to Mars* and made the flight feel suspiciously like a simulation. I gripped the armrest over Arizona and clawed through *The Bicentennial Man* by Isaac Asimov to get my mind off the sudden turbulence. Mr. Toad's Wild Ride.

I was certain a natural man would have understood and reacted to this deep magic of aerial technology with an uncontrollable desire to dance, all spasmodic and filled with trembling fear, or else howl with joy and amazement like a banshee. But I, the unnatural man, the bastard of Titusville, white renegade of Hickory Hills, haughty son destined for prep school paradise while my pathetic classmates rotted in the heat and sweltering humidity of the hell that is Florida, I was off to meet Kickshaw the Great.

I sat there, faintly dizzy, and moment to moment lived a dreadful fantasy: the fear, the horror, of puke, of acrid vomit in my throat, choking me, puke convulsively erupting and spattering everywhere, puke ejaculating into the little paper bag in retch after torrid retch as my mind exploded over enemy territory.

That bag. I kept obsessively looking at its white edge poking obscenely out of the sleeve of the seat. I did not touch it; I was uncertain if I was permitted to pull it out until the moment of the crisis, and so it sat there and I could do nothing but look. But its very existence spoke of the horror of air sickness, and reminded me of endless TV stories, of hours of air distress played out. In those days people smoked on planes, and the faint, evanescent wisp of tobacco was everpresent. It made me want to retch.

But the smile of a woman who boarded at Houston and now sat next to me, a woman whose butt was wider than my shoulders, who I imagined as a gracious cow princess of the Texas Lowlands, reassured me. She seemed so confident it was possible to do this airplane thing, commanded me through her calm to trust in the machine, in Engineering as a belief system. And at least I was out of Florida! That was my dominant thought now after the melodrama of my departure and a few hours of white noise and sips of Coca Cola. She smelled of grandmother.

"So you're going to California?" she said.

"Yeah, I'm going to see my dad."

"All by yourself?"

"Sure."

"That's wonderful. I'm going to see my son. He lives in West Valley. Have you heard of it?"

"No ma'am."

"What does your dad do for a living?"

"Oh, he's an actor. At least part of the time."

"Really? That's amazing!"

"Yes." I warmed to my theme. "He lives in Hollywood. He's had some minor roles on *Star Trek* and other shows. You know, episodic television. He got fried by an alien in one of the recent episodes."

"That's amazing!" she said again. I did not think she would be familiar with *Star Trek* and probably, perhaps fortunately, she was not. So I kept lying.

"Yes," I said. "He's really something, my dad. He makes so much money he can afford to send me to prep school. He owns a Mercedes Benz and a Hollywood bungalow."

The cow woman stopped talking after that; perhaps money was not an accepted subject of discussion in her brutal rangeland subculture.

***

As we got closer, minute by minute my fear and anxiety departed. The little white puke bag suddenly became just what it was in objective reality, a small wax paper bag, harmless. It felt so good to think I could find some normality in California with my Dad. That was my dominant thought. I didn't actually know much and just hoped it would all work out. But I didn't tell Mrs. Texas Longhorn that.

Shelly the air waitress buttoned down the cabin for landing after a laconic message from the pilot, his jumbled words largely indecipherable to my ears over static. Glorious Earth met us lovingly with a jolt, the gigantic magic bullet bounding down out of control and into her caress. But then it was done, all so suddenly, and we were down. Returned to the joyful rutting earth. Earth, mother earth. I leaped up from my seat without saying goodbye to anyone.

***

"Robbie! Over here!"

My father waved, waiting at the gate, all smiles, and gave me a hug. He was like a great brown bear, Smokey the Bear, his arms swallowed me up with huge kindness. Richard, who liked to be called "Dick" with all the associated connotations fully intact, was suddenly so very familiar. I presumably had blocked out his face from my mind or else infantile amnesia had erased it; but the face I saw matched my expectations and I felt a great sense of relief, even a burst of affection, towards him.

There he was in the flesh, my father, my own father at last, not fathead Sam of the thick finger squad, but tall and well-built, even handsome. My Dad. At age 38 he was like a Norfolk Island Pine that has grown up weathering the winds of the coastline and is now strong beyond strength, a trunk not possible to fell. His scent, a mixture of Old Spice aftershave and perspiration, seemed hauntingly familiar. It evoked times that I had no conscious memory of, but there was a hidden reality, a hidden past, that came with this man.

"Robbie, this is my friend Lawrence," he said.

"Call me Larry," said the thin little man, and he held out his hand. I had not really noticed him up until that moment, but he was clearly *with* my father. He was smiling and friendly, a bit younger than my father, even by a generation, but considerably older than I was, with smooth features— my father had a killer mustache, as was very much the 1970s fashion—but Larry was clean shaven at that moment with dark hair and a half-Asian face. He grinned like a pirate.

"Hi, Larry," I said. "I love the tooth." We shook hands, a real handshake, like two men.

"Nice," said my father. "Oh crap! I forgot to bring the Nikon."

"You're right, Dick. How did we forget that! Well, we can get a photo soon. I'll see to it."

"I leave a lot of details like that to Larry, son. He's a maven for information and a fountain of facts. And he has a style sense like you've never seen."

"Oh, listen to him flatter." But Larry smiled with his eyes. When he did that you could see his gold tooth peeking out, and his face had a twist to it, such that one side was different from the other. The "other" side had a gold earring, like Sinbad the Sailor, while the near side, the leeward side where the wind blew, was more open and "normal." An intriguing combination of parts, that face. Larry was not easy to forget. When he walked, the smoothness to his stride was such that he seemed to glide. This effect was so prominent it sometimes caused observers to mistake him for a celebrity. His propensity to dress to a tee, in an era of sloppiness and sloth, increased this sense of anxiety in the observer about impending contact with celebrity, with fame. "Surely I know this guy from somewhere," was a common intuition. But always with me, he was calm and gentle. Almost motherly, even though I know that sounds like a cliché. He was detail-oriented, too; and I believe, immediately decided I needed more clothes.

My father looked at his watch. I noticed it seemed to be a very nice one; the watch face itself appeared to be encrusted with small jewels; it was only much later when he was away and I wondered about it, ticking on his dresser when the house was quiet—the damn thing was a Rolex.

He seemed keen to get moving. "Let's collect your luggage and then maybe we can go and find a place to talk. There's a few things I need to say, little buddy."

"Sure, Dad."

"You hear that, Larry? Dad. I'm Dad."

"You sure are, Dick. Tricky Dick reproduced. And now we see the benefits of it. You appear to be a fine progeny, Robert. May I call you Robbie?"

"Of course," I said.

We made our way down to the baggage carousel and collected my two bags—they contained basically everything I owned—a lot of books in one—and then we found a place to sit.

"Son, there's a few things we should talk about."

"Sure Dad."

"Well, I don't know if I am very good at explaining. But Larry and I, we're together, you see. Larry lives with me."

I shrugged. "Oh yeah? Well, that's cool."

My father seemed a little bit confused by this response. The phaser had apparently been set on mild stun. He looked at Larry, who then smiled and said, "What your father's trying to say, Robbie, is that your Dad and I are gay. Do you know what that means?"

"Not a hundred percent," I said truthfully. "Does Mom know about this?" I said, looking at my father.

He seemed a bit flustered. "Uh...well..."

Larry crossed his arms and made a face at my father; this gesture, oddly enough, made me connect better with him; Larry was clearly thinking exactly like I was. "Honesty is always the best policy, Dick," he said. "Or should we call you tricky Dick?"

My father looked a bit depressed. "Yeah, I know."

"Cheer up, Dad," I said. "I won't rat you out." I had not told him anything about my exit from Florida, and actually the details were not something I planned to share with him at all. Not if I could help it. I was already feeling ill about all that. I merely explained that my mother agreed I could spend the whole summer. "I'm really stoked, Dad. This is all good."

***

The fact is I was a little freaked out by what my father and Larry had said. 'Oh my fucking God. My father is a faggot.' That was my instantaneous first reaction. But I was trying to be cool. I could not put a label on what I was feeling; we did not have words then. It was just a cloudy, obscure fear about being different, or perhaps the fear of cracking up, like milk mixed into hot black coffee and then the milk suddenly breaks. Curds and whey and vomit. I felt a sinking sensation that perhaps my father was a weirdo, that he had something wrong with him, and perhaps whatever that was, it might be in me, too. I was momentarily terrified by this thought. After all, I was his son, his natural son, and the product of his genetic material. Or so it would seem. I suddenly wondered if maybe some sort of paternity test needed to be performed. If he was really my father and "gay" and only liked men, what did that mean about me? Was I going to turn out to be that way someday too? And if he was a fag, how did it come about that he got my mother pregnant? Did he actually do the deed, even? Or did he infect her somehow, like an alien parasite digging into an animalcule's vacuole? I began to contemplate various sci-fi scenarios. And then I considered the possibility that the thing was someone's fault. Perhaps my mother's fault. Perhaps he once loved women but now had switched to men? And if so, did my poor mother somehow turn him off or make him gay by doing the wrong things in bed, the wrong or inadequate sexual things? It made me think about my mother and that pig

Sam, and how I now hated him. Those two had fucked. Yes, fucked, even the thought of it was impossible for me to imagine. Partly because I had never actually done that, but partly because their bodies, their shapes, seemed incongruous. Sex. The physics of it. And made two children somehow; and perhaps more would come, sneaking into my room, looking through my things, and then ratting me out. Oh what a horror. But somehow my mom and real dad had also been doing that, in some distant prehistoric period, perhaps the Cretaceous, and I was the unholy Saturnalian result. And what, exactly, was this gay business, what was that all about, anyway? What the hell was going on?

These were the sorts of absurd questions that ran through my head. I felt like Bambi trying to avoid Godzilla. A burning explode-mobile spaceship had crashed into me. The photon torpedoes exploded one by one inside my head.

However, another completely different and distinct part of my mind was actually elated. My dad was a fag, yes, and that shame was no doubt a concern, something to keep hidden, but he was also "gay," which probably meant he was wildly counter-culture, he was hip, he was cool. He was *into some things*. And this gay guy Larry, who was clearly like, super-gay, well, gosh, he was just a trip. He was interesting, out there, so out, so opposite of Baptist KKK Florida, and I had no idea what to expect, but surely this was going to be an interesting summer.

It is a fact that my fears, my worry and anxiety, passed quickly. As we drove up from Los Angeles towards Santa Barbara, I had some time to cool down and calm down. There was a breeze off the sea, and California, I beamed, was just so *kick-ass*. God. It was suddenly all that I had expected, filled with sunlight and smog and dirt and filth and the joy of commerce. Larry intentionally sat in the back seat, even though it was his car, so I could ride shotgun with my dad, which was cool, and I quickly relaxed into the drive-as-destination, the American car experience, life behind the wheel, life at 70 miles an hour. There was music in the car, too, good music to my ears, and Rod Stewart's *Maggie May* belted out the speakers of Larry's Camaro.

It was Larry who made things work. Larry, at every step, was building a handrail for me to hold. My dad was like a bear who broke chairs by sitting in them; but Larry had it all in the palm of his hand, and then some. Their old place on De La Vina Street in Santa Barbara was funky but fun, and it seemed Larry was the interior decorator and had a fantastic style sense. Architecturally the house had a San Francisco feel, but at the time I did not know that. It was about as 70s as you can imagine, though: electric candles on an oversized wooden table that was literally a prepared slice of a huge tree, rings and all; and there was a bean bag chair, or several of them; earthtone towels and actual earthenware majolica tableware in a sunny kitchen, and avocado wall tiles in the bathroom, stained glass in the front door, a great California brown bear in gentle colors was depicted, that made me think of Smokey the Bear; and we laughed seeing it and the vague similarity to my father that it seemed to present; and beads, even some macrame on the wall. Beautiful wood. I had my own room, which was a novelty (previously I had shared a room with my younger stepbrother Sam Jr.), and Larry had put in some cool touches for me like a poster from the recent Fleetwood Mac *Tusk* tour, which he thought I might like (I was yet to even hear Fleetwood Mac, I had no idea, that's how behind the times I was) and a six-foot-tall Ficus and a few smaller ferns "to make oxygen in your room," he said. He even had selected another poster—Farrah Fawcett, the original red swimsuit with nipple pop—and had positioned it on the wall in a place easily visible from the bed. I was in heaven.

The art was also Larry's. A lot of it was distinctly gay—I have to admit—very attractive male bodies, not leather fuck boys, but just graceful attractive nude men. Drawings mostly. Nothing overtly sexual—no erections. Nothing that rose to the level of a Mapplethorpe—but clearly, very attractive male models. Some of it reflected the academic sensibility; if they had been female models, no one would have thought of them as out of bounds. But these were men with beautiful natural bodies and pubic hair and detailed dicks, all drawn from life.

"So where did all this art come from?" I said.

"Well, some of it is mine," Larry said.

"What? You mean you drew this stuff?"

"Larry is a regular artist, son," said my dad. "He's the real deal. We even met in an art gallery. Didn't we, Spanky?"

Larry laughed. "We did, but it wasn't my show. More's the pity."

"Wow, what's that?" I said, looking at a drawing in the living room. The weird but wonderful drawing held court in the room from a central location on the wall above the couch. It was chalk on black felt paper, a sort of baby crawling and a barking dog. It looked like graffiti, but the style was memorable. The whole thing was carefully framed in a white wooden frame.

"That's a Keith Haring," said Larry. "I visited New York last year for a show and met him. He's a street artist now, but he's going to be big someday, obviously. That came from the subway. I basically stole it. He's already got a lot of attention."

"That's so cool."

"Yeah, I got to hang out with him. Nice guy."

"Is he? I mean—"

"Yeah. Robbie. You can say it."

"Is he gay?"

Larry scratched his forehead. "Well, I sure hope so."

But I have not even talked about the biggest thing, the thing for which Larry got the most points with me: the guitars. Larry had several, and they were real beauties. There was a music room, even; things like amplifiers, which in truth I knew nothing about but it all looked impressive. And he said, "Are you into music at all, Robbie?" I was bashful and downcast. I really was into it, though. I wanted very much to learn how to play guitar, because it seemed so cool, but I was too shy to do much about it. It seemed so intimidating to go into a music store and try out a thing like that with people looking at me.

"So what's that one," I said, pointing to the nearest guitar.

"That's a Stratocaster," Larry said.

"And that one?"

"That's a Les Paul Gold Top—a Gibson. Your dad bought me that as a gift last year."

"Wow."

"Oh, you haven't even heard them yet. Here, let's get you set up." And then Larry proceeded to fit me out with the Stat, shortening the strap a bit. "OK, take this pick. Now just try strumming. Don't worry about the frets yet."

I brushed the pick a few times over the strings, and then Larry turned on the amplifier. There was a sudden rush of sound from the amp in front of me that I felt in my chest. "Whoa. That's really loud!"

"Yeah, it can go a lot louder. We can't turn it up, really. The neighbors would go nuts. That's only 4 on the dial."

"Only 4? Oh my God!"

"Let's see if I can teach you some chords."

***

It was the morning of the third day and I felt a bit like I imagined a proper California rock star would feel. I was lounging in bed; Larry and my dad had both gone off to their respective work sites, my dad to his real estate office, and Larry to his "art space" studio where all kinds of Hijinx might be going on, drawing from nude life models, painting, sculpting, rock and roll jams—I had no idea and could only imagine. Larry was entering into a musical phase, my dad had said.

And so I was home, it was summertime, and not much to worry about yet for school other than the huge reading list I was supposed to be working through. Life was good.

Larry had helpfully furnished my room with a few useful items, including a street map of Santa Barbara that I planned to make use of that afternoon. It was time for me to get out and about, I felt. But Larry had also provided something else—perhaps as a joke—for I soon learned Larry was something of a trickster. It was wrapped in a brown paper bag with the annotation, "Have fun, Robbie! From Dad." But I guessed that it was Larry's handwriting immediately.

I broke into the bag and found a copy of Playboy for the month of June, 1979. Oh my, oh my. I got up and checked the house—everything was quiet, even the street traffic on De La Vina seemed subdued as my hour of revelation approached, and the front door locked tight, good. I hurried back to my room and closed the door. My first dive into a Playboy. I braced myself for a wonderful bout of onanistic, guilt-free pleasure.

About ten minutes passed and I thought I heard the front door open; was there a key in the lock and the door lock turning? Or was it my paranoia? At first I thought, no, it couldn't be. No way. I went back to my own enjoyment. The pull of the pampered photoshoot boobs on me was too great to let go. Then I heard, quite distinctly, "*Esos bastardos!*" and "*Pinches jotos, siempre con sus cosas...*" It was a woman's voice, and I thought perhaps she was robbing my dad's place. The door to my room then burst open.

"*Pequeño bastardo!*" Cried the woman. "*¿Qué estás haciendo aquí?* Who the hell are you?" she said finally, in English.

"I'm Robbie!" I sputtered.

"Robbie? Are you one of Larry's fuck boys?" she said.

"What? No! I'm Richard's son."

"Son? Ehh...."

"*Hijo! Hijo!*" I screamed.

"*¿El idiota tramposo tiene un hijo?*" then she seemed to understand. She began to laugh.

The woman was older in my eyes, late 30s, not unattractive with her big floppy tits, but nothing to write home about either, and I guessed she was the hired help—my dad had not mentioned anything about a maid. But then I realized I was naked. I was, shall we say, caught in *flagrante delicto*. She seemed to be looking closely at my face and then down at my exposure. Perhaps there was some family resemblance with my father—in my face, I mean. Then the old cow caught sight of the magazine on the bed and just shook her head at me. "*Demonio sexual!*" She crossed herself religiously as I waved my arms at her vigorously to get out.

"You dirty boy!" she said, finally. "Just like your father," and closed the door with a bang.

Whatever erotic feeling I previously had, was suddenly gone out of me, for now I had been caught. My face was red in the bathroom mirror. I got a shower and got out of the house pretty quick.

That was how I met Conchita, the maid. My dad and Larry got a huge laugh out of the whole thing when I told the story that night.

"You could have at least given me a hint," I said.

"Honestly son, I didn't think of it."

"Conchita is a considerable expense, but I draw the line at washing your dad's shorts," said Larry.

***

That summer was a time of exploration—of all kinds, I guess—and it changed me, primarily through freedom. Probably too much freedom. My experience of that phenomenon had up to then been limited to which box of cereal to choose on Saturday mornings at the Publix; but now I had free time, free will, and no obvious constraints other than common sense and cash. My father did not particularly care if I said 'fuck,' or whether I ate this or that, or when or if I retired at night. There was beer in the fridge, and although I was not interested in it, he would not have been upset if I had taken one. But he did have some rules and some basic constraints, like not bothering him and Larry in their bedroom. I got that, I respected that. There was a waterbed in there, and other wild things, things on the wall, things in the closet, and it was not my territory. Yes, I peeked when they were out. I felt like a tenant in a freak show but I could get past it because of the joy all the freedom brought into my heart.

My father cared about the big things, like if I was feeling upbeat and motivated, if I had ideas, if I could speak with wit, argue a point, or have something to add to a conversation. If I was silent or reticent he would probe for more.

"Clever boy, you must have considered this?"

"Not really."

"You, should, it will make money someday."

Yes, he cared about money. He thought about money a lot. He was impressed that I had had my paper route and I told him everything, even about the Johnsons and the hundred-dollar bill. I had never told that story to anyone and here I was, sitting on his living room shag carpet, spilling all, like my mother at a coffee klatch. His only comment was, "you got past it, you overcame a challenge. You won." It pleased him to no end that I had experienced employment, and self-employment at that. "A hundred-dollar bill!" He returned to this many times, his face shining, and seemed to believe it was a fortuitous omen.

"Work will set you free, Robbie!" he said one day.

"That's just what the Nazis told the Jews," said Larry.

"Nonsense!"

I don't think my dad understood the reference.

We spent a lot of time in conversation, but it was usually in the context of some social activity. He was not loquacious in private; there he tended to become introspective and self-absorbed. He would occasionally seem down and retreat into his own private world. But out in a public space, especially after a glass of wine or a can of Coors Light, he would open up. He was able to tell jokes. Some of them were dirty, a few were pointed and sarcastic. My father also loved to flaunt his wealth in ways that I thought silly. He liked going to nice restaurants, for example we would go, the three of us, to Luigi's on State Street, an Italian restaurant that was so authentic you expected to see mobsters loitering at the bar. My father would enter the restaurant like a king, upright, erect, and point in the general direction of Lorenzo's section.

"Lorenzo's section is full, sir, why not try—"

"Absolutely not, we will wait."

No other server would do. And of course, Lorenzo's section was deep in the back of the place, which for an Italian restaurant, is where the most respected made men and Capos sat, so they could keep an eye on the front door and speak in cautious tones. My dad had no difficulty hobnobbing with the clientele there. He was not a made man, but a self-made man, which is much the same in those circles. He loved to be seen and was always selling. "Always be selling, Robbie," he liked to say. When Lorenzo had taken our order, and the Chianti was brought out, I marveled at the bottle, it was wrapped in a straw basket. "Chianti is from Tuscany, son. That's in Italy."

"I've heard of Tuscany, Dad."

"You hear that, Lorenzo? He calls me Dad! This is my son, Roberto, he's just out from exile in Florida. He's going to Kickshaw."

"Private school!" exclaimed the old waiter. "Very good. Very good. Does Roberto wish to try a glass of our Chianti?"

"Robbie, would you like a glass?" my father asked.

"Yes please," I said. "Thank-you, sir."

"He is very polite, your son."

"He's intelligent, too," said my father. "He conned a nigger out of a hundred-dollar bill."

"So he is good with money like his Papa."

"Indeed. And he understands how to use a slide rule."

"Really?" said the waiter. "Bene, bene. He will be a scientist or an engineer."

I washed down my pasta with the wine and soaked up the praise like sauce on bread. The warmth filled me with a sense of exhilaration and, in truth, a bit of a buzz. 'So this is alcohol,' I thought.

"You like the wine, Robbie?" asked Larry.

"I feel warm," I said. "Flushed, even."

"It's the glow of the grape. But you see what happens to me." Larry's face was flushing.

"It's the Jap in him, Robbie."

"It's true, Asians tend to flush from alcohol. Not all, but it's a thing."

"Your Dad was from Japan, Larry?"

"My mother. She was born in Hawaii, actually. He was a sailor who almost got his nuts shot off at Pearl Harbor."

***

"Dad," I said. "Why did you turn gay?"

It was a Friday night. We were back from Luigi's having enjoyed more Chianti and their fantastic garlic bread and now sat watching a *Kung Fu* re-run.

"Robbie, do I really have to answer that?"

Dad was well into a sixer of Coors Light, so I thought maybe he would be ready to open up about a few things.

"I don't know, Dad. I think so."

"But why?"

"Because I'm trying to figure things out. For myself. I'm worried I might be gay. Larry says I'm not—"

"You're not," came Larry from in the kitchen.

"—But there are obvious questions. We've never talked about this. I feel like it's time. Was it because of something Mom did?"

"No, son. It's nothing to do with your mother. It was long before I met her."

"Well, then?"

This is where Larry came out and joined us. "Well Dick?"

"Well what?"

"Let's hear it. Interested parties want to know." He was smiling and steepled his hands together, as if he was going to hear something amusing. "How did the great Dick Gray turn gay?" He flopped onto the couch. "We're all ears."

"Oh my.... It's a bit of a story. This was all a long time ago in a galaxy far, far away. Those days seem like the era of the cave man. Anyway. One night I snuck out of the house. I was probably about twelve. My objective was to see a porno movie. An X-Rated movie. I had heard about it from my friends at school. In Portland back then, out by Division Street, there was this porno theatre. I guess they still exist. I had to sneak out of the house very quietly, make sure my parents were asleep and creep out. I found my bike—I had it set up away from the house, see, and I rode and rode my little kid bike. Finally I found the street and then I could see the theatre in the harsh streetlight. I tried to get in, but they wouldn't sell me a ticket. I stepped up to the booth. There was this grungy old guy who looked like a bum in the booth. I said, 'One please,' and he just looked at me and laughed. 'Get out of here, kid. This ain't for you.'

"'But I want to see.'

"'You wanna see something?' he said. 'Go buy a magazine, you punk kid.' He snarled at me. 'Get outta here!'

"I wandered away, feeling foolish, but I didn't leave. I kind of cased the joint. I went around the back. I saw some guys going in and out of the back door. I figured, I'll just wait for someone to open the door, and then slip in. So I did that.

"I went into the theatre and found a place to sit. The lights were just going down. I noticed there were a bunch of guys, actually the whole audience was men of various descriptions. And I was very aroused, you know? Because I thought

I was finally going to see an X-Rated movie. I was so excited and pent up I thought I would burst.

"The movie began to play, and my eyes were glued to the screen. And I was puzzled. I didn't understand at first. But then I looked over, and this guy just down the aisle from me, he had his equipment out and was rubbing it. I was shocked. But then, it seemed as if everyone was doing it, they all started to masturbate, too. Suddenly, to my horror, I realized this was a gay movie. It was gay porn. And all these guys, they were masturbating to this gay porn. On screen, instead of hot girl, there was a guy, a naked guy, and he was having sex with another naked guy. And then, well, there was a lot of sex going on of all kinds, and it was all guy on guy. Guys doing things to each other—I won't say what all to you, Robbie. You're too young.

"Anyway, I didn't know what to do. Because, you see, I was still very aroused, but I was also very disappointed. I felt cheated. I really wanted, you know, a sexual release. It was like my head was going to explode. Something had to give. But a tiny part of my brain hesitated. I questioned my arousal." He paused as if remembering. "You see, if it had been a straight porno, I probably would have just immediately joined in with the other guys and masturbated without questioning it too much. But now, I was grossed out but also aroused. It was sex after all. I was conflicted. With all that going on, I had to decide what to do and I guess I just went along with it. Like in that Star Trek episode, you know, I wanted a piece of the action."

"A piece of the action? You were just going with the flow? Is that what you're trying to say?"

"Well, yes, Robbie. I was going with the flow. Everybody else was doing it so I did it too. When in Rome, you know. So I pulled out my equipment and rubbed it to the gay porn. I got to where I liked it. I went back to that theatre a few more times. And then, well, there was a guy, he wasn't that old, he was a good-looking guy about Larry's age, maybe less. His name escapes me right now. He asked me outside.

We talked, and he said I was too young and I didn't belong there. He was trying to mother me, you know? He said this was for grown ups. He had seen me masturbating, and he didn't think I should be there. He was worried for me. I respected that, I could see he was good guy. I even considered if maybe... Anyway, I had kinda got a taste for it by that point."

"You were ruined!" said Larry. "It reminds me of Francis Bacon. He was ruined at age 16."

"Who's Francis Bacon?" I said.

"He's a painter, Robbie," said my dad.

"Yeah," said Larry. "A pretty fucked up one, too. But he had a great talent. His art is some of the most shocking of the 20th century. His father caught him wearing his mother's clothes, and had the stable boys whip him as a punishment. So guess what happened?"

"Uh, he got interested in horses?"

"Sort of. He started having relations with the stable boys. They'd whip him."

But I was not convinced. I looked hard at my dad. "So you watched gay porn, and it turned you gay? Dad, that doesn't seem credible. It's like something Anita Bryant would say."

Larry laughed.

My father lowered his head and frowned. "Well, gosh, Robbie. You asked me, and that's what happened. It's a true story. I was turned gay by watching gay porn. It happened."

***

I didn't know what to think about my father's explanation because it went against some of my own ideas about psychology. I just didn't think watching gay porn in a movie theatre could turn someone gay, any more than reading Moby Dick could turn you into a whale. And Larry seemed to be of the same mind.

On the other hand, I'd never seen gay porn. Maybe exposing a boy to a lot of dicks over and over *could* turn you gay. That worried me. I also knew that a young boy in a state of arousal lets down his inhibitions and thinks all kinds of thoughts. I certainly had some "ideas" when I was wanking away in the privacy of my room, thinking about my mother in the shower, and then attempting to hit the ceiling, as *Mad Magazine* once suggested in an article I had read at Scout camp. Anyway, that's why I did what I did in secret and never admitted to anything. It was all hiding and shame and something to keep to myself.

But guys like Hedda Henry, they enjoyed spending time together in groups, ogling naked chicks in porn mags and talking about them endlessly. They probably even talked about their own equipment. Did they touch themselves? I guess things like that could happen, especially at a boys school. I thought it was pretty fucked up to do that, though. I felt guilty as hell even imagining guy on guy, much less to contemplate doing it.

In the end, I regretted asking my dad about his story, because it was his private life and none of my business anyway. He had revealed a part of his life, something important to him, and I had doubted him. It was a mistake, and he clearly felt bad, but now it was too late to rewind to cassette.

***

It was move-in day, and my dad drove me up to the school about 10 a.m. For some reason Larry was busy, and couldn't go, it was just me and Dick. My father was dressed in his weekend clothes but still looked pretty sharp. His prominent chest hair sprouted and his chest was further decorated with a small mounted white and black yin yang symbol hanging from a thin gold chain; but his smart white blazer and chinos, with topsiders below, made him look like a preppie. He was relaxed and looked strong and confident then. It's the way I like to remember him. He drove with one big arm on the wheel and the other arm aped the frame of the open window, his elbow down and hand on the frame. We were in the Beamer. I had not been in that car very often, and it smelled like it had been recently detailed, but Dad thought it would be more appropriate to make a good first impression on whomever might be milling about. He really only used the Beamer for work.

My dad's preference in cars actually leaned towards old Volkswagens, the kind of car he used to fix when he was a lowly auto mechanic, and he treated his old Beetles (he had three, in various states of discomfiture, if not full decomposition) as if they were beloved delinquent children. Feral. He was very much a car guy, and known to occasionally borrow a Porsche for a special weekend. Larry said my father knew how to drive fast; that he could even drive a track with confidence if required. But I'm getting distracted.

Kickshaw School for Boys was the full name of the school, if I have not mentioned that before. It was indeed a boarding school, but the entire complement of students was only 200—approximately 50 boys per grade, in years 9 through 12. We had my stuff in the back but there wasn't much. My clothes, a big stack of books, mostly science fiction.

"It's a very elite school, son," my father was saying. "You're going to meet a lot of kids from well-placed families, and those kids, they will be friends for life. They will even become business contacts. It's what they call the old boy network."

"But what's the use of it?"

"That's how the world works, Robbie. You've got to know people."

"But what about you, Dad?"

He laughed. "I had to do things the hard way, son."

"Well, yeah. So, what if maybe I want to be like you?" By this point I had a serious man-crush on my father. 'I idolized him,' would be fair. I even thought his being gay, which at first was such a nightmare, was about as cool as it got. And then there was Larry. Larry was like a secret magus of subterranean blues knowledge and cool and the best uncle a dude ever had. I had two dads, closet-secret Dad and out-of-the-closet guitar Dad. It was like winning the jackpot.

But my father was suddenly serious. "Oh Robbie, don't say that. I mean it. I never even went to college. I'm just a glorified grease monkey. This is something I want for you. This school thing. Imagine if you could get into Stanford or Cal-Tech. Sometimes kids from Kickshaw get into Harvard."

"Really?" I said. I was beginning to get a little nervous. I didn't consider myself much of an intellect. My main talent seemed to be masturbation. Little did I know many of the kids I would meet at Kickshaw were ignoramuses. Having money (in the sense of generational wealth), as I learned later, has little or nothing to do with intelligence.

We left Southbound 101 and took an overpass onto a road headed up towards the foothills. I could see them in the distance as we rolled past a suburb of smallish houses. "Not exactly hills like white elephants," I sighed.

"What?"

"Oh nothing, Dad. It's just from one of the books I had to read over the summer."

"Oh yeah, right. The book list. Damn, I was supposed to check if you read those?"

"Don't worry, Dad." The booklist had been a pain in the ass for me but I read all thirty books that had been on the list. I actually enjoyed the Hemingway more than some of the others. Previously I had been rather aloof to his machismo minimalism. "Larry asked me about it like, a million times."

"Ah. Good man, that Spanky."

We had turned a few times and entered the agricultural areas, there were lemon trees and up higher, avocado. The hills were close now and behind them, mountains. It was glorious and sunny. We reached a cut out on the left and turning, saw the first indications of the school: a large brick and concrete sign that said the word "Kickshaw" in large capitals and then "Preparatory School for Boys" in smaller letters. The road, which was now a private road, but recently blackened asphalt and wide enough for two lanes of traffic, led steadily up the side of a hill. It wound up and down and got steep in places, eventually flattening out at a fork near the top of the hill. We took the right fork, and it led up to a flatter area with buildings and the school grounds. I did not know it then, but the other fork was simply a longer, more roundabout way to get to the same place. A loop, in other words.

My dad slowed the beamer and then eventually came to a complete stop, like a man in a reverie. He had seen the brochure; it was like a Florida land deal dream that had been sold to him—but had not been up to the school before; in that sense he was just as much a virgin to Kickshaw that day as I was. "Wow," was all he said. He started driving again and we followed the main road, which was lined with gigantic, fully mature Eucalyptus trees; I thought they must have been at least 100 years old. The smell of the trees engulfed me, as I had rolled down my window and was letting the air soak in. My dad peered around as he drove and I hoped he would successfully stay on the road, as I could see on the right side, in places where there was a slope with grass and what looked a little like hotels down farther. There was an access road to get down there somehow.

"Are those the dorms?" I said.

"Good question."

We eventually reached a pleasant tree-lined area, like a village square, with parked cars and people milling about. My dad had a quick conversation with an older boy wearing a blue sash. The boy looked at a clipboard and then gestured back behind him, pointing. My dad returned and gestured for me to come out.

"Neville here says we can walk the rest of the way. Thanks Neville."

"Sure, just walk down this path and then around, that's High House and Lido. High House is the top floor."

We grabbed a few things from the trunk of the Beamer and headed down the path. I could see a few other boys doing similar things. The dorms on this side looked older and I did not have a word for it—today I would say more European—than the newer construction we had passed earlier. It turned out these buildings were considerably older. Brick but painted a pale shade of cream, like a marshmallow, but with ivy growing prodigiously on the side, they had a wholesome feeling. We walked towards what looked like the entrance and went inside. There was a flight of stairs, and two floors of dormitory. At the top, a man, obviously the inhabitant of the Master's apartment he sat in front of, and dressed like a preppie, was cutting pole beans from a bag on a cutting board. "Greetings," he said. "Welcome to Kickshaw!"

My dad stopped to speak with him but I was more interested in where my room was. Walking past open doors and other boys moving in, I found my door, which was at the extreme end of the hall on the left. I did not open it. My dad eventually made his way down the hall.

"That was one of the teachers, his name is Martin."

"They're called Masters, Dad."

"Masters, yes."

"I'll meet them all later," I said. "Check out this room." I didn't knock—I had no idea—but then I realized someone was there ahead of me. The room was a double after all; perhaps I should have expected it. "Hey," I said. "Sorry I didn't knock."

"Hey," said the boy. "I'm Jonah. Jonah Archer." He seemed to be waxing a surfboard.

"Robbie Gray," I said. "This is my dad."

"Hey Jonah," said my dad, shaking hands with him. "Wow, a real surfer dude. Very cool!"

Jonah seemed to flush with pleasure at this. "I hope you don't mind. I already picked this side."

"No, by no means," I said, looking around. "This is nice." And it was. There were two wood framed windows with twelve small panes of glass each; Jonah had opened them both; and two desks with wooden chairs and two single beds; and even a fireplace (although I found out a bit later we were not allowed to use it).

I was impressed by Jonah and also a little taken aback. He was a total dude: longish hair, stereo already set up and with a big milk crate of records, and he had already put up a poster. It was of Farrah Fawcett, not the original famous one in the red swimsuit and nipples, but the only slightly less famous one with the tank top and nipples.

We brought up my stuff, what little there was, and my dad, looking at the layout Jonah had, said, "It looks like we need to get you some more stuff, Robbie."

"Nah, I'm fine. I just need to get this shelf up and put my books on it."

"OK if you say so. Well, son, I've got to get going."

I said goodbye to my dad and then set about installing the much-discussed shelf, which actually was not that big and was the only thing I had for stuff. I felt like a starving Bangladeshi farmer. Meanwhile Jonah had set down the board and now busied himself reading a magazine. I soon realized it was a *Playboy* after he flipped open the centerfold. "Check her out, Robbie," he said. "What a pair, huh?"

"Wow, that's a *Playboy*?"

"Yeah, don't worry. Happy to share. I've got a whole stack."

"Gosh," I said. "I guess I've been too shy to try and buy those."

He laughed. "So where are you from?"

"My dad lives in Santa Barbara. My parents split up so, you know, I was out with my mom in Florida."

"That's cool. I'm from Malibu."

"Wow. So that explains the surfboard?"

He laughed. "I guess."

Jonah was my first friend at Kickshaw, and that friendship came at an important time, because amongst all the feelings I had in this new place, inferiority was a prominent and recurring motif. They had a lot of things I lacked: they were hip Californians, most of them, but beyond that, they were surfers, cool guys who had dated, maybe even had fingered a pussy, and some of them could even drive. Hell, some of them had their own trust fund Beamers, cars as good as my dad's.

Jonah was about my height, although he had a lot more meat on him—I was a skinny little strip of a kid, a Slim Jim, with short-cropped hair and cheap clothes my mom had bought from JCPenney and Sears. Sure, over a period of time Larry helped dress me—after that first day my dad figured out I needed more appropriate clothing, and dispatched Larry to assist in that noble and desperate cause. But Jonah was cool about it. He could have just ignored me, and went about his business, talked to his own well-established friend group, and not talked to the geek in the corner reading Arthur C. Clarke; or he could have made fun of me, which certainly was the fate of many of the new boys, like James Goldberg, a Jew, who quickly became known as 'Fish' (short for Gefilte fish) and kept that nickname like an Auschwitz tattoo emblazoned on his forehead for the next three years. You see, I was a sophomore, I was coming to Kickshaw in the 10th grade; but Jonah and many of the other boys had been there for 9th grade; so they had everything wired, they all knew the drill. I was the fresh meat. There were about ten of us, the new boys, and we were uniformly mistreated in the first few weeks. But Jonah had no real part in that.

We talked a little about music initially, and it was clear that I knew nothing about it. Jonah was really into Queen, and I foolishly asked if it was a gay group, and got a long

explanation about Freddy Mercury, and the absolute genius of Brian May's use of VOX Amps. And he was also
quite solid on the B52's (which was very normal and true of
many that year) but also Cheap Trick and Journey. He had
actually seen some of these bands play. At the time I had no
idea what those groups even sounded like; in my mother's
house, in Sam's house, we didn't have a stereo, and nights
usually involved watching television. I had never been to a
rock concert, a fact that Jonah often repeated in wonder and
astonishment: "Seriously? You've never been to a show?"

"No, no I have not," I had to admit.

"My God, it's like you're from the moon."

"Yeah. Florida. My step-father works in the aerospace industry. You know, rockets and stuff."

"Right."

I wanted to say it was a fucking hellscape out of a Flannery O'Connor novel, but that seemed too strong at the first
introduction. So I was sure I was a hopeless case, probably
grouped in with the nerds whose parents were working in
Saudi Arabia. I was told we had a few of those.

But Jonah soon saw my potential. He quickly observed
that my essays in English class were getting top marks; my
easy mastery of Algebra (which I already had taught myself,
in the main) made me stand out as well. And then in my
science class, I was often the one who put up his hand, having already understood simple harmonic motion and the basics of Newtonian physics and the sort of things Heinrich
Henler, the German Physics master, had on his syllabus.

Now, Jonah was in those classes, which were very small
affairs, ten or twelve students deep at the most; so there was
no way to fake it or stay in the back of the class, even though
some boys tried. It wasn't like old Dent Head's science class
back in Titusville. But I liked school, I liked learning, and I
wanted to do well, at least in those early days. After all, my
father, unlike the fathers of these boys, had been an auto
mechanic; his hands used to get dirty, he once stank of
grease, even if now he had gone up in the world. My father

worked hard and by hook or crook had come up with the money for me to be here, perhaps through a windfall, or other amazing misadventure, even a deal with land barons or criminals. I had no idea. But I was deeply conscious of this social divide and in those early days I was terrified of letting my father down. (Or perhaps, worse than that, of being inadequate—of being unable to stack up to these wealthy-fathered surfer dudes.)

And so Jonah no doubt saw a way to improve his own somewhat lackluster outing. In the evenings he would probe my knowledge and had no qualms about asking for answers to certain questions; and I, in turn, had no problem at all sharing my knowledge. Indeed, I was grateful, because it meant I had value, and Jonah, who had previously not introduced me to his own circle, soon found occasion to do that. His friend group was the Malibu Mafia—not the famous group of Jewish men who opposed the Vietnam War and funded Daniel Ellsberg's legal defense in the 1970s; but rather, the many surfer dudes from his hometown of Malibu, and also those who hailed from further south—Newport Beach, Huntington Beach, that whole stretch of good surf that was the Southern California expanse, the joy zone of surfer paradisiacal experience.

Surfing was like a religion, but I did not know the creed, so Jonah helpfully gave me a script to assist me in these introductions. He would always introduce me as a Santa Barbara native, that my father made good money selling real estate, and explained what to say when asked about Rincon, a subject of local knowledge that always came up eventually. I learned Rincon was a world historical wonder in regard to point breaks—one of the best. The break there was apparently similar to the one in *Apocalypse Now*, a movie that was all the buzz that year (but that I had not seen). He even coached me how to speak the correct lingo, words like tub-

ular and gnarly and radical, and what to avoid in a conversation, which was basically anything geeky or political or
spiritual or philosophical or anything not surf-related.

I was eternally grateful for this initial help. Even as a senior three years later, I always felt close to Jonah, though our
paths gradually crossed less often and something happened
that I'll talk about later. We were only roommates that first
year. I knew I would never be a surfer dude, and that the
guys in Jonah's clique were not my kind: most of those guys
were surf-nazis who thought Hitler was a clever social ar-
chitect, but I didn't care. It was all good. And Jonah did the
extraordinary thing of speaking to me when these guys
came to see him, causing me to be included in the conversation. On days like that I made certain Jonah knew a satisfactory understanding of the next day's lessons. We did not
share all the same classes. But I did what I could.

***

I suppose the logical thing now is to describe what a typical
school day at Kickshaw School for Boys was like back then.
Things have changed, I'm sure, but one thing would have
remained the same: going to a boarding school is an entirely
different experience from going to public school. There's a
feeling of being embedded in a place if you wake up there in
the morning and go to sleep there at night. It becomes
home, which is never how it feels at a public school. You're
really in it, or up to your neck in it, depending on your
karma or your connections. After I met Christian and he
taught me about Bob Dylan, I came to understand when
Dylan described Life as being like a bum laying in the gutter
and next to him, standing on the sidewalk, is a rich man in
a suit. Those two worlds can be inches apart and yet worlds
away. I understood Dylan to mean that in the same "world"
we all inhabit are actually millions or even billions, an in-
finity of different, even unique, worlds.

And in each of those worlds, I knew, at the center, the core, is a soul. That soul—for the sake of argument it is a human soul, but the fact is even a cockroach can be said to inhabit a world, filled with experience and taste and touch and feelings and knowledge—that soul is trapped in a body, and that body is under the continuous pressure of desire, of needs and wants. Hunger and thirst, cold or heat, the need to escape from the elements into safety and security, but most importantly, the need for love. Love, yes, love is of critical importance and essential for survival. It is the most important need of all. A lot of times people forget about that and think only of money.

But the thing is, every single one of those worlds is completely cut off and distinct from all the others: each world has its own world-line, each has its own pathway that it travels in space and in time. And the soul trapped within that world-line can only hang on and go along for the ride. A Space Mountain; a Tower of Terror. Well, it also fights back, it wails and screams sometimes and refuses to capitulate to the predestined path. But unfortunately that makes no difference, whatever happens, whatever complaint is made, or cry of pain, or agonizing moment of humiliation and failure, that world-line continues on, rolling like a marble, or floating like a piece of driftwood in a mountain stream going down, down, and down, until it reaches the sea.

***

Jonah was in the habit of lounging around in board shorts, and he had a gorgeous back that was free of any kind of blemish, and bronzed by the sun, sea, and sand to a deep golden brown, the color of a perfectly turned pancake. His body type was of the kind that had a well-developed latissimus dorsi, so that his back had an almost arrowhead form when he was upright; but the top of his trapezius was not over-large (in other words, his neck did not have the appearance of a fat-head weight-lifter neck or jarhead neck). His legs were compact and the thighs gave the appearance of strength, but not speed; he was not a runner, but rather a swimmer. This body type is something I saw again and again in the surfers.

Like me, Jonah also wore glasses, but he preferred a kind of aviator look whereas I was a total nerd in wire square frames. He also had sunglasses—I think they were actual Ray-Ban Wayfarers—but around school in the classrooms he sported his aviator rims. His hair was long for that time period but not ridiculously long, as mine would become.

Jonah's surfboard held an important position on his side of the room; not stuffed under the bed and out of sight but boldly propped up and pointed, erect. It stood near the stereo, visible to all, a proud testament to his physicality and Zen-like ambition in search of the perfect wave.

Now, the only surfboard that I had ever seen was the kind used by Greg Brady of *The Brady Bunch* in their Hawaiian adventure: the longboard. But I quickly learned that what the guys preferred was a much shorter board. Often they had two or three fins rather than one; and they did not have much curve (which is called 'the rocker,' like on a rocking chair). These short boards were very maneuverable, almost like a skateboard, and good for tricks. I used to watch Jonah surf, like a girl or a groupie, going down and observing from the Rincon picnic tables, until he said that I was too gay and I should either get a board and surf, too, or else stay at Kickshaw. But I enjoyed watching and being a spectator. Sometimes my Dad would go, too, or Larry and my dad and I, all three of us. My dad had met Jonah, and he was excited to see him surfing too. He even offered to buy me a board. But I laughed and said that was a bad idea. "I'll drown for sure, Dad." On those occasions my dad would bring fried chicken and French fries in white Styrofoam takeouts, perhaps from Carrows, and cans of Coors in a plastic cooler, and I was eligible to drink a beer if I wanted; but I usually abstained and stuck with Coca-Cola.

Jonah's board was fiberglass, like all of them, apparently it floated better than wood and was considerably lighter. I think also the small-sized board was just easier to get into a car for transport than the bigger boards.

"Mr. Zog's Sex Wax?" I said.

"Of course. What other kind of wax would you use?"

"I see, yeah, if you put it like that."

Jonah spent an inordinate amount of time waxing his board, or so it seemed to me. Sometimes he even melted off the existing wax and then lovingly reapplied fresh. It was during one of these waxing sessions that Joey O'Dell burst into the room.

"Hey, man! Hey dudes!"

"Hey Joey," I said. Joey was a bit of a hothead; he was always going off about something. He had customized his surfboard with an inconspicuous black swastika at the base. Today he was going off about the Grounds Crew. "There's beaners crawling all over the school, man! Why can't they hire some better people!"

"What's wrong with Mexicans?" I said.

"Oh, Florida boy, you don't know how it is here. We're choking in them. They're like rats."

I shook my head. "You sound like a Klansman."

Jonah was not interested in getting involved. "Cut it out, Joey," he mumbled.

"Yeah, Joey, why don't you fuck off."

It was Christian Benoit in the open doorway. He was a tough Lido kid, no surfer but a genuine San Francisco kid, and a new sophomore, too. Except that no one fucked with him. Not even seniors. He apparently had come up to say hello and caught the stink of what Joey was putting off. He didn't seem to like it.

"What's your problem, man?" said Joey.

"Just get out."

"Yeah dude, I'm out, I'm out."

***

I did not become friends with Christian Benoit (who that
year we almost universally called Ben Wa, after the sex toy)
immediately. He was initially oriented towards sport and
so was entirely connected to the guys on his team—he
played Soccer, with his preferred position being center or
center midfielder, even occasionally playing forward, and
then in the spring, he would suit up for Lacrosse. Eventually
he even attained the captaincy. He liked to play attack with
an aggressive, full-contact style and strong stick work for
which he was universally admired. His body was well-
suited to these sports; he was not tall, but his calves, thighs,
and core were all designed for running, as if that had been
the plan, and he easily produced bursts of speed and feats
of agility. He was like a young Greek god, his long blond
hair waving in the breeze, thighs pumping, as he drove in a
goal or hammered a shot at a wincing goalie.

I knew nothing about either sport, such things as soccer
balls and the esoteric lacrosse stick being completely unknown to me. I knew what a football was (in theory), and
that was about it. I also thought team sports were stupid,
and the people playing and watching them must be even
stupider. That claim, I said, was easily proved with science;
but no one would do the experiment for fear of being beaten
up. The only kind of sport that I had even a vague appreci-
ation for was track and field; and that interest came from
my somewhat absurd romanticism about the Olympics.
We, like everybody else, watched the Olympics on TV religiously. And perhaps other individual sports such as tennis
were at least interesting; they represented individual and
personal bests. My mother had the interesting nugget of going to the same school as Billie Jean King; she had even spoken to her. So naturally when the Battle of the Sexes happened, we watched that on television and cheered for her.

So tennis was OK, and I even had some lessons somewhere along the line.

But even then, long before Kickshaw, my interest was merely to observe. Due to my not giving a fuck about sports and my general wimpiness and pathetic skinny boy appearance, I am sure Christian did not initially consider me friend material.

Our casual intimacy began in the most natural way, due to his ubiquitous presence in Lido, which as I have said was the dorm directly below High House. I'd see his big frame, like a tyrannosaur, on the stairs or coming in the back stair, maybe in the dark scuttling across the lawn when we were all supposed to be in the sack, and sometimes I'd bravely make eye-contact and smile. He was cool to me, then, and in his own zone.

Just to explain a little more about the building, because it will be featured a lot later, the totality of the 'ancestral pile' (as Sherlock Holmes would have said), was two stories tall with heavy red roof tiles and was organized into an L-shape, with one wing going South and the other towards the East. In the center of the 'L,' on both the first and second floors, were apartments of masters—normally unmarried males. By master, I mean teacher. (The teachers were all called "Masters," which presumably was a nod to some antiquated and draconian British school system tradition). The top floors of the 'L' were High House; the bottom floors were Lido, except that at some point in the history of the building, the majority of the east wing of Lido had been converted into offices. The Headmaster, and old Kickshaw himself, now an antiquarian hobbling like King Lear in black-framed round coke-bottle glasses, had their offices there; other offices were for the Dean of Students and the Alumni Affairs team, i.e., the money grubbers.

Perhaps I should also mention there was a narrow stone stairwell like an escape hatch at the end of each stem on the 'L.' It meant my room was near a quick exit, and also an exit that did not pass in front of the doorways of said Masters.

Anyway, Christian's room had an inward-facing window on the southern stem of the 'L' down in Lido while Jonah and I were at the extreme south end one floor up. I was down in Lido a lot that year and looked out that window in Christian's room many times, staring off into space. Christian's window faced the pleasant green of the grounds and had a view of the chapel, the south wall of the "Schoolhouse" dorms, and further on, the dining hall.

Like me, Christian had come as a 10th grader. Unlike me, his older brother had also attended Kickshaw for a time, so Christian had been there before on a visit and had a good general idea of what was expected of him.

Christian's father seems to have been an exceptional man (at least in the eyes of his son). He graduated from Harvard Business School with an MBA that he achieved in his late 40s. Christian enjoyed telling that story, I heard it more than once. His father, he said, was a man with no formal education, did not even graduate from high school, yet he had made an appointment with the Dean of the Harvard Business School, and explained his background and his educational goals (by that stage he was running a Fortune 500 company) and by force of personality walked out of that meeting an admitted student. At Harvard. "No need for him to bother with a B.A.," Christian said, laughing.

"Yes," I said. "But it was Harvard Business, not Harvard Law or Harvard Medicine."

"It's still impressive, though, don't you think?"

"Of course. Business is a place where the force of personality can operate. That doesn't work everywhere."

But he would have none of it. He believed his father had successfully overcome the very system which he, Christian, was now in preparation to enter, and had thus shown his dominance and mastery of the entire educational game. Christian was proud of his father and wanted very much to please him. He found this difficult. The older son had been through a tragedy, and the younger son was in his shadow.

So there was something deep and bitter, something Freudian, that must have burned in the pit of Christian's stomach. I eventually met the old man much later, but the circumstances were not good. Of the mother I knew nothing. We only spoke very briefly once, and then in a crisis.

It must have been karma, then, perhaps mine, or perhaps his; but the connection, the 'inciting incident,' is a moment lost in the mists of time. I could make something up about it, and it might strengthen the story, but that would not be fair to either of us, Christian or myself. What is most likely to have happened was this: I had discovered Frisbee, because Larry had one and he and my Dad and I would once in a while go out to the park near the house and have a throw. After a certain point in time my dad and I would add in smoking a joint first, which of course brightened the experience considerably, if it also dimmed my accuracy and caused Larry anxiety.

Christian loved frisbee, he played *frisbee golf*, which was entirely new to me at the time, and he would also play 3 *Flies Up* over by the Hermitage where there was a steep downward sloping grade and it was possible to throw for a long distance, the frisbee catching air and finally floating downwards far down the path, or ending up though misadventure on the roof of the '27 house, the loathsome den of the Freshmen. And it is likely that I joined such a game and because of my deep study of the Great Circle, my paper-throwing Zen, I had developed an athletic motion in my body; a single one, to be sure, but still, it was an athleticism; and this motion of repeatedly throwing papers was miraculously carried over to Frisbee.

Yes, I was good at it. That was a bit strange. Frisbee was a revelation, and a California thing, a useful accreditation, and I got some street cred for that. I could produce a seriously long throw through the Kung Fu magic of my left arm. I could even throw a Frisbee with either hand, which Ben Wa considered worthy of a Journeyman. So it probably happened in that way; that first spark of connection and attention.

But things were much deeper than that and what I saw in Christian, in my friend Christian, my blood brother, who so much later seemed to suffer like his namesake, what I saw in him was a guy who knew so much more than I did about being cool—about music, sports, drugs, the mysteries of the counterculture—that I immediately granted him iconic status, he became my idol. Someone to listen to, to hang out with if that were at all possible, or if it could be allowed. And it seemed for Christian that perhaps, just possibly, I fit the bill of a side-kick, a weeny Patroclus, because even though I was a geek in the beginning, as I grew my hair out and began to wear the crazy, super trendy but fashionable clothes that Larry helped me acquire, thrift shop fantasies, and as I showed a willingness to perform devotions and even offer full adoration towards his skills and knowledge, a bright continuing narrative in which Christian was the star whose opinions were the gold dust to be mined and from whom lessons could be learned—eager lessons—from all that he must have decided that I was OK.

I think I have left out that Christian was from Palo Alto, that old Benoit Senior was in the technology business of some kind, a Trillionaire or money pig, and Christian knew everything there was to know about San Fran, and had been to Berkeley countless times. Ah, San Francisco, that name meant something mystical to me; and to him as well, although for different reasons. For me it was about City Lights Bookstore, a place even I back in Florida had heard of and imagined; but for Christian there were many landmarks and places, record stores, paraphernalia shops, and, of course, a few connections—dealers.

Christian's real esoterica, I would have to say, that thing so important to our relationship, was his great love and fascination for music; and he communicated that love to me as a teacher infuses a student. Even above pot, in those days it was all about the music. The music worthy of note to the kids was Rock and Roll, and Christian rebelled deeply against the wishes of his father by embracing the Beatles. Yes, the Beatles and the Stones. The father could not accept that any music to surface during the British Invasion had value. Apparently he could not stand the concept of electric guitar at all. He was a Jazzman, an aficionado of the trumpet and the saxophone, of swing, and not exactly unmusical, and so there was all that mystery of Jazz for Christian to absorb, which he did. But Christian and I were not born in 1940; I didn't know who Benny Goodman was and frankly didn't care. Clarinet? Our musical gods were completely different and perhaps even somewhat antagonistic towards the Jazz greats, almost like two drugs that act like agonists towards each other and cannot be mixed without producing the most horrifying side-effects.

I should not overplay this analogy, for Christian himself would not abide it. Christian certainly had the music of Weather Report represented in his prodigious album collection, all organized alphabetically in milk crates, and even something from John McLachlan, of the Mahavishnu Orchestra, although he did not rate that worthy very highly. More of an intellectual curiosity than anything else. It was not that Jazz had no place, he would have said, it was just that the combination of Jazz and Rock was a complexity that only the future could create and Fusion was not yet that answer. Later, when Steely Dan came to the fore, Christian said he had finally found his link to Jazz. But the father would have none of it.

The other esoterica that Christian brought to the party, the secret clandestine knowledge that meant the world to me, was how to smoke pot. How to party. Christian had learnt his deep and sneaky weedcraft from his older brother, and he loved to get stoned. It was a joyful thing for him. Everything about pot pleased and enthralled him. And it is certainly true that there are few things more cool when you're 16 than smoking a joint with some pals and then playing some great tunes, going deep into the mystic.

But for all things in life there is a first time, a time before of virginity and innocence, a later time of 'nowness,' of action and experience, and then finally (with a little luck or else random, mindless and unseeing probability on one's side), a time of wisdom, of supremacy.

And that was how I saw my time with Christian. He taught me many things that were cool, and also even the essence of Cool itself, through music, but the most personal and intense thing was the pot smoking, like a ritual, and we got high together almost daily.

Of course, this was completely forbidden and would have got me expelled immediately. So there was that: the fear, the anxiety, and the immense joy of being on the wrong side of the law.[2]

***

I have to admit that the first time I got high was not with Christian at all, but with Dick. Yes, my dad was a bit of a pothead, it turned out, and it was a great way for him to unwind after the rigors of a complex real estate deal, but he was like the teacher in *Animal House*, the one played by Donald Sutherland. My dad's generation saw weed as an evil, as

---

[2] *I would like to say, at this point, that even though the world has changed in 40 years, and drugs are dangerous to growing bodies and minds, and yes, using is bad; still, everyone should smoke pot at least a few times in their lives and probably a lot more often than that. The world would be a much more peaceful place if everyone were stoned on a regular basis. Rockets might not successfully get into space, but minds would. Very few fist fights ever happen between stoned people. Almost none. Contrast this to alcohol, which can have hideous social side-effects, even inducing people to violence. Alcohol destroys the senses. Weed seems to entice and enhance them. - DRS*

Reefer Madness. So for my dad to get stoned, a lot of preparation and care had to go into it. My dad was not much of a planner, but he put a lot of time into his appearance, which takes considerable planning; and he thought carefully about people, what they needed, what they wanted, and what his role could be in that equation; and so he weighed and measured people in the same way a baker measures flour and sugar. I could never master those skills; people always overwhelmed me and I would eventually give in to their stronger vibe. I had no moxie, no mojo. That's true to some extent even now, which is why I admired him greatly, because he had these things that I did not understand. But later, when I just wanted to score some pot and he wouldn't help, I went away thinking he was a drag.

In the beginning, though, I was like a scatterbrained virgin, overwhelmed by every energy, trying to keep my head above water. I'd just been living with him and Larry for a few weeks that first summer, when I began to notice my dad slipping out to the garage. He didn't say much, and he seemed to do it when Larry was distracted or elsewhere. One day we were deep in a discussion that interested him greatly: the future of China. "Robbie, the day is going to come when China becomes an international power. Nixon opened up China, but there's so much to come."

"Have you been to China, Dad?"

"No," he said. "But I'd love to go some day. There's money to be made, son. I'm looking into it. Maybe we'll import something, and have our own business of some kind. Maybe you can help?"

It was evening and Larry had gone out, possibly buying some Chinese take-away for the three of us.

"I'm sure you can do it Dad. You and Larry are like superheroes to me." I must have impressed him a little, or touched him inside, because he gave me a look. After a minute he said, "Tell you what, come with me, buddy boy."

I followed him and we went down the stairs and into the garage. Along the back wall of the garage were some shelves above the washer and dryer, and above these was a wooden box with a lid. It was a beautiful wooden box the color of red wine, polished and burnished, and had some carvings; perhaps it had come from Bali or somewhere like that.

My dad opened the box and took out a translucent brown plastic tube about the thickness of a turkey baster, looking for all the world like a piece from a chemistry set. There was a hole in the tube where a black rubber cork fitted, and from there protruded a small bowl on a glass stalk. My father went over to the sink and put some water into the device.

"What's that?" I said.

"This is a bong. You'll see how it works in a minute. Take a look at this." My dad produced a little baggie of loose green leafy material, the color of oregano, and proceeded to crush some of it up by rolling it in his fingers, catching the disintegrated fragments in a small white ceramic bowl. He then stuffed a wad of the contents into the bowl of the bong.

"Watch how this works, buddy boy." He then sparked up the bowl using a lighter: it suddenly burst into flame with a click, and then as he drew in on the bong, a sort of bubbling sound could be heard, even as the shredded herb burned like a coal. I could see smoke rising in the glass tube as he sucked on the end of the bong.

It seemed that he drew on the bong endlessly, but finally he stopped. He coughed, then, and released an enormous exhale of smoke into the garage. The smell was sweet, like an herb, but not like any specific herb that I knew; however it reminded me of something I had detected when I was around the remedial seniors from old Dent Head's science class, especially Tommy. Yes, I remembered them talking about getting stoned. So this was it.

My dad was obviously super-cool.

"What do you think, son, would you like to try it?"

"Well, OK, Dad. Is that Reefer?"

"It sure is, son."

"All right. What do I do?"

"Let me get things set up for you." My dad loaded the bong and then handed me the lighter. "It will work best if you control the fire. You just need to get it lit."

I started sucking on the bong and could feel the draw, and then sparked the lighter and held it to the bowl. I could see the weed ignite. Suddenly I got a big blast of smoke. I stopped and choked up.

"It's OK son, just hold it in if you can, otherwise you're doing it!"

I kept smoking and we each did a few more "bong hits," as he called them. "What do you think, little buddy?" He said.

"I can feel it, I think." In truth, my dad's idea of pot was somewhat lacking. He was only smoking leaves, shit weed that he had picked up somehow. So the effect was not exactly brain-shattering, but it was a nice buzz, not really so different from wine or beer.

"Let's put all this equipment away carefully, I don't want—I mean—"

"I get it, Dad. You don't want Larry to know."

"Oh, Larry always knows, son. But if it's not obvious, if there's no mess, then he doesn't throw a fit about it. Larry is very anti-drugs."

"Why is that?"

"I guess too many of his friends from the hippie days either freaked out or dropped out or went KIA. You know, Killed In Action. They overdosed."

So Larry was seriously anti-drug, and I got it. It made sense. But my father's basic outlook on life was to tolerate, and Larry, too, believed deeply in the concept of toleration in all things. So although Larry scoffed and guffawed when he heard we had smoked in the garage, that first time, he was also willing to joke around and was even, perhaps, proud that I had matriculated. "So you smoked a hookah with your old man, did you? Well, there's a first time for everything. Just don't let it rule your life. People like that are not worth having around, it's too much pain. Don't be that guy, Robbie."

***

They say that it is good practice to introduce all of your characters in the beginning, lest the narrative become too confusing for the reader. But there were so many potential characters at Kickshaw—it was in some sense a storehouse and bottomless pit of comedic and tragic figures—my childhood fountain—and it would be difficult to introduce even a handful all at once. However there is one who I must mention now, as we met early on. He was my first friend at Kickshaw besides Jonah (who was my roommate, and thus, in a sense, a given). And that was William. Not Bill or Willy, but William is what he preferred. William Brennan. I called him William J. Brennan, on account of his progressive demeanor and judicial bearing, and I think he liked this. I met William in the following way: I was stalking through High House on the far side and came across an open door. This was very early on. William was inside and sitting on the floor in his room, and a few other boys were there, Tony Perkins, for one.

"Alright," William was saying. "Tony, your mad professor is standing at the mouth of a dark cave filled with bats. There's a putrid stink of batshit and the air smells damp. The walls of the cave are wet, and you can see a gleam like they're made of alabaster. Inside, you hear the faint sound of dripping water. What do you do?"

Tony adjusted his coke bottle glasses and squinted at a little leather-bound pad he held in his thick hand. "Okay, uh... I take out my Ruhmkorff lamp and wind it up."

The boy sitting next to Tony grinned. Ryan was his name. "My elf has Darkvision. I don't need no rotten Ruhmkorff lamp." He rolled a weird looking die, just a single one, and it bounced on the carpet. "I stride in confidently."

William arched an eyebrow in that way he had, like a Charley McCarthy. "With no fear?"

"Yeah, man. No fear. I'm a rogue. I'm sneaky as."

"You're also very stab-able," Tony said. "What if there's, like, a goblin ambush or a blob monster on the ceiling?"

Ryan scoffed. "Then I take them out!"

William sighed. "Okay, okay, let me check something..." He flipped through his notes, then smiled. "As soon as you step inside, Ryan, you hear a *click* under your boot."

Ryan froze. "Uh-oh."

William's grin widened. "Roll a Dexterity saving throw."

Ryan groaned and grabbed his die. "This is gonna hurt, isn't it?"

Tony chuckled. "Called it."

I didn't really know what was going on, and those guys didn't stop playing to say hello. But I listened for a while. Finally William said, "Hey man."

"Hey," I said. "Is this...?"

"D & D. It's cool, huh?"

"I see." I didn't, but I figured it was some sort of game. "Is this like, a thing from San Francisco?"

"No," William said, looking up at me. "It was invented by some guys in Wisconsin."

Ryan said, "They made beaucoup bucks off it, too."

"Well, that makes sense," I said. "Not a shit-ton of things to do in Wisconsin."

They all looked at me.

"Hey! I'm from Wisconsin!" said Tony. "And I plan to burn you with my death eyes!"

I said, "Uh, sure," and moved on. Tony never did seem to come out of character, even when he wasn't playing D & D, which I found a bit worrisome, and when I looked back I could hear the three had already gone back to their play acting.

For a while this fantasy play made me think these guys were infants, and I avoided them, especially Tony, who was a Junior and lived across the hall from William.

A few days later I was on a walk around the campus and saw William sitting alone on the vast soccer field out past the swimming pool and the tennis courts (yes, we had both). He was wearing a straw hat. He looked a bit like Vincent van Gogh in a field from that distance. I walked in his direction. Eventually when I got close enough I called out, "Dude. What are you up to?"

"Oh, just sketching."

I came up and looked over his shoulder. "Wow," I said. "That's really good."

He was working on a landscape drawing of the foothills. I could see he was an experienced draftsman; the lines were those of a person who knew how to draw, not just a scribbler.

"So you like art?" I said.

"Sure. Who doesn't?"

"Oh, I guess I know a few."

He chuckled. "That's unfortunate."

"Yeah."

He sketched for a while and I slumped down nearby. I looked out with him at the horizon. It was early in the day, I'd say midmorning, and the sun illuminated the hills. There was a cool breeze, it was still Fall. You could see some mid range hills, and then the Santa Ynez mountains in the background behind the hills. I didn't say anything, and after a while he said, "You know, Gauguin, when he was in Tahiti, noticed that the islanders would sometimes sit, just looking at the sea, or whatever, for hours. And in that time, they felt no need to make conversation. They would sit quietly, silently. Just for hours. He thought that was remarkable, he wrote about it in one of his letters. Did you know that?"

"You're saying they would just sit, contentedly, like dogs laying in the sun? Were they sleeping?"

He laughed. "Well, I wouldn't suggest *that* exactly. I'm saying they were different; they were indigenous people. Their understanding of the world was not like ours. They were definitely not sleeping."

"So they were content."

"Perhaps."

"Was their lifestyle better, you think? Did they have something we lack?"

"I think they have something we lack, yes, certainly that's true."

"But perhaps, living on an island, they were just under-stimulated. Perhaps they were bored out of their minds. Or perhaps they had long before run out of things to say."

He laughed. "That is a very euro-centric thing to say."

"Hmm."

We sat for a while. He sketched. I just daydreamed. I noticed that I felt quite comfortable in his human presence. That was not always the case with humans in general. Eventually I said, "I wonder what it's like back there."

"You mean in the foothills?"

"Sure."

"Well, you can find out. The seniors are known to go on walkabout up there. I understand there's a creek, and a swimming hole."

"Really," I said. "Interesting."

"Oh yes. You know the dean—"

"Stacks?" I said.

"Right. He went up there for a weekend. Took his young wife. Have you seen her?"

"No."

"They live in the apartment at the north-end of Long House."

"Really?"

"Yes."

"I've not seen the woman. The wife. I'm surprised, actually. I thought the dorms were all-male."

"Oh they are. But he's the Dean. Imagine what he would do to you if you bothered his wife. She's quite attractive, blond, probably about 25 or 26."

"My goodness," I said.

He sketched for a while.

"Anyway, Stacks went up there. It was observed that they only took one sleeping bag."

"One sleeping bag," I murmured. "Well, perhaps they're newlyweds."

"Perhaps."

I was babbling now. "I don't think I could sleep with someone in that manner. Wrapped around another person. I think I thrash around a lot in my sleep. Our heads would butt together. Someone would get seriously hurt."

"I thrash around, too. But I'm not entirely sure their plan was sleep," he said. We both laughed.

***

Kickshaw's system was to give every student an advisor, half-parent and half-confessor, and I heard mine was Martin Quinn. Every weekday we had morning assembly in the big Henderson Theater, and the way that worked was we sat in rows but more or less in groups clustered around our advisors, who each anchored a zone of camaraderie. So the very first day of class Martin beckoned to me as I was looking for where to sit. "Robbie Gray? Over here!"

However I did not interact much with Martin except that the Masters who lived in the dorms, like Martin, were also the dorm "parents," and did bed checks to see that bodies were in beds. So I saw him then. That is, I saw his face silhouette in our dorm room doorway at night. But it was not until the advisor house party that we actually had a conversation.

It was the first weekend and I was still getting adjusted to dorm life. Martin had organized a barbeque. I passed into his man-cave through a front door that had been propped open with a chunk of alabaster that looked like it had tits, and was confronted by more art and books than seemed reasonable in such a small space. Inside it was already crowded. A diamond needle was softly scratching vinyl somewhere on an unseen stereo; I could not really place it except to say it must be Italian Opera.

It turned out that among Martin's advisees were both William and Jonah, which was a relief. I weaved my way in their direction. There were a few more faces from High House and Lido too, guffawing and laughing. Over in the corner, conspicuous as a bandaged thumb, stood the only black boy in the room. He was actually the only black boy in the whole school as far as I was aware. Downfaced, skinny like a strip of lean bacon, he looked intently at nothing. Martin was at pains to introduce him.

"This is Calvin, everybody. He's a new sophomore, like some of you. Did you want to say anything about yourself, Calvin?"

"Oh, not really."

The bacon strip didn't look up. I had the odd impression he was wearing a tight band around his chest, like a sort of brassiere, under his shirt. But it was just a fleeting impression; an intuition. What I noticed consciously was Calvin's shirt, which bloomed with fine crochet work that effloresced at the collar and wrists. Now the bacon spoke up, a plaintive word or two.

"Except—that it's just so wonderful to be up here...it's nature, God's creation. But also kind of lonely."

"That's not unusual, Calvin," said Martin. "Everyone takes some time to adjust and make friends. Give it a few weeks yet."

The barbeque was in full swing, and I had already made waves by complaining about the lack of vegetarian food.

"Hey, Martin, there's nothing for a vegetarian to eat here."

"Do we have some of those?" he said.

"You're a vegetarian?" said Jonah. "I didn't know that."

"Well, I'm not *actually* a vegetarian. Yet." I said. "But I have an ambition to become one."

Martin put his hand to his chin. "I suppose it's a bit of a chicken or egg problem, if all the available food options are meat you have no choice, and cannot actualize your goal," said Martin. "We are not being supportive enough. But hopefully you won't starve tonight. I do have some noodle salad...let me see. Come with me, Robbie!"

"Oh, don't trouble about it," I said. By this point I was becoming aware of what was on the grill.

"No, no," he said. "That's not for you. Now that I am aware of your dietary requirements, we must do something about it."

He would not take no for an answer. And as a result I missed out on the barbeque ribs—incredible looking and smelling baby-back ribs—like something out of deep Cajun country. Oh, my mouth watered. Instead, that evening I was made to subsist on cold macaroni clogged with mayonnaise and some dubious romaine lettuce heads Martin found in a deep recess within his fridge.

"Next time, I'll be sure to have more for the vegetarians," he said with a smile. Martin had a devilish grin sometimes and it was difficult to know when he was bullshitting me. But as a bullshitter myself, I was pretty sure he was giving me the treatment.

After we were all eating, Martin said a few words of welcome. "My door is always open. Well, maybe not always. Basically, if my door is closed that means I'm either asserting my inherent right to privacy, or else I am with a lady. Or wished I was. Either way, consider me unavailable to you. I mean, available."

We laughed.

"We're all boys here, and boys will be boys. My attitude about things is to live and let live, and I practice a philosophy of tolerance. Everyone should be tolerant of other people. So, for example, I made a point of helping Robbie to achieve his goals of becoming a vegetarian. I did not force those horrible ribs on him."

More laughter at this.

"However," he went on, "what I can condone is limited, and there are school rules to contend with. Ultimately, every boy is responsible for living up to the school credo, which is that if you work hard, you can achieve anything. Well, anyway, that's the end of my pep talk. Anyone have any questions?"

"Sure, uh, what's with the church music?" said Jonah.

"Oh, thanks for asking. So you like Opera, do you, Jonah?"

"It's uh, very inspiring," he said.

"Inspiring? Well, yes. I suppose it is. I like classical music in general, but Opera most of all. Ah, La Traviata! Don't worry, after a few months of hearing it, you will all become aficionados." He said this with a grin, and was met by general sarcasm and guffaws. But everyone could see he was a right guy.

***

As a Kickshaw sophomore I was initially busy learning the basics, like where my classes were, who the masters were, and what expectations the school had for me. I tried to figure out where I fit in, as all new members of a family must do.

But as time passed, my natural inclination to explore—something I think is etched in the hearts of every teenage boy—began to manifest. As with the family, eventually there is a desire to see what lies beyond.

For one thing, we were sometimes granted leave—liberty— to go off-campus. It was a privilege, not a right, and many a Kickshaw boy agonized about losing that privilege for some minor infraction or rule-breaking; but when it was granted then freedom reigned supreme.

And with liberty came the existential problem of how to get off the campus. For some, this amounted to no more than a phone call to friends or family, or even a taxi, and others had the joy of riding a moped into Carpinteria. But I had no such options, so I had to walk. Sometimes I hitch-hiked, although it was not recommended and may have violated some minor Kickshaw policy to do it.

That first day I successfully signed the off-campus liberty sheet, as the Dean, Charlie Stacks, looked on and winked, I skipped back to my room and collected my mainly empty wallet and a few coins, and then started off in the direction of Long House. I knew from Jonah's explanations that the path would lead downhill, past a few free-standing domiciles—one of these was apparently the Dean's—and snake along the side of the Mesa, eventually becoming a fire road paved with dust and rimmed with sage. That road led around until it looped back and found asphalt of the main thoroughfare leading up; but before that, there lay a cut to the right that headed down, a trail. It meandered and branched, like a goat trail; but the goats had been students. 'If you take this path,' Jonah said, 'eventually it pops out at the foot of the Mesa, right in front of the Sauvage's house.'

For this reason the whole area was called, at least by me, the *Forest Sauvage*, though it bore little resemblance to what is described in *The Once and Future King*. I must explain that Mr. and Mrs. Sauvage were caretakers, fellow Scots who had followed out old Kickshaw from the U.K. all the way to California; they were thus presumably Kickshaw's oldest and dearest friends. But they said Mr. Sauvage was dead; now only his wife remained. She was a kind old woman, apparently half blind, and yet she still prepared and served the Senior Coffee in the evenings. I would see her moving slowly pushing a cart in the direction of the Branson Library, the old, original library under the Schoolhouse dorms, where Kickshaw used to read to the boys in the evenings. 'A captive audience!' I thought.

I took this trail, and trudged happily across the *Forest Sauvage*, hoping for adventure on my first solo trip into town. It was a glowing afternoon, it did not feel like Fall yet in Southern California, and I was soon perspiring. The scent of sage, that specific scent of the foothills, enveloped me, and I wondered if anyone could be more happy. Suddenly I heard a voice off to the right. It seemed there were several voices, but when I reached a goat trail crossing, I could smell pot, and the voices stopped. I paused, considering if I should crash the party. But it was early in my Kickshaw career and I knew basically no one. So I kept walking.

The trail eventually bottomed out. I could clearly see the back of the Sauvage's cottage. It was positioned in such a way that anyone who reached the big sign at the start of the private road that led up the Mesa, would also see the cottage; but that also meant someone in the cottage would see the visitor, should they choose to make it their business to look.

I reached the road. This was Casitas Pass Road, a long ribbon that ran back into hills and even around the back of Carpinteria. But here, there was very little through traffic. An occasional farmer would block the road while sitting on a tractor. There were no cars at the moment, the world was curiously silent; and I could see lemon trees with yellow eyes sleeping in an orchard on the far side. I started walking, then, not really too concerned with reaching any particular destination, but headed in the direction I knew went towards Carpinteria; that is, to the right. To the left the road led further along the orchards and then there would be a turn that went up the foot hill; and somewhere up there Heinrich the physics master and his elderly wife lived, inhabiting an idyllic life far removed from the horrors of World War II, which we all assumed Herr Henler had participated in to the full. He was SS for sure.

Suddenly my thoughts were interrupted by the sound of a struggling air-cooled engine. The tiny engine was embedded in an old VW Beetle, like a ragged WWII era contraption, the kind my dad collected and had once worked on as a mechanic.

I looked back over my shoulder, because I was walking in good boy-scout fashion facing imaginary oncoming traffic, while the existentially real VW was rapidly overtaking my position. I would soon be outflanked.

"Oh no!" I said.

It was Heinrich, I could clearly make him out peering through round glasses and gripping the steering wheel like a she-devil. I was not exactly ready to encounter him here, out in the wild, and me on liberty. But the Beetle rapidly slowed, finally coming to a complete halt in the middle of the road. He had rolled down the window; or otherwise was driving with it rolled down. "Young Master Gray! May I give you a lift into town?"

I smiled. "Certainly, sir." I went around to the side and got in.

He immediately gunned the engine and the car began to move. After a moment he said, "What do you think of Kickshaw so far?"

"Very different to my old school."

"Oh, where was that?"

"Back in Florida, sir. Where my mother lives. I used to go to Titusville High, it is in Central Florida."

"I understand Florida is a nice place to retire."

"I wouldn't know, sir."

He looked over at me and said, "You have good manners. You may call me Heine, if you like. But only if I can call you Robbie."

"But in class we always say 'Master,'" I said. "I thought perhaps it was the rule."

He chuckled. "No. The rule is that I call you Mr. Gray, and you call me Master Henler. But if you like, we can be more informal. That is our choice as men."

"So Heine is the diminutive of Heinrich?"

"Or Einer. But I prefer Heine."

"Isn't there a famous author named 'Heinrich' who is also a Heine? But that is his last name. It is all a bit confusing."

The old master seemed surprised. "You have heard of the poet Heine?"

"Well, yes. I spend a lot of time in the library. Or did, anyway. Not much else to do back in Titusville except watch rockets occasionally blast off and hope they explode."

I could see he was still not quite convinced. He looked at me as if I might be pulling his leg. "Hmm," he said.

"Isn't he the one who said, 'They start by burning books, and end up burning bodies?'"

Suddenly I felt the car swerve wildly. Old Heinrich, who was now Heine (I never had the nerve to call him Einer) had pulled violently at the wheel of the small car and seemed to be in considerable distress. "*Dort, wo man Bücher verbrennt, verbrennt man am Ende auch Menschen*," he said in a small voice. The car slowed—he must have taken his foot completely off the gas pedal—and coasted slowly forward and finally to a stop. He seemed almost in a state of shock.

"Are you alright, sir?" I said.

"Oh, I am sorry dear boy. You do not understand. This quotation, it was important to us in the war years. We saw things then, terrible things."

I didn't say anything.

"Yes, I'm sorry," In his distress, he took a handkerchief from his right coat pocket and wiped his eyes. "Please give me a moment."

"Of course." It had never occurred to me that Master Henler actually was, for real, in Nazi Germany. He did seem very old; certainly old enough for this to be true, but it raised many questions. However, my immediate concern was to make a mental note to stop calling him 'Himmler,' which now took on an additional urgency. I could not help but think our childish talk and laughter about the SS was cruel. Much more likely was the possibility he had been brutalized and terrorized, and thus felt the need to flee to America. What if he was a Jew? Was he in a camp? Or perhaps, was he a soldier, a conscript? Now he was old and suddenly reminded of the terror, of unspeakable things. I had made a serious mistake.

But old Heine was now recovering. Instead of being angry and killing me with a hidden Luger pistol from the glove box, he smiled. His face changed. "So, at least we have established you are a young man of culture. That is astonishing. Not every boy at Kickshaw..." This thought seemed to dry up, but he continued, "May I ask, who is your advisor?"

"My advisor? Oh, that's Martin Quinn."

"Ah yes, young Martin. He's a veteran, but then you knew that, of course."

I did not, but I lied and said, "Naturally."

Master Heine then collected his wits, dried his eyes again, and finally looked at the road, which was still empty, and put the car back into gear. We bumped forward slowly, gaining speed, and the little Volkswagen began to surge as he changed gears. "Let us progress," he said.

"Thank-you. By the way, it was most kind of you to stop."

"It is my pleasure. And I will tell Martin, who is also a man of culture, that I have found someone he may want to put a little more attention into."

"Oh, that's not necessary." I did not like the idea that I had drawn unnecessary attention to myself; after all, I was a newcomer. I knew nothing. "Not necessary at all!"

"But it is. Martin is actually an old student of mine. You see, he went to Kickshaw also. And then he was drafted and went to Vietnam, and then finally University on the G.I. Bill."

We 'progressed' on down inevitably to the Freeway, US-101, the majestic concrete double stripe smear running up and down the California coastline.

"I am going to the Albertsons, Robbie. You see? Right over there. Where can I drop you?"

"Oh, just anywhere is fine. Yes, the shopping center."

I waved goodbye as he moved on shaky legs slowly towards the grocery. I didn't really have a destination, Carpinteria was unknown to me. What an adventure! The joy of being free flooded over me, but at the same time I felt curiously alienated, even a little afraid. The small corner of anxiety came from a feeling I could not have explained then. Only now, so many years later, I understand it was an effect of being alone. Suddenly, I was just myself, and the truth was, I didn't know who that was. Was I the son of a faggot? Was I the funny joker mysterioso I imagined or hoped I was? Was I a scholar? Was I a rich white boy? A creature of privilege? Perhaps I was a child, a fool, a nobody? I had no idea. Somehow these days I seemed always to react to others, and that defined me. It was what was supposed to happen. But now, alone here in this little bedroom community, no friends, no car, no money to speak of, just salt air and sky, I had nothing to react to and no one to try to convince. I was just me.

I walked for a while and it seemed my feet took me inevitably in the direction of the sea. Perhaps the detectable scent of salt air drew me forward. I had come down from the hills, like Moses carrying nothing, and my destination was a Red Sea. Or at least it was a sea, a beautiful sea of my imagination, the Pacific. The Atlantic, I always thought, was so fucking forgettable. This was different. I felt like I was home. I just sat on the beach for most of the day. It was heaven.

***

On a Saturday morning a few weeks later I ate a breakfast of heavily buttered and jammed whole wheat toast and frozen concentrated orange juice, and observed the glory of the day from the windows of the dining hall. Heading back towards our room, I found Jonah was up and out—surfing, obviously. Yes, the board was gone and there was a void on the far wall where his wetsuit customarily resided, like a black scarecrow.

I was inclined to dive into Jonah's stack of Playboy magazines, as the whole of the dorm seemed very quiet, but I

knew where that would lead, and I decided to go on an explore instead. I changed into some shorts and put on my
older pair of canvas high tops and set out from the back
stairs. No need to sign out; I wasn't really going off campus.
At least not in theory.

The *Forest Sauvage* was my destination—of course, but I
meant to investigate further down the hill. Instead of going
the usual way in the direction of the Moon Flower, the secret hideout of the seniors, I went to the end of Long House
and sat for a moment on the grass near the edge of the drop
off. It was not too steep at that point, but there was no trail
to speak of. I paused and waited and watched. Things
seemed quiet enough; this particular spot was shielded
from view on the left by some trees and to the right it was
only the dorms, and no one seemed to be out on their balcony. I went over the side, moving quickly, working my way
down to find cover about 50 yards below.

Once I was out of sight of the top of the Mesa, I rested for
a minute and got my bearings. I figured I'd keep going down
a bit. There was a road, called Jefferson Canyon, that ran
along the north side of the Mesa property. I knew if I hit the
road I was at the bottom. But meanwhile there was plenty
of unexplored territory in between.

After a while, I began to miss my trusty machete. It was
my constant companion in the Florida Wasteland, and
would have been useful. I stopped for a minute because I
thought I heard something unexpected: water. Not flowing,
but the sound of a sprinkler. Perhaps I had made a wrong
turn? But no, up ahead I could now see the beginnings of a
path running along the side of the hill. A gray metal pipe ran
about four feet in the air along the path, and attached to the
pipe, directly in front of me, there appeared to be a sprinkler
head. This was the source of the noise. A trickle of water
bubbled from the head as if at this moment the pressure of
the flow was minimal; but I could see evidence that at times,

the outflow was plentiful, enough to drive the head in an arc of about 90 degrees.

I stepped onto the path. It was clear that it was only occasionally serviced, no doubt by someone from Chickie's crew, but there were no footprints, and the path itself was of solid dry clay with small pebbles here and there—the stuff of the Mesa itself.

I observed that the path ran very slightly downhill, and I thought at first the plumbing might be part of an agricultural system, for irrigation, but then I noticed the type of plants growing where the water sprayed: nasturtiums, primarily. And an abundance of tomato plants, volunteering in grotesque spots here and there, cherry tomatoes ripe and unripe scattered on the ground like cannon shot, and then nettles. Lots and lots of nettles. "Ah, a shit-sprayer!" I said to myself. Yes, it was obvious now. This was indeed an irrigation system, but it irrigated only as a side-effect. The purpose of the outflow was to distribute the gray water, the wastewater, from the toilets and sinks and showers of the dormitories. It had not occurred to me until now that Kickshaw was not attached to the Carpinteria sewer. We were too high, perhaps, or Santa Barbara County had not got around to building a municipal sewer this far out.

The tomatoes were the giveaway: those durable little seeds were capable of passing through unscathed the assholes of the Kickshaw crowd, and then survive the water treatment process, whatever it was, and found themselves still viable. It was something that pleased me immensely for reasons that I could not really fathom. So the seeds lived; and they travelled down the pipe only to be projected out onto the side of the hill, into wet and well fertilized soil. Meanwhile the nasturtiums might have arrived by a similar route; I thought the nettles were from seed blown in, but they made sense, somehow. I supposed they loved the nutrient rich damp where many other plants would not thrive.

But the nettles were also quite painful, as I instantly found out when I brushed against one of them. My left leg below the knee was suddenly on fire. It occurred to me that I was surrounded by them, and also that the shit-sprayer outflow, while it did not exactly stink, probably was not that great to get all over my shoes. I stopped and thought about what to do. Finally I figured I would follow the shit-sprayer path for a while. It seemed to me that on my return journey, I could go the other way on the path and see where it led, probably by some *commodius vicus* of recirculation back to the top of the Mesa.

I had not gone more than a hundred yards when I saw it. There was a garden hose. Someone had removed the sprayer head from the pipe and did a bit of plumbing sufficient to mount a hose onto it. It snaked down the hillside. I did not immediately think through what this might mean.

I went a bit further down the path, and began to hear a low rumbling in the gray pipe, and then the pipe itself vibrated much more than I would have anticipated, as if it were about to come to life; and finally with a joyful release, staccato blasts of fluid began to ejaculate at full force from the sprayer heads. The heads were equipped with spring mounted triggers that moved the outflow chk,chk,chk,chk,chk, blast after blast, in sequence to point in a new but always counter-clockwise direction. I realized I was about to get sprayed, and moved on the double out of the trajectory. The shit-sprayer path was no longer a safe way forward, I thought, and I dove off it into the bush, heading downhill. At some distance now, the sound of the sprayers became faint, and I had a sense of disorientation; I was not so high up on the hillside anymore, and I could see much less, and the growth was very thick. But I soon realized my error: I was completely surrounded by a dense green forest of a singular plant species, something like a vine, with lobed leaves similar to an oak. I had a bad feeling about it, but then I crossed paths again with the hose. Not having any real curiosity, but by this point urgently wanting to find my way out to the street that must be somewhere below, I followed it now, pushing aside the dense green growth that was everywhere.

That's when the hose ended. The shit-sprayer effluent coursed out onto the ground and the end flopped like when the head is cut off a worm. The expelled fluid flowed into some rough trenching, now. I followed the trenching, pushing back hedges of overgrowth, and landed at the base of the largest marijuana plants I had ever seen. They were taller than I was, perhaps 8 to 10 feet in height in some cases. There were a number of them, and I knew immediately they were pot plants by the shape of the leaves, but mainly by the sweet odor. They had a strongly resinous smell that is hard to describe but very easy to recognize if you have ever smelled it.

I gazed in wonder at this magic shit-sprayer pot farm hidden in the thickest part of the *Forest Sauvage*; but unfortunately my excitement was tempered by the realization that I was surely trespassing, and fear overwhelmed me. I ran the other way, back up the hill for a while, out of breath, and went through more and more of the dense, green lobed vine that seemed to be everywhere, pushing through it, running my hands over my eyes, which now seemed strangely irritated, and wishing I had better clothes or equipment, or even a water bottle. Where was my machete! I struggled back up the hill, mainly following the hose, and came at last to the shit-sprayer path once more. I figured this would at least get me back to the Mesa. It did, eventually. But it seemed to go on much further than I expected.

The path with the pipe topped out on the far end of the Mesa, past Long House and High House, past the Hermitage, and further on, even past '27 House. There I found the pumping station—Shit-Sprayer's End—and what I guessed was the water treatment plant. It was not overlarge, and naturally out of sight for cosmetic reasons. I was exhausted, but just able to walk around the structure and emerge, completely innocent in appearance, I hoped, although I am sure I was somewhat disheveled, if not an all-out wreck. I looked at my canvas high tops, which were now completely fouled and soaked. Ruined. As I walked they creaked. Before I got back to High House I took them off and discarded them in the bushes before I crashed in our room. Jonah had not returned. I contemplated the Penthouse I knew was under Jonah's bed (I thought Penthouse was gross, but there was no doubt you got to see the whole taco). However, my eyes were not working somehow. I figured I was just dead tired. I took a nap.

***

After a few hours I began to really feel ill.

I had not been to the school infirmary before. I shuffled up to the door and pushed it open, as the sign said, "come in." I could barely make it out.

"Yes," said an old matron with a nurse's cap. "What have we here?" She was sitting behind a small desk, like a child would use, near a lamp, and seemed to be reading a leather-bound book, likely the Bible. The room was fairly dark beyond the lamp, it seemed lit for cocktails, not CPR. There were a few cots in a row and then in the back I saw a shadowy hallway that no doubt led to perdition.

"I think I've got a problem," I croaked.

"Oh? Well, come on in then."

It was Mrs. Standish, the nurse. She led me into the infirmary by the hand and set me on a stool as she gently helped me remove my shirt. "Oh, my." The nettles had really done a number on my legs and my right hand; but my main concern was that my eyes were watering and seemed to be almost swollen shut.

"Yes, I see." she said. "That looks like a nettle sting. And those, too. And the swelling looks a lot like Poison Oak. Have you been down on the trails?"

"Uh-huh."

"Do you think you rubbed your eyes?"

"Yes. Most likely," I said.

"That would explain why they're almost closed. Can you breathe OK?"

"I think so," I said.

"I'm going to help you into a shower. Try to wash your face and eyes. Use soap first on your hands for a while, then wash up as best you can. We'll put some calamine lotion on after. Poison Ivy contains a caustic oil. You can help yourself most by trying to wash off as much of it as you can."

"But it hurts!"

"Yes, it will sting a little. Especially the nettles. But do what you can with the bar of soap. It will help, believe me. You're in for a few days of it, unfortunately."

I struggled with the pain as I felt my way to the shower and she turned on the water. "I think these clothes, I'll put them in a bag so you can wash them later. They're probably covered in the oil that causes the rash."

She helped the invalid into the shower, where I stood reeling, and I groaned and moaned as I came out, looking for all the world like a wrinkled hairless rat. A lab rat.

"What am I to wear?" I moaned.

"Just lie down for a while on one of the cots and pull the sheet over you," she said. "Rest. I'll have one of Ciccariello's boys go and get you some clothes."

I don't think I have introduced Albert Ciccariello, who we all called Chickie. He was the work-gang boss of the all-Mexican building and grounds crew, some sort of Arab-Italian mix, and he'd worked at the school forever, reporting to the Head of Buildings and Grounds, who was of course always a white man, currently Glen Thompson. Thompson was also the basketball coach, the kind of guy who refused to call Mohammad Ali by his name and still said Cassius Clay. But unlike him, Ciccariello was liked.

I once had to go and ask Ciccariello for help to get a frisbee off a roof. I went down to his office.

"Sir," I said, "I have a problem."

He turned around, cigarette dangling, and said, "Yes, most of us do. It's the human condition." But he eventually did get someone to help after considerable discussion and allocution about the dangers of wild flying disks.

I estimated Ciccariello's age at about 55 years old, but he was small and wiry and then further shrunken by his addiction to black coffee and nicotine. Heavy exposure to the California sun rounded out the shrinking ray effect of his diet and lifestyle. He had become miniaturized. He was a wop, is what the guys all said (I never said stuff like that) but he was cool. His 'office'—basically a big shed where the tools and other trappings of grounds work were stored, that is, the Buildings and Grounds Sheds—was right next to the Infirmary. He had put up a makeshift desk for himself, something he cobbled together from two -by-fours and old sawn planks, and liked to sit with his feet up on this rickety platform, puffing away. Sometimes he would sit up and ground out his butts in a huge, filthy brown ashtray.

A peculiarity of Chickie was that because his office was also close to the designated smoking area (the one place on school grounds where students with permission from their parents to smoke tobacco were allowed to do that) and because he himself was such a continual smoker, and a frequenter of the smoking area himself—often you could bum a smoke off him—he had formed a little group of addict wayward youth who clustered around him, or loafed in his shed, coughing up phlegm, chatting and joking, spitting like snakes, or swearing like small demented sailors, as they indulged their tobacconist vice. These were the "Ciccariello's boys" that she was referring to. Think Fagin's boys but with a lot more money.

I lay on one of the cot beds in the peaceful, darkened infirmary and rested, listening to the casual chatter and four-letter words emanating softly from the smoking area, and almost fell asleep while the nurse gently rubbed calamine lotion over my arms and legs and torso. It was relaxing, almost sensual, for her to do that, and because of the intimacy of it, it gave me pleasure mixed amongst the hypersensitivity of the chemically burnt skin; but in my mind she was ancient and so I had no sense of anything improper or sexual about it; I was drifting off. It was so peaceful. I just lay there in the calm and quiet, dim light hiding everything, as she rubbed the lotion, while I occasionally let out a little sigh of relief, and she let out a little "ah," each time I sighed.

Unfortunately I began to feel myself becoming erect. She had not touched me there, but all the rubbing in that general area must have had some effect. My eyes were still weepy and it felt good to keep them closed. 'Oh no,' I thought. 'What if she sees.' I kept trying to suppress it, but it seemed like the more I tried to make it go away the more intense my erection became. It just got bigger and bigger.

"Now, now, there, there Robbie. That will do."

'Oh no!' I thought. She had seen my erection. All I could think of was how big it was (it's not that I have a penis other than ordinary size, but *from inside*, as it were, it felt big, then) and I imagined her, too, how she was looking at it. Staring at it. If anything, it was even bigger now, probably (in my imagination) visibly throbbing. It just felt tighter and tighter.

"It's all right, Robbie. Nothing to be embarrassed about. I've seen my share of penises."

Hearing her say the word 'penis,' and how she was so comfortable around erect ones, seemed to do something to me. I heard her startle. And then after a while, "Oh my goodness."

I cried out. "Oh no, oh God!" It was happening and it was going everywhere.

"Just calm down. That's all right. My Lord, what a mess," she said absently to herself. "I'll get a washcloth. Silly boy. Just rest now." She laughed then, looking back at me, a woman's laugh when she saw a dollop of jism on my face, and that laugh completely deflated me in an instant. I was suddenly a small naked boy, age 5, standing in a distant bathroom, my mother, younger then, chiding me for something embarrassing I had done or imagined doing, as she sat peeing on a toilet seat with a string hanging out of her crotch.

"*The Incident*," as I called it, was a self-*cause célèbre* and source of shame for the rest of my days at Kickshaw, a secret carefully hidden. A secret I hoped no one else would ever, ever learn. What had happened, the truth, was far worse than what had happened to Johnny Winkle, that unfortunate in the class of '76 who we heard was dragged out into the hallway naked when caught masturbating. Yes, far, far worse than Johnny: I had forcibly ejaculated in front of the school nurse, like an absolute wanker. Like a DEVO mongoloid. She had seen everything.

For a long time I imagined in terror what would happen if Mrs. Standish were to tell people—of course, she must be doing that, spreading the story far and wide, telling it in the teacher's lounge, laughing about it with that big-titted Ms. Snodgrass, the fantastic young jewess we had for English and Photography, who everyone fantasized about constantly. My terrified imagination ran wild.

Every time I would see Mrs. Standish, for months and years, perhaps at an assembly, perhaps in the school parking lot, in the Chapel, or on the green, and forever after, it seemed to me she also smiled in that same special way. Smiled and laughed. Giggled. At those times I would flush and become bashful and not know what to say, thinking about her touching me, and then walk in the other direction as fast as possible. But it was not always possible, and on one or two occasions I had to actually speak to her.

Anyway, after a while, after she cleaned me up, after I calmed down, perhaps an hour, maybe two, I heard the door to infirmary open and the doorbell (which was an actual bell) jingled, and then Sheldon Witherspoon, one of

Chickie's "boys," and a senior no less, came in bearing some of my clothes, a shirt, belt, and pants.

"Hey Robbie, here you go, I had to rummage around a bit. Found your porn stash in the bottom drawer, but not much in the way of underwear."

"Well that's just great, Sheldon." He smelled of cigarettes, which was no great thing in my mind.

Sheldon came a bit closer and then whispered. "Did you see anything interesting down there?"

"Oh, not much," I said. "Kinda stinks down there."

"Naturally," he said. "It's a shit-sprayer after all."

I was lying, of course. Not about the stink, but about the bud. I had been thinking rather steadily about the pot farm I stumbled into and what I should say or do about it. But now it seemed Sheldon might already be onto me.

"Well, anyway," he said. "Next time, ask me, I'll give you a bit of a tour." He winked. "Not a word, now. Toodles."

***

For a while I was out of commission, obviously, but that wasn't so bad. After a few days I was back to class and undergoing the brunt of jokes about my skin rash. I kept thinking about the marijuana, but eventually came to the conclusion that keeping my big mouth shut was probably the best policy. Someone—certainly Sheldon—knew about it and they knew I knew. Which was bad. I didn't want to be implicated; but I also didn't want to be run over by a Beamer filled with angry pot-head seniors. I had no idea, so my imagination continued to run wild.

But also, I admit, the craving for bud was there in me. I coveted the weed. They say pot isn't addictive; well, perhaps not. But pleasure is. I cursed myself for not having the wherewithal to pick a few buds. Payment for my troubles. And even beyond that, what would Jonah think? What would Christian say about it? Was there a way for me to profit from it without getting my ass kicked or my head shot off?

***

The final friend I have to introduce now is Cadogan West. I didn't really click with Cadogan for a long time. He was in High House with us, and in fact he was near Jonah on purpose due to their friendship from freshman year. I guess they had been roommates. In '27 House. So he was tight with Jonah, but not as a surfer. His vibe came from an entirely different place. I remember giving him shit about his name when he came to see Jonah.

"So, you're in Sherlock Holmes, huh? Steal any plans lately?"

"Oh," he said. "You know about that."

"Sure do. Probably got the book right here... But I won't let on if people ride you about it. I imagine they do."

"Not as often as you might think. People don't fucking read. Ninety percent of them would rather choke on a carrot than crack a book. I'm Cadogan. Pleased to meet you." He held out his hand and smiled. I took his hand. His grip was like that of a wrestler.

Cadogan was small and wiry with a face already ravaged by acne, and he would continue to get an occasional angry pimple during the entire time of our acquaintance.

According to Jonah, Cad's father was rich, tremendously wealthy, or as Kurt Vonnegut said in *Breakfast of Champions*, "fabulously well to do." The man didn't just develop property, he was behind the creation of an entire *city* that was called, appropriately enough, West Valley.

But there was no "valley." It was flat for miles around, completely featureless except for the prickly pear. And *West* Valley was located *east* of Los Angeles, out past San Bernardino but not quite to Barstow. The distance was certainly drivable to LA, if you could manage 90 miles an hour, which was what people did out there, and in other words, it was a bedroom community for the terminally car cultured: not so close as to be inundated with the problems of LA, like "wetbacks, gang bangers, and niggers on crack," as his father is supposed to have said. But still comfy and private and white. Cadogan West *père* was apparently in the Klan as a youth back in Georgia and Cadogan *fils* said his father had once described witnessing a lynching. He thought it was very satisfactory.

Yes, there was something about Cadogan senior that his son despised; so I knew for every story there was probably a bit more that was not forthcoming; an even dirtier, darker truth hidden by a dark story. Shade hidden by shade.

Cadogan didn't talk much about his wealthy family though, in part because his father assured him of nothing during his lifetime and probably hardly knew his son existed; and then he was suddenly dead, dead of a heart attack, an eater of steak and drinker of bourbon poleaxed in his prime, laid out on a fucking golf course or maybe with a fork in hand, or stuck up his ass, Cadogan would never clarify that point; and it was the mother, youngish and still reasonably attractive, who now had all the money and the exquisitely built 20-room ranch home on ten acres in the middle of absolutely nowhere. The mother and the son in Erewhon. And the young son was a quick study.

"It did not seem possible there could be so many guys out in a place like West Valley," he told me. "But there were. I grew to dislike it immensely. I disliked everything about it. Me, I like greenery. I like snow, even. Plants. Animals. California has always been a disappointment, for me, Robbie. So you see, money can't buy you everything." And then he'd sing "*Can't buy me love, love, no, no, no, nooo!*"

***

"Robbie, can you read your essay about Edgar Allan Poe's *The Tell-tale Heart* to the class, please?"

"Of course, Ms. Snodgrass. I'd love to."

Lori Snodgrass taught one of the Sophomore English sections—by chance, Jonah, Cadogan, and I were all in that class—and also Photography, which was a subject that Jonah loved possibly as much as surfing. Christian and William J. Brennan were in a different English class.

"Robbie, are you staring at me?"

"No, Sorry, Ma'am."

"You seemed to be daydreaming."

"Undoubtedly," I said.

Lori was a beautiful woman. She was what I later understood to be a Sephardic Jew, her family had roots in Spain. The skin on her face and hands was silky and smooth, but her eyebrows were dark and the kind that get plucked, and her hair was rich and black; I could not opine about the rest of her dermis, because every other part of her body, it seemed, lay covered under a layer of cloth at all times. It was not the hijab or head scarf, not that, but it was a very modest attire, to be sure. Prim and proper. She also had small-rimmed reading glasses that tended to exacerbate the effect of propriety and aged her by a few years. Even her feet, which I took considerable interest in, were wrapped in close-fitting shoes over tight-fitting socks, so that no part of her body was sun-exposed. I hypothesized she might be allergic to sunlight, like a vampiric creature, but surely the concern was us. The allergy was to us: the prying eyes of the obsessively horny teenage boys she had to deal with on a daily basis.

Not that we were anything but gentlemen, at least within earshot of the poor woman. But my point in all this is just to say that she was not ugly or old or fat or possessed of any other attribute that would preclude vigorous sexual activity as part of her daily routine. We imagined her like a Spanish Brigitte Bardot, who claimed to need it every day. And sex, being the biological reason for existence from the point of view of a 16-year-old boy, yes, sex was the *raison d'être*. We were all certain she was soaking in hormones and danced nude somewhere for money or pleasure. What her actual daily routines were, or what her lifestyle was actually like, her private life, her interests and passions, even what she liked to eat for breakfast, none of us knew. Our young imaginations ran wild. Cadogan was convinced her pubic hair was as dense and coarse as a bristle brush, and willing to bet money on his assertion if someone could prove its veracity.

Of course, the actual truth, which was probably entirely different, was completely obscured and distorted by our fantasy and so quite impossible for us to perceive.

In this day and age obsessing over a woman's physical attributes is considered crude, sexist, perhaps even a form of harassment. But I cannot pass over the truth about Lori. It would be unfair to her, and also skew the narrative, if I did not talk about the elephant in the room, or rather, the two of them.

Yes, the Boobs. Impressively big boobs. Big enough that they had to be holstered; big enough to be bolted on with heavy straps, like a ship moored to a pier with prodigious ropes. Her hips and thighs were relatively slender, perhaps from youthfulness, which caused her upper body development to seem even larger than it was.

"She's like a juggernaut," was Jonah's way of expressing it. "You could lose an eye to one of those."

"Those are Mastodon-sized udders," was Cadogan's take. "Far too large for a normal guy to handle. It would take a specialist to even know how to hold them."

"Imagine being under those and having her slap you in the face. What a wakeup call," said Jonah.

"She's so busy covering up that it just accentuates the whole effect," I said. "Poor woman."

"Oh, don't feel sorry for her," said Cadogan. "You know how many women spend good money to have doctors create what she has been given naturally? There's an entire cosmetic surgical industry forming right now. And in fact, they could be fake."

"That seems highly unlikely."

"Why? A million women would love to look like her. And where desire leads, money follows."

"But she doesn't seem that comfortable. Inhibited, I would say. At times, she seems awkward."

Jonah laughed. "In need of a good bonk, more like it."

Cadogan turned the chair around and sat using the chair back as an armrest for his elbows. "Perhaps you should encourage her to dress a bit more provocatively, Robbie. You seem to be connecting. I've watched you in class."

"Oh, don't be silly."

"It's true," said Jonah. "She does seem to like you."

I was blushing now. "She just likes the fact I can write. I turn in my assignments on time."

Jonah and Cadogan both looked at each other and shook their heads. They knew I was a virgin. It's true that I was terribly shy around girls. My experiences with Cecilia were not entirely Platonic, but our friendship was only sexual by proxy, by projection as seen by others. I was too young. But now...

"Talk to her. Ask her out."

"Oh, you guys." I shook my head vigorously.

It was Jonah who first approached her with overt amorous intent. He took his best shot. "Miss Snodgrass, have you been to Rincon?"

"Not too often. I think once."

"What would you think about taking some shots of me surfing?"

"Hmm. That sounds like fun."

"Really? Uh, OK, how about this Saturday?"

Things went as Jonah hoped, and she appeared at the appointed place and time; he mounted into the passenger side of her yellow Chrysler LeBaron convertible like a king, and they drove off together. I saw the car going down Mesa road on the far side, over by the Chapel. I could see his surfboard in the back.

But a few hours later Jonah returned, his face downcast.

"There you are!" I said. "How did things go?"

"Oh, she got some shots in, but she laughed when I suggested we should have a swim together. She didn't even put on a bathing suit. It was just the usual cover-up."

Cadogan then made his own efforts, which were much more subtle and complex and applied the shit-fuckery of girlie seduction. For reasons I can't explain, Cadogan seemed to naturally appeal to women; either that or he had the gift of gab. Or something. Perhaps he had been professionally trained as a spy. Because he got on very well. As I will narrate later, Cadogan managed to bone more than one of the women on campus—and technically there are none to bone.

But with Boob, as he called her, he got stonewalled. He would push and pull, and she would just laugh or make fun of him. Not outright jokes, but just asides to his youth, or gentle, tittering laughter. She suggested certain skin care products for his acne, as an example.

One afternoon Cadogan was passing through. Jonah and I were hanging out with the dorm room door open, and you could hear Martin Quinn's opera from all the way down the hall. And we started talking about her.

"You know, Robbie, I got held back after class today, and Boob just trashed my paper. It's covered in red ink. She decided to go over it line by line."

"Unfortunate," I said.

"Brutal." said Jonah.

"Indeed. And then she said, 'Let's look at Robbie's paper. That's right. Just have a look how concise this is. It's half the length of your paper but says more. You see how he has paragraphs for each topic and covers the ground. It's all very clear and well-argued. And then here, you see how he makes this observation that ties it all together. Whereas, you, you flop all over.' She praised you, dude, she praised you outright."

I smiled. "Sounds about right."

And this is where Cadogan's special genius came into play. I could see his mind beginning to turn over. He was imagining the how, the where, and the when. "Robbie," he said. "I think we can use that. Yes... Let me see..." He began pacing.

Jonah looked over at me and smiled. "He's thinking," he said.

"He does that, doesn't he?" I said.

"We need some sort of literary event. Perhaps the 500th birthday of someone—"

"Shakespeare?" I said.

"Exactly, someone like that. And you invite Miss Boob. To some sort of gathering. Where you...you read something you have written. And then you thank the audience and single out Boob as your inspiration."

"Right," I sighed. "That doesn't even sound remotely plausible."

"Hmm. OK. I've got another idea. It could get you into her, but it's high risk. I don't know if you have the nads."

"Let's hear it," said Jonah.

"We will have to draw on a curious bit of intel—gossip, I suppose—that I heard when I was having a smoke in Chickie Boy's Smoking Room."

Jonah frowned. "I thought you committed to quit smoking, Cad."

"I did. But once in a while it feels good to have a smoke. It's just that first puff, really, and then it's all downhill from there. Anyway, I was sitting quietly, no one else was around. And I overheard Standish telling Boob a little story. Over in the infirmary."

I was looking on in horror. "No. No!"

Cadogan glanced at me. "It's only Jonah, Robbie. And we can swear him to silence."

"No! No, dude!"

Cadogan chuckled. "So Standish is talking about rashes, I don't know how it came up but they're conversing about something and Standish says the boys sometimes go down to the trails and there's poison oak. Lots of it. And then she laughs and starts telling a story about a recent incident, where a boy—she doesn't use his name—a boy is completely covered in poison oak rash and comes into the infirmary. And when she applies calamine lotion—"

"No, Cadogan!"

"And when she applies calamine lotion, and just inadvertently," he went on, "the boy becomes erect. Then in his confusion and panic, he ejaculates. Not from anything she has done, of course, according to her, but spontaneously. Just from being sensitive. An incredible happy ending."

I covered my face with my hands.

Jonah was tittering with laughter. "And what did Snot Rag say?"

"Oh, she was laughing hysterically about it. Couldn't stop."

"No, No!" I cried.

"So it's all true," said Cadogan.

"No, it was just a thing that happened. She was rubbing calamine lotion over the majority of my body. I was tired, exhausted, and my eyes were closed. I got hard somehow. It wouldn't stop."

Jonah couldn't seem to hold back. "She's only like, 500 years old, man."

"Yes," Cadogan said. "Astounding. You successfully got Standish, that old bag, to give you a hand job. Who could have imagined."

"No!" I said. "It wasn't like that."

"But the best part is still to come." Cadogan was gleeful. "Standish then said the ejaculation was so strong that some of the jizz hit the back wall of the infirmary. She had to wipe it off the wall with a sponge."

"Oh no way," said Jonah. "Holy hell!"

"It's true. They went on to discuss how that might have happened. Apparently Standish thought your urethra must be scarred at the opening, causing the hole to be more like a gun barrel. They had a long discussion about your manhood, Robbie, and penises in general. She even talked about your ball sack."

"No way, man. You're embellishing."

"Well, perhaps just a tiny bit. Anyway, the point is, Boob was entranced. She's fascinated and intrigued with you. So now, for the revenge. The women have been laughing at your manhood, but this is your way to even the score. Now listen to this..."

That night I got to work writing a short story about an incident that happened to a boy I knew—I tried to frame it that way. But I intentionally allowed myself to write something that bordered on pornography. Or what I imagined to be. I wove in an older woman, a teacher, with Catalonian features and a delicious, curvaceous figure. The boy became entangled in poison ivy and his whole body had to be tended to, well, you know the rest.

The next task was to ask Lori out. Cadogan had explained it was crucial she read the story when we were at her place. I had to find a way for her to take me there, or just possibly, to show up cold at her house. I didn't think I could do that. "Miss Snodgrass?"

"Yes, Mr. Gray?"

"You can call me, Robbie, you know," I said.

She was smiling. "All right. Thank-you for that. You may call me Lori in that case."

"I was wondering if we could go somewhere and, well, I wrote a short story. I wanted to have your opinion."

"Sure. But why not just give it to me and I'll read it this weekend?"

"I wanted to be there when you read it."

"Oh?" Her brow furrowed but gradually her face relaxed until a Mona Lisa smile appeared. "I see."

I thought maybe I had completely blown it.

"Tell you what," she said. "Why don't I pick you up on Sunday morning."

"Really?" I was completely surprised. "Uh, that sounds great."

"Be sure to sign out for weekend Liberty. OK?"

"Absolutely."

So things seemed to be working, and not only that, but it even seemed easy. I didn't understand it, and I even began to imagine it actually was just that easy. I must have been missing out all this time. I started to feel good. I was nervous, of course, but Cadogan kept pumping me full of courage for doing what had to be done. "You must teach Boob a lesson, Robbie. There's no other way. Give it to her. Release onto her boobs if you can."

Sunday finally came and I obsessed over the details of what to eat for breakfast and what clothes and tried to comb my hair, which was an absurd, impossible task. It was growing out nicely (much to the dismay of old Kickshaw) but I lacked conditioner. I gave up and focused on clothing. I had a nice shirt that Larry bought me, I suppose it was a Hawaiian shirt, one with Balinese dancing girls, and the old comfortable jeans seemed best. I was not a "penny loafer" guy or a "boat shoe" topsider guy, like so many of the Kickshaw boys. I loved my Chuck Taylor All Stars. So all stars it would be.

Twenty minutes before the appointed hour I sat out on the back stairs, so I could watch for Lori's car. The idea of her coming up to the dorm room was too much for me so I kept a lookout. Finally there it was, the Chrysler, like a yellow moth among the greenery of the lawn. She saw me and waved. I rushed down, then remembered the story, and ran back up to the room, grasped the hand-printed paper, and dashed back out. Soon we were rolling. I looked over at Lori and she looked radiant. "You look good. I mean, you look great," I stuttered.

"Thank-you. You look good yourself. Relax, I'll take you for a little drive and then we'll go to my place."

I was overcome with excitement and the sudden unexpected pleasure, entirely new to me, of being in a convertible. I had no idea. The wind blew back my hair, and I noticed Lori had a scarf over her head but otherwise there was a lot more skin. She was wearing a black tank top. I could clearly see her arms and the outline of her bra, the thick edges of the straps showing on her shoulders. She was wearing shorts, the Levi kind that had been cut off, and the edges were now ragged, and she was driving barefoot. It was not easy to talk with the car in motion so I just kept quiet. Occasionally she would point to some landmark, we were driving through the back of Carpinteria and then out in the direction of Summerland, which is a little community just to the North. We never got quite that far, she pulled into the Polo Club, and then went around to some condos behind it.

"Is that where you live?" I said.

"Yes, it's just a rental. But I like it out here. There are horses."

"So you're into Polo?" I said, rather lamely.

"Oh by no means." She parked. "But I know someone who's into it. He's kind of teaching me how to understand it. Well, here we are." She slipped on some sandals and I watched her lean over. I got out and followed. We walked up a flight of stairs and I was two steps behind her, staring at her butt, which filled the Levi shorts in a way that seemed very grown-up woman, not girl. I felt totally out of my depth. She unlocked the door to a condo a few doors to the left; we went in.

"This is nice," I said.

"Yeah. Why don't you sit down. I'll make some tea. I've probably got a coke in the fridge...let me see..." She was bending over again and looking around in the open fridge, so I forced myself to stop my own looking and went to the dining table, and then I thought I should sit on the couch. But I finally moved to a chair opposite the couch. She came out eventually with tea in two mugs and put one down on the little coffee table for me. "Well, I guess you have a story you want me to read."

"Yes, uh, definitely."

And then I heard something. "Honey buns, are you back?"

"In the living room," she said.

Then to my horror, I realized we were not alone. It was a man's voice. An older man. And I thought I recognized it. The bedroom door opened and out came a familiar face, but I had never seen it outside the context of Lido and High House. It was Martin Quinn.

"Martin?" I sputtered.

"Hey Robbie," he responded, and sat down with Lori on the couch. The way that he sat, smiling, and close to her, within her personal space, with his arm on the top of the upholstered couch, but behind and around her, as she smiled at me, made everything clear.

"Oh crap," I said.

"Robbie has a short story he wants me to read," she said.

Martin continued to smile. "That sounds like it might be interesting."

"No," I said. "Not that interesting." I was already getting up to leave.

"Don't rush off, Robbie," said Martin. "There's going to be some Polo in a bit if you want to watch it. Lori has a really cool pad, we can see the action from the balcony."

"No," I said. "I'm not much for Polo. I don't even like the shirts." I made it about as far as the door when Lori stopped me. "Robbie, wait."

"What," I said.

"Well, how will you get back to Kickshaw?"

"I don't know."

"But I can get Martin to take you in a bit."

"No," I said. "That won't be necessary. My dad lives in SB. I can go to his place and get a ride. Or something."

"Hmm. Tell you what, let's go for a little walk. OK?"

"I don't think so."

"Please?" she said.

"Fine."

She told Martin we were going out for a walk and we went downstairs.

I felt a strong need to get out of there. Either that or cry. "So long, Miss Snodgrass."

"Wait, Robbie. Wait. I played a bit of a trick on you, I know. I wanted to apologize for that. Come on, let's walk down to the grounds."

There was no Polo on quite yet, the place was just starting to open up. A truck pulled up with a horse trailer on the back; a horse was inside peeking its head out the front.

"It looks somewhat fierce," I said.

"What does?"

"That horse."

"I don't know much about Polo," she said again.

"It's the game of kings," I said. "That's how it is described. Seems like a game of wack-a-mole to me. They use big sticks to hit a ball around."

"It seems a bit silly."

"Pretty fuckin' stupid if you ask me."

Lori beckoned to me with her hand. She opened and closed her hand, palm up. "Come. Please. Come and sit on this bench."

"Fine."

We sat for a minute in silence, looking at the field. There was a fresh grass smell in the sun that percolated up like coffee, and the smell of horse dung. A man came by wearing a polo uniform, or at least part of one. They have funny hats. He looked at Lori steadily as he walked by.

"You see," she said.

"What, that dude eyeing you?"

"Yes."

"I imagine you get that a lot."

"Oh, you have no idea." She leaned back on the bleachers. "It really kind of sucks. I have no desire to attract attention. That kind of attention is like a poison. I think for most women that's true. We really don't want it."

"That's interesting," I said. "I thought it was every woman's dream."

She just shook her head. "No, Robbie."

We sat for a while longer, and then she said, "Can I read your story now?"

I shook my head. "There's no point."

"But why not?"

"It's part of a con. It was Cadogan's idea."

"Ah yes, Cadogan. I think he fancies himself quite a ladies man."

"Well, he's already made out with at least two girls on campus. And you've seen Kickshaw. I mean, there's no girls."

"My goodness. He is quite the stud. But I'd still like to read it."

"I'm embarrassed, Lori. It's erotic. Or at least it's supposed to be. It's supposed to be sexual. I, I have never written anything like that before. I've never even said that word to a woman before."

I was talking about the word 'sexual.' I felt completely alienated. But it seemed that in response, as I moved further and further away from her emotionally, as if she knew how I felt, she opened. I could see her begin to open.

"You know, Robbie, you are my best student. In my English section. In photography, it's Jonah. He's got talent, a really good eye. But you are my best writer. I think some day you could be a novelist. Or be whatever you want to be. You're really smart, but you're also kind. That is a wonderful combination."

I didn't say anything. Slowly, I dug out the paper, it was folded up in my front pocket and had to be uncrinkled. "Don't laugh, OK?" I said, and handed it to her.

She unfolded the paper and started reading and after a while I could see she wanted to laugh. I crossed my arms and frowned and looked elsewhere. And when there was some chuckling, I finally said "Stifle yourself, Edith."

But I finally looked back and she was smiling at me. "Oh Robbie. They're only breasts. If you really want to see them I'll let you see. You certainly deserve it."

"So you're going to flash me right here? Don't tease. You know? That's not fair." I had taken on a rather grim attitude. Maybe being gay would be easier than this, I thought.

"You don't have a girlfriend yet?"

"No. I almost had one, back in Florida. But she decided to go with the jock instead."

"Ah, right. It happens."

"It does. Anyway, this has been fun."

"OK, Robbie. I'm glad you came out. Even though maybe it was not what you expected. Thanks for letting me read this."

I reached out for it and she reluctantly handed it back. "I wouldn't mind keeping this. It's like a love letter. I never got too many of those when I was young."

"No," I said. "I think I better keep it."

"That's fine." Then she had an idea. "I know. I'll give you extra-credit if you want," she said, smiling.

"Bye, Lori," I said.

"I'll see you in class!" she called out, after I'd put some distance between us. I looked back after a while and I could see Martin was with her. He waved.

Boy, what a reaming that was.

PART THREE — Long Showers

A girl and a boy fell in love,
And they set about trying to shove,
But the later the hour,
The tighter the flower—
They said it 'a sign from above.'

I'm going to hazard a few third-person omniscient sections in this part,
because some of this is reconstruction, perhaps almost dream se-
quences, and it just makes sense to narrate it that way. The reasons
will hopefully become clear as we go forward.

— DRS

***

Christian came in with the mist of morning clinging to his damp clothes; he'd been "out of bounds" again. It was just the usual stuff, a quick trip to town to buy a quarter bag from the new connection he had found—this freaky tulip farmer in the Carpinteria hinterland who had a magic greenhouse out back of his Casitas Pass roadhouse hideaway; plus a few other supplies from the all-night liquor store, there and back again using his stashed Peugeot. That moped was getting a lot of miles.

Back in his room, all was peace and quiet, and he breathed a sigh of relief. But he decided he wanted a quick shower and a brush of the teeth. 'You have to take care of your teeth,' he thought. 'Some things can't wait.' In his mind he saw someone he secretly feared: his grandmother, now long dead, who had no teeth at all, and put the disgusting dentures into the bowl beside the bed, just like in the Polident commercials. He didn't want to be like that; the image horrified him. It was like he could *see* the smell of decay, and it even had a color: his grandmother's face and teeth were spangled a fierce blue.

Going down the hall, he was puzzled to find a light on in the bathroom and a shower going somewhere inside. 'That's odd,' he thought. 'I wonder who.' He went on in and then saw it was Susan.

Their eyes met. She let out a little girlish "Eeeeeeeh" like a barn owl chick. Eyes bulging, mouth gaping, she tried to cover her smooth, brown naked body with her hands. The effort was completely ineffectual, and he just stood there, staring. Finally she said "Christian, go! Please!"

But Christian only had eyes for her big, dangling dick.

***

Susan woke up very early, as per usual. The mellow brown of the oak wall paneling all around her in the small room reminded her of a cloister cell. This cloister effect was heightened by the fact that the room had only one window, at the far end. It was a nice window, and like the one in Christian's room, it faced East and had a partial view of the chapel and the dining hall. But the room was still basically a cloister. I suppose a lot of dormitories feel like that.

Her bed, like all the others in Lido, had a cast iron frame painted gray and a single mattress. I don't remember these beds having a box spring, but they were generally comfortable, and that night she lay still, peacefully and blissfully asleep.

3 a.m. came like a dream-buster.

She woke up spontaneously before the alarm because that is how the human body adapts to such requirements: initially we need an alarm clock, but eventually we become so habituated to a routine, no matter how hard, that crutches like the chime of an alarm clock become unnecessary. Even, eventually, annoyances. Because we demand the freedom to overcome adversity.

She rose up in bed, then, and stretched her thin arms, and set about automatically saying a prayer. That was the routine every morning at 3 a.m. and sometimes, when she was feeling particularly ardent, at midnight as well. There were of course the ordinary prayers at the appointed times: 6 a.m., 9 a.m., noon, 3 p.m., and at the dinner hour. Then a 9 p.m. prayer before bed. She called it her prayer cycle, her 'Work of God.' It must be done and will be done.

Getting out of bed, she put on a robe and slippers and picked up her kit to make her way silently to the door, opened it a crack, peeked out to check the coast was clear, and went into the hallway. The lights were out but she knew the way by heart, and actually her room was well located for her purposes. She went into the bathroom and used the toilet in a stall, flushed, then turned on the light in the shower room. She disrobed, then, and stood naked, a small brown almost childlike body against the creamy electric light in the cavernous, tiled shower room, all the surfaces too bright and gleaming, and turned on the water to one of the projecting shower heads, the closest one. The water felt good on her thin body, the heat penetrated into her and soothed her internally, and the water snaked, eventually cascading down and running on the tiled floor towards the brass drain cover. The steam from the hot water percolated in the air for a while making chaotic patterns and some of it escaped out into the other room where the line of sinks stood waiting.

Susan did this ritual every morning. She didn't want to shower with the boys. After all, she was a girl. Girls need their privacy, she reasoned. That all seemed quite proper to her. But suddenly, someone was there. 'Oh no,' she thought. 'Maybe they are just using the toilet. Maybe it is all right...'

But then Christian had burst in, his lean sinuous body, an athlete's body, tan and gorgeous, was suddenly nude in front of her.

She was stunned by how beautiful he was, but also terribly ashamed of her exposure. 'No!' she thought. 'Not him!'

Wailing now, she cried out. "Christian, go! Please!"

But he just stood there, staring. Finally he turned and left.

**

I myself have never been particularly sanguine with group showers, and would prefer to have my privacy; but I was not motivated enough to get up early in the morning to achieve it the way Susan did. I know that there is nothing wrong with the human body, but for whatever reason I just feel like doing certain things in private: defecation, urination, washing and bathing. Sometimes I even feel like eating is something I'd rather do alone. I don't pee in urinals, just out of habit, unless I have to, because I like to sit down. Urinals also tend to stink of piss, so there's that. And indeed my father always said, "Why stand when you can sit down?"

As far as showering with other boys, well, it offered an opportunity to observe their dicks and the extent of their pubic hair and their overall physical development, their bodies taken as sculptural forms, which was certainly interesting to me and I think everyone is naturally curious about such things. There's nothing 'gay' about curiosity over the human body, especially when it comes to attractive ones. It's natural and normal. At least I think so. But I can say that I would rather have left those boys, especially the older boys with their bigger dicks, to their own devices in complete privacy. I did not feel then, and still do not feel now, any compelling reason to compare notes.

So that was the way it was in my mind, that was how I thought about it. We all showered together, although at random, showers were not at any prescribed time. And it was really no big deal at all and Susan seemed to make too much out of it. That was the general consensus. She had a dick after all. Christian could attest to that. And apparently a dick to be proud of. We did not understand her problem.

***

It was actually Martin Quinn, in the beginning, who asked me to befriend her.

"He's not making any friends, Robbie."

"Yeah, I know. The fact is, he's, you know, kind of weird."

"In what way?" asked Martin.

"He's kind of a pansy."

"Robbie. That's not right. This is a disadvantaged kid. My friend, Father Ferapont, who is a priest down in L.A., he recommended Calvin for Kickshaw. Through the Diversity program. Calvin comes from a hard background, he's from Watts. You know anything about Watts?"

"No," I said.

"It's a tough neighborhood. There's a history of police violence, of police brutality. That's not an easy place to grow up."

"Fine," I said. "What do you want me to do?"

"Just talk to him once in a while. Be his friend, just a little. I'm not saying pal around."

So I told Martin I would do that. But I found excuses to avoid doing it for a long while.

Because Susan was in my Aikido class, I had occasion to speak with her. Not that we really ever sat down and talked about anything of consequence. But we were on speaking terms. Susan was a misfit even among the misfits of Mr. Morris's Aikido class. She really wasn't that motivated. Her Gi, white and ironed, barely fit over her slim shoulders, and her belt sagged or else was not tied properly to form in a square knot. But one day we were sparring and I slipped and tumbled down on top of her. She smiled at me in a way that reminded me, just for a brief moment, of Cecilia.

I got up quickly and turned away to kind of get my head together and then swiveled around. "Are you alright?"

"Yes, I'm fine." She was adjusting her hair for some reason, in a way that no boy would do. "Come on, let's go again," she said, and charged at me, laughing.

That night it occurred to me that Susan was in a very similar situation to Valentine Michael Smith, the protagonist in *Stranger in a Strange Land*: she was from Watts, an area of LA that was infamous for the Watts riots of 1965. So Susan was from another planet, so to speak. Planet Black People. Susan also had other qualities that made me think of Heinlein's early work about Mars: she really was kind of like an alien in her appearance and attitudes. She seemed so different. But this connection to the strange did not disturb me, quite the opposite. I thought that perhaps I had started to *grok* Susan: I thought maybe I was starting to understand her. Or at least, to sympathize. No one likes being called a gay butt hole.

I impulsively decided to knock on Susan's door. She opened it rather timidly.

"Hi," I said. "Do you mind if we talk?"

She smiled and shook her head. "Not at all."

I went in. It was exactly like Ben Wa's room down the hall but smelled oddly of lilac and there was a lot more negative space: the room was mostly empty and unadorned. It occurred to me how large Christian's record collection actually was seeing a Lido room without all those crates. I did notice a small crucifix hanging on the wall.

"Why don't you sit in the chair," she said. Susan herself plopped onto the bed.

"I just came by because I thought you might like this book. Have you ever read Heinlein?"

"Oh, I'm not much for science fiction."

"Well, you might like this one. It's called *Stranger in a Strange Land*."

She laughed. "Oh how funny! What's it about?"

"It's about a boy who is ship-wrecked alone on Mars and raised by Martians. He is found and returns to Earth, but he's basically a Martian, all his ideas are different. And he sort of starts a new religion. He ends up changing the way people think about a lot of things on Earth."

"Hmm. I don't know if that's right for me, Robbie."

My idea of connection with Susan seemed to not be going as well as I had hoped. I thought I'd have to go back to Martin and report that it wasn't working, and that I had failed. I had tried, but failed. Perhaps this was visible on my face, and I looked sad, because after a few seconds she said, "But I'd like to read it. That's actually really nice of you to think of me. You came here, and no one else does that. You came and offered me something, a book. A book is a message, isn't it?"

I had no idea what she meant, but I said "Sure. Very much so. It can be."

"Good. Very good. Yes, let me read it. I will do that immediately."

It was a strange interaction, but I just went with it. I handed her the book and departed and we did not speak for a few days. But she must have read at least some of it, because we talked about it soon after.

"Hey Robbie, thanks for the book."

"Sure, what did you think of Smith?"

"Oh, I liked that his name was Valentine. What a beautiful name. I read the whole thing. But don't quiz me, please!" She laughed.

"Right. No quiz."

"I—I have a special name, too, Robbie."

"Oh? You mean like a nickname?"

"Sort of."

"OK. What is it?"

"Susan."

"Susan," I said. "Well, that's kind of like the boy named Sue."

"What?"

She didn't seem to get the reference. But that didn't bother me. "So you want me to call you Susan then?"

"Really?"

"Yes, really."

She smiled. "Oh, that's so nice of you. I can't believe it."

"You should try to be who you want to be. Or, rather, you should be who you are. We should all do that, you know what I mean?"

"Wow, Robbie. You are so inspiring sometimes." And she did something I did not expect, which was to give me a hug. I didn't go crazy over it; I just let her do what she wanted. She seemed happy. It's not easy to make someone happy in this world even for a minute or an hour. Even at that age I understood this. So I considered my book offering a success.

However, I must clarify, I didn't understand this Calvin Tyrone Gay was actually the girl, Susan. Not quite yet. I thought it was just a private fantasy she was telling me, a homosexual fantasy; as we all have feelings and transitory fantasies; and I had no belief in her. No faith. But that un-derstanding, that certainty, slowly dawned on me over a period of time. Eventually I could not get "she" out of my head. By that time it was so obvious that he was a she, and I was so comfortable with the idea, I could not formulate it in any other way.

Yes. Once I started to look at Calvin as indeed a Susan, it all made sense.

***

One day Susan and I were sitting out on the lawn after Ai-kido and she just started talking about her life. I was going on about how my dad had called from California and I didn't remember him, and he offered to send me to private school. And that I had accepted.

"I feel like there's something fated in it," I said.

Susan smiled. "My confessor thought coming to Kick-shaw would help 'straighten me out,'" she said.

"Straighten you out?"

"Yeah. He thinks I'm confused. He doesn't say that exactly, but I can see it in his eyes."

"Well..." I was going to say, 'Yes sometimes you seem pretty confused.' But I thought that would be rude. So instead I said, "You mean, like not knowing what to do with your life?"

"Oh, no, that's not it. I know exactly what I'm supposed to do with my life."

"Right. Go to college. Is that it?"

She looked at me. "College? Well, I suppose it might come to that. But it does not really seem required for my sort of future."

I was now completely flummoxed.

"Sorry, Robbie. You don't understand. God tells me what I am to do with my life. He has a plan. I don't know the whole plan but he tells me bit by bit."

"Really?"

"You don't believe me." It was a statement, not a question.

I hedged. "It's not really about me believing, is it? It's what you believe."

"Let me explain how it works. Now first of all, do you agree not to tell? You won't tell on me? Because I think people would be jealous, some of them might be very jealous, and I don't want that. It would be a terrible sin for me to seem superior. Very few have this."

I put up my left hand in the air and my right out straight, as if it were resting on a bible. "I swear."

"You are making fun. Well, anyway."

"You don't have to tell."

"No, I want to."

She paused for a minute as if to consider. "Have you ever had something happen that you were pretty sure meant the world was speaking to you? Like for example everything around you is falling apart, and then out of the blue, you get a lifeline?"

"Like for example an offer to go to school two thousand miles away, from a man I hardly remembered?"

"Yes. Yes... Sometimes things and objects manifest, but usually it is a human being, a person, who speaks. Only it is not that person, not their lower self, but their higher self. God in them. And they sometimes get carried away, because as you might guess, when some higher power speaks through you, that gives a kind of madness."

"Right. I see." I didn't, and had no idea what she was talking about, but I wanted to be a friend, so I said, "Yes, obviously that would be euphoric. Sounds like the oracles in ancient Greece. But can you give me another example?"

"Sure. I'll tell you how I came to Kickshaw. I didn't want to. I was really fearful."

"Oh?"

"Yeah. Don't be angry, Robbie. But it's all white people here. There's nobody like me. I'm alone here."

"Uh, yeah. I get that. I don't actually like that myself. And I'm white."

This joke seemed to fall flat with Susan. She never had much of a sense of humor.

"I miss black faces," she said, with a sigh. "In LA, if you saw a white person in my neighborhood, it was 9 times out of 10 a cop in riot gear. Everyone there hates white people."

"Hmm..."

"I don't hate them though! I'm just afraid of them."

"You're afraid?"

"Yeah."

"But what about me?"

She laughed. "Well, no, you're not that threatening, Robbie. Sometimes I don't even consider you to be white."

"Hmmm," I said.

"I also miss my church. There's one or two, you know, Catholics, up here on the Mesa, but no one who even prays the Rosary. There's not that serious."

"I see."

"But anyway, my confessor is very wise, a very great man, and I guess he knew someone, he applied for some sort of grant program, diversity thingy. My father laughed and said it was idiotic."

"That seems cruel," I said.

"It was. God put me into his hands. My mother died. I'm not even sure we are blood relatives, but I still call him Dad." She paused. "But God also arranged for me to leave him. He was not a good man. He was violent. He sold drugs, things like that. I was worried he'd make me do disgusting things for money. And I think he would have, he was about to, which is why God intervened."

I didn't know what to say, so I said something rather stupid. "Well, you know, nobody's perfect."

"I suppose. Anyway, one day the formal letter arrived; it was the first letter I had ever seen where we had to sign for it. And it was addressed to me. I was so excited."

"Wow. That's a pretty good story. Better than mine."

We sat for a while in silence. I thought maybe she was going to say something hard, because her face contorted.

"I want to tell you something, Robbie. Will you keep a confidence?"

"Yes. Of course."

"Really."

"I promise," I said.

"People don't understand me, Robbie."

"You mean about—" I sort of let this die because I was not too comfortable where it led. It touched dangerously close on a question I had about myself as well. But I soldiered on. "Do you mean, because you're gay?"

"Oh Robbie," she cried. "You don't understand. I'm not gay. I'm a girl. On the inside I'm a girl. I'm a girl in a boy's body. I like boys. But that's not because I'm gay. It's because I'm a girl. I have the wrong equipment. It's all so wrong, you see. A terrible mistake, perhaps. But no. There are no mistakes. It must be His Will."

I sat thinking about this trying to digest it.

Slowly, I put the pieces together. "So you mean, you're a transsexual, like in *Rocky Horror Picture Show*? You have a guy's equipment, but you—"

She looked at me rather blankly. "I don't know that one."

I chuckled and lifted my eyebrows. "You've never seen *Rocky Horror*? Seriously?"

She shook her head. "It sounds kind of weird."

"No," I said, "Not at all. You definitely need to see that show."

***

So I started to formulate this big plan, I was excited about it, I thought this was going to really help Susan, it would open her up. In those days I was always trying to do things to help other people; I had not yet learned that helping people is almost impossible, that people are the way they are due to karma and the trend of mind in them from one incarnation after another, which is impossible to alter. Trying to help someone who does not want to be helped is like helping a train to stop by throwing a bucket of cold water on it. It makes a splash and rolls off; the train, however, is unscathed; it is not even wet; the water you threw evaporates. But I did not know all that until much later.

'Maybe she'll meet some people who can relate to her or who she can relate to,' I thought. 'This could change everything.'

It took some time to organize that trip, and I was a little uncomfortable about it, because even though I had been a few times by this point, it was always with guys like Jonah, for whom *Rocky Horror* was a regular thing, a celebration of the weird and raw and wild and wacky on a Saturday night, preferably at midnight. The thing was, when Jonah was put in the position of actually dealing with weird—and Susan was pretty weird—he had no interest in it at all; but when it was a movie with Susan Sarandon and Tim Curry and Meat Loaf, well, that was all fine.

So I figured I'd better go alone with Susan, just me and her. I didn't even tell Jonah I had plans to go. We were still roomies at that point, of course. Jonah was the one who had taken me the first time; it was a thing going on then, a sensation actually, going on in LA at a few hip, avant-garde theaters. It was really cool and I was so grateful that I even let him in on my secret: that my dad was gay. Jonah didn't care. He said "Yeah, there's a lot of that going around. I wouldn't mention it too often up at Kickshaw, though."

But even so, I didn't invite Jonah. I didn't even tell him. This was to be a special remedial trip, a mission of mercy, you might say, to help Susan.

I had no car at the time, and the thing was in Santa Barbara at the Arlington, playing at midnight, and I immediately thought maybe Larry could take us. But it turned out that Larry was not down with the *Rocky Horror*.

"Too campy," he said. "I'm not really that amused by cross-dressing, Robbie."

Of course I should have known this, and I don't know why I assumed he would like the picture. Larry had a profound style-sense. It made perfect sense that he would not go for the over-the-top. He was a gay man, but he was also an impeccable one, even an elite.

And so it was my dad who took us. He even sat with us and he seemed to think the movie was hilarious, he was laughing the whole time. "This is crazy, Robbie! But why are people throwing toast?"

"I don't know, Dad."

"Look! That guy's in drag and dancing to the music up by the stage. They seem to be acting things out."

People were shouting lines, like "Great Scott!" and "He's a credit to your genius, master," and other insanities I can't even remember. Given a few drinks my dad would have easily been right in the middle of it.

But Susan was not having a good time. At first, she didn't seem to understand what was happening.

"I'm not into horror movies, Robbie."

"Don't worry, it's just a setup. It's a musical."

"OK." She put her hands on her cheeks and kind of slumped down—she wasn't very tall to begin with—and seemed to withdraw into herself.

As the movie progressed, she appeared to grow more and more uncomfortable. Bored, most of the time, I would say. When we got to *Sweet Transvestite*, she said "This is gross!" which I thought was a bad sign.

The movie wound its way down to the end and we left the theater, my father still buoyant and frothy.

"That was pretty cool, Robbie," he said. "You showed me something. I had no idea."

"Thanks Dad."

"What did you think, Susan?" he said. I had explained to my dad about the whole 'Susan' thing and how she was a girl in a boy's body, and to be cool about it. And he was like "Yeah, OK, son. I'm not going to make waves for you. Are you trying to make it with her? I mean, are you attracted? Because I'm not sure that would be a good idea. Trannies are mostly total head-cases, at least in my limited experience."

"No, Dad, no," I said. "That's not how this is. I'm trying to, you know, be a friend. She seems to need one. I like girls."

"But you say she is a girl, really."

"NO, I mean, I like girls that, you know, don't have dicks."

He thought about that and then laughed. "Yeah. OK, well that's really big of you son. I'm impressed actually. You're quite the gentleman to try to help someone."

"Now you're just riding me," I said.

"No, Robbie. You are a prince among men."

I don't think he believed me, as by this point he understood I was a master of BS—a chip off the old block, he often said—but it didn't matter, and regardless, he really was very cool about the whole thing. He tried to draw Susan out in conversation in the car several times but it wasn't easy. They ended up discussing the Watts riots (as she was from Watts) and he told stories about having to drive through there to get to his workplace, which at the time was the Texaco oil refinery. "Robbie was just three years old at the time," he said. "I was working at an oil refinery down there in Long Beach and had to drive through there. I used to carry a baseball bat in my car. Also my .45."

What he didn't say was when he had told the story to me, when we were alone, the baseball bat was his "nigger stick." But he had been cool. He had toned things down to try and make Susan comfortable. But it did not do much good with her; she was unreachable.

"Watts was swarming with angry rioters," he said.

"Oh my," said Susan. "That sounds scary. You were afraid for your life?"

"Nah, it was just the world gone crazy. But sometimes I was scared, sure."

"We feel that way mainly about the cops. But I never thought that they might also be afraid."

"I guess," he said. "The LAPD is known for its brutality. Maybe that does hide fear. But frankly, I think they're the aggressors. I mean, just try being gay."

"Oh my," she said.

"So you have a gun, Dad?" I said, trying to change the subject. "I didn't know."

"Yeah, son, I was in the Coast Guard."

"To get out of going to Vietnam?"

"Oh hell yeah. Exactly. Who wants to go and kill the yellow man? But I was not brave like Cassius Clay. He went to prison, you know. The best years of his boxing career, stolen from him. Fucking unreal. But no, instead of protesting, I opted for the Coast Guard. It wasn't so bad."

"But you were still a shooter."

"Oh, sure, shooting is good times, son. Lots of fun. We should go sometime down to the range. I'll teach you how to shoot. I've even got a marksmanship ribbon for the pistol. I can disassemble a .45 automatic with my eyes closed."

"Did you ever shoot anybody, Dad?" I said. I was joking, but he answered with a straight face.

"Not anyone who didn't deserve it." He was driving and had one hand on the wheel. He glanced over at me and winked.

Susan looked at him queerly for a minute, and then broke up. "Oh, you're pulling my leg!"

We all laughed.

***

This is where we get to the part I wasn't sure I was going to write about. But, what the hell.

After the show my dad didn't take us back up to campus but instead we went to his place in Santa Barbara. I guess it was my place too, I had a bedroom there, but somehow I always thought of it as his and Larry's.

Soon Susan and I were in my room. My dad had signed off for the night and gave me a mischievous wink, but I shook my head vigorously at him.

I closed the door and looked at her. She had her back to me and was looking around my room. Her eyes lit on the Farrah Fawcett poster. And I suddenly felt embarrassed, like it was somehow wrong; after all, I'd certainly wanked off enough times to it. But Susan turned around then and looked at me. She seemed to be giggling. "Oh Robbie, I guess you're a normal boy."

"Well, I'm glad you think so," was all I could get out.

"But where am I going to sleep?"

"We could be together...if you wanted," I said.

"I don't think so, Robbie."

"But why not?"

"Come and sit on the bed," she said. She plopped herself down, like a small brown elf, and took my hand.

"Robbie, I know you have been trying to do things for me. And I'm appreciative. I really am. God sent you to me. You remember, that first day when you came bearing the weird book? I knew then that God was sending me an important message."

"Yeah?"

"Yes. The message was not actually the book, though, it was you. You have been my only friend at Kickshaw. Really, no, that is true. You are the only one who cares. God sent you, because I really needed someone. But—not for this."

I didn't quite know what was going on, but it had started to feel a bit like what happened with Cecilia.

"Oh no, you're not dumping me, are you?"

She didn't say anything then, but I got the drift.

"So are you saying you have someone?"

"No, Robbie. But there's someone in my heart."

"Right."

***

It was a day when a lot of things had gone wrong for Christian. He got caught out by Martin, who was wise in the ways of the world but ordinarily would turn a blind eye. But this day Martin knocked, and Christian could not get the pipe put away fast enough. They made eye contact and Martin shook his head.

"I'm not going to bust you," he said. "Everyone gets one Get Out of Jail Free card from me. I know how it is. But you have to make a serious effort to do better. If I catch you again, I'll have to take it to Charlie."

By "Charlie," he meant Charlie Stacks, the Dean of Students. Stacks was relatively young, with a hot young wife (more on her later) and no doubt, probably, a very reasonable guy off campus, but he was known as a hard-ass and a brutal enforcer up on the Mesa. We called him "Clint" because he looked a lot like Clint Eastwood and had some mannerisms that (at least in our imaginative fantasy) re-called the Spaghetti Western. He was known for a zero-tol-erance attitude about weed, and even beer.

So that was bad. And earlier in the day there had been other problems. The soccer practice was going well until he slipped and got stepped on. The cleats drove into the side of his head. He thought his right eardrum was going to ex-plode. But he wouldn't come off the field. Instead he took out his frustration on Fish, who was a marginal footballer at best but wanted to play....

That night, without the support of a nice bong hit to help him sleep, he tossed and turned. Even both disks of the White Album in the headphones couldn't do the trick.

Time passed as it does on a sleepless night, drawn out like an infinite series of prickly, iridescent seconds. And eventu-ally Christian figured he just had to spark a bowl. He thought about the bag of dirt-weed he had procured the week before, but it was not doing much for him. 'Fuck it,' he thought. 'Time for something special.'

Christian opened his secret stash panel, a spot on the floor in the closet that he'd fashioned in week one, and took out a little cigar box. Inside he rummaged, mainly by feel—the room was dark—and found a little chunk of hashish that he got as a gift from his older brother the last time he was in Palo Alto. He worked this into the "pen pipe," which was able to completely seal the load in a chamber, and then opened the window sufficiently wide that he could blow the smoke out of the room. The night air rushed in and felt refreshing. His synesthesia kicked in then, and the cool air seemed to faintly glow. Sparking the lighter, he took an ex-perimental drag and kept going until the hash began to burn. When he got enough of the acrid smoke out he held it manfully, eventually exhaling in controlled fashion out the window. The blasts of smoke looked green and ghostly. This went on for a while. And he began to feel a bit better.

Moroccan hashish is a very special high, not something for everyday, but more like an emergency break-the-glass type of deal. And Christian, feeling he needed something more, that his situation this day was particularly unfair, as it was in general unfair, probably something about his father—just kept hitting on that pen pipe over and over until the contents in the brass chamber had turned to dust. Gone.

He was pretty stoned now. The angels were certainly spinning in the Moroccan architecture, geometric patterns vibrating as if to an unknown, highly operatic score within his head. The walls were glowing blue.

Then suddenly he heard something, a noise, in the hallway. Instantly he became completely still as his heart leaped. He quietly grabbed a piece of gum and started chewing mechanically. It felt dry on his tongue but he kept chewing, trying to get the acrid smell off his breath. Meanwhile, listening, after a moment he realized the Lido shower had come on. He peered in the darkness at the radium dials of his alarm clock: 3:02 a.m.

'Well, I'll be,' he thought. 'It's banana dick that thinks she's a girl. Banana dick girl...gay butt hole.' He slowly stood up, kind of pulled himself up, head rushing, colors flashing, and put on a robe. He grabbed his kit and moved to the door, opening it very quietly. Going into the hall, he calmly entered the bathroom, pushing the door back slowly and then closing it behind him.

He took off his robe and hung it on a hook, dropped his boxers, and set his kit down. Calmly, in a relaxed mood, feeling better than he had all day, he went into the shower room, where the light was on. It was very bright in there; he had to shield his eyes for a moment. He felt the warmth of the steam on his chest.

'Long showers are the best,' he thought.

Susan was in the second shower to the right in the big open room, the water coursing down her body, her long dick dangling. She turned and saw him. This time, she did not say anything. Her hands automatically went to cover herself, but then slowly, inch by inch, they fell to her side.

Christian was standing with his finger to his lips. His other hand was behind him. He made no sound. First of all, he turned on his own shower, and washed up, but he had his eyes on her the whole time. Then, slowly, he came over to her. His body showed his attraction. Gently he put his hands on her torso, first the right hand and then the left, and ran his fingers over her wet skin. The drops of water splashed on and on, glinting blue and green, turquoise, in his mind, and then seemed to radiate heat and light. He took the bar of soap and began to lather her body. She looked down, almost demure, as he did this, and then lifted her eyes to his face.

"Christian...Christian," she said.

PART FOUR — A Conspiracy of Ground Meat

A boy found his balls were too big,
And stuffed them inside of his wig
But out with a shout,
Came his balls in a rout,
And that was the end of his twig.

I had an ambitious agenda for the fast-approaching summer sandwiched between Sophomore and Junior Year, but there was one overriding impulse: try to get laid. I would also work and save money, so I could fund my various appetites and new requirements like visits to the record store. But getting laid seemed to be the top priority. I had my reasons.

My failure with Susan, which had produced a bad case of blue balls that night after the *Rocky Horror* screening, was part of it. It was not really the rejection—I understood—there was someone else—but the truth of the matter, which was that I realized I was suddenly willing to *do* things with Susan. Sexual things. Yes, I was ready to try.

At first I wanted to blame *Rocky Horror*. Susan Sarandon's fantastic body had aroused me, perhaps Frank-n-Furter's, too. But I knew that was absurd. It was just a movie. Susan had said no, leaving me dejected and frustrated and (probably obvious to her) fully erect, only to deflate slowly in the silence of rejection, like a flat tire.

Sure, I was now regularly going into the 7-Eleven, stoned out of my mind, armed with a few sweaty coins with which to buy porn mags, as the store clerk sighed and scolded me, and that was a kind of progress; I was becoming bold about my passions, almost heedless of the consequences. For me this was progress away from anxiety. But I realized I had not progressed much beyond poor Hedda Henry, the boy I punched repeatedly in the face to little effect, the masturbator who looked so much like a dick head. Henry's taste in pornography was grotesque, and he was a grotesque youth, a product of the grotesqueries of the South. As time passed I felt sorry for him—but I was not that far behind. It was a question of degree. Yes, even at that age I had a certain minimal level of self-knowledge. I knew, not in a way I could express, to be sure, but on some level, that I had a long road ahead to be who I wanted to be; that there was more. And sex was a part of that equation. Sex was a problem.

I shared some of these private thoughts and confusions with William. In my mind he was wise. Or, at least, he was wiser than anyone else at Kickshaw. He was like the Wizard cabbie in *Taxi Driver*. He knew things.

"It's like Diogenes," he said. "When caught masturbating in the marketplace, he famously replied 'If only hunger could be satisfied by rubbing the belly.' Apparently he was fine with it. So there are philosophers who embraced it. But most have said to abstain, which seems absurd. On some level we are animals, after all. Nature will have its way."

"But I want to be free."

"Free of desire?"

"Yes. Free of desire."

"That sounds like Buddhism."

"Yeah."

"But you haven't, you know—"

"No, I haven't been with a girl."

"Well, Robbie, sex with a girl is ten times better than masturbation."

"Ten times?" I was incredulous.

William smiled. "Uh-huh. I think you better wait a while before deciding you want to give up on sex entirely."

So that was something to think about. And the summer was coming.

***

My dad's place was quiet these days, except for Conchita occasionally dropping in and swearing at me as she folded my boxers. Larry was away more. He was now working hard to make his band, Larry and the Linguals, into a viable unit. Larry's sound was apparently a little bit like the *Sex Pistols*; it was punk, but with an LA edge. He liked X, the Go Gos, and The Bags, and aspired to that kind of sound. It was way too intense for me; I was still deep in musical development, just getting to the point that I liked hard rock. I have a clear memory of listening to *Who's Next* that summer and having it finally click. I wasn't ready for punk. Nevertheless I asked if I could go to a show. It seemed like a great way to maybe meet a cool punker chick; one that would put out; maybe she'd even have a tattoo....

"No, Robbie. No way. Your dad would kill me. It's the LA bar scene. I don't think you're ready for that; it's very crude. Besides, you're not 18. If we ever do an underage show I'll let you know."

Maybe Larry could see that I was bummed out by being shut down cold, so in a more conciliatory tone he said, "Since you're interested, I do have something for you...give me a sec...." He disappeared for a few minutes and came back with something in a plain brown paper bag. "Here, Robbie. Your very own copy."

It was an album. There was a picture of Larry on the cover looking very butch in aviator shades, a leather Trilby, and matching vest, almost like a Japanese Lou Reed, and the title said:

Larry and the Linguals
Hollywood Useless

"Holy Hell!" I said. "Did you get a record contract, Larry?"
"Nah, it's just a vanity printing. It's a demo. We wanted to see something on vinyl."
"Has Dad seen this?"

"Not yet, so mum's the word. Your dad actually put up the cash for this. So I want to surprise him. And by the way, I think he's got something for you, too..."

***

My dad was keen to help me get a summer job, it seemed he knew everybody, and he introduced me to a Carrows manager who was willing to put me to work; but I had no car. So it did not seem feasible to me and for a while I pushed back. America is many things, but one thing it is most certainly, and that is a car culture. And yes, it was obvious a car would help get me laid.

It was Larry, I think, who planted the idea in my dad's head, as he did with so many things; Robbie is going to need a car for the summer. And my dad listened. One day he said, "Hey Robbie, what are you up to?"

"Not much, Dad."

"Well then, come with me."

We got in one of his antique decrepit VW Beetles and cruised down breezy sultry SB streets to his new property. He called it "De La Vina" simply after the street it was on— we were up about 10 blocks—but the real name was "*Rancho Bravos Bungalows*."

"That's very macho, Dad," I said.

"I think so too, son. Larry makes jokes about it. 'Strong stuff, that property,' he says. 'Better not get bunged up,' and so forth. But it's a great opportunity. The cashflow looks to be fantastic!"

By this point my dad had got enough money together to buy a pretty serious investment property, and this was it. It was a group of cute little freestanding units, bungalows or cottages, perhaps 20 in all, in a rancho style, on a strip of land that spanned all the way between De La Vina and Bath Streets. This property was the only complete strip of land between the two streets, and he was convinced some day it would be worth millions just for the land. It also had a good-sized parking lot, ostensibly for the residents, where he now decided to park some of his growing car collection. While he drove, he wanted an update on things.

"So you're thinking about a job for the summer?"

"Yeah, Dad. I need money. The ten bucks a week from you hardly buys a loose joint."

"I know I'm a bit tight about things like that, but it's for your own good. If I just keep giving you cash, well, we know where that goes."

He was referring to my rapidly expanding drug habit, which coincidentally he benefited from largely, I had upgraded his pot from loose leaf off a street peddler that was half oregano, to sinsemilla worthy of *Hotel California* by the Eagles. I didn't much like that kind of weed; it was far too stoney and bright. I was sentimentally attached to the Colombian shit-weed of my initial experiments with Christian, brown water-cured pot that came up in bales from Mexico (the kind of thing Cheech and Chong would have smoked) full of stems and seeds. But my dad liked the fresh resinous bud. Once he learned about it, he was hooked.

My father was feeling the pressure of work, it seemed, or something, and that summer I noticed his consumption of alcohol increased. The pot, booze, and even a little cocaine now and then (something I was not allowed, but I did try once with Christian when we went to see George Carlin at UCSB—not a rock show, but a show, my first real show)— yes, all of that, I could see my father was burning the candle down. But whenever I said something he would just laugh it off. "I'm fine, buddy boy. Perfect even. Nothing to worry. It's just a bit of a slump. *Rancho Bravos* took a lot of cash to put together. But it will pay off big in time. Buying assets is key." In fact, according to Larry the property cost more than $800,000, a princely sum in those days.

Anyway, we pulled into *Rancho Bravos*—there was a sign out front and everything— and drove slowly down the long private road that ran through the center of the property in the direction of Bath Street. On either side were the little bungalows. I saw a few eyes looking out here and there, but mostly it was quiet.

"Wow, those are very cool, Dad."

"Yeah, they're cute units. You'd be amazed what kind of rent I'm getting."

"I see, so those are all rented out?"

"Yep. I'm a slum lord now, little buddy."

"Slum lord?"

"Yeah, that's how things are. Wetbacks, Asians, poor white trash, lowlife types, some of them. I have to make sure no one is dealing. We wouldn't want that, now would we, Robbie?"

"No, that would not be good."

"We've got to keep up appearances. But the place is a goldmine. And then there's a nice garage in the back here. Kind of my own private parking lot, if you know what I mean."

I soon saw what he meant: five or six of the cars were his, including an RV, three more VW Beetles in addition to the one we were in, and then a new car I had not seen before. "What's that one Dad? Is that yours?"

"No, buddy boy. That's yours."

I was flummoxed. "Whoa. Dad!" It was a VW camper, a '63. It was very stripped-down but in great shape. "That's like, a collectable car, Dad."

"Yeah, well, try not to crash it."

We got out and I looked into the window. "I like the simplicity."

"You can take that van apart with just three tools, son, and put it back together as well. Of course, it's not even got a radio. And it's a manual transmission. Can you drive a stick?"

"Sure, of course," I said. The fact was, I had never driven a stick, but I assumed it was easy. "How hard can it be?"

My dad laughed. "That's the spirit. Well, son, here's the keys. I will leave you to it. I need to get going."

"Oh, uh—you don't want to give me any pointers?"

He looked rather hesitantly around, and I had the distinct impression he didn't want to run into the residents. I could not understand why. Finally he said, "Well, OK. Hop in. Just a quick lesson. Now, that over there is the clutch. What you have to do is press that down when you want to change gears. When the clutch is released, you will feel the gears come into effect. You have to move through them. So, for example you start in first, then move into second, and so on."

"OK. Should I try it?"

"Sure. But I think it's best you do that on your own. I think if I'm here it will just make you nervous."

"OK. Thanks, Dad." I was still uncertain but figured he must be right. And obviously, he wanted to get going.

What followed was about two hours of me tearing and grinding gears until I finally got out onto De La Vina Street. And then that was terrifying. I drove around the block and then came back in and slowly rolled towards the parking lot again, only to have my spot, where the van had been, taken by someone else. "Well crap," I said to myself.

Meanwhile a guy came out of a nearby bungalow and walked over. He was an older Asian, a small wisp of a man, wearing a baseball hat and old person clothes. "So, you try park back here, huh?"

I turned the key and the engine stopped. I said, "Yeah, I was just here."

"I know," he said. "I been listening to you for two, maybe three hours. You no drive this car?"

"Well, my dad just gave it to me."

"Oh. Your dad. Is that Tricky Dick?"

"Tricky Dick," I repeated. "Yeah, that's him."

The man's face changed. "He no good landlord. We not like him. He take up all the parking. That our parking according to lease."

"Oh," I said. "I'm sorry. I didn't know."

"Probably you best get going. Take new gift van elsewhere."

I wasn't sure what to do by this point. In fact, I had been considering if I should park the van back where it was and just leave.

"But, well, I don't know how to drive a stick."

"It easy. I show you."

Without another word the man walked around to the passenger side and got in. "Start her up," he said.

I turned the key.

"Now, your problem, you not understand clutch. Clutch not like trigger on gun. You must be smooth, push down, only then move gear shift. Use motion like in Tai Chi. Smooth, big circle. Then, gently lift clutch until you feel engine begin to engage. It like ten-speed bicycle. Easy once you have idea. Now you try. Forward, first gear."

I took the emergency brake off and then pushed the clutch in and moved the stick.

"OK, now gently on clutch," he said.

I slowly let out the clutch. The car began to move and I thought I could feel what he meant. But I had to slam on the brakes because now we were going too fast.

"Stop!" he said. "Now, gently, slowly, push in clutch. OK. Now. Put car in reverse."

I tried this and it was less smooth, but it worked.

"OK, you almost ready to go. First gear, second gear. You go down De La Vina, then find freeway. You have lot of fun on freeway." He laughed now, a wicked sort of laugh. He opened the passenger door and got out. "Good luck, sonny." And then he turned away. He didn't look back.

I said "shit!" and then did what I had to do. I instantly forgot about the guy. I didn't even say thank you.

He was right, the freeway was 'a lot of fun' if you mean fun in hell. But I was now driving a stick. 'God damn,' I thought. 'I have a car!' I was soaked with sweat. Suddenly I felt like a true American.

***

That summer I worked a lot less than I planned. It was such a blast to have a van that I spent a lot of time just driving. Too much, actually. I was burning through gasoline like anything. I went up to Isla Vista for the day and wandered around looking for hippie chicks without finding them, and then on another day I drove up to El Capitán State Beach. It sits soaking in sun to the north, where nudie bathers lounge tanning their glands. I also spent time in Summerland watching the surfers do tricks so close to the rocks it seemed crazy. I parked the van at Carpinteria State Beach and hung out and abortively roasted corn in a barbeque pit while scraping tar off the soles of my feet. The corn didn't really get cooked through and through, but I ate it. I was convinced I wanted to be a vegetarian, as hard as it might be. I did eventually do some shifts at Carrows and earned a few bucks that way. Unfortunately I thought working in a restaurant sucked. Too greasy, too much meat. I needed another idea for money but for a while, it didn't come.

And then a bad thing happened. I started thinking about the plot of weed I had seen that day on the trails, well hidden in the *Forest Sauvage*. For a while, I was able to push the idea down; but eventually my own craving for weed and my need for cash hatched a plan in my microcephalic brain.

Yep. I started thinking about ripping off whoever was growing the weed. It was an insanely stupid idea, I realized, and yet, in my mind I was already calculating how much bud might be down there. If it was still there. I also had the foolish idea that as a minor I was immune from prosecution. Somehow I was "still a kid" and so my shenanigans could always be explained away, I thought, as stupidity and simple hooliganism.

Of course, this was largely wrong. I was contemplating stealing at least several pounds of pot. A cop, busting a kid with that much weed, would logically assume it was intended for sale—which was true. I had glowing ideas about myself as a sort of super-stud teen drug kingpin. I knew plenty of kids who would buy. And now I had a van and could make my way to LA, to Malibu, to Berkeley—anywhere I wanted to go with my big bag of buds, like Santa on a mad delivery.

The plan was soon put into motion. I waited until a night when the moon would be new and the sky as dark as possible. I got some equipment together: a backpack, a big black plastic bag, some secateurs, and then for clothing, I figured I'd wear two layers. The top layer was more or less disposable, including a black balaclava. I found some swimming goggles of my dad's out in the garage. I figured those would protect my eyes if I could avoid doing something stupid.

Driving out to Carpinteria, I took the freeway and then motored boldly up Casitas Pass Road. It was well past 2 a.m. and the road was empty as a Kickshaw Freshman's head. I yawned a few times as I got close to the turn out for the school. My plan was to park at the base of the hill, down by the Sauvage's cottage. Surely old brain-dead Mrs. Sauvage would be sound asleep. I stashed the van as best I could behind some trees that were on the turnout near the cottage. Then I got fully suited up and grabbed the pack and headed out. I walked up the path that led into the *Forest Sauvage*. I knew I had to go a fair way up the hillside, then cut across and find the shit-sprayer path. I had quietly sussed this out previously, not with any intent to steal the weed, then, but simply to further make a mental map of the terrain. The Moon Flower, which was the senior's hillside hangout, was up there, and I'd seen it. Christian and I were curious enough to find it: a well-built octagon of seating with a view of the stars. The perfect party spot, especially on a morning like this. But now I was on a mission and could not afford to get distracted. I stood and listened for a while at the cut-out that headed down to the shit-sprayer path. It was still like a tomb down there. Except for a few night sounds the only noise was my labored breathing.

I made my way down to the hose, mainly by feel. I was too paranoid to use a flashlight. Following it down, I came to the endless poison oak—I smiled under my balaclava, thinking I'd outsmarted it, and then thought about squirting on Nurse Standish. Well, only Cadogan and Jonah and now Lori and undoubtedly Martin, who would have been curious, knew my dreadful shame.

After what seemed an interminable trek, I finally popped suddenly into a small clearing. Yes. There were plants here. I noticed about half of them were smaller. Inspecting these I saw they were immature. But over to the right I could see several adult plants. They were thick with flowers. I could see them, dark on dark, as silhouettes against the night sky, and smell them, thick with resin. 'Jackpot!' I said to myself.

I set to work on one of the plants, cutting off stems covered with buds, and quickly realized my small pack could hold only a fraction of what was available. 'Well, fuck it,' I thought. 'I'll load up as best I can.'

I was soon tired, covered in sweat and grime, and it was getting late, I certainly did not want to be up here when dawn broke. That would be a disaster. My pack felt full such that no more would go. Suddenly I was filled with fear: I realized I was committed; I was doing it. There was no going back on this. I stank of pot and the resin covered my hands and clothes. A sniffer dog would eat me alive. The sense of finality and dread pushed me into wakefulness, and I had a surge of adrenaline. I started back up, following the clandestine shit-sprayer hose, and then huffed and puffed along the trail, past the Moon Flower cutout, until I was near the bottom. I stopped and listened. The coast seemed clear. I moved towards the van. But then to my horror, a light came on in the Sauvage's cottage. I started to move faster, and even got as far as my van, but had to struggle first with getting the gloves off and then fumbling for the key. To my horror it seemed I couldn't find it.

"Stop right there," said a voice. I turned and saw a small figure in the dark. I thought at first the figure held a stick, but no, it was a gun. "Come with me to the cottage. Get moving. I'm within my rights to shoot you."

"I don't see how," I said. "I haven't done anything wrong!"

"Oh no?" said the voice. I heard a very peculiar laugh. I did not understand in the dark how to conceptualize it. It sounded like a jack in the box voice, or a doll voice. "We'll see. No, pick that up, bring the bag. Get moving."

I moved slowly, totally defeated now, my heart hammering in my chest. "You first," the voice said. "In."

I went into the cottage. My eyes were temporarily blinded by the brilliance of the electric light, even though it was only a front door light. I had never been in the Sauvage's cottage and had no idea what to expect; but inside it looked very much as I would have imagined: a place where old people lived; or had lived.

I got a poke in the back, then, from what felt like a cold hard metal object, and moved further into the small house. I could see the outlines of a kitchen further on. I turned and got the shock of my life. "You!"

"Who are you?" She said. She was squinting at me. "Take that ski mask off."

I fumbled with the mask. "I'm Robbie. Robbie Gray," I sputtered.

It was Mrs. Sauvage. Old brain-dead, now fully alive and alert. She stood firmly, holding the rifle, pointing it at me in an extremely businesslike manner. An old robe covered her flimsy nightgown, the bottom of which hung down flapping in the breeze. Her saggy feet were wrapped in ancient, corroded slippers.

"I'm Robbie Gray, from Kickshaw," I said again. "I have seen you many times in the cafeteria, but we've never spoken before."

"I see," she said. She peered at me in the darkness and her face seemed to close off. "I don't remember you."

"But I'm a sophomore, ma'am! Or I was, I will be in my junior year. Please don't shoot me! I'll never get to try your coffee!"

This seemed to make her chuckle. "Very good. Hmm," she said. "I see. You're a BS artist."

Of course, my first thought was to try to bullshit my way out of things and my mouth began to run. "I'm sorry if I disturbed you. I—I was on a trek up to the Gobernador Creek. In the foothills. It's beautiful up there this time of year."

"Nice try, sonny," She said. "I saw you park your van a few hours ago." She was still pointing the gun at me and she waved it like a wand at my bag. "What's in that pack?"

"It's just my stuff, you know, my sleeping bag."

"Boy, this rifle is loaded. This is no toy."

"But you, you wouldn't shoot a kid, would you? I'm just a hiker. I'm a Kickshaw student. I live in Santa Barbara. I'm a local boy. I love surfing and the beach and everything."

"I think you're something else."

"But you wouldn't. You're, you're—"

"An old lady?" She chuckled. "It's true I guess. Somehow I got old. Well, I am within my rights to shoot an intruder. If I have to shoot you, then I will just tell the cops you broke in and frightened me half to death."

I could see I was royally screwed. But I still didn't understand the situation. "Fine," I said. "I'll show what's in the bag. But what's in here, it might shock you. I found it when I was up on the hill side. It was a complete surprise."

"Go on, get on with it. Open it!"

I opened the pack slowly, unzipping the top flap, and spread open the top, so that the contents were visible. Some of the buds then spilled out onto her kitchen floor; it was raining weed. "You see? It's just an herb. An interesting herb. It's oregano I think."

"No, boy. That's not oregano. It looks like pot."

"Oh, I don't think so."

"Stop lying."

"But ma'am, it's nothing to interest you."

She laughed. That was weird. And actually, looking back, that was the strangest part of the whole affair.

"So you think an old lady like me would have no interest in pot?"

"Well, no, you're, you're..." My voice trailed off. "Are you saying this is yours?"

"Ah, so a tiny little light bulb has now gone off in your tiny little head. Eh, sonny?"

I still couldn't get a handle on it. And I told her so. "I can't grok this."

"Grok? What kind of word is that?"

"It's from Heinlein."

"Heinlein?"

"He's a great science fiction writer. It means to 'understand deeply.'"

"Sit down," she said. "Dining room table. Put your hands on the table. Heinlein. He thinks Heinlein is a great writer. What nonsense."

I sat down and put my hands flat on the table. Meanwhile, Mrs. gun-wielding maniac granny hefted my pack and pulled the black liner plastic trash bag out, freeing it from the pack, which toppled over onto the floor. Then she lumbered slowly off, the trash bag in tow, dragging it, until she disappeared into a bedroom. I sat and squirmed, thinking about making a dash for it. "Don't do anything stupid," I could hear her say. Finally she came back. She wasn't pointing the rifle at me anymore—it was a nice rifle, perhaps a Winchester, and was like something out of the *Wild, Wild West*—but she was still holding the gun. I asked the obvious question.

"Are you going to call the cops?"

She smiled then. "You still don't get it."

"I'm sorry." I was feeling pretty depressed. I admit it, yes. "What are you going to do with me?" I was crying now. I blubbered for a while.

She watched me cry. After a time, she scowled. "Oh don't be stupid, boy. I've seen a million stupid boys. I'm not going to hurt you. Would you like a cup of tea?"

"What? Oh...OK."

"What did you say your name was?" She was moving around now in the kitchen, lighting the stove with a match. She had leaned the rifle against the wall, but it was not far away.

"I'm Robbie, Ma'am."

"Robbie. Well, son, you see how slowly I move? Hmm?"

"Yes Ma'am."

"That's because I have arthritis. It's really bad sometimes. But the medicine, that herb you were trying to steal, that helps my arthritis. It's the only thing that seems to help the inflammation." She worked for a while getting cups ready with tea bags. "This hot tea will do you some good. But I would be careful not to touch your face. I think you may have already done."

"Oh no!" I said.

"Yes. The Poison Oak is something fierce up there. You were very foolish."

"I had a run in with it about four months ago. When school was in session..."

"Ah yes. I don't suppose you're the boy the nurse talked about? The one who, well, shot his wad, so to speak." She laughed in the way women sometimes do.

"Oh my God. You heard that story? Even you?"

"Of course. That kind of thing tends to get around. We were talking about it with the cafeteria staff just a few days ago."

"Oh my God," I said again. "Well, just shoot me. I think I would prefer the rifle bullet."

She cackled like an old hen and moved to the table slowly with the large copper kettle. It was so hot I could see the radiant heat emanating off the bottom. I was convinced she was going to drop it and scald me, her, or us both. But somehow she made it on her unsteady legs and poured the hot water into the two cups. She looked over at me. "Do you take sugar?"

"Yes Ma'am."

"I'm sorry, I don't have any milk or cream."

"Please don't be sorry. I woke you up. That was wrong."

"What you did son, was to try to steal my medicine. I need that just to keep moving. Otherwise I'd be bedridden. And then what? I'd be done for."

I realized now the full import of what had happened. I wasn't ripping off some asshole senior like Sheldon Witherspoon, or some no-name, anonymous thugs. I was attempting to steal from an old woman, an invalid, living on her pension, and what I tried to take was her critically necessary medicine. I was stunned.

She looked at me over her teacup. "So you are thinking now, eh? The thinking cap is on."

"I, I don't know what to say. I have made a terrible mistake."

"Well," she said, "I am glad you are starting to come to terms with the magnitude of your crime. I have a few of the older boys helping me."

"Seniors," I said.

"Yes of course, seniors. They love me. I make them their coffee and serve it every night except on weekends. Every year I take one or two into my confidence."

"Sheldon?" I said.

"Hmm. Yes. He is one; or was. He matriculated. I need to bring a few new boys into my secret."

I thought for a minute. "But Ma'am! What about me?"

She shook her head. "What was your name again?"

"Robbie, ma'am," I said patiently. "This is good tea, by the way. I cannot wait to try your coffee." I took a sip, then. And actually it tasted pretty good at that early hour.

"The thing is, Robbie, look, you tried to steal my medicine. I don't know it is very wise trusting you. What were you going to do with it?"

"I am ashamed, ma'am, to say."

"Well?"

"I was going to sell it."

"But that is a serious crime."

"But you're growing it! That's illegal!" I said weakly.

"Yes. It is. But no cop is going to bust an old lady, age 90, over some pot plants that aren't even on her property."

"So you own this cottage."

"Yes," she said. "Yes, by arrangement with Harold."

"Who?"

"Harold Kickshaw. You know, he used to be Headmaster but now he's got a hired lackey to do that. He still bumbles around on campus, though. Harold the Schoolmaster! Harold the bumbler. Harold the fool!"

"Oh, I see. Yes. We just call him Kickshaw."

"After I die, the cottage reverts back to Harold. But for now at least I have a roof over my head. It's hard to be old and alone, Robbie."

We sat for a while in silence and I concentrated on my tea, not looking at her. She seemed to be considering it. Either that, or daydreaming. "You are too young to have met my husband. He, Harold and I were once polyamorous."

"I'm sorry?"

"Polyamorous. Look it up sometime."

"Yes ma'am."

"Harold and my husband used to be quite a pair."

"I see," I said. I wondered if she could possibly mean what I thought. Kickshaw was gay? Or least, had done the deed? Maybe that explained the boy's school. And old Mrs. Sauvage had, what, watched? Applauded? Done them both? My head was reeling.

"Well, I've considered your idea," she said. "I don't think I can use you to help me, but, I would like to get your word, as a gentleman, that you will not say anything about the medicine."

"Oh course, ma'am. I'm terribly sorry. If I had understood the situation I would never have tried to—do what I did."

"Every once in a while—and this is to be very rare—you may drop by and say hello. I'll give you a lid. Just don't smoke it on campus. That would be against the rules. Is that a good enough incentive for you to keep silent? For my sake? Or rather, for both our sakes?"

"Yes, ma'am, of course! That is very generous of you. Very generous."

"I think so. All my boys have been satisfied. They get a taste now and then and it satisfies them. But I also know you have the itch. You have that look about you. Try to stay away from hard drugs. Now you pick up those buds on the floor there and put them into your pocket. That's right. That will do. Try not to do anything stupid from now on. Agreed?"

"Yes ma'am."

"You can see yourself out now."

***

I shudder to think about the rest of that summer; my dad stalwartly refused to hand over more than ten dollars a week of play money, and that wouldn't even fill the tank of the van, so I ended up having to work double shifts at the Wendy's down on lower Bath Street. I could walk there, for one thing. My plan to get laid was also going nowhere.

There was a sweet little chick with big eyes and blond locks, who wore her hat at a jaunty angle, and worked the register on alternate days. Unintelligent, I have to say, but beggars can't be choosers. My eyes were on her a lot. I was too shy to say much, though. One day I got up the courage when she was having lunch.

"Hey, Sharon?"

She looked up from her Dave's Single with juice running down her chin. "Robbie? How you goin?"

"I was wondering—see, I bought these tickets to Joan Armatrading. You want to go?"

"Well, when is it?"

"It's tonight."

"What? Not tonight!"

And I ended up going alone. Pat Metheny opened that show. I spent most of the set in my car, feeling sorry for myself.

But talk about bad karma: the job involved lugging huge plastic bags of ground beef from the walk-in out into the cramped back station, and then loading the bloody ground flesh into a patty machine that might have been created from plans found in a Stephen King novel. I had to then get the thing running and watch as it crapped out those delightful Wendy's "Hot 'n Juicy" by the stack. Finally the output must be carefully packed into more plastic and returned to the walk-in. After hours of doing that, I was covered in the blood of some unfortunate steer who in a different reality I could have called friend. I went home stinking, ever so slightly, no matter how much I washed. It got so bad even Larry noticed. "We need to get some bleach into those clothes, Robbie. Good Lord. Or else find you another line of work."

"It's a conspiracy!" I said.

"A conspiracy?"

"Yes. A Conspiracy of Meat. I stink!"

Larry laughed. "That sounds like a pretty good name for a band. But yeah, you're never going to get laid smelling like that."

And suddenly I was a confirmed vegetarian. Even Martin's glorious ribs seemed like a non-starter.

PART FIVE — Inner Astronauts

A man made his way from Toledo,
With a swollen hard rock of torpedo,
He busted his way,
Through whorehouse they say,
Looking for Frito Bandito.

"So you're back," said Dean Stacks.

"Yeah, nice to see you too," I said.

It was the first full day of Junior year, and classes were on. I found myself curiously filled with anticipation, even if the sight of the Dean so early in the morning was off-putting. Previously my summers were an escape from school and I had counted down the days until the time of freedom when I roamed the Wasteland or planned toilet paper attacks on errant neighbors; but now when I thought of school, even if I was safe in the custody of a dad watching *Kung Fu*, or hanging out with Larry and his wild punk band at a practice, I only wanted to go back. I missed my friends, and looked forward to seeing William and Christian in particular.

The class I was looking forward to the most was called simply 'Ideas.' I'd heard a lot about it. Ideas was unusual in a number of ways, and based on the various descriptions I had heard, I did not understand how the class even got into the curriculum.

It was an eastern philosophy and metaphysics class, something probably only imaginable in California in the 1970s, but it was set up like a study of comparative literature and had a Literati (and perhaps even Illuminati) feel to it. The Master was also very unusual, perhaps unique, and did not fit with the theory of an elitist sausage grinder intent on macerating corporate cannon fodder.

That first day, when we all stood outside and then filed into the classroom, I admit I had some anxiety. My father had earlier mentioned he knew this master; that they were friends but had drifted apart. This worried me because of my secret: the unfortunate fact my father was, as the expression went, gayer than a three-dollar bill. I worried about what this new teacher might say or think about him and about me; and worse, what he might spill or reveal as a joke or otherwise somehow compromise my newly found and hard-fought status as a cool guy, as a dude. My hair was all grown out. Larry had dressed me to the nines, but it was a punker look, a rocker look, and very much at odds with the Preppie aesthetic of the school. I was a known pothead and music aficionado. My connection with Larry and the Linguals had even slipped out. I wanted all of that to be me, to be mine, my identity. My father did not always fit into that beautiful image.

***

The Ideas classroom was one of those under the Infirmary Dormitory. (This was not the same building where I had inadvertently ejaculated, but rather, a much older building that had also once been an Infirmary). The classrooms on this floor were at ground level, with entry through graceful wooden doors on the side facing the main road, the road festooned with Eucalyptus trees that I thought of as Paradise Alley. On the far side, these classrooms all had windows made of many panes of glass, with doors that could open out onto a covered walk (although often these were locked). The walkway lay under vaulted supports of white stucco that fronted a vast well-maintained green lawn. That lawn was where Mr. Morris had his little Aikido class on Tuesday and Thursday afternoons, and I knew it well, if only for having my face planted repeatedly into the dirt there. Yeah, Aikido was my sport. I could not stand any of the other options. Great Circles.

During the school day various classes brought busy movement of many student-ant feet to those classrooms; I remember having both English and Anthropology in that particular room at some stage or other of my education at Kickshaw. It was a classroom full of light on most days, not direct sunlight, but abundant filtered light, which diffused
through the room due to the multi-paned glass; but otherwise there was very little in the room save chairs. The chairs
were of the type that provides a built-in writing surface,
and we sometimes struggled with the awkwardness of a
chair suddenly too small for a rapidly growing body; but
they had a flexibility and simplicity that a full desk would
not.

The Master had caused these chair-desks to be organized
into a circle, so that we all sat facing each other, and he,
himself, sat amongst us in one of the chairs, like a humble
servant intent on showing his equanimity. This tactic gave
the room a distinctly Arthurian feel, although there was no
central table, but rather a void, a contemplative void. And
this was apt, because sometimes the content of the lesson
really was the Void.

Meanwhile the Master's desk, which ordinarily maintained a prominent position front and center in most of the
classrooms, a mainstay and anchor, was absent; and this
gave the space a distinctly egalitarian sensibility and perhaps a feeling of being incomplete. The ubiquitous chalk-
board, Slate black and cool to the touch, stood somewhat
forlorn on the wall in this room, lonely for attention, where
in so many of the others it was the backdrop of the Master's
desk, like a movie prop, and held important scribbles.

So yes, we filed in on the first day. I was happy to see Cadogan and William J. Brennan. This is going to be an enjoy-
able class, I thought.

A man walked briskly through the door. He was bearded
and wore a white turban. In the past I had not had occasion
to observe him before except at a distance; but now he was
in front of us. Up close and personal, as it were. He was an

Indian man, obviously, but in entirely western clothes except for the white binding on his immense head, a fine black suit and thin black tie under a crisp white collar, with polished black Oxfords on his feet. I guessed he was about 55 to 60 years of age. His stride was strong and his posture upright and correct but he was fast developing a paunch.

He went to the forlorn slate board, currently bereft of any writing, clean as if writing had not yet been invented, and produced his name in bold letters. When he was done, he turned around and said, "Good morning. I am Ramakrishna Onkar Ji. But you may call me Ram. This is Ideas 101. There is an Ideas 201 section as well, that is normally for the seniors. Any questions so far? Anyone think they might be in the wrong place?"

We looked around at each other. It seemed everyone was determined to soldier on.

"Very well. If there are no questions, we will set about the process of introductions. I will tell you a little about myself, and what the course is to achieve, and my expectations for you. And after that, perhaps we will say a little bit about each other. Question?"

Cadogan had put up his hand. "Mr. Onkar Ji, are we to address you as Master Onkar?"

"Thank you, and your name is?"

"Cadogan West."

"Well then, Mr. West. You are to call me Ram, and I will call you Cadogan, if you permit it. Or possibly Cad, as you have that caddish look about you."

This produced some general laughter in the classroom. Cadogan's eyebrows went up and his lips bunched, but he nodded in agreement.

"Just to explain, the "Ji" is an honorific, translated, it basically means "Mister." The other parts of my name all mean God. So for example, "Ram' means God. Krishna also means God. Even Onkar, is a word that means "Lord of Om" which presumably means God. So, that is why I am very humble about my name. Obviously I have a long ways to go before I am God. Also, my name, it seems some boys cannot bring themselves to pronounce it."

More laughter.

"So just 'Ram' will do. Simple, precise. Now, as to my-self—" here Ram went to one of the open desks in the circle and sat down. He looked rather small when he was seated, an effect exacerbated by the student-sized chair and desk. "For myself, I was born in the Punjab in India, in 1934. I grew up in a very turbulent period. India was seeking inde-pendence from the British, and there was war and revolu-tion. Then a wave of sectarian violence swept over every-thing—Hindus against Muslims, Muslims against Hindus. That civil war then led to India being partitioned into a pre-dominantly Hindu area, which we now just call India, and Pakistan, which was all the area that was predominantly Muslim. Later, Pakistan itself split again, and one part be-came Bangladesh, which I think you have heard about from George Harrison and Ravi Shankar."

This produced a general chuckle.

"Yes, I occasionally make jokes. I also know who the Beat-les are. Anyway, I grew up in situations that, as you can im-agine, were sometimes very hard. But I was not really inter-ested in politics or making money and so on. I was inter-ested in the spiritual life."

Someone put up a hand.

"Yes?"

"Are you a Brahmin?"

"An excellent question. No, I am not a Brahmin. Brahmins are Hindus. Hindu society has traditionally been divided into four castes, and there is a fifth caste, the untouchables. The highest caste is called Brahmin. So no, I was not a Brah-min, because I am not a Hindu by birth. I am what is called a Sikh."

"What's a Sikh?" I said.

"Sikhism is a religion. It is based on the teachings of the Ten Gurus. India has many different religions, not just Hin-duism and Islam. There's a lot going on. As we will see. But to complete my story, after the Partition, I decided I wanted to move to the West. It was difficult to do that during the Cold War period. So much war, isn't there? But anyway, about ten years ago I emigrated to the United States. I eventually became a citizen. So, now you are all stuck with me."

This caused more laughter.

"In India I went to school to study literature. Western literature, of course, as was the custom. And I achieved an advanced degree, or work in the Indian public service, which is a common destination for educated people. But I grew tired of books. So I rebelled and left academia to do something I loved: I became a mechanic. Even today I love racing and driving cars. Anyway, when I came to America, I worked as an auto mechanic. In fact, I think I know someone's father...." He looked around, and then at me. "Perhaps you?"

"My father used to be an auto mechanic," I said.

"Richard Gray?"

"That's him."

"Very good! You must be Robbie."

"Yes. Pleased to meet you."

"Yes, likewise. We used to call your father Tricky Dick." Laughter.

"Yeah," I said. "He still goes by that."

"Very good. Well, to complete my story, I am also a member of the Theosophical Lodge in Santa Barbara. The Lodge was approached a few years back to see if there was anyone with a background in Eastern matters. So, somehow, I came to find myself teaching every Tuesday and Thursday up here on this splendid Hill. Anyway, that is enough about me. Unless there are questions, let's turn to the class itself."

We spent some time discussing what an "Idea" actually was, and then Ram explained that we would be reading the great books, many of them Eastern, or Eastern-influenced, to see what ideas might be in them. "Books like *Siddhartha* and *Steppenwolf* by Hermann Hesse. And *The Way of Zen* by

Alan Watts. A little later, if we build up to it, we may read *The Bhagavad Gita*. This is a core Hindu text, the spiritual part, you might say, of what is in the *Mahabharata*."

"So is this a kind of a counter-culture class?" said Cadogan.

Ram scratched his chin through his beard. "Perhaps. I suppose it goes without saying that ideas are always somewhat counter, if by culture you mean the status quo. But our purpose is not to be revolutionaries. At least, not yet. You are too young to be revolutionaries. First, learn, become inner astronauts, climb the visionary mountain. Then, with understanding, with a view of the horizon, the destination—only then should you act. You are in the early learning stage. In fact, Kickshaw is a wonderful opportunity to soak your young brains in knowledge, just like Madge soaking her hands in Palmolive."

More laughter. Everyone seemed pleased with the Ideas class, until Ram explained that in addition to the reading, we would be writing essays. "Very lengthy essays!" Ram said to groans. "It will be an exploration of both heart and mind! In a space of safety, you can express your inner heart!" he said loudly, his arms spread wide, as we hurried out.

***

It was Christian who began it, seeking interesting safe spaces in which to smoke a joint unmolested, or just relax out of sight and out of mind. His idea of an inner astronaut was quite different from Ram's, I thought. Christian regularly snuck off campus—something I had not dared to do—and his bravado in the face of danger was exciting to witness. Of course, it was incredibly mad, and expulsion was a real possibility if he got caught. But he seemed to thrive on risk. Having a safe space on campus would just make our own kind of inner astronautics—the kind with bong hits—all that much easier.

So we set out to explore and discover. It was like fort building, the sort of thing kids do quite by natural urge. We were a bit older, but somehow it felt right, like a game, to find the secret perfect hideout. It was on one of these forays that I made an important discovery.

I have described the "Schoolhouse" building, which included the "Infirmary" dormitory above and classrooms below, and attached to that was the old Branson Library, where the senior coffee was held. It was observed that this building had a furnace room or sub-basement. I was curious about that. One day I looked around and found it was currently used primarily as a laundry. But at the back stood a large fire door. It was evident there was more. Perhaps a furnace or some other work area lay behind the big red metal sliding door.

I also noticed at the end of the Branson there was a little access panel, about man-sized, and I could see down into it. It looked like there was a crawl space that led underneath the library. Conjecturing there might be an access to interior works, much like the Great Pyramid of Giza was known to have secret passages, I decided I would explore it.

It was necessary to wait for the appropriate moment. I wanted to go in daylight, because a flashlight would probably give off too much visible light back through the passage, so I waited for a day when the school was mostly deserted. Sunday morning served this purpose. I walked over to the back of the Branson and sat down next to the access panel. It was down in a sort of culvert made of old concrete a few feet in height. I just sat down and relaxed as if I was waiting for someone. Meanwhile I made a scan of the area and used all my senses to detect any living being in the immediate vicinity. But the scene was quiet. I then took the plunge. Quickly I dropped into the culvert and lifted the grill. It was not even locked. I carefully crawled into the passage and slipped the grill back into place from below.

Looking now for the first time, I could see this was indeed an access passage that led under the library. It was a crawlspace, but I could easily navigate on my hands and knees. I followed the passage and it gradually became darker. But I rested, then, and listened, and allowed my eyes to adjust. I moved forward to a join, with a passage going left and another to the right. In my imagination the right passage should go to the laundry sub-basement I had checked out previously. I crept down the right-hand passage. Eventually I could see it coming to an end. There was a dim light. I reached the end of the crawlspace and looked out into another room, not that big, and yes, there on the far wall I could see this side of the big red metal sliding door that was locked on the other side with a padlock. I dropped down slowly onto the floor of the room. I could see very little and looked for a light. I found a switch on the far side, after stumbling into a table. The room was a work area; I could see tools on a workbench, perhaps for the building and grounds crew. There seemed to be stacks of chairs and piles of metal pipes and other bits stacked and packed away to the side.

Suddenly I heard voices in the sub-basement, on the other side of the red door. I flicked off the light and stood in silence. I realized, to my horror, that laundry soap and bleach and other accoutrements of the laundry process were in evidence in the room where I now stood, and I felt panic welling up inside. Perhaps some staff did laundry on a Sunday? Up from Carpinteria to look after an urgent need for tableclothes in the senior coffee? Old Kickshaw demanding out-of-hours service for a mess he'd made?

But as I listened, I could hear the voices had a familiar tone, and I could make out words like 'dude,' and 'gnarly.' After what seemed was a dryer being emptied, the playful voices guffawed and then trailed off as footsteps made themselves scarce.

I took a breath, then, and slumped down into one of the chairs at the table before me. Suddenly from that vantage point I could make out the glint of a key chain. Some light was coming in through a crack at the top of the red metal sliding door, and it fell on what appeared to be a fat ring of keys. I had a mental flashback to the moment in *Journey to the Center of the Earth*, when a bead of light snakes down at the critical moment to reveal the entrance way to the underworld. I got up and gingerly lifted the keyring off its hook. The keys were numbered, and mostly uniform as to the kind of lock they would service, but some had quite intriguing labels written on miniscule scraps of paper and then taped onto the top of the key. One said "Hitch bd." Which might mean the back door to the Hitchcock Theater building. Another said, "Chem 132." I thought that might refer to the janitor's closet in the Chemistry Lab.

"Holy crap," I thought. I had a hard decision to make. Should I take one or two keys, and just test them, then return if I wanted more; or should I abscond with the lot and hope someone would assume they had been mislaid?

Being lazy, and also perhaps greedy, I opted for the latter. If I was caught with the keys, I could always say I had just found them laying in the grass somewhere and intended to return them. But then forgot to do that. Or something. I was convinced I could create a better story about that given time.

Having decided not just to trespass on school property, but now to go rogue as a thief, I forged my resolve and set out. I had to clamber back up the access way, which turned out to be more difficult than it seemed if I was not going to leave something as obvious as a chair under the entrance to the passage. Finally I got up into the opening and began to crawl. I realized I was soaking in sweat and my clothing was already grimy from crawling in the concrete passage. Which was bad. And I now had a heavy key ring to tote along with me, one that did not fit into my pants pocket. If only I had brought a day pack!

I was too cowardly to just carry the key ring around and bluff my way if someone saw it, so I left it in the bushes near the culvert and went back to my room. I was in Long House this year, which kind of sucked, but that's what I got. At least it was a room with a view, and in the evenings my balcony looked out on the sunset, with Santa Barbara and the sea in the distance. Meanwhile Christian had made it into the Hermitage, which was a small dorm of only 12 singles. The Master was old Mr. Bright, who taught American History.

I returned after a shower—luckily the dorms were more or less deserted from weekend liberty and people out and about—and picked up the key ring, hiding it in my backpack. I then went immediately in the direction of the Hermitage, intent on showing Christian my incredible find.

"Mr. Gray," someone said. I turned and saw the considerable bulk of Franklin Bright's body emerging from his apartment.

"Good morning, sir," I said.

"Yes it is. I trust you are in good spirits?"

"Yes, sir."

"As you know, I am your advisor this year. We should meet soon to discuss how things are going."

"Yes, of course," I said. "I am looking forward to—having you as my advisor. I'm fascinated by American History."

"Oh really," he said. The rotund man seemed to suddenly become lighter. "That is most encouraging!"

"Yes sir, in fact, I was thinking I would take the AP History test." This was complete BS manufactured on the spot, of course, but I actually did like history. I had heard Master Bright was a real hard-ass.

"Really? That is manna from heaven, as far as I am concerned," he was saying. "As a Junior, no less. Well, that is wonderful to hear. Let's discuss the details in the coming week. Perhaps I can get you into one of my sections."

"Very good, sir. Speak soon!" And with that I darted into the Hermitage entrance. I was painfully conscious of the jingling coming from my pack. Of course, probably no one except myself could hear the tintinnabulation; it seemed to be more than half inside my brain. I dropped down the flight of stairs to the bottom floor and gently tapped on his door, once, twice, three times, and after a minute he said, "Who is it?"

"It's me, dude," I said.

He then opened the door and peeked out. "Hey, dude!"

I went in and we sat, he on his throne comfy chair, which was an actual recliner he had scored from a senior at the end of the previous year, and me on the bed. "Check this out!" I said. I pulled out the key ring. It seemed even heavier than when I first hefted it as if the gravity of our affairs had added mass.

"Well, well, well," he said. "Someone get lazy and leave that lying around? My, my, is that what I think it is?"

"I haven't tried any of the keys yet. I don't know what to do, actually. Do you think if it is missed they will start a search?"

"Hmm." Christian leaned back and considered. "It's not out of the question, but I guess we've got all day, or even until tomorrow morning, to figure it out. Let's first try a key or two to find out if those are still good. Hell's Bells, my man!"

"Oh yeah."

We had to do some research to see if we could match keys to room or office numbers. The most interesting keys from my point of view were the ones related to the chem and biology labs, the music room, and the Headmaster's office. The Alumni office was also interesting.

"What would you want with the Headmaster's office?"

"Oh, I don't know," I stammered. I was thinking about Dr. Kickshaw and his dalliance with Mr. Sauvage. "Probably all kinds of interesting information in there."

"That's very bold, dude. Axis Bold As Love, my man."

"Hell yeah, why not?" I was engaging in pure bravado and hyperbole, of course. The chances of me actually getting up the courage to break into the Headmaster's office were probably zero to none. But I was keen on visiting the chemistry closet.

For Christian, the keys he thought were most interesting were to the Sheds—the name for the place where the majority of the sporting equipment was stored, and also other kinds of useful building and grounds gear. Tools and such. He was also curious about the Rayburn Theater. "There's probably lots of weird spaces in there. It's huge. You wanna go see?"

"Sure," I said.

The Rayburn Theater was the biggest building on campus, and it sat at the bottom of a path that lay catty-cornered to the Hermitage; so it really was just a short walk past '27 House and then a casual glide to the back of the big building. The sun continued to shine, and the wind blew calmly. It was a gorgeous day for a break-in. Christian produced some cover by bringing a frisbee, and we tossed our way around, eventually finding ourselves as if by chance at the back of the building.

Having already secreted the key he guessed was right from the ring, Christian looked around and, seeing the coast was clear, tried the key. It didn't seem to work.

"Crap," I said.

"Ah, but let me try another..." He produced a second key and inserted it. This one worked. He looked at me with a grin and then glanced around. "You ready for this, dude?"

I nodded. Actually I was terrified. What if other people were inside? It did not seem impossible on a Sunday. We walked inside, moving quietly, not talking or laughing, as we were on a mission. The place was very familiar—we were there almost every school day—but now, it was silent and echoed our footsteps. There was an airy sense of space.

"Come and see something I noticed," said Christian.

We walked around to the side and went up a flight of stairs. It led to an upper deck that had a view over the seating in the theater. Christian pointed to a void, an opening at floor level, that looked like it went somewhere. "Wait here," he whispered. He got down on his hands and knees and crawled into the void. I could see there must be something, because he kept crawling and soon his entire body was inside.

I became fidgety but after a moment his hand appeared as if magically detached and waved me forward. I got down on my hands and knees and crawled in. It was completely dark but I could hear Christian's breathing. He lit his lighter, and now I could see the interior of the space.

"Cool!" I whispered.

"It's not that useful in itself," Christian said. "But I think if I cut a panel out of this wall board, there's probably an interesting space behind here."

There was a distant click-clack. It echoed in the empty theater. I knew immediately what it was: one of the entrances towards the front of the theater had been unlocked and opened, and when it closed, it produced that well-known sound. We both froze, listening. For a while, nothing seemed to be happening, but I could clearly make out movement down below, as if someone was walking in the theater.

"Crap," whispered Christian. "Stay calm."

Time passed second by second, perhaps dilated by the adrenaline pumping in my system. Music suddenly pulsed, a loud, somewhat distorted sound. It took a few seconds to figure out what it was: opera. The sound was tinny and brass, as if from a small record player (which indeed was the case). Someone had set up a little phonograph on the stage and set a record spinning. Meanwhile, as we listened, a live voice, a human voice, male, strong, and definitely a tenor. Someone was singing to the music.

Christian was much braver than I was. He slowly began to crawl out of the void. I pulled at his leg but he kept going. Eventually he disappeared completely. After a moment I could see his hand in silhouette, prompting me to emerge.

I was afraid to do so, petrified we would get caught. But slowly I emerged. I then crawled to where Christian was sitting. He was smiling. "Just peek for a moment and look who it is," he whispered.

I plucked up my courage and slowly peeked over the top of the wall. 'Oh, Christ on a cracker,' I thought. 'It's Martin!' And it was. He was standing on the stage, his arms akimbo, and as the aria rose in strength, his arms extended up and his voice rose in power, filling the space.

Martin was a pretty good tenor, as far as I could tell. But now Christian had removed his shoes and slowly was crawling towards the back of the theater. I had no choice but to follow. After what seemed an interminable crawl, we reached the far stairwell and then descended, step by step, in our socks, to finally reach the exit. Christian gently pushed it open—it was a fire exit, fortunately it was not alarmed—and we slipped out.

"What the hell was that?" Christian said.

"Rigoletto."

"Rigoletto?"

"Yep. Verdi. The lady is fickle."

"Ah. I see," Christian nodded. "It's a song about a girl."

"Yep. Another song about a girl."

We learned later that Lori had dumped Martin. *C'est la vie.*

PART SIX — Mr. Chunkie and the Dragon's Den

There once was a boy who did stone,
And found himself lost in the zone,
But the thing of it was,
He just wanted a buzz,
And a friend, and a place to call home.

"We need to score, dudely," said Christian, as he scraped his pipe for resin. He was prying black goop out of the pen pipe and collecting it onto a piece of clean white paper. "We're down to the brass tacks."

"But smoking black crud?"

"Well, who do you know in the big wide world? Your dad?"

"No," I said. "That's a non-starter right now." Larry had put his foot down again about weed. Even my dad was on a tight leash. The garage bong had been thrown in the trash.

"Here goes nothing," Christian said, clutching the bowl and hitting it with his lighter. He coughed pretty hard. "Ugh. Lordy!"

"How is it?" I said.

"Not bad. Dude, don't you know a few seniors? Those burnouts?"

He meant AJ and Ringo. Yeah, I knew them. Normally Kickshaw seniors had nothing to do with underclassmen, but we came up with them in the dorms—AJ had been in Lido and Ringo up in High House, and I always had a kind of due deference that they appreciated. They liked my hairstyle, too, which by then was quite long for the times. It was like big brother little brother stuff, or like back in old Dent Head's class with Charlie and Tommy. And they were druggies. Maybe as a last resort.

AJ was Alan Jensen, but we never called him anything but his initials, and Ringo was Ronald Bryant, but we called him Ringo due to his demeanor and hairstyle. These two were best friends and I used them more or less interchangeably as advisors on drugs and music and all knowledge of things in the forbidden realm. These days you can just google something or ask the AI and have it say sorry that's off-limits, but back then, we relied on people; the rock star people amongst us; if you wanted to know if Carlos Castaneda was on the level, or what it was like to eat magic mushrooms, or how to prepare coke for snorting, you went to that one guy who probably knew, broached the subject in a tentative manner, and hoped for the best.

AJ was the one who turned me on to Reggae, and I then transmitted this particular Jamaican virus to Christian, who was a bit more circumspect—yes, Christian was a musical snob, a rock and roll suicide no doubt, but even he was eventually won over by the buoyant positivity of the pot-smoking dreadlocked fiends. The great Bob Marley, who everyone there agreed was The King. AJ had actually seen him in concert.

"You really saw him?" I said.

"Yeah. In 1976 at the Roxy."

"Was that a good show?"

"Oh yeah, man. It was the best show I've ever seen."

"The *best*?" I said.

"Yes. And I've been to a lot of shows."

"He has," said Ringo.

AJ began to wax poetic, as he occasionally did about music. "I've seen the Rolling Stones. The Grateful Dead two or three or maybe ten times. But the vibe of the music at that Bob Marley show, it just was all love, man, you know? It was all love and positivity. And the crowd, man. The crowd was just loving it."

Ringo was a bit more academic in a kind of Timothy Leary sense—had dropped acid—something Christian and I aspired to but had not yet achieved. And he loved Blue Oyster Cult. "Don't fear the Reaper, man!" That was his catch phrase. He was applying to Cal Tech and likely to get in, and eventually would go on to a postdoc in Chemistry. But at this moment, he was still down deep in the dorms at Kickshaw, struggling with his addictions and (quite secretly) occasional bouts of depression that came and went in blank obscurity.

One day I was up in his room and he whispered, "check this out," and then beckoned me to look into his closet. There, in the dark behind his dirty clothes pile, was a little block wrapped with damp straw and bound with string. I could see a few mushrooms growing on it like eyes on a toy newt.

"LBMs," he said.

"LBMs?"

"Yes, Little Brown Mushrooms."

"But are they...?"

"I'll never tell," he said, his eyebrows twitching.

So these guys were cool, twilight idols, Shades of the 70s, and now they were seniors, clothed in the immense power of Kickshaw's final stages: SAT and Advanced Placement testing, college admissions, ladies in waiting to the great promise of freedom that is graduation and matriculation into the tertiary: University.

Even as I was getting up the courage to talk to them, AJ surprised me in the dining hall.

"Hey man, come up to my room for a word, will you?"

"Of course," I said.

"You know where it is?"

"I've got an idea." He was up in the Infirmary, a dark cavern of a dorm I had walked through exactly once.

I wasted no time heading up there after classes. I knocked, and he opened the door in this, the most quiet and sedate of all the dorms. He was smiling his million-dollar AJ dealmaker smile. "Hey man, there you are, come on in."

"So what's up?" I was a little surprised to see Ringo already there. But then he did live in the same dorm.

"Thanks for coming man. Here's the situation. My older brother has run into a cash crunch. He's got to pay his rent and due to some unforeseen circumstances with roommates, and such, he's short on cash. So, he asked me to hit up some of the more with-it kids. If you can give him a loan for a week or two, he can pay you back either in cash, or in hashish."

Ringo wasn't saying anything, but his eyes lit up, shaggy eyebrows twitching and his head nodded back and forth violently, like 'yeah man.' I didn't question it. I had some money left from doing yard work at *Rancho Bravos*, capped with a Ben Franklin from Larry—an early Christmas present—so I said, "Sure AJ. I'm in. Happy to help."

"How much do you think you can loan him?"

"Well, how about $200? Would that help?"

"Yeah, $300 would be better."

"OK, man. I can go $300."

AJ got happy then. "Alright. Alright! Well, get back to me. Maybe tonight?"

"Yeah, I'll drop by after dinner."

"Thanks Robbie. Or are you going by Sutra now?"

"Yeah. That's just a joke from Ideas class. But yeah."

"Sutra!" said Ringo. "Very cool. You should put that on a tee shirt, man."

So I got the cash for AJ from out of my top desk drawer and I didn't think too much about it until later that night when I told Christian I was unsuccessful.

"I tried to talk to him about weed, but he needed money for his brother's rent."

Christian laughed. "Oh dude, you don't get it. You're so innocent."

"Huh?"

He opened his door quickly and looked out to check the hall was clear, and then sat back down. "Yeah. They're doing a drug deal."

"What? You mean—"

"It's fine. AJ's brother probably has an opportunity and they're just putting together as much cash as they can. Or maybe he already has the hash and is now in the process of distribution. These things happen. AJ's bro went to Kickshaw for a time, did you know that?"

"No."

"Well, he also got expelled. He can't come up to campus. So AJ is probably helping him out."

"Uh-oh."

"Nah. You should consider yourself lucky. AJ thought of you. But don't tell anybody else, dude. Know what I mean?"

"Holy crap," I said. It suddenly dawned on me. "Those dudes used me. They lied. It was all bullshit."

"It was a sale. Hopefully you don't get ripped off. We might just get some hash! Think of it."

"Is it good?"

"Oh hell yeah."

"Yeah. OK. I guess we'll see." I was tight lipped.

After that I was a bit more circumspect, a bit more jaded, around the pair. Seniors or no. And maybe other people in general. It was a good lesson.

But that was how we got Mr. Chunkie. Christian, who was always quite creative at naming things and inventing new words, called it 'Chunkerton' after the 'Chunky' chocolate candy bar. The lump of hash certainly was as big as a Chunky, and roughly the same dimensions. I didn't have a scale—but Christian sure did. He carefully disrobed the pale block from its shroud of aluminum foil and deposited the block on the device. It seemed to sag under the load.

"Check it out! It's almost 30 grams!"

"That's more than an ounce," I said.

"It is. Mr. Chunkie! My, my, my. That sure is a lot of hash." He carefully repackaged the block. "I'm going to cut off a working slice, OK?"

"Definitely."

"You had better stash this bad boy carefully, Sutra."

"I've got a good idea about that," I said.

He handed Mr. Chunkie back to me and then put the pale blond gummy of hash into a film canister. "We need to celebrate, don't you think?"

"Sure. But I've got to hold it until the weekend."

"What?"

"I've got a paper to write!"

"All right, dude. All right. We'll go down to—oh, wait, you haven't seen the Dragon's Den yet."

"No."

"We'll go this weekend."

***

The *Forest Sauvage* had many byways and hidden off ramps to mischief and madness, and that sunny Saturday Christian led me down the main trail past Long House until we came to a new cut. Here Christian stopped, surveying the path behind us. We were completely alone as far as I could tell. "Be careful not to wear this down. Watch how I do it—push this sage plant back." We traversed an entirely new trail that plunged steeply down and then made an abrupt right turn, then again left. Eventually we came to a sort of ledge. I could see the footing was treacherous over a gorge of ten or twelve feet in depth. It was necessary to jump at this point. Christian did this easily; I followed suit but with a lot less finesse. He watched approvingly as I bounded over the rim. "Crap on a cracker," I said. "Yeah, we don't want anyone coming this way."

We stopped at a vantage point, and I audibly gasped.

"Welcome to the Dragon's Den," he said.

"Whoa!" Down below, I could see a dug out on the steep face. Someone had installed a few boards that might have marginally stabilized the hillside; and then, incredibly, the spot had been furnished. A couch had somehow materialized there. It was about the size of a loveseat, and beside it was a red, white-lidded cooler. There was even a little wooden table—just a milk crate with a board, but it would serve.

"Have a seat, dudely."

We cozied in, and Christian proceeded to extract a ceramic bong from the cooler. It was shaped like a dragon with the mouth open and upright, and in the mouth was a brass bowl. The air hole on the bong was at the front, on the chest. "Meet the Dragon."

"Ah yes. Now I get it."

"Let me put some water in this."

"You seem to have thought of everything. But did you bring the main ingredient?"

"Oh, crap!" he cried out. Then after a moment he chuckled. "Got you! No, I didn't forget. Mr. Chunkie's smaller sister, Chunkie Cutie, has made the trip with us." Here he excreted the black, grey-lidded film canister from his front jeans pocket and popped it on the table like a magic trick.

While he was getting the paraphernalia ready, I checked out the view, which was expansive: I could easily see the distant Catalina Islands laid out, as the crystal sky stood unusually clear that morning. Normally shrouded in mist, the Santa Barbara hills were magnified as under a lens to the East.

"Let's smoke this," Christian said. His eyes gleamed in the flash of the lighter as the bong gargled.

Those were good times, and I like to remember Christian in that place, a secret place of hidden beauty, where one moment of perfection could spread out into untold, unspoken joy. But that is not how life can be all the time. The wheel of Karma is inexorable.

***

"They've shot him!"

"What?" I said.

"They've shot him!" Christian repeated. "John Lennon, they assassinated him! He's dead!"

It was December 8th, 1980. For Christian, Lennon's assassination was as hard to cope with as the death of Martin Luther King Jr. or maybe Jesus—he was shaken to the core. I stood there, not knowing what to say.

We spent the day talking in whispers, not doing much, and there were others at Kickshaw who were hurt, too. Shock, dismay, could be read on the faces of students and Masters alike. We even had a special service in the Chapel that night and sang Beatles songs. Martin Quinn seemed especially aware of Christian's suffering, and he said, "Robbie, can you keep an eye on Christian?"

"Sure," I said. "If you mean about Lennon, he's bumming out all right. But I don't think he would do anything, well, brash."

"I don't know," said Martin. He looked thoughtful as he gazed at Christian, openly weeping by himself out by the Dining Hall. "Just keep an eye on him for me, OK?"

"I will," I said.

"And what about you?"

"Me?" But I had no funny retort. I just shook my head.

That night Christian made one of his late-night sojourns into Carpinteria. He knocked on my door very late, perhaps 1 a.m. I got up and peeked out.

"It's me, dudely," he whispered.

I let him in and he sat on the bed in the dark. "Hey man. Let's drink to John." He was holding a paper bag in the way a wino does.

"OK, man."

He took a shot himself from the hidden bottle and then handed it to me. "Go easy."

I took a small drink and it burned. "Ugh, what is it?"

"Whisky."

"I've never drunk whiskey before," I whispered.

"Don't hold it in your mouth. Just gulp it down," he said. "It'll burn, but that works with, you know, how we feel."

"Yeah. OK."

I wasn't as broken up as Christian was, but I did feel sad, and Christian was my best friend. I took a big swig off the bottle. I almost choked; the liquor burnt in my throat. Christian put his hand on my mouth to quiet me. "Shhh," he said.

I sent Christian off to bed eventually. We did, maybe five or six shots. Later that morning—probably I was dreaming—I thought I heard the shower on downstairs. "Maybe Christian is trying to get cleaned up," I thought.

I slept late, and woke up with my mouth feeling like a blow torch, and missed my first period class to go and retch.

But I told Martin Christian was fine. "He's on the mend," I said. "He's working through this his way." And that next day it seemed that he did show a smile.

"It will be Christmas break soon," said Martin.

***

Before Christmas came we had the obligatory Junior Christmas Show, which was a series of skits put on by the class for the entertainment of all in the Rayburn Theater. William figured largely in this, and I could see his creativity was flowing. The guy had a tremendous imagination. He wrote most of the skits including an introductory bit where he portrayed Rod Serling from *The Twilight Zone*.

"Meet the Man With No Name, age 33, who some call Clint. Dean of Students at Kickshaw School For Boys. A man who prides himself on

knowing every face that's ever sat in assembly, and every liberty ever granted on the signup sheet. But this morning, things have changed."

"In a school where boys vanish and girls appear in their place— where wedding rings no longer fit and voices rise an octave—Clint is about to discover that identity is a fragile thing, and that gender may be more illusion than anyone believes. For Dean Stacks has just stepped into...the Twilight Zone."

The school was transformed, *Twilight Zone* style, into a girl's school, and one by one surfer boys were turning into girls in drag. The dialog, which unfortunately I can no longer remember, was hilarious. But the funniest part came when Cadogan, wearing a blond wig, dress, and pancake makeup, acted out a scene with "Clint," the cowboy Dean, played by Jonah in Western attire. Cadogan cried out, "Oh Clint, what is there for me here?" We laughed and laughed in that hysterical way that happens when you know what you are doing is over the edge.

Stacks and his wife were in the audience, and clearly unhappy about this portrayal. I could see that the Dean's left eye was twitching, even as his perpetual iron smile was burned onto his face like a brand. His wife's face was downcast. I felt sorry for her.

Afterwards, it seemed that "Clint" had had words with William and Cadogan, but I didn't hear what was said. William looked apologetic, but Cadogan sneered and shook his head.

"Great performance!" I said.

"Sutra, you pud! You should have seen his face!"

I had a sense of foreboding about this, because I knew Clint was a real bastard. But I didn't know the half of it.

PART SEVEN — Night of the Living Chick

A girl began working a job,
To stroke at the end of a fob,
But the fob was too big,
To fit in her rig,
So she took out her heat on the hob.

Isabella came into my life the way lovers often do: mysteriously, and with no clear explanation. It was just meant to be, and so it happened. That was how I felt. She could have been walking down the street and then bump into me as I tried to tie my shoe; or she could have been shot out of a cannon and end up crash-landing on top of the camper, only to be scooped into my arms. Whatever the outward process, she would have somehow been inserted into my life and into my heart. Perhaps that sounds a bit strange or absurdly impossibly romantic, but I am quite sure I am right about this. Some things are just Fate.

Cecilia was like that, too. I could never have predicted her. I was intensely afraid of Black people and ended up in love with a Black girl, the meekest and most mild of girls, but still a forbidden fruit, a banned and taboo experience. Up to this point I had never admitted to anyone my first love was, in the parlance of the bigots, a nigger. I had no way to frame my experience; and I did not think other people would understand what had happened. I didn't even tell my dad or Larry the whole story. Only my mother knew all, and she was now divorced from my life.

My experience with Cecilia did not teach me that racism was wrong or absurd, but rather that what I valued in human beings had nothing to do with race or outward circumstances—nothing at all. Rather, what I valued most in life were people who are like me, people who live in this world like strangers in a strange land; people who float on the water of this world like a lotus, rather than tread water with most of their bodies submerged, trying in vain to keep their heads above the surface of a putrid sea.

And then of course, there was Susan, who was the great contradiction. I did not understand her at all. I had done everything, made every sacrifice to create the perfect moment; I was ready to rub Susan's girl-cock, or even suck on it, if that was what had been called for. But no. The Saint, the girl in that puny male body, trapped and spread-eagled in a continuous crucifix that we call gender, would not have me. I wanted to joyfully penetrate her while she lay spread-eagled on that crucifix, with all the guilt and uptightness that such an act entailed.

That was not to be, and my foray into the world of the wild thing was abortive at best. But at least I had tried. I was 'friend material.' Apparently sent by God to be one. And a friend in need is a friend indeed. Well, OK then. But there were other karmas waiting.

***

It was the time of year of the school dance. Kickshaw was an all-boys school, but there were a few all-girl schools in Santa Barbara, or at least, in Santa Barbara county. That was only logical, I suppose, this notion of reciprocal preparatory institutions. Perhaps a standing arrangement with those schools was in place, because on a particular evening, at the appointed time, several busloads of girls—prep-school girls, young ladies, women—pick your poison—lumbered up in buses to the Mesa. I have no idea how those chartered buses navigated the narrow road up to the top of the Mesa without going off the ledge, but somehow they eventually did.

This explosion of skirts and the associated blast of Yin energy then drifted by diffusion and gentle persuasion onto the Kickshaw school grounds, scattering for a time, as on the wind, only later to coalesce around the dining hall, which had tonight been converted into a makeshift light show and dance hall. It was like a weird invasion from Mars, everywhere I walked, everywhere I looked, there were girl faces and girl bodies. Stray girl-parts protruded everywhere. Some of the guys were giddy, like Felix, who had already put on his best suit and was sporting a red power tie as he prattled on, dancing a little jig in the hall-way. But others who were less comfortable or less familiar with the power of Yin, avoided the feelings and the sensations the girl-meat brought on. It was too much all at once.

To me, there was something gross about the idea of a bunch of rich Kickshaw dudes getting girls bussed in so they could pretend to socialize and then greedily cop a feel. Maybe not third base, but clutching a tit. Why not just have co-ed schools if it were useful for us to connect with girls, with young women? But to that there was no answer.

Old Kickshaw himself seemed to revel in these sordid so-cial events. He saw nothing out of the ordinary in the girl-meat cavalcade. On arrival of the girls he would set out to walk the grounds and see them in their finery, admiring and waving his hand and sometimes chatting with the chaper-ones. These tended to be spinster-like women almost as old as Old Kickshaw, and almost as deaf. Or at least it seemed that way to me.

On this particular dance-night Jonah thought the girl-crop was less than satisfactory and expressed his discon-tent in the harshest terms. "Oh no, not Santa Anita again! Those bitches!"

"What, you aren't into them?" I said.

"It's really slim pickings, dude. Have you not been follow-ing along?"

By this stage, Jonah had moved into Long House too, but was on a different floor, and I was visiting as he had some questions about old Norwich's English test.

"No," I said. "The truth is these dances sort of give me the creeps."

"Well, it's always a mixed bag; but sometimes there's better pickings. This crop is mainly local girls from Carp. They're far from satisfactory, although a few will put out. There's some Mexican girls," he said. "They tend to not put out. Catholics, I guess. But there is one..."

By Carp what he meant was of course Carpinteria, the sleepy seaside town that lay, like a woman, at the feet of the angry elitist foothills. We looked down on it imperiously every morning.

"Mexicans, huh?" I said. "Joey will be thrilled."

"Yeah. There's these two sisters with a rep. Carmelita is the older sister, she's known to be quite friendly. That was two years ago, though. I think she's graduated. But the younger sister might do. Isabella."

"That's a nice name," I said.

"She finds favor in my eyes, if you know what I mean. Great titties."

"Well, good luck with that." I was aware that Jonah had suffered with blue balls from the last dance-night and I considered making a joke, as frustration seemed often to be the name of the game with these events. But I thought I'd leave it alone for the moment. There would be time for that yet. When he was limping around like a stray dog with rickets.

Me, I planned to completely ignore the dance. Not actually sign up for a pass to leave campus for the weekend, in flight, like a frightened nerd, but just lay low, perhaps diving into *Ringworld*, or revisiting *Rendezvous With Rama*, or even wasting time in the *Hitchhiker's Guide to the Galaxy*. By this stage I was also into the books Ram suggested in Ideas, like the *Bhagavad Gita*, which I considered light reading. We had even been on a field trip to the Theosophists Lodge where some of these wonderful secret books and other esoterica, like sandalwood incense, could be found for purchase. I bought *The Gospel of Thomas* on that trip but had not yet cracked the cover.

I was pretty sure Christian was going to the dance because he mentioned a girl who was coming up for the
event— "Not one of the skanks from Santa Anita," he said.
"It's Jill, I met her in SB a few weeks ago."

"That's pretty cool," I said.

"Yeah. It was all very iconic. You know, like it was meant
to be. I was in that used record shop down on State Street."

"Paradice Records?"

"That's the one. She's into the Beatles, man. I'm so stoked."

"Yeah, I can see that. Well, don't get expelled."

"Ah, you know me."

I did, in fact, know him, and I was certain he had a new
hideout or hideaway escape all set up and ready for this Jill.
I was happy for him but it meant he wouldn't be around to
share a bong hit to help get me through this monstrous
Night of the Living Chick.

So I put my headphones on and listened to *Who's Next* at 11
on the dial and contemplated the drumming of Keith Moon,
which Christian described as "lead drums." He was not
wrong and Moon was clearly the lead in that band. Idly, I
glanced at book covers, dosed in my chair, and then finally
gave up and decided I'd stroll around the grounds like Mrs.
Robinson in a straitjacket. It was dance-night, so that was
completely fine, there was no rule that prevented me from
wandering the grounds as there was on a school night, and
it was only 10pm anyway.

I walked up from the Long House and idled for a while,
looking out at the dark forest below, then past the Hermitage, past Mr. Bright's domicile—the light was on—and
walked slowly up the main road, observing the sky through
the Eucalyptus that stood on parade. The clouds obscured
the stars and eventually a mist settled in from the sea and
made it doubly hard to see the objects that Aristotle believed were souls. There was a gentle breeze now and then,
and the leaves in the trees rustled, but otherwise the only
noise came from across the campus and to the right, where

on the other side of the Branson Library the dance was in full swing. The Bee Gees were throbbing in cacophony at the moment to some form of strobe light.

I descended down the stairs that lead towards the science classrooms, past the little snack shack, and eventually wound on down towards the Rayburn Theater. Christian had made considerable progress, he said, on the super new hideaway hangout, but I had not seen it yet. I wondered if he was up there right now with the new girl he was so excited about, Jill. He claimed to have dragged a mattress up there, which seemed physically impossible. But then Christian tended to attempt the impossible.

I turned, because I heard someone. At first I thought it was a wounded animal or a dying bird. But it was a girl. She was weeping in low, soft undulated cries that were not quite moans. "Hello?" I said. "Someone there?"

There was no answer, but the crying stopped. I walked over in that direction towards a bench and saw a girl slumped over, essentially she was lying on the bench on her back, one leg bent. Her dress was not looking too good. Not torn, but not on her as it should be. I assumed there would be a boy with her so I said, "Oh, sorry," and turned away, but then she said "No, I'm the one who is sorry." She sniffled. "I'm just over here crying. Take no notice. All is well. Remain calm."

I stopped and turned around, then. She had quoted *Animal House*. "Um. Sorry to intrude. Are you in need of assistance?"

She laughed then, because apparently that was a funny thing for a Kickshaw boy to say.

"Oh, I think I've had about enough 'assistance' from you guys tonight. Thanks though."

I was silent. "Are you Isabella?"

"What?" She lifted herself up a bit and looked at me. "Do I know you?"

"No," I said. "You're Mexican, I'm guessing. Someone described a beautiful girl to me. Maybe you have a sister?"

She shook her head in disgust. "You guys. Real piece of work this place. I guess word gets around. No, I'm not Mexican. I was born in San Diego. My dad is a cop. OK?"

I didn't say anything. We were both silent for a moment. It was dark. "That building over there, the first door, it's the Chemistry classroom, there's a sink and water, soap, you could, you know, clean up if you wanted."

"What, you got a key or something?"

"Something like that." I didn't let on that I had a key, that would be too much information to have out in the open. But I wanted to help. "I can get in. If you wanted. We'd have to keep the lights off, though."

"I don't think I want to do that. But thanks."

"Well, OK then. I hope you're alright."

I turned to leave, just a little. But I didn't leave. She was pulling herself together while we talked and had now sat up and put her bra back on—I realized somewhat stupidly that her actions implied it was off—and through some magic of adjustment under her dress her breasts were now once again holstered, and then her arms popped back out of her sleeves. "What's your name?" she said.

"I'm Robbie, but people call me Sutra."

"Sutra?"

"Yeah."

"You mean like Buddhism?"

"Yeah."

"Come over here."

I moved closer and she made room for me on the bench. "Sit. Here," she said, pointing to the spot on the bench next to her. It was like she was talking to a dog, but I didn't mind. I was a mutt alright. I sat and it was warm from her body, that spot. I could smell her body odour, a musky smell that I hypothesized was the smell of sex—of girl parts. It mixed with the night air that was full of jasmine. I noticed she wasn't wearing any shoes.

"What do you think about these dances," she said.

Impulsively I said, "I think they're kind of stupid." I wasn't sure if that was the right thing to say, but my attitude at that moment was one of openness and truth. The fact is, Isabella—yes, this was Isabella, the girl Jonah had mentioned—even though she had not acknowledged that to me quite yet—Isabella was incredibly beautiful. In my eyes at least. Very much as Jonah had intimated from his offhand quote from *The Golden Voyage of Sinbad*, a movie I knew well, but of course modern readers would not. In that movie Sinbad dreams of an exotic damsel of tremendous beauty who has a Cyclops eye tattoo on her palm; and then a few days later, meets that same woman and takes possession of her as a slave. But now, I was encountering my own exotic woman and she was no slave. I was deeply conscious that unlike Sinbad, I was untested and uninteresting. I had nothing to offer and I was abashed. She was so beautiful in her distress.

An ethnic mixture to be sure, I thought, a hybrid, Latino, maybe, but perhaps her father was white, or black, or something like that. At that time I did not understand the unique role of the indigenous genetic contribution from the South American continent in the people of the Latino diaspora. Later when I saw a picture of Isabella's mother, it dawned on me how native-looking her features were.

I don't think Beauty is an objective attribute, except in some scientific sense of proportion and symmetry. To a male adult baboon, the red swollen behind of a female baboon in oestrus is no doubt beautiful; but not to me. Still, Isabella's gentle face and soft brown skin, her almond eyes and naturally full lashes—her face had no makeup whatsoever, and yet was perfect, radiant, even in her dishevelled and disorganized state—seeing her face moved me to a higher plane. I could not lie to her. "I think it's a fucking joke. Girls should not be brought here in cattle cars like whores as entertainment for rich white kids. I feel guilty about that. I am sorry."

She laughed. "Well. Yes. Don't feel guilty. Or sorry. But you've got it about right. That's what we are. Cattle. Udders. Our school gets money for doing this. I suppose that's whorish."

I realized I had insulted her. "Oh Christ, what did I say. Good Lord, I am such an idiot."

She put out her hand and touched my arm, and I looked at her, because I had been looking down. She shook her head in the negative. "It's fine. Calm down. So, what's this deal with your name?"

"You mean why do they call me Sutra? Oh, that's a funny story."

"Oh really. OK. Amuse me."

"See, I take this class called Ideas. It's taught by this Indian dude named Ramakrishna Onkar Ji. He's really cool. We just call him Ram. Because, you know, most of the guys can't pronounce his name." I was looking at her to see if she was listening, because I thought maybe what I was saying was nonsense. But she was looking at me closely, so I averted my eyes again. "So anyway, one day I was in class and Cadogan, he's a buddy of mine, he asked a question about the Dharma and I said, 'well, according to the *Diamond Sutra*, all is Void there is no Dharma,' and then everyone laughed, even Ram, and Cadogan, he started calling me that. He'd be like, 'Sutra, you dumb pud, pass the ketchup.' And I just went with it and then the other guys did and now even some of the teachers call me that. You know, the masters."

"I see. That's a pretty good story. So you've read the *Diamond Sutra*, have you?"

"Yeah. I mean yes." I was feeling a bit self-conscious by now.

"Have you ever read *Dharma Bums* by Jack Kerouac?"

"Of course," I said. I was lying, but I'd read *On The Road* and *The Subterraneans*, so I figured his books were all pretty much like that. And I had read a few of the other Beats, although not as many as I would later. I was put off of *Dharma Bums* because I didn't know much about Gary Snyder and I thought it was mostly about him.

"Sutra, do you think you could walk me to an actual bathroom? Is there a toilet somewhere around here? I could use one."

"Yeah. Actually there is. Kinda dumb of me not to have remembered. There's one over there," I pointed, "That's the snack shack. There's a bathroom back behind there. I don't think it's for girls though."

"That's OK, it will do. Any port in a storm, as they say."

"They do say," I said.

"Walk me over there, would you? I'm a little unsteady. For some reason. Take my hand."

I didn't ask her anything about "that reason" and the truth was, I didn't want to know, for fear it might lead back to Jonah and then I would probably end up having a bad impression of him forever. If he had done something to this beautiful genetic hybrid, possibly an android or fembot, who had read the *Diamond Sutra* and understood about Kerouac, if he had done something that hurt her—even the concept of him touching her had now become unthinkable. So, I just didn't think about it. It's funny what you can suppress if it doesn't work to your benefit. We walked slowly and at her pace and I held her hand in a very formal way, like the hand of a princess. Finally we got up the steps.

"Wait here," she said. "I'll need you to walk with me in a bit."

"Sure. No problem." I waited and she spent some time in the toilet, more than I imagined would be required; but then I remembered this was a girl and I knew nothing about them; and finally she came out looking a little more composed. She had washed her face and it still glinted.

"Tell me a little about this Chemistry room you somehow magically have access to."

"Oh. Well...there's some pretty nice chemicals in there. Christian and I made some gunpowder recently, just as an experiment. That was fun. And next door, in the Biology room, we've got some microscopes that are very cool. Have you ever seen an amoeba?"

"No. Not a live one. Tell me something interesting about amoebas."

"Something interesting about an amoeba?"

"Yes."

I was feeling a little put on the spot. "Well, I think the most interesting thing about them is that when an amoeba is hungry, it moves a lot faster than when it has already eaten. In other words, it expends *more* energy, not less, when it is hungry. Its metabolism accelerates, even as it has less to work with. After it eats, it is far less interested in doing anything. They even become quiescent. But they should be full of energy."

She thought about that. "Yes. I see. It sounds like you want to be a scientist."

"I really love science, especially biology, zoology. But in order to study zoology, you know, like in college, you have to do vivisection. And unfortunately that goes against my belief system."

"Oh? That's interesting."

I got up my courage and said, "Shall we walk a little more?"

"Yes. Take me down there." She pointed in the direction of the Hermitage. "Is there a place we can see the view?"

"I think so, sure."

We walked slowly, not holding hands now, but I had a sense of dread she might fall in the dark or somehow get hurt. It was like walking with a China doll, or when I broke my sister's toy and she cried. There was a sitting place on the edge of the Mesa that had a good view from a bench, but it seemed a pair of bodies had already taken that spot. I heard the slurp of tongues.

"Ugh," I said.

"How about over there?" She pointed to the north. "What's that?"

"Oh, that's the shit sprayer pump."

"Shit sprayer?"

"Yeah, Kickshaw treats its own water and pumps it down there. It gets sprayed all over the hillside."

"You're joking!"

"No, I've been down there."

"Let's check it out."

"Well, OK."

We walked down the dark path and I showed her the pumping station. It was fenced off but you could see basically what was going on. A single dim bulb glowed on a pole high above.

"Let's sit here," she said. There was a concrete ledge. Not exactly clean but it was a place to sit. She didn't seem to care. She looked out and her face seemed to change. "Whoa. That's a view, I'd say."

She was right, or course, from this spot it was possible to see over the whole of Carpinteria, and then from there out into the dark Pacific. Without stars, everything was illuminated only by the lights of the city. But Santa Barbara was in the distance, and then Goleta, and beyond.

"Do you sometimes hear the ocean?"

"Not the ocean, I think," I said. "But the fog horn. From Anacapa. Sometimes in the wee hours of morning."

"Ah. It must be nice."

I didn't say anything for a while. I was becoming conscious of the fact I was with a girl.

"So, do you have a girlfriend?" she said.

"No."

"No? Are you gay?"

"Uh! Well what kind of question is that?"

"Oh, I see. I hit a sore spot."

"No, not, not really." I could not dissemble with her. "My father."

"Your father?"

"Yeah, yeah. My father. He's gay. OK? He's a faggot."

"Oh. Don't say it like that. He's your father. So you worry a little bit."

"Not really. He's totally fucking cool. I just don't want everyone to know. He claims he was turned gay by watching gay porn."

"Gay porn? I'm not sure how watching porn would turn someone gay. That's like something Anita Bryant would say."

"Exactly!" I said. "That's what I said. But he's convinced that's what happened. Anyway, I have no girlfriend. I did fall in love once, though."

"Really? What was that like?"

"It was good. But it also created complications and led to suffering. You know, exactly like the Buddha says."

She laughed. "Complications."

"Yes."

"What was she like?"

"I don't know if I really want to say." But Isabella had a way of wrapping me around her little finger. I could not deny her anything. "She was black, OK? A black girl. She lived on my street. We did science together. I gave her a slide rule."

"Your first love was a black girl? You gave her a slide rule?"

I looked at her. "You seem incredulous. That's not very nice. Maybe I should explain I'm from Florida. They have black people there. Also occasionally a slide rule or two drops out of the sky. They are picked up and collected by the children, who use them to deduce new mathematical theorems for fun as the rockets take off. Occasionally the rockets explode. But that is not due to the children."

"Right."

We looked at the skyline some more.

"That's pretty cool, Sutra."

"What is?"

"You gave a girl a slide rule."

"Well yeah. It was very cool. You know, logarithms."

"I have a theory," she said, "that Science is a religion. Have you ever thought about that?"

"No."

"Well?"

"Well what? Science and religion? I thought maybe those were opposites. But you know, happy to be taught otherwise."

"Science is a belief system just like religion. It is supposedly in pursuit of truths, perhaps even eternal truths. And it has a catechism, a creed."

I thought for a minute. "Ah, the scientific method."

"Exactly. It also has saints, like Einstein and Darwin, and martyrs like Madam Curie, who died of radiation poisoning. And it has churches and monasteries—places of research, academic institutes. The people there are like monks and priests, high priests of technology."

"But what about God?"

"Oh, yes. Science has a god. The god of Science is Objectivity."

"Hmm...Objectivity."

"Scientists believe so strongly in their god that they are willing to abnegate themselves completely. They are willing to deny subjectivity—they're own consciousness —for the sake of an objective view of things."

I looked over at the distant bench, the one we were interested in, and someone with a flashlight had approached the bench. The pair who were sitting had now scattered like birds frightened by a fox.

"So you see," she said, "Science is very similar to a religion. People even say they believe in Science, just as they say they believe in Jesus or whoever."

I could hear footsteps now, and the flashlight seemed to swing wildly back and forth, like a pendulum.

"What's going on over here?" said a voice. It was Mr. Bright, the rotund American History teacher. He seemed winded from walking. With him was an older woman who

I assumed was a chaperone from Santa Anita. She spoke in an old voice but the voice was strident. "Isabella! This is not a proper place for a Santa Anita student at night."

Isabella was none too pleased. "Put that light down! Robert and I are having an in-depth discussion about science and religion. I do not appreciate this intrusion."

"But Isabella," said the chaperone.

"I am sorry, young lady," said Mr. Bright. "We did not mean to intrude on an important conversation. I am not surprised. Mister Gray here is one of our best students, Marylin. A prodigy of literature and a maven of understanding. I am currently attempting to recruit him for American History 201. He's so advanced I feel comfortable having him skip 101 entirely."

"Is that so, Franklin?" The woman seemed mollified. "Indeed. Very good then."

"However," he said, turning back to us, "I must inform you both that the return coach will be loading soon. It is getting late. It is after midnight."

"Really?" I said. I suddenly realized this precious time with a girl had almost evaporated, leaving me dry and empty, or rather just exactly as I was before except now, I felt changed. It had happened so quickly. "Sorry, I had no idea. I guess we lost track of time."

"Yes." The fat man turned the flashlight back on and began to trudge off into the dark. "We will leave you now but please begin your ascent."

"Thank-you Master Bright," I said.

We began to "ascend" as Frank indicated we must. We got near the buses that were parked in the main parking lot, not so far from the Hermitage. I realized it really was late and the dance had now collapsed into a sullen silence. The light show seemed to be stuck on one color, it had become monochrome. Closing time.

"This is fine, Sutra. You can leave me here."

"Uh, OK. Well, I guess I'll say good night then. Thanks for talking. It was, you know, it was really good. I mean, it was nice meeting you," I said. I started to walk away. I was holding the index finger of one hand with the other hand, my face down. I noticed it was quite dark. Aristotle's star souls still refused to make an appearance and the sky was blank like a slate. Even the city lights were dimmed.

"Wait. You idiot," she said.

I turned, just a little. "What?" I said.

She shook her head. "Go and get me a sharpie, something permanent, or a ball point pen. But a sharpie would be best."

"Uh, OK." I rushed off to comply. I stopped and turned on my heel. "Do you need paper, too?"

She laughed and shook her head.

When I returned, she grabbed hold of my arm and wrote in big letters anyone would be able to read, in indelible ink:

ISABELLA TORRES - 275-1374

"I'm Isabella, as you guessed. I want to see you again." She said this simply, without fanfare. She didn't touch me or give me a kiss or anything, but she looked into my eyes for a moment. Then she put her hand on my chest. She let it rest there, very gently, just the fingertips, I noticed they were quite feminine, and I was kind of stoked, and probably smiled, but then she filliped me on the sternum with her thumb and middle finger.

"Ouch," I said.

"And read *Dharma Bums*, there will be a quiz."

"But I—"

"Yeah, right. Now, when you call, if my dad answers, you say 'I found a scarf and we think it's Isabella's, she left it up here at Kickshaw. I would like to return it to her.' Now repeat what I just said."

"I found a scarf, we think it's Isabella's, she left it up here at Kickshaw. At the Mesa. I'd like to return it to her."

"Correct."

"But what if he says, what color is it?"

"Ah, now you're getting into the swing of things. Let's see, say it's green with little white birds on it."

"It's green with little white birds on it. Got it."

"Good." She paused and we just stood there for a minute not saying anything. Oddly I did not feel any uneasiness about that. It was all so natural, like we had been acquainted for years. We might have been waiting for a bus, which in some sense was what was happening. The bus driver had now materialized, it seemed, and one or two girls were milling around. Then Isabella sighed.

"It's time. Good night, Robert Sutra," she said. She gave me a little kiss on the cheek and I could smell her warmth. Her face had been so close to mine that it entirely filled my eyes with her darkened form. Her eyes. I felt a rush inside my body and then my face flushed hot. "Gosh," I said in a whisper. William had said sex with a girl was far better than masturbation. But this was not sex, this was something else.

Then she turned and walked to the bus. I had one last glimpse of her slender form on the bus-step and then her face turned my way. Her eyes glinted. "Call me," she said.

The next day I was a barnyard sensation. Word gets around very quickly. Long House is not a close-knit House, so nothing happened there, but once I wandered into breakfast over at the dining hall, everyone could see. I didn't figure there was any point in trying to cover it up. AJ and Ringo were huddled over trays, sipping coffee, and AJ was smiling.

Ringo stared for a moment and then went stiff. "*J'accuse!*" he shouted. Everyone turned towards me as he kept gesticulating wildly, almost knocking over his chair, while AJ guffawed. "Dude!" he said, "don't you know that chick's father is a Narc?"

"Nah," I said. "I'm sure he's not DEA. Maybe just an ordinary cop on the beat."

"Oh, man," he said. "You are so in for it."

But Jonah's reaction was the most puzzling, or perhaps the most interesting. He was *perplexed*. It was like in *A Country Doctor* when the Doctor is lost in a snowstorm; that was what Jonah looked like. He'd look and look in my direction, somewhat surreptitiously, as if he couldn't figure out how I had had time to interact with any girl at all, let alone that one. I did not choose to enlighten him, and he didn't ask, so somehow the subject didn't come up, then or ever. But it was always sort of in the back of my mind. And perhaps, for him as well. After that time, for a long while, we were both on tenterhooks around each other, we tiptoed around each other like new friends in need of a kind word.

Cadogan, on the other hand, was deeply impressed. He immediately slapped me on the back. "Holy hell, Sutra!" he exclaimed. "You barnyard fucker. That's the ticket!"

***

It took a few days for me to summon the courage to actually call Isabella. The whole Halcyon experience, those few moments with an ideal young woman, and then the aftermath of celebrity on campus, the shock of recognition that I now had to go through with it and actually date a girl—it was all too much to take seriously. I really needed a bong hit.

"Sutra's in love, man," said Cadogan to anyone who would listen, as if this was a mysterious revelation from above he needed to share, a sort of Gospel.

However, it's quite possible I would have blown off the whole thing and just hid in my books and fantasies, had Cadogan not regularly checked in on me to see my progress.

"The call."

"What?"

"The call. It's time, dude."

"But it's only been two days."

"Fine. I'll check back tomorrow at dinner. Don't pussy out, man, you can do this."

So at length, I summoned the courage to find a phone. The truth is, I actually wrote out some responses. I tried to game it a little bit in my head. I didn't have the self-confidence to just call cold, with no support. No, I would have bombed out hard for sure. It was a good thing though. Torres senior picked up. He was a real bastard.

"Hello? This is Robbie Gray...Yes sir. I met Isabella up at Kickshaw...No, no sir. You see she has left a scarf up here and I'd like to return it to her....at her convenience. Yes, I know Carpinteria sir, My father sells real estate. The scarf? Well, sir, it's green. Green with little white birds on it.... Yes sir. I'll hold."

Finally Isabella came on the line. "Hi Robbie, just wait a minute....*sigue, papá.*" She was shooing him out of the room so we could speak. Then she laughed a low chuckle that sounded like a flugelhorn on a warm summer morning. "You did it. OK then, Sutra. So what's your plan?"

This response did not connect to my thinking, exactly, I had no plan, my goal (which seemed hard enough) had been just to get her on the line. Now I had to think fast. 'What the fuck do guys do on dates?' I wondered, desperately. "You're really putting me on the spot," I mumbled. "Oh," she said. "That's a great idea. Yes, The Spot! That will do nicely. Good idea, Robbie Sutra. So what time, maybe Sunday at 1 p.m.? Lunchtime?"

"Uh, sure. All good. Thanks Isabella."

"You can call me Isa, if you like, Sutra. I go by Isa. It's only the teachers and my father who say Isabella."

"Uh, sure. OK, Isa. See you on Sunday."

"Bye, Robbie Sutra!" She laughed and hung up.

***

"What the hell is the Spot?" I said to Cadogan. I wasn't even sure what I had committed to.

"Oh that's perfect for an initial meetup," he said. "I don't think I could have suggested a better place in Carp. Easy to get to, not too expensive, long wait time for food so you have plenty of time to hang out...and then you can walk down to the beach...yes. It's perfect!" he said again.

"But what is it?"

"Oh, The Spot? It's a little hamburger joint. Kind of famous, actually."

"Well crap, I'm a vegetarian now."

"Oh stop whining. Buy some French fries. Listen, Robbie," he said. "I'm going to do for you what no one ever did for me. I'm going to tell you how to talk to girls."

"Oh dude. This is hard enough as it is."

"No, seriously. I'll teach you the basics. Just really simple. You ready?"

I didn't think Cadogan would go away until I heard him out, so I said, "Sure. Tell me."

"OK, first of all, a little theory. When you are talking to someone, anyone, there is the question of dominance. It's natural, very normal."

"Sure."

"The person who speaks first is actually giving up dominance. So for example, if you approach a girl and say hello, and then she responds, you have given up dominance. But in return you have also made her feel safe. You have demonstrated by speaking first, that she is safe with you, you are no threat."

"I'm not sure I'm following, but go on."

"Take the opposite situation. Suppose you approach a girl but say nothing. She can't tell what your deal is. Are you a threat? Are you a danger? That's exciting, she'll have chills thinking about it later. So she will then speak first: 'Robbie, is that you?' It's just biology, really. Women want to feel safe with a man, but they also want to be dominated, controlled. Not in the sense like that—I mean they want to be with someone who is strong. They want to be directed, guided through life. Life is hard; someone who knows where to go, what to do, is what they want to find. They spend years seeking a strong man. That, to a woman, is what a man is. Maybe that way of saying it sounds better."

"Strong. OK. But I'm not strong."

"Well, I don't know, Robbie. Everyone has something they are good at."

"I'm not good at shit."

"You're a good writer."

"Yeah."

"You're reasonably quick. Quick thinking."

"Yeah."

"When you're with a woman, slow down. Don't speak quickly. Don't walk quickly. Be calm. Thinking fast, sure. But everything else, let it slow down. Always take time to assess the situation. Don't change your mind about things. Never backtrack, never do-over. If you have an opinion, stick to it. Be solid, be secure in yourself."

"Right."

"What a woman wants is a guy who, if the shit goes down, she feels like maybe he is going to stand up for her. He's not going to lose his shit and run around like a decapitated chicken. He has cojones."

"Right. You're making me think of Aikido."

"That's it. Martial Arts. Strong. But not a dickhead. Quiet, reserved. Giving. Always giving. But not shy. Willing to take when that is called for."

"Man, this is hard," I said.

Cadogan laughed. "Nah. Just think of it like a story, a romance novel, where the winner gets the girl and the losers all look on, wondering what the hell happened. It's your romance novel. It unwinds, it always was, it always was meant to be."

"OK, I like that bit. Is that all?"

Cadogan laughed. "No, of course not. But it will get you going. Remember. Let her say hello first. You're in charge. Oh, one more thing."

"Yeah?"

"You'll need money. Lots and lots of money."

I groaned.

Cadogan scratched his head. "Sutra, you pud. Be sure you pay for the food. Never go Dutch. That's just for pussies. Real men pay for the meal."

***

Sunday approached and my level of anxiety rose as the hours passed by. I had been caught by surprise on that fateful night with Isa; that was why it was possible for me to be so open and forward. 'And I spoke first,' I realized. 'But she dominated me. She was in charge.' Well, perhaps that was the way I liked it. She was strong. But I had been strong, I had spoken with conviction, I had been interesting, and she eventually had opened herself to me, even to give me her number and a demand that I call it. Traditionally that was the absolute proof of success. It was like that even in the movies, even on television. So it had all worked; almost by pure dumb luck, I had succeeded.

But now, in the context of a traditional date, of protocol and expectations, I was sure I would screw things up royally.

Suddenly I realized I had not yet accomplished one of Isabella's commands—basically the only real demand—which was to read *Dharma Bums*. 'Holy crap!' I thought. 'Now I'm in for it.'

I asked around in the dorm, which of course was futile. Run-walking over to the school library, I pushed on the door only to find it locked. Peering in the window, I could see the lights were off. 'Of course,' I said to myself. 'It's Sunday morning. Who the hell reads on a Sunday around here.'

I considered walking over to the Bosworth's—Mrs. Judy Bosworth was the librarian—but their residence was on the far side of campus and old Bradly Bosworth, who taught Greek or Latin or some such nonsense, was a known ball breaker. I didn't feel like explaining my desperate love-needs situation to him. Who might have a copy? Who? I thought maybe William was worth a try.

"*Dharma Bums*? No, I don't think so...let's see." William rummaged amongst his books. "Here's an old beat up copy of *On The Road*. It's Kerouac at least, does that help?"

"No, I've read that one. It's got to be *Dharma Bums*."

"I'm sorry, Sutra. But you know who might have a copy?"

"Who?"

"Martin. Martin Quinn."

"You think so?"

"Oh very possibly. Haven't you been in his place? He's got a lot of books and he's the right age for the Beats after all."

"I guess." I'd been in Martin's apartment, of course, but didn't bother to pay attention to his furnishings. "I do remember a big bookshelf."

"He also went to UC Berkeley, you know. That's got to count for something."

"Sure."

I was out of William's dorm room like a shot and down the hall. Martin's "door was always open," he liked to say, but I had never actually put that particular statement to the test. And it was a weekend. I knocked rather timidly.

Nothing happened. I tried again; this time I basically pounded on the door. Then I noticed a bell. I rang it.

Nothing. I was just about to give up when the door gave way. Martin Quinn's bleary head peeked out at me. "Robbie! Or should I say Sutra? Are you out of your mind? What's going on? It's Sunday morning."

"I'm sorry Martin, but I have a bit of a crisis."

"Oh," he said. He paused. "Well, don't just stand there, come on in."

He led me into his man cave and I could see the remains
of the night still on the table. Wine bottles, mostly empty. I
could detect the smell of good cooking hovering in the general vicinity, like a tasty ghost. It looked like he had enter-
tained, too; probably some fantastic babe from the Polo
Club he had spirited up here and then whisked away, like
Cinderella, before the clock struck. "I'm really sorry," I said
again. "But I have to read a book immediately and I wondered if you might have it?"

"You have to read a book immediately?"

"Yes." I pointed my finger emphatically. "Right now. It's
life or death."

Martin didn't question the reasoning. In fact, it seemed he
completely understood, without explanation, how such a
thing might be necessary. He scratched his chin. "What
book?"

"*Dharma Bums*," I said.

"*Dharma Bums*," repeated Martin. "Hm."

"It's by Jack Kerouac!" I said, like an idiot.

His eyebrows went up. "Yes," he said. "Yes indeed it is..."

"Do you have it? Sorry, I mean, I was just wondering if you
can help me to find a copy. It's uh...it's important. To me."

Martin didn't say anything for a minute. "Why don't you
sit down. I'm just waking up. I know, I know," he said, looking at me. He waved his arms helplessly. "But some things
take their own time. Give me a minute to get cleaned up."

I then realized he was just in a bathrobe. He looked like
shit warmed over, actually. Probably had a splitting head-
ache. I began to realize he might not be alone.

"Sit down, Robbie. Don't worry, I've got you covered."

"But—you mean you have it?"

By now he had wandered back into the bowels of his
apartment. I dared not follow. I could hear him rummaging
and moving around, doing normal waking up morning
things. And then after a while the shower came on. There
was nothing to do but sit on the sofa. I plopped down and

sighed, but then I noticed a considerable number of books in the shelving along the far wall. Jumping up, I began to scour his bookcase. Martin had a lot of interesting books and I was surprised and a little abashed that I had never made use of him as an intellectual resource. Master Henler, old Heine, had said he was "a man of culture," but of course that observation just passed through my head, in one ear, and out the other. Now I was discovering that Martin Quinn had a well-worn copy of *The Lord of the Rings*, in three ancient volumes, but also apparently had not only heard of Stanislav Lem, but had some of his original works. They looked to be in a foreign language.

Martin had returned and I felt his eyes on my back. I swiveled around. "Holy shit, Martin, this looks like a copy of *The Cyberiad* in the original language."

"*Cyberiada*. It's in Polish, which I can't read, but it was too much of a temptation to pass up when I saw it in a used bookstore. I was in Krakow at the time. The illustrations are great. I have a lot of Lem but the bulk of his work is not even translated yet. But I thought you were here for the Beats."

"Yes, Yes, the Kerouac!"

"Come with me," he said.

We went back into his bedroom—it was surprisingly large and well lit—and there on a shelf appeared to be a collection of many different authors.

"Burroughs, Ferlinghetti, Allen Ginsberg? Look at all these!" I exclaimed. "And about ten books by Jack Kerouac...there it is!" I said.

"I have some of Gary Snyder's poems, too, if you are interested. The Jaffy character in *Dharma Bums* is based on Snyder. *Turtle Island* is one of his books, *Cold Mountain* poems, that's a translation of Han Shan he did."

"Holy Hell!" I said.

Martin smiled. "So, Robbie, tell me..."

I looked over at him.

"Why do you need to read the Kerouac today, on this beautiful warm Sunday morning?"

I sighed. "I told a girl I'd read it. But I lied. I'm seeing her today. We—it's a date."

"Ah," he said. He smiled again. "So you have to bone up on Kerouac."

"Oh, I know a lot already," I said, bounding up, hitting my head on the lamp. "I just need to, well—"

"It's OK," he said. "Not that one, that's a later edition. Take this one." He pulled out a shabby volume from the shelf. "Be careful with it."

It was a small paperback, a Signet Edition. "1959?" I said.

"That's the original paperback, Robbie. First edition. It's not signed or anything. But it's still pretty cool."

I read, "*From the pagan depths of Frisco's Bohemian bars to the dizzying heights of the snow-capped Sierras...The Dharma Bums!*"

"Sounds about right," said Martin.

"But this is probably valuable, I don't know."

"It's OK. I know you'll look after it. You can show it to your lady friend."

"Yeah. That would be pretty cool," I said.

"What's her name?"

"Isa," I said. "Isabella Torres."

His eyes widened. I thought maybe he'd heard something. 'Yes, of course,' I thought. 'He knows.' But what he said instead was, "*Torres* means towers in Spanish." He paused. "Sometimes it means fortifications."

"Oh, yes," I chuckled. "Yes. She's fortified alright."

Martin was silent for a minute. "Well, you best get on then. You have a lot of reading to do. I think you should at least take Cold Mountain Poems, too."

"OK," I said. "Thanks Martin, this is big. I owe you."

***

I caught a ride down to Carp and walked from the shopping center at Casitas Pass Road towards Linden Avenue. The day started out overcast, but the gloom had lifted and hot sun shone down on my bare head. I saw myself in the reflective glass of a store window and took a moment to study my face. My hair was absurdly long, but just in the spirit of rebellion I refused to cut it. 'I look like a vagrant,' I thought. 'Or a clown.' I was wearing Levis and a black Journey t-shirt, with black Chuck Taylor All-Stars on my feet—just very stripped-down. Cadogan wanted to dress me, but I said no.

"I have to be comfortable in my own skin, Cad. I have to be me."

"Sutra, you pud! Total slob. At least tuck in that shirt."

But I didn't.

I knew The Spot would be on Linden, so I wandered down in the direction of the beach. I had no watch—I hate watches—but I had a good internal sense of time. I wasn't late. There it was: The Spot. I laughed. It was funky as all hell. Tiny, with a billboard menu on the front face and a little window to order from, and wooden picnic tables in a corral on the side.

And there she was. Isabella in the flesh. She was looking off, her back to me, not having seen me yet. And of course, there was a dude.

'What the fuck,' I thought. 'Of course.'

But no, in a moment he moved off. He was wearing an apron, I realized. A greasy white apron. And looked like a Mexican. Yes, they had been speaking Spanish. He was no threat. But the adrenaline was bursting in my bloodstream.

Maybe that was why, instead of calling out, I approached her table. I slowed down a bit. I came around to the side she was facing, so my back was to the ocean-side. Suddenly she saw me, but I didn't say anything. I sat down slowly and put my little daypack on the picnic table. I still hadn't said anything. I sat and faced her. Put my arm on the table and propped up my head with it. Finally, she said, "Sutra. Robbie Sutra. What are you thinking about?"

"Oh, it's just something Cadogan told me. When you're dating you're not supposed to speak first. He said to try and make you speak first."

She looked puzzled. "That's weird."

"I'm really happy to be here," I said.

"Yeah?"

I nodded. "And I have things to show you. But all that can wait." I thought about how good it would be to show Isabella the books, the precious cargo that Martin had loaned me. I was radiant. It was just a moment, but it was mine.

She was still looking at me, almost incredulous. "OK."

"You hungry?" I said.

"Yeah. Yeah, I think so. What about you?"

"Starved."

"Good. Come on, let's look at the menu..." She took my hand then. 'Isa is holding hands with me,' I thought. I was calm for no obvious reason. We stood in front of that little place and gawked at the absurd menu, it was silently hawking tamales and onion rings and milkshakes, with burgers as the entrée, and I was one big grin. It was like windmilling a guitar Pete Townshend-style. They must have thought I was stoned, or something.

***

Ideas class became an oasis of Eastern escapism for me in those days. I loved all things Eastern: Japanese rock gardens, Chinese Kung Fu, the novels of James Clavell, the smooth round faces and folded epicanthes of Asian women wrapped in silk. My sensibilities about these things were all deeply at odds with what had just happened historically (because in living memory were not a few Americans who hated the "Jap" and despised the "Chink.") But that wasn't my fault. Then, on top of this love of the East, of things

Asian, Ram added in a new ingredient to this Seven Treasure Soup of culture and other-than-Western-ness—India. The deepest, darkest secrets of mankind were all there—there and I suppose, in Africa, but Africa was too black for me. Too stained with the crime and sin of slavery, and so psychologically I would never go there or contemplate seeing Africa, even as a tourist.

India, on the other hand, held out its magic like a handful of jewels. Tempting, alluring like a strange but beautiful woman, like a woman with three breasts.

All that being said, you might expect I had no interest in things Western. Because they are opposites, right? But you would be wrong. It is natural and normal today for everyone to specialize; everything about our world, then and now, screams of specialization; but my specialization was to be a generalist and I only wanted passion and truth and the specifics did not matter. Yes, I only wanted what I was passionate about, and what I thought might contain truth: I wanted to swallow the entire cup even as much of the wine poured down my face. At that age I unknowingly followed the passionate diktat of Stendhal, who said whatever did not move him was not worth spending time on. And there were things in Western literature, in the Western Zeitgeist, that moved me, things like European history, or the unique biographies of the American Founding Fathers, or the more recent history of technology that had achieved the unthinkable—almost spiritual—journey to the moon, the history of science, the history of the great art. There were also things, horrible things, terrible fever dreams, to be discovered there, like the Holocaust; the dawning realization that we were destroying the planet; but like a story by Edgar Allan Poe, those studies had their own sick fascination.

All of this lay before me like a plate of oysters on ice. And Kickshaw existed (at least ostensibly) to keep that banquet stocked, to keep the plates coming.

But as in all things, the promise is not necessarily fulfilled, and the limitations of people, of other people, came to my attention over and over. And then, of course, my own limitations, my own laziness, my own stupidity, my own craven nature soon became a factor.

***

Master Norwich taught Junior Year English. Norwich was the head of the little Kickshaw English Department. During the summer I had already scanned the textbook, which was a collection of short stories. I knew we would be reading these and writing essays about them, and I eagerly looked down the table of contents. I sighed. It was a depressing list: names like James Thurber, Guy Maupassant, Stephen Crane, some Hemingway, which was welcome but I already knew Hemingway, and a few stories from authors that I did not know but could not hold out much hope for. And then my eyes stopped on one particular name: Kafka. Franz Kafka. And the story was *A Country Doctor*.

'Ah!' I thought. *I was in great perplexity...* 'Well, at least there will be something interesting to look forward to.'

Now, old Norwich, who had the gene for male pattern baldness but incompletely expressed, so that his head was a round smooth dome ringed by a fringe of hair, which sometimes grew too long, just faintly reminiscent of Bozo the Clown—had organized things in such a way that logic and reason prevailed among the dunderheads; we started reading at the beginning of the book, one story a week, and then he said we would have to write a two-or-three-page essay. Perhaps we were to pull out the "theme" or something suitably literary like that.

And each Thursday, old Norwich would write the next week's story on the dusty slate—just to make things clear to the less intelligent or less interested of what to do next. During class he sat quietly and calmly at the master's desk at the front of the room, framing the slate, and being of short stature, he was not always easy to see behind the big sarcophagus.

Still, it was a good class, in my way of thinking. The possibility of literature, of discussion. And Cad and William J. Brennan and some others were there.

"Master Norwich?"

"Yes Mr. Brennan?"

"Why are there so few women writers represented in this selection of stories?"

"A fair question," he said, setting down his pen. "We would need to find a specialized selection dedicated to writers of the female sex to really explore that genre. They are not at all that common, I am afraid. We do have Flannery O'Connor in the queue. A personal favorite."

And the Kafka—it was about three quarters of the way to the end of the reader! Far down the line. Many stories in front of it, queued up, that I would have to pass through, like rowing in mud to get to the only one that I thought was really interesting, the jewel at the bottom of the mud. The mysterious, the enigmatic. I mean good lord the author wasn't even an American!

Weeks passed, vocabulary words like "turgid" and "gesticulate" were discussed, actual lists of vocabulary words were written out, because Norwich was a great believer in lists for vocabulary building. I did not mind this task at all. And essays were written and judged, and assignments turned in, or assignments were late; or Cadogan was seen to be struggling; or disaster would strike and we would all of us fail to find the theme.

William J. Brennan, who even then styled himself a writer and revealed to me he harbored the secret flame, the ambition to be a poet, while we were discussing Hemingway— possibly *A Movable Feast*—told me in whispers that old Norwich had submitted a story to *The New Yorker*. It came back with the note, "We like this very much, please, please just re-write it one more time."

But Norwich, William said, stoutly refused to even consider it. Perhaps in humble humility and resignation, perhaps in pride.

William had gleaned this intelligence from his intimacy with the old fart, who was very much like him in temperament—soft spoken, but practical and sturdy, as well as a lover of *The New Yorker*. William was from back east anyway, despite his stint in Hawaii. No doubt they had discussed the magazine at some point, and that is when old Norwich admitted his attempt.

These details about the English Master increased my hope that he was truly a lover of literature in the way that I was, even if *The New Yorker* was in my view a rag for nabobs to wipe their asses with. Great things were indeed possible. It was not all hopeless. I expressed some of this to William, and he reflected my interest, but that was all.

Finally, yes finally—the day arrived. A great day, meant to be filled with triumph. The dullards would be exposed to something glorious; their small little brains would be rendered into great perplexity. Assuredly they would be perplexed.

We had consumed the penultimate story, something by O. Henry, no doubt, and old Norwich strode to the slate and wrote out in his clean cursive hand the title of the next story for us to read. I prepared myself for a vision. But it was not right. The black slate-mirror was cracked.

"What?" I ask myself. "*The Lottery* by Shirley Jackson?"

I flipped through the reader wildly. Yes, he had skipped over the jewel. He had gone on, plodded, like a sleepwalking man, to the next story.

After class I waited, crestfallen—and indeed, in great perplexity. Perhaps an error had been made? Even a bureaucratic error, a typo in the syllabus? A mysterious signal emanating from immeasurably far within the kingdom, and now misfired?

"Master Norwich," I raised my voice to get over the hub-bub of the departing minions. "Sir, I think you have made a mistake."

"Oh?" The Master turned his head as the other students paraded out the door, unaware, and uninterested, moving into the fine air. It was a beautiful morning—to them.

"Yes, sir, the next story is actually *A Country Doctor*. The Kafka. You have missed it."

"I know. But I don't understand it. So we're going to skip that one."

This grim admission was met with shock on my part. "You don't understand it? So we're skipping it?" I repeated his words like an idiot. It seemed obvious to me if someone does not understand something, that is the one thing they should be looking into. But no. I did not say those words. I did not say, "You idiot! Allow me to explain it to you!" Instead I just stood there, as if expecting an explanation, and began to chirp like a bird. "So we don't get to read it?"

"That is what I say." Old Norwich was packing up his bag. I suddenly perceived it was dilapidated; the strap did not close and he left it hanging loose. Norwich's clothes also struck me as old and needing attention. Did I imagine it, or was one of his coat buttons missing? His shoes were unpolished, a dull grey. But he plodded on. He said: "How can I teach something I don't understand? It would be unjust." Or words to that effect. It was difficult for me to hear him because he sometimes mumbled or spoke into his hand. He was a shy man, and I forgave him for that. But I was getting the drift. He simply did not understand Kafka—yes. Because he was in fact Gregor Samsa. It was mind boggling.

This humbling statement from the great man was all the more unacceptable coming from the chief proponent of literature, of literary knowledge, at Kickshaw. If he did not understand, then no one did.

'What a hideous failure of a man!' My anger knew no bounds. In a flash I understood odious Kickshaw, taken as an institution, was intent on depriving me of knowledge, of truth, of beauty. It obscured, it hid the truth, under a blanket of the banal, and claims to finery, to elitism. My father had paid so much for me to come here, a ridiculous sum, an amount that Larry had jokingly said could buy a nice house in Mexico or feed a thousand starving Biafrans, and I had toiled in this place of eucalyptus and sunsets, and I had dreamed of something, a world bigger, a world beyond. Beyond Florida, beyond thick-fingered idiots. Beyond bigots and houses built on sand. But now all was known; yes, the school, like all things in my immediate vicinity, the school was here to keep me down.

I stumbled out of the classroom blinking like an owl, and fell into the sunlight. I had already read the story, of course, and its meaning seemed crystal clear to me. What could possibly be hard to understand? The mystical horses, the maid unwillingly fucked by the groom. The child with the bleeding wound. It was all so clear!

***

That was one of the salutary, painful, bittersweet moments of my Junior year: I finally grasped the scope of my education at Kickshaw. The "Masters" were nothing more than simple men, men who had retreated from the world, into this cloister of pleasant conversation and daily duties and dreamy views of distant vistas, and peace amongst plenty. Ram alone, among all of them, seemed free of many of their constraints. But even Ram was merely a "Master." I needed a *real* Master, a spiritual teacher. A Guru. Meanwhile the stirring world of life below throbbed in my ears, demanding my attention. Somewhere down there, Isabella lay nude in her bed, like a proud young goddess, child of the Mayan Kukulkan. I could see in my imagination her face, her brown eyes, their irises tightening as she rose up and stretched her strong young body in the morning light. Somewhere the sea rumbled and churned, pounding rock and surging over sand. Somewhere stone idols stood on mountain peaks or perhaps stared eyeless from lonely island platforms, waiting.

'Man,' I thought. 'This is bad.' I wasn't sure I was going to make it to the 12th Grade at Kickshaw.

PART EIGHT — Death by Hand Job

A fag had just buried his rod,
In the ass of another man's bod,
When he looked with a cry,
Through the side of his eye,
At the size of the other man's cock.

"He's left me, Robbie!"

My dad was in pretty bad shape. But I have to go back a bit to tell it properly. It was the summer after Junior year, and I was home, by which I mean, I was at my dad's place in Santa Barbara. My hopes of spending a long, luxurious season in the sun with a well-oiled Isabella beside me, bikini blanket bingo, down at Rincon, watching the surfers frolic in the waves, and later, much later, laying in the back of my van with the shades pulled down, rocking the sides like a cheap motel bed, with Isabella's lips glued onto mine—had long before been dashed: Isa was with her Oaxacan mother down in San Diego and not coming back until the fall. Out of reach.

But it was still summer, and I was still in possession of a fantastic 1963 camper van and a little bit of sweaty cash saved up, and a baggy full of weed, good bud, Thai Stick in fact, and I was living the high life, no major complaints, if not somewhat concerned about my old man.

Dad and Larry were already at loggerheads about his steadily increasing drug use. Things finally came unglued when he decided to make pot brownies. I don't know what put that insane idea into his head. Larry was in LA on yet another *Linguals* gig, so I suppose he was feeling lonely, or mischievous, or some combination of both. I found him conspiring with a baking pan and a mixer in the kitchen. I should explain it was Larry who normally did the cooking;

Dick had little or no idea. I thought maybe he'd burn the house down.

"Dad," I said, looking over his shoulder. "Seriously? That's a lot of pot to put in, don't you think?" I was none too keen on him using up our collective house stash on this project, yes the weed was bought with his money, but through Christian's and my crazy tulip-grower connection, so I was making an ambit claim.

"It's all good, son! Don't be a party-pooper!"

So I guess he went hog wild.

I woke up with Larry's face over mine, he was shaking me awake. "Your father is at it again!" he said. "Wake up, would you? I need your help."

Together we went down to his office, he had somehow made it in to work under his own power by driving the beamer. I was shocked to see the front end had a large dent—the whole front fender was bent in. "Oh, no," I said.

I went through the waiting area and into the office interior, and I found him on the couch in the back, dazed and incoherent. I came back out even as Larry was talking to a few guys in suits out front. I had not even noticed them.

"We have an appointment with Tricky Dick," the main guy was saying, while the others laughed. "He said he had a deal for us. We want to go in on *Rancho Bravos*. Have you seen him?"

"Sorry," said Larry. "I'm afraid Dick is out of the office today. He's sick."

The guy and his buddies left, thank goodness, and the office door banged shut behind them. I locked the door.

Going back into the private area, I had another look at Dad. He'd cut himself shaving, which left a trace of blood on his face, and his eyes were glazed like a cat's eyes. He seemed to be in a trance.

"What do we do, Larry?" I said. "Should we call for an ambulance?"

"No, I don't think so," he said. "There would be too many questions. Let's get him into the car....Come on, Dick, we'll take you home."

I couldn't believe how heavy my dad was, it took both Larry and I on either side lifting to get him up and going. "Sorry, son," he mumbled. "I'm just too high...just too high...stupid brownies...never doing that again...ugh..."

We got him into the car—we were in Larry's ride—and he lay on the back seat mumbling.

Larry was pissed off, I can tell you. "I don't know what to do with him, Robbie. I had to drive all the way back from LA for this bullshit."

"He just got too high. I told him not to do it. I swear I did."

We drove for a while and Dick rolled over and we heard a splat. The acrid smell of vomit filled the air.

"Ugh..." I said. "I'm sorry, Larry."

"It's not your fault, little dude. Just make sure he's still breathing."

***

Things seemed to settle down after that, and maybe for a few weeks something like normality returned: my dad joking around and Larry laughing his sarcastic laugh. In fact things were so good I went off for the weekend—ostensibly to visit Jonah and some of the other Malibu Mafia down in LA, but really I was pining for Isa. I had fantasies of driving all the way down to San Diego, a place I'd never visited. Surprising her. Meeting the Mexicali mother. But something stopped me.

I was at Jonah's; he was still living at home. His parents were away—part of the reason he was having a party—but no matter. We weren't planning to do any major damage. Jonah's parents had a beach house, and where he lived was a sort of granny flat off the side of the main house (next to the pool), and that's where I stayed. I won't describe the weekend—doesn't matter. The only thing that mattered, or that really stands out, I found a picture of Jonah and Isabella. It was just a polaroid, just an informal shot of the two of them standing together. But (in my imagination at least) it was recent. They were smiling. His arm was around her shoulder and her arm wrapped comfortably around his waist.

I considered stealing the picture, yelling and carrying on, like the idiot I was, or punching Jonah in the face, or doing something even more stupid like running him over with the microbus. But it was all a kind of temporary insanity, and I knew it. It was just the "complications" I had once told Isabella about, the pain and the stupidity of wrong understanding, of not grokking the Four Noble Truths. I sighed.

So I didn't say anything to Jonah; nothing at all. And I made sure to leave the evidence exactly where I had found it, upside down on the desk in the main house.

'What am I doing in here, anyway?' I thought. 'It's not my house. Why am I even here? I'm just a probe, poking my head or maybe my dick into the wrong hole.'

And as for the weekend, it went just fine, I guess—Joey O'Dell managed to set fire to himself and had to be put out by rolling him on the concrete. I did that, acting quickly as the others just looked on in horror, stoned or stunned, drunk or stupid. We tossed him in the pool for good measure. He came out bedraggled and spent like an errant cupid, a house cat lost in a hurricane and finally found.

"Damn!" said Joey. "What happened?"

"Idiot! You don't spray lighter fluid on a lit barbeque!" was Jonah's response.

But Joey was fine, just his hair a bit singed. And his eyebrows burnt off. In a half-hour he was laughing again. It had been fun to bang his head on the ground (apparently I was the only one at the party who understood anything about fire safety. I guess reading eventually does come in handy).

So that was the weekend. It was like the Marx Brothers with beer and bong hits. But I wasn't laughing anymore.

And I didn't make the drive to surprise Isabella down in San Diego after all. I guess I just didn't have the confidence, or maybe the audacity, to do that after seeing the polaroid, the oh so innocent picture of my love and my erstwhile roommate. My buddy, my pal.

***

So I motored back to my dad's place and the detente had been shattered as if by sneak-attack nukes: I found him lying on his side naked and motionless on the living room floor.

'Is he dead?' I thought. I rushed to his over-large carcass fearing the worst. "Dad! Dad! Wake up! What happened?"

"He's gone, Robbie. Larry's gone."

"Gone? But why?"

He didn't answer me. He seemed to be weeping.

Looking around I could see the place was a complete mess: bong water spilled all over the rug, bong tipped over, burnt matches and ash trays with cigarette butts and Coors Light beer cans and unwashed dishes on the dining room table, and the place was trashed. I wondered idly why Conchita hadn't been through. I checked the various places my Dad kept drugs and found them all ransacked.

"You didn't make more brownies, did you?"

He was definitely crying. But this time I noticed the gun.

Yes, curled up in a fetal position, like an enormous infant made of pale white putty on the whiter plush shag carpet—now soiled, and he was naked, his dick hanging limp—I could see he was holding his 1911 Series .45. The metal of the prodigious pistol pressed to his belly.

"Uh, Dad?"

"He's left me, Robbie. He's gone….gone…."

I got real quiet and came and sat down near him. I didn't say anything. After a while, he seemed more steady.

"I'm thirsty son. So thirsty…"

"Let me get you some water, Dad. Just…be calm."

I went to the kitchen and turned on the tap to put some water into a beer glass, when there was a loud retort. I dropped the glass, which broke in the sink, water splashing and glass flying everywhere.

"Oh shit," I said. I had cut my hand on the glass. I wrapped my hand in a dish towel. I was kind of afraid to go back into the room, and my ears were ringing from the shot, but (to my credit, I think) I did.

And then I almost laughed, which of course would have been the totally wrong thing. But my father had sat himself up, and from that drunken position he found himself facing the Marantz stack, with its shiny chromium controls; that glorious music machine, and next to it was the big bin of Larry's records. My father had put a bullet through the crate. It was the album cover of Larry and the Linguals, of course, that he was shooting at, *Hollywood Useless*, which never charted (The Linguals eventually did get a record deal, but to no avail). He could see Larry's face, was reacting to it. I guess it enraged him, or whatever.

But the pistol shot wasn't like on TV. The crate full of records more or less exploded, and shredded remains of vinyl, album covers, and debris now littered the area along with the over-turned crate. The bullet had not stopped for a few measly records; it passed through the wall behind and kept going. I found the slug in the garage, where it had knocked over his heavy toolbox, leaving a dent in the steel. That was some gun.

I just stared for a minute at him and then slowly walked over and very gently, put my not-bleeding hand on the weapon. It was warm, and I noticed the room now stank of gunpowder.

Very gently, I lifted it away from him. He didn't stop me. I didn't know how to get the clip out—all the war movies from those days didn't teach me much—but I did think to hide it.

So, that was a bummer of a day.

No, he wouldn't talk about it. I don't think we ever really talked about it. But he did eventually say Conchita had quit and we'd have to do for ourselves for a while.

"She's gone, too. Larry gone, Conchita gone...I guess the shit has hit the fan."

"Don't worry, Dad," I said. "I can, you know, do some laundry or something. We'll order take out."

I didn't much like Conchita, even with her big sagging tits popping out of a ragged bra all the time when she bent over, or her endless hilarious swearing in Spanish filled with curse words that I tried hard to remember for later use.

Conchita also smoked cigarettes where she wasn't supposed to, rubbing out the butts on the wrong surfaces, which drove Larry nuts; and generally was in the way whenever I needed 'me' time—usually when I got home with a new porn mag from the 7-Eleven. But it sure was handy to have the laundry done and someone to do the dishes.

I hung round for a few hours, tending to my hand and kind of keeping an eye out, to make sure my dad wasn't going any further down the drain. I tried to think who I should call, but no one really came to mind. Oddly, I thought of my mother. He seemed to calm down, though. Maybe the gunshot had cleared his head a little. He eventually crawled off to his bedroom and I turned out the light for him with the shades down. After a while I heard gentle snoring. Luckily no one reported the shot to the police; or at least, no uniformed Gestapo showed up banging on the door to ask about faggots killing each other. My hand hurt and my head was full of fear as I tried on a few stories, just for size.

I had an idea where to find Larry, but when I got there his studio was cold and dark. I told myself I'd have to come back later. But I checked back after 7 o'clock that night and he was still a no-show. Of course I had no real idea where else he might be. I realized my father's life with Larry was a lot less open to me than I thought.

Suddenly I was, like, a grown-up, and dealing with grown-up things. I can't say I was too pleased by that.

It took a week for me to eventually find Larry. It was necessary to drive down to Los Angeles once again. I learned the *Linguals* had a gig at Club 88, not from my dad but just from looking in the newspaper. Club 88 is where *X* and some of the other LA Punk sounds got their start.

That drive to LA was always a nightmare for me. I'd done it a few times to go and see rock concerts with Christian. The Volkswagen microbus was great on a hillside, but with a top speed of 50 miles an hour in fourth gear, it made for a terrifying freeway experience. In those days, the speed limit on the 101 was a full 70-miles-an-hour—great for the 18-wheelers that tore down the road trying to make a deadline, high on Dexedrine, but less good for me.

Somehow, I managed to find the Santa Monica offramp. I didn't know if I could get into the 88, but to my surprise, it wasn't a problem. Maybe I looked older in my agitation.

A band was on stage and generating an auditory assault through what looked like 100-watt Marshalls, like the one Larry had. It was the kind of sound that (as a *Doonesbury* cartoon said) could have sterilized frog embryos at 100 yards. I felt the low frequencies move my internal organs. The drummer was wild and out of control, a gonzo sort of drummer who hit the cymbals too often, the bass player danced like a druggie zombie, while the singer pounded his head up and down maniacally to the rhythm, as if his very life depended on it. His black hair shone red under the colored stage light, a gold tooth glinting as he shouted inaudible screeds of concrete lyrics.

It was Larry, alright, but another side of Larry that I had never seen in full effect. His stage presence was more frightening, I would say, than anything else. I guess I didn't understand punk yet. It was like the record but louder. A lot louder.

I hung around, mainly in the back with the drunks, wishing I had brought some ear plugs, and when *The Linguals* had finished their set I tried to wander back into the dressing rooms to find them. No luck. A burly-looking bouncer shrouded in black leather stopped me.

"You can't go back there, kid."

"But I'm Robbie Gray, I'm with Larry. I need to talk to him."

"I don't think so."

"No seriously," I said. "Can't you tell him I'm here? It's important." I didn't think that was going to work but after an interminable wait the bouncer came back.

"He doesn't want to talk, kid. He says you should go home."

There was nothing to do but go outside. It was dark and there were kids milling around, punker kids maybe, it was Santa Monica, not such a bad area, I guess, but I was totally out of my element. Mentally I was fried. I thought about going for a walk down to the pier (I could see the water glint in the distance) but it just all seemed so pointless.

"Still here?" said a voice. It was Larry.

"Yeah, man. Hey Larry!" I felt a gush of affection for him. "I've been looking all over for you!"

He walked over and I wanted to give him a hug, but he pushed back on that idea by lifting his hand.

I looked at him like a stranger. "Can we sit in my van and talk for a few minutes?"

"Yeah," he said. "I guess we'd better. And then please head home."

We got into my van and closed the doors. I was holding the keys like a rosary. "I saw some of your show, Larry."

"Oh? That's good. So what did you think?"

"It was like the record. But louder."

He laughed, "Yeah. That's the general idea." He paused. "So, why'd you come down, really?"

"Dad's bumming out. He won't say what happened."

"How do you figure that's any of your business?"

"I don't know."

"It's not, you know."

"Yeah. Sorry."

We sat for a while in the van, not going anywhere. I moved the keys from one hand to the other. After a while Larry sort of broke down.

"It's over with me and your dad, Robbie."

"It's over?"

"Yeah. We're done. I'll come and get my things eventually."

"But what did he do?"

"Like I said, it's not your business."

"But I want to know. I need to know."

"Oh? Well. OK. What did he do? He cheated on me."

"Dad cheated?"

"That's what I said."

"You mean like, gay cheated?"

"He cheated."

"I'm sure he's sorry, Larry. I mean, you know him. He makes mistakes all the time. He's a human being. But I know he loves you. I love you, too."

He sighed. "You're making this so hard, Robbie."

"I'm sorry."

He hung his head. "I walked in and caught him in the act, you know. He cheated on me. In the worst way imaginable."

"He had someone in our house?" That idea bothered me for some reason more than I expected.

"No, Robbie. Much worse. Much worse than a stranger in the house. That I could probably deal with. But this!"

He kind of spat the words out. "And it was going on for a long time. Years even."

I tried to think what that might mean but I was mystified. I guess my face showed it.

"It was the bitch," he said. "The wetback bitch."

"Who?"

"You know. That god-damned Conchita."

***

I had never been to Conchita's place. Funny, I didn't really think about her as having a domicile. She was just this Mexican lady who came in as if through a door in the ether, did the cleaning and laundry, and then went on her way, dematerializing into the Santa Barbara haze, only to rematerialize later when needed. She cursed a lot in Spanish, which was hilarious, but otherwise there was nothing distinguishing about her. Big boobs, sure, and I looked at her ass every chance I got, but so what? I looked at every woman's ass and in fact all men, I knew, looked at all women's asses, even the old ugly ones, every chance they got, and there were even men who looked at other men's asses, too. I assumed women were the same. That was just human nature. Everyone looked at everyone else's ass.

So Conchita was no threat, not exactly a homewrecker. My dad had enough money, I reasoned, to buy ten Conchita's; we could get her to come back, if that was what it took, we could give her a bonus or something. I had no idea why Larry went totally bonkers; but that could be fixed as well. My dad could apologize and they could go to Hawaii for a honeymoon and visit his childhood haunts. Or whatever. I still believed I could fix it all with words if I just tried hard enough.

But I was in for a shock when I saw the address: she lived in *Rancho Bravos*. My dad had apparently paid his sex slave maid, in part, with a rent reduction.

I stood in front of her cottage—number 18, it was towards the back—trying to get my bearings and figure out what I was going to say. I still had the crazy idea that maybe things could be made right.

The cottage didn't look much different from the others—the lawn wasn't mowed, and the door seemed dirty, but who was I to judge?

I pressed the buzzer but it didn't seem to do anything so I knocked. A man opened the door. He looked like a stereo-typical *machismo hombre*, not old but not young, pomade in his black hair, stained wifebeater, loose pants with a belt, cigarette butt stuck in his teeth.

"Hi," I said. "I'm Robbie. I am looking for Conchita."

"Conchita?" he said.

"Yeah. Do you know her? *¿la conoces?*" I said.

"*Sí. Mi esposa.* You can speak Ingles, kid. So, Let me guess, you are the son of Tricky Dick?"

"Uh, yeah," I said. Things were getting weird faster than I expected.

"Well you ain't getting no rent. *Oye Conchita,*" he said over his shoulder, "*¿quién está aquí? Es el hijo de Tricky Dick.*"

"I'm not here about that," I said.

"No? Then what you want?"

"I'm just looking for Conchita."

Then Conchita appeared. She was half-dressed, her tits hanging out of a skimpy robe, and none too happy to see me. "What are you doing here?" she shouted.

"I, I just wanted to apologize."

"You? You apologize?" She said. "For what? What you do?"

"I wanted to say that I don't know what happened, but whatever it was, we are sorry."

"*Él se está disculpando,*" she said to the man.

"*Ah, ¿lo es?* Tell him what Tricky Dick was doing."

"Your father, he a bad man."

"Oh?" I said. "I'm sorry. I didn't know."

"He says he doesn't know," she said. "But of course, you not know. But you should know. You old enough to be a man, you look at me, you look at me dirty."

"She say she feel your eyes, man."

"Tricky Dick," she said, "he pay me for hand job. I give him hand job after I clean and do the laundry. For long time, years even. Always the dirty. He make me do it every time. And he cheat my pay, he let me rent, but little pay."

"I'm very sorry," I said. "We're sorry."

"But then he want me do more for him," she went on. "He argue with that devil Larry, they argue. And then he want more, he want—" She made a gesture as if her hand was curled around the shaft of a pole, and I got the idea. Her scummy dude laughed.

"He force me," she said. "Do it or move out. That's wrong. Then devil Larry catch us. He was very angry. I laugh at him. I tell Larry, call him fag, make him cry."

"He a faggot, loco faggot, eh?" laughed the creep.

"I'm sorry, Conchita. Very sorry."

"Give us *dinero*, kid," said the guy. He held out his hand. "Money. You sorry, give money."

"I don't have any money," I said. "I didn't come to give you money."

The guy shook his head in disgust. He threw his cigarette butt out the door past my head. A bit of the ash seemed to get in my eye. I teared up.

"Just go away, Tricky Dick Jr.," said Conchita. "Go." She pointed her finger, jabbing it at my chest. "I no work for you no more. I not a whore. Got a man. Got kids. *Vete a la mierda!*"

The door slammed, punctuating the finality of my failure. I walked away shaking, with the rather odd sensation—a feeling of creepy surprise, emotions that I didn't want or expect—that maybe Conchita was more attractive than I realized. She was certainly younger than I had believed. I guess in reality I had never looked into her face steadily for long enough to really see her. He knew her ass better than her face.

The thought that she was a secret sex worker that my dad had abused over and over, endless hand jobs, ejaculate squirting on her face as she squinted, which I suppose should have made me hurt or unhappy to hear, was later that night a source of intense arousal. I felt guilty about that, guilty as all hell. Conchita's brown skin, the deep curve of her breasts swaying free under that flimsy bathrobe—I had just seen more of her than ever as she stood next to her filthy pig of a man, with crying brats clinging behind.

That pig also had touched her; he might be touching her at this very moment, his jism squirting across her face. It was wrong. But I also wondered secretly if I had missed out. Was she some sort of brown-skinned Madonna? Did I secretly want her to do the same things to me?

"Nah," I said to myself. "That would be death by hand job." My father was apparently an idiot.

***

The rest of the summer was about the move. My dad said he wanted to make a change, spoke of downsizing, starting afresh, noises like that. But in reality he just needed to get out of Santa Barbara.

What had happened was this: the problems at the *Rancho Bravos* property that were hinted at by the little Asian man and now Conchita, had spilled over into the public view. Yes, the *Cottage Renter's Association*, as they called themselves, the collected renters of the 20 little units with De La Vina addresses, plus the two that fronted on Bath Street, had come together in a rare show of unity about how bad the landlord was.

"He never fixes anything. My rent is $600 a month, if you can imagine, for this one room shack, and the sink has been broken since I moved in."

That was from one of the disgruntled renters, a Mrs. Simper, who spoke to KEYT Channel 3, the NBC Affiliate, at the street protest. Yes, there was a protest and everything, cars honking support, signs calling out problems. The story got picked up by several other stations in California. "Tricky Dick," as this errant landlord was called, was named and shamed by the television station. It seemed everyone now knew.

"Richard Gray, according to court documents, a real estate agent and entrepreneur," the reporter said.

And so my father was named and shamed. The rent strike, as they called it, by the *Cottage Renter's Association*, hurt him financially, hurt the bottom line. Basically they stopped paying rent completely. But the TV news story was what really hurt, because it hurt his pride.

It motivated his exit, I thought, from the De La Vina Street place, the one with electric candles, where he, I and Larry had been together as a sort of New Age Cali gay family.

I was sentimental about that; and it sat vacant for a time, later to be sold off, probably to a nice straight Mormon couple from Utah with eight piglets in the litter. The beautiful gay drawings gone away with Larry, guitars too, all except one that he left for me, a small acoustic steel six-string I had admired more than once, and swore I would practice on, and then the poster of Farrah Fawcett. But I put that into the dumpster. My tastes were changing and times were changing. I was about to become a Kickshaw Senior. The wife of Lee Majors was of no interest to me. I pined for darker meat.

Meanwhile over the July 4th long weekend we moved into a condo in Carpinteria—much to my joy—as it would be a lot easier for me to catch a ride home on weekend liberty. And easier to access my van for those late-night adventures with Christian. And, of course, I imagined how close I would be to Isabella's. I had never been inside, but over that summer I would often drive down her street, slowly, and loiter for a few moments by her house, just to think about her. I saw her father once puttering around, too.

He looked to be about seven feet tall.

PART NINE — The Piano Murder Mystery

The winter of our discontent,
Was the time of a constant lament,
The Seniors were high,
On the pie in the sky,
But their futures were laid in cement.

"Seniors at last! I guess we've arrived," I said to William and Cadogan. We were lounging in The Branson after the Sunday formal dinner, the first for the senior year. Somehow I had managed to smear mushroom gravy on my new silk tie, the one my dad gifted me when we were cleaning out his closet for the move to Carpinteria. It was wide and floral and I tied it that day in a single Windsor. The single was always my preference.

As a sophomore, I had no idea how to tie a tie; my dad did the duty on my behalf and I spent the first 50 evenings pulling it over as a slip-on; but eventually came the crisis and then Jonah laughingly taught me. That moment in time now felt like Rome or Mesopotamia, archeology, ancient history, but it was really only the High House. Two light years distant. Two centuries.

I looked around the old library that now served mainly as the scene of the nightly Senior coffee. It had a warm lived in feeling and a working fireplace (not lit at this moment). Not too shabby! William slouched comfortably nearby. I could see he had let his hair grow out over the summer, and his rug had taken on a life of its own. "That's quite an afro you've got there," I said.

"You might try it, permanent waves and all, I'm told the ladies love them."

"That's what Ray Davies says."

William was adapting to school life without Tony, who had graduated. I guessed William was now a D & D master of one, but that was wrong; I found him up in the same old room (he had kept to it, unlike most kids who liked to move dorm rooms). I looked in and he was playing D & D with some freshmen, as if time had collapsed or there had been an eternal return. But he seemed older somehow, despite the fro.

"And Cadogan, you're looking very dapper," I said.

Cadogan was standing erect, and looked thinner in the face. He was sporting a sharkskin suit and some shiny black boots. For some reason he was all apologies. "It's a present from my mother," he said. "I'm not necessarily a sharkskin kind of guy."

"That material, it has a sheen to it," I said. I reached over and ran my finger over the surface. "Is that silk?"

"Don't be silly. Sharkskin is wool mixed with Rayon." He shook his head muttering. "Silk suit. What do you take me for. Christ." Everyone knew Cadogan's family was wealthy but perhaps this rankled now that he was closer to receiving his trust fund proceeds: it would mean he had to actually grow up. But I didn't tease him about it. At least not that much.

"Hello boys!"

It was Mrs. Sauvage. I almost fell over. "I didn't hear the cart," I said to no one.

The old woman was small of stature but broad in girth, and not exactly frail. "I hope the summer has been good to you all."

Laughing and talking, the new seniors now made a joyful bee line for the coffee, with Sauvage, *le femme ancienne*, mother-henning over the whole affair. She greeted each boy and cooed and clucked. I felt a little sick; it was like watching Field Marshal von Goering reviewing the SS Waffen. Formerly I had no taste for coffee, but this year I was definitely into it; a legacy of my concert driving experiences in the Van. So, yes, I stood my turn in line like a member of the Stoa. Finally my turn came.

"Robbie, is it?" she said.

"Yes ma'am."

"I'm surprised you haven't been expelled yet."

This generated considerable laughter from the other boys. "Sounds like you know Robbie already," said Felix.

"We've met. Well, Robbie, let me get you some cream for your coffee."

"Thank-you ma'am. But I like it black."

"Oh do you? Perhaps you are secretly a good European. They drink no milk after 10 a.m."

"Yes, ma'am. Maybe in another life."

"He's a polite one," she said. "I always liked that in my boys."

***

Senior year only took a few weeks to melt down Three-Mile-Island-style. The term started out well enough. After all, every one of us aspired to be a Kickshaw Senior.

So, yes, becoming a senior was a joy. We reveled while the sophomores and most especially the freshmen toiled.

But about three weeks into the new Fall term, we had what I called the Failed Spartacus Moment. What happened was that at morning assembly, Francis Remus, the music master, stormed onto the stage. Everyone became quiet. No one had ever seen the big man like this.

"Who did it!" he shouted. "Who did it!"

No one answered.

"Mr. Remus, calm yourself," said the Headmaster. "What's happened."

Remus was pacing up and down on the stage. "I went this morning to the music room and found that, sometime during the night or early hours of the morning, a person or persons, still at large, went into the room and clandestinely played piano."

"That doesn't sound so bad."

"No," he said. "But they also decided to smoke. That in itself is bad enough. But then they set the burning cigarette on the piano top. Apparently they just left the burning cigarette there; they forgot all about it. The cigarette burned down, and by morning the entire top of the grand had caught fire. The varnish, you see, it's flammable. The instrument is ruined!"

Remus turned to the assembly and continued shouting. "I want to know who it was! Who did this!"

No one spoke up, perhaps because in that moment Remus was frankly terrifying to behold. But he continued to rant. He would not be mollified. "I want to know now. Someone here did this. Someone needs to be a man, and come forward. You have destroyed an incredible musical instrument, a Steinway Concert Model D Grand Piano. You have no idea of the value of such an instrument. I want to know who did it! Stand up! Be a man!"

Finally, as the morning was wearing on, I stood up and shouted, "I am Spartacus!"

Everyone looked in my direction. I thought at least a few other people would join in and claim to be Spartacus. It's not like the Kirk Douglas movie was unknown to this crowd. But no. The room was silent as a church. And Remus lasered in on me like a rabid dog. "You! You did this?"

"No, I just said 'I am Spartacus.' This is ridiculous. You will never find out what happened by yelling at people." I slumped down, then, feeling very ill that my comrades were hardly comrades in arms, but merely pathetic cowards in the face of abuse. No one deserves to be yelled at. But Remus, having found a target, did not seem to be able to let it go. "Come to the Headmaster's office at once, Robert Gray!" And stormed off.

The assembly seemed to have truncated itself; everyone was talking at once or else running for the exits. Finally the Headmaster came over and said, "Robbie that was kind of foolish. Were you trying to belittle him?"

"Oh, don't be an idiot."

"What did you say?"

"You heard me. If you want to know what happened, put Stacks on it. He'll sniff it out."

"That is very rude and insubordinate, Mr. Gray."

"And Mr. Remus was also very rude, don't you think?"

"Be that as it may, you have not impressed me this morning. Come to my office."

"Don't be ridiculous," I said. "I have class."

The Headmaster seemed incredulous that I had refused to cooperate. "But I have told you to report to my office."

"Well, that's just too bad. If Francis wants to talk to me, he needs to do it with respect. He needs to cool down, obviously. And you need to tell him so."

The Headmaster didn't say anything. I suspected he agreed with me but was unwilling to say that out loud, or at least not here with others watching and listening. I realized that perhaps twenty students had gathered around us and were listening.

"All right, everyone," he said, looking around, "Please go to class. I'm sure there will be more to say about all this tonight."

I started walking, but he said, "Robbie, hold up there."

I didn't turn around, but I just stopped and waited.

"Do you have anything to say?"

"Yes," I said. "Sorry about—all that. I apologize. I have my own problems—the summer was not exactly great—problems at home—and I don't need Francis Remus to unload his problems on me."

"I see. Well, apology accepted." He considered. "You don't smoke cigarettes, do you?"

"No," I said. "I don't think my dad would approve." That was true enough, he hated tobacco cigarettes.

"I have a list of all those with smoking approval."

"I know. It's not that long of a list. And you also have a good idea who would spend time in the music room out of bounds. Right?"

"Perhaps. I have some thoughts."

"Like I said, I'm sure the Dean will smoke out whoever it is. That person is clearly a coward. I am not that."

The Headmaster suppressed a smile. "I can see that now. But do you know who it is? Come now, Robbie."

I shook my head. "I think it's a terrible crime to kill a piano. Worse than killing a man. If I knew, I would definitely say."

Of course, I was lying. I suddenly knew who it was, or at least I had a pretty good idea—an intuition. And I was overwhelmed by a sense of dread. But I could not tell the Headmaster about that. I shook my head again and raised my hands in a gesture of surrender.

"Very well then. Off to class."

***

To clear up the mystery I will have to go back to the previous school year, all the way back to the Spring of Junior Year.

On a cool day in March Mr. Remus sat at the baby grand piano in his living room and played staccato plonks on the black and whites while singing in a broad, open, baritone voice. *"Martha, my dear, you have always been my in-spir-ation-please!"*

It was Saturday morning, a few of us there, I was ostensibly listening, but in reality we were all waiting for Mrs. Remus to fully assemble the troops for our day's adventure. A few boys were yet to materialize. And one girl.

Team Remus consisted of Elantra, the indefatigable wife and mother, who did advisor duty to a swath of boys; Francis, the Kickshaw music teacher, who also served as an advisor, and Julie, the young vixen, their blonde waif daughter, age 15 going on 25, who Cadogan had recently taken notice of. Our task for the day was to drive south and visit a destination a little beyond Laguna Beach, a city called San

Juan Capistrano. There we would experience the wonder of the return of the Capistrano Swallows.

I remember considering the sign-up sheet—these were normally to be found posted on the dining hall pin boards or near the weekend sign out sheet—and thinking, 'No, I'll just hang out this weekend,' but then Ram in Ideas said that he was going, and thought some of us in the class should go, too. "Oh yes, I have been several times. It's a glorious thing to observe. The Mission is ancient for a building in California, from the Spanish period, and there is a sacred feeling about it. Franciscan monks used to preach there. And on a day, traditionally March 19th, a sunny day in the early spring, birds that have flown all the way from Argentina finally arrive, completing a vast migration. There, in mud nests they construct under the eaves of the church, they breed, and the cycle of life continues."

"But Ram," said William, "That colonial period was horrible for the native people."

"I have no doubt," he said. "But I think you should judge the Mission and the grounds for yourself. Some places just have a certain feeling about them, a feeling of the sacred. You do not have to go to the Ganges for that. Even here in California."

William was skeptical, but for whatever reason, Cadogan chimed in. "I'll go," he said. After that I thought it might be worth seeing.

"Sutra, stay after class, will you?" said Ram.

"Sure, Ram," I said.

"Sutra, there is someone I think would benefit from this trip. Do you know who I am thinking of?"

I did not immediately register on this question, so he prompted me further. "I am thinking of Calvin. He's a Catholic. He might really enjoy this."

"Hmm. OK. But it's an open signup. If Calvin wants to go, can't he just do that?"

"But he's very shy, apparently. I've seen him. He's alone a lot, I gather. Perhaps you could suggest it?"

"Sure," I said. "But I don't know it will do much good. She, I mean he, doesn't seem to want to socialize much."

"Why did you say she?"

Ram was a very perceptive fellow. He also probably knew more than he was letting on. He tugged at his beard and his eyes glinted. So I said, "I'm not sure I should betray a confidence."

"I see. But perhaps this is a way for you to help Calvin. As I often say, Robbie, actually helping another person is the hardest thing one can achieve in this world. And, arguably, helping others is more important even than the search for self-knowledge. In fact, one could say, truly, that helping another person is the demonstration of self-knowledge. Truth is highest, but true living is higher."

I sighed. When Ram was in this state of mind, when he was manifesting some higher power and his eyes began to resemble those of an Andrei Rublev icon, there was not much to do other than go along. "All right. How to say this...Calvin is one of those people who believe they are wrongly sexed. Calvin is a boy on the outside, but a girl on the inside—in her thoughts. Everyone thinks she's gay, but that's not it."

"And you know this how?"

"Because we talked about it. She told me in confidence her secret name, and I even agreed to call her that. Once I started doing that, eventually I started seeing Calvin as 'Susan' and now I always think of her as a girl. I can't think of her in any other way."

Ram considered. "So you see the inner self. That is good. I'm not sure Kickshaw is a healthy place for someone like that. However, as a Catholic, he, or she, would probably enjoy seeing the Mission. Will you ask—her?"

"Of course."

But I did not have to do that, actually, because Ram was so curious that he approached Susan after Aikido that very afternoon. I saw them sit down on a bench out by the Dining Hall. I could not hear what was said. But I could see they were having an animated discussion and I more or less spied on them, not overtly. I just pretended to be reading my trusty *Return of the King* from a discrete distance. Susan's thin arms were gesticulating, and then Ram shook his head, in the negative, and pointed his index finger vigorously at his forehead. He was explaining some inner truth; but Susan crossed herself. When she did this, Ram caught sight of her right hand, the hand with the palm that had been perforated with a ten-penny nail. It seemed they discussed this stigmata. Ram appeared to be deeply moved; tears welled in his eyes and he wiped them on his sleeve.

Later, he told me "It is arranged, Robbie, she will sign up for the trip. I think you are right; I sense a feminine presence there. But this is not good. She is too fragile for this world."

***

Nevertheless, on the morning of the trip Susan appeared, and Mrs. Remus greeted her warmly with a hug.

"I didn't get a hug," said Cadogan more or less to himself, sarcastically, to which Francis, who heard him, promptly responded by saying, "No? Oh, well, then, come here!" and insisted on giving him a bear hug. Mr. Remus was at least six-foot four, so Cadogan, who was of medium build, was more or less engulfed. I thought that was hilarious.

"Alright," said Francis, "I think we are now complete. And we're raring to go! Everyone please pile into the van. Julie, sit near the front."

The ride took on the ribbon of freeway known as 101 down through Los Angeles, and I always looked for the moment we topped out over the pass into the bowl, the great basin of L.A.

"What are you looking for, Sutra?" said Ram. He was sitting next to me, on my right, and Cadogan was on my left.

"I watch for that moment when you can see the smog line. I've always done that since I was little."

"I thought you grew up in Florida," said Cadogan.

"I did, but my parents got divorced. I was born not so far from here, in Long Beach."

"So you are an ocean person," said Ram. "That explains much."

"Hmm."

"As you know," he continued, "the people who live near the sea tend towards a rich spiritual nature. Look at the Vikings with their complex mythology."

"Naturally," said Cadogan. "If you risk your life at sea, you need strong gods."

"Very perceptive, Cad," he said. "The Vikings also had strong instincts. Their gods reflected the Viking's inner vicissitudes. Their desires." As he said this, I thought I saw him glance at young Julie. Of course, Cadogan had been cautiously sizing her up. I realized in that moment that the entire reason Cad had come on the trip had to do with this rather prurient interest.

Meanwhile Susan was given the place of honor—she got to ride shotgun. Mrs. Remus insisted, and sat immediately behind her, occasionally making conversation. It evolved that Team Remus was Catholic. Elantra told stories of visiting Papal Rome, touring the museums and Saint Peter's Basilica. Susan seemed to be in good spirits. She was chatting now with Julie. I had not seen her interact with a girl before.

We arrived at about 11 a.m. and I could see some festivities already in progress. "I've got tickets for everyone," said Elantra. "We'll meet up for lunch about 1 p.m., OK?"

The Mission celebrated St. Joseph's Day on this date, and I suppose due to some serendipity, the swallows were integrated into that Feast.

"Who's St. Joseph," said Cadogan.

"Uh, that's, you know, the father of Jesus," I said.

"The guy who boned Mary?" Cadogan said this so that Susan and Julie could both hear.

"No, you silly," said Julie. "She was a virgin. God was his father."

"That's some very impressive impregnation."

This response from Cadogan produced titters from both the girl and the other girl.

I left them to follow Ram, who was walking slowly, holding his chin with one hand and the other holding his elbow. He looked around at the Mission walls, walking slowly. We could see a lot of mud bird nests, but no birds.

We walked into the structure and I noticed a coolness under the stonework that felt good on my face. I could see there was a covered area that opened out into a walled court. Inside, in the shade was an elderly woman sitting erect on a loveseat that had been placed there; in front of her were a few rows of chairs, and in the chairs were children.

The woman was in the middle of a talk about the native people that once lived in this area to a group of children. We did not want to interrupt, but she herself beckoned to us. "It's alright! Come join us if you wish!"

Ram smiled and moved forward and I tagged along. We sat in the back row, which was empty, and she continued to narrate something of the history of the Acjachemen Nation. "My people say we have lived here since the beginning of time. And that is not so far from wrong, because the archaeologists say we were here for thousands of years. Our settlements spanned much of this valley and beyond into the nearby counties."

"The people lived peacefully, they considered the Earth to be sacred and the source of life. They also made connections through marriage with peoples from other areas, and that strengthened the bonds of friendship among them."

"When the Spanish came, they set about converting us to their religion, Christianity. Never mind that we had our

own religion and many rituals and rites that people prac-
ticed. But sadly, almost all those have now been lost. We no
longer know much about them."

"But why were they lost?" asked a child.

"Because the Spanish took the children and baptized
them, and then kept them away from their parents, raising
them in dormitories. They were kept here, at the Mission.
This was to prevent them learning the rituals and religious
ideas of the Acjachemen."

"The Spanish transformed the countryside here into graz-
ing land and the population of cattle grew; they also began
work on the Mission that you see now, although it would
take many years to become what you see today."

"Unfortunately, at the same time, diseases brought by the
Spaniards began to decimate the people. Their numbers
dropped away. Eventually the few that remained were de-
clared "free" and allowed to live their own lives not under
control of the priests and monks, but they had little true
freedom and continued to be used for labour, and to tend
crops for the invaders. In the mid-1800's, around 1850, the
Americans won California and all this territory came under
American control. Unfortunately, the Americans continued
the same destructive practices not in the name of religion,
but simply to own and occupy the valuable land for its own
sake. Diseases like smallpox continued to kill more of the
people. What small amount of land the Acjachemen could
claim legally, was lost over time to Anglos moving into the
area from the Eastern United States. The remnant of the
Spanish, the Californios, lost most of their ranchos by this
period."

"That sounds very sad," said another child.

"It is, my darling. But we can learn much from our history,
even if most of our rich culture was erased. Should I tell you
one of the stories of our people? This is one that we still
know."

Some of the children nodded.

"Alright then. Here we go."

***

As the old woman was telling the story, which was sing-song and in an unknown language and filled with delightful gestures and cooing, I noticed that one by one, the children departed. They slipped away quietly, like mice. It was as if the story was insufficient to retain their attention. A few stayed, but finally by the end, all had left. Only Ram and I remained. We clapped.

"Thank you," she said. "Are you visiting the area?"

"A school trip," said Ram.

"Well, thank you for listening. You have come on a good day. The swallows are coming."

"We haven't seen any yet," I ventured.

"Yes. But I feel them," she said. "They are near."

"You can really feel them?" I said.

Ram gave me a look, and whispered, "That is not polite." But the old woman smiled.

"No, it is a fine question. What is your name?"

"Robbie, ma'am."

"I have lived near here my whole life, Robbie. It could be that I just have that yearly cycle inside me, like a habit, and it tells me when they will come. But I am also an old person, as you see, and I think because I am closer to death, that I feel more of that world than the eye or the ear reveals about this one. So yes, in my heart I think I can feel them. They are close. You see, they are spirit beings. My people considered them sacred."

Just completely by chance, I am sure, at that moment a bird seemed to fly close to us. It circled around a few times and then settled on the ledge of the roof only a few yards away.

"It's a swallow!" I cried.

Ram and the old woman both laughed.

"So it is," she said. "Wait a moment."

Then with a rush, we could hear a fluttering sound, and more birds began to arrive. One after another. Soon it was like a wave and the sky was filled with beaks and flapping things.

Ram and I said goodbye to the old woman after thanking her and made our way out into the courtyard. Swallows were now everywhere and I was afraid I might somehow step on one or lose an eye to a sharp beak. We were standing watching, and I could see Team Remus over on the other side of the Mission gawking at the swallows. Francis Remus was joking and smiling while holding hands with his wife. Cadogan continued to chat with Julie and Susan.

Ram looked over at me. "Cadogan certainly has a way with the ladies," he said.

"Something like that."

At that moment something memorable happened. Susan had been tossing bits of bread at the swallows to no effect; apparently they were insectivores and not interested in bread. But she had now moved out into the open, and multiple swallows seemed to fly around her in a rush to enter the courtyard. Soon there were ten or fifteen birds. She became concerned and started to run. "They're after me!" she cried. She was flapping her thin arms. We laughed.

"Sort of a reverse St. Francis, isn't she," I said.

***

It was two months later, towards the end of May, and Team Remus was holding a school-year-end barbeque at their compound. Cadogan was one of Mrs. Remus's advisees and he invited me to come along.

"But I don't do much barbeque anymore," I said. "Regrettably. I love barbeque sauce. But so it goes."

"Just tag along. There's a little something to show you."

"Sure, OK."

We walked down the Eucalyptus Parade and chatted idly. The Team Remus compound consisted of the main house, a detached garage, and then a sort of granny flat positioned towards the back (it was on the playing field side). After we said hello and spent some time hanging out, Cadogan eyed me. I was just working my way into a hunk of flavourless potato salad. I set the plate on the picnic table and got up and went with him. I was trying to be casual.

"Mrs. Remus, may I use your bathroom?" I said.

"Of course dear, just go inside."

Cadogan then met me in the house in a few minutes. I knew why he had invited me: it seemed there was something he wanted to show me, perhaps in Julie's room. He nodded his head silently, and I was surprised when he led me out the back door. We were walking towards the little granny flat. Cadogan seemed to know his way around. He didn't knock.

"Isn't someone possibly there?" I said.

"No, Julie is at school."

"Of course. She goes to public school down in Carp."

"Correct. Well, what do you think of it?"

I looked around at what was plainly a teenage girl's room: girl pictures of teen idols on the wall and even a unicorn poster. There was the little school-girl sized desk and chair, and a futon on the floor, and some dirty clothes tossed around. There was some makeup, too, something I knew not much about. "I presume this is lipstick?"

"Yes, she's learning. Experimenting. All opposed by her hippie nature-worshiping parents."

I picked up a bra off the dirty clothes pile. "This is padded," I said.

"It's a training bra, Sutra, you pud. Put that down."

Cadogan looked at the desk. "Come over here. Check this out."

It was a little diary, like a daily planner, with a pink faux leather cover embossed with a rainbow unicorn pony. He opened it up. It was the 12th that day. He flipped back a page or two in the diary. "The 10th, I think...yes...there, you see?"

The page he was looking at was blank. But very small, in the bottom right corner, almost at the limit of vision, a diminutive '69' had been scrawled there. A child's hand, a girl's hand, obviously. In pencil.

"Oh my goodness, Cadogan," I said.

"She's a breeder."

"You really are a cad!"

"No, no, she's driving. I swear! I'm just the teacher. She's a total savage. I have to keep telling her to be cautious. Sometimes I think she wants to get caught."

We headed out, quietly going back through the house, and I couldn't help thinking Cadogan was out of his mind. I had no idea he had taken things to this extreme. We rejoined the barbeque for a while—I never made any more progress on the potato salad, the plate sat forlorn and forgotten as I looked around, somewhat in shock, at the other boys and old man Remus laughing and joking. Finally, we walked back towards Long House.

"So you make the midnight trek to fairyland often?" I said.

"Not that often."

"Hmm. Well dude, I'd say that's a mighty big risk you're taking. The unicorn is a Christian symbol of purity, as I'm sure Ram would explain."

He made that expression where the eyebrows raise, the lips purse, and the arms extend, hands outstretched. Kind of like 'yes, but?' "I'm just doing what comes naturally."

"Right. Hmm. I sure hope she doesn't get pregnant."

Cadogan chuckled. "Oh, I won't go that far. After all, she's underage."

"Uh-huh."

He was steepling his fingers now. "I'm not completely irresponsible. You know. Besides."

"Besides what?"

"It's a lot harder to get a girl pregnant than you might think. You really have to work at it."

I laughed. "I guess I have no idea. But I didn't realize. I thought the jizz goes into the hole. Whence onward and upward, to join with egg in holy matrimony."

"Yes, yes, that's the short story version. But it has to be the right time of the month, and the sperm has to actually go in, not get splatted on the wall or killed by spermicide, or stopped by a rubber, or run down your leg, and so many other things have to happen. The angels have to sing."

"Exactly. The angels have to sing."

After a while he said, "She's a Catholic, you pud. They're absolute breeders, Sutra!" And then he was on the stairs for the dorm.

***

Fast-forward the cassette to the start of Senior Year. Cadogan knew I could access a key to the Rayburn Theater. I don't know if I told him or he ferreted out the secret of the Missing Key Mystery, or what, but however it happened, a day came when he wanted to borrow the key.

"Come on, Sutra, I know you've got a key."

"But we don't loan it out."

"We? Oh I see, so this is a conspiracy, you and Christian no doubt. But, look, this is for a good cause. Very educational."

I shook my head. "Let me guess...it involves the youngest member of Team Remus in some sort of late-night game of twister? Naked twister? Unicorn horseback riding?"

"Oh, by no means."

"So you, I guess, are learning to play the castanets and want to get into the music rooms to practice? Braless bongos perhaps? But just at 2 a.m.?"

"I need it for 24 hours...maybe a few days. Tops."

"Fine. Give me a day to collect it from the...trustee."

***

I spoke with Christian the next day and he was loath to let go the precious item. "The Crash Pad really came in handy at the end of last year. I wouldn't want to lose access." The Crash Pad, as he called it, was the space we had discovered together in junior year. He had put in considerable clandestine efforts, first carefully cutting through the wall board in a way that was clean, and then secondly building out the space within with boards, cardboard, and finally somehow he had dragged a mattress all the way up there and got it through the entrance. The first time I saw the space I was just stunned. So I understood his reticence.

"Look," I said. "I'll make sure it comes back. It's Cadogan after all, he's a good guy, if slightly mad. OK, totally mad." I had not divulged all I knew, even to Christian, but certain rumours were easily spread and word tends to get around in such a small community.

"Yeah, I agree. About him being nuts, I mean." He fished out and then slowly handed over the key, which was stashed under a brick behind his bed. In due course, the next day Cadogan took possession of the key.

That was then. I didn't actually connect Cadogan to Mr. Remus's outburst and the Great Piano Immolation, not immediately. I knew he smoked a cigarette once in a while, I'd seen him, but it was not something he was known for, and I couldn't connect smoking with the girl. It didn't make sense to me.

But it turned out that there *was* a connection. It seemed that Julie was fast turning into a rebel, sexual exploration was just one part of that; she was getting into punk—claimed now to love the Sex Pistols—and wanted to get a piercing (which Francis had outright rejected) and since her parents didn't smoke, naturally that was another point on which experimentation was required. According to Cadogan, it was her idea, not his, to smoke in the music room.

"My dad will totally hate this," she said to him, as she blew smoke up at the pristine, high-vaulted ceiling.

"She laughed, the little devil," he said.

The day before—or rather the night before, as they lay together on her futon, his jizz "not going in," but out, collected on her washcloth, she asked him to bring some cigarettes to their next rendezvous.

"After the first puff it's all downhill from there," he told her.

"But I want to try it. Come on, Cad. Can't you get some? Please? Pretty please?"

"I can bum a few. Chickie is always good for a smoke."

"Let's meet in the music room," she told him. "It'll piss off my dad something fierce!"

I was pretty conflicted about this whole situation, now that Remus had set his sights on me—he was still carrying on the next day, giving me the evil eye at the assembly and at dinner that night. He seemed to have gone out of his mind. It was just a piano, and kids do stupid things. But I had a sense I would need to speak with him eventually.

I told Cadogan about that. He was in the process of shakily returning the Rayburn key. "You better take this dude," he said, as he secreted the key into my upturned hand. "I have no idea what's going to happen. But here you go. If I were you I'd hide that deep. Or lose it over the side of the mesa."

"Not a bad idea. But the key's trustee wants it back." I looked around—we were sitting on the lawn after Ideas class—and I said, "So…What happened?"

"What do you mean?"

"Oh come on, dude. Spill it."

He was tense, not his usual confident Jokerman self—and spoke quite softly. "We clowned around for a while on the sofa. It was getting late. We had already done some stuff; her top was off and she was jumping around, doing some gymnastic type moves. And then she played some things on the piano that way—little tease, with her tits out—actually she's a pretty good piano player—her parents insisted she learn, even though she says she had no interest in it. That's when she wanted to try a smoke. She said, 'go ahead, light one for me. Put it in my mouth.' I was playing with her titties and she was smoking, the cig hanging out of her mouth, like a pro, as she pounded on the keys, some ragtime tune. She must have set it on the piano at some point. I don't even remember that happening. But by then we were—"

Someone walked by and we both became quiet. Then Cadogan said, "You can never talk about this, Sutra."

"I know," I said. "It's way over the top even for you."

"You pud."

***

"I think you need to tell what you know, Mr. Gray." It was Remus again; he wouldn't let it go. We were in the Headmaster's office, and I was feeling picked on. I knew there was no way around it, however. It was predictable. Everything about Kickshaw was becoming that way.

But I knew this was extremely sensitive territory. I imagined by this stage in their 'relationship,' Cadogan had penetrated every orifice in nubile Julie's sweet angel body, pushing her to depths of depravity not seen since the Marquis de Sade. And she a willing participant. His cum staining her sheets and clogging the little drain that stood in the granny flat's half-bath. If Remus ever got wind of *that*, things might come to physical blows—or Cadogan might end up in reform school.

"Look," I said, "I've already told the Headmaster that I don't know anything. Besides, the right thing is for Dean Stacks to deal with this problem. From my point of view you are overstepping. You're just the music teacher. I have a mind to complain."

"To whom would you complain, Robbie?" Asked the Headmaster.

"To my dad, for starters. He was looking at making a sizable contribution to the school's alumni fund when I graduate."

"That's very much appreciated, I'm sure," said Remus. "But it's not going to get you off the hook here." His eyes were positively red, as if he had eaten too much red dye number 3 or blasted himself with a Martian heat ray.

"Well. OK," I said. "First of all, the cigarette."

The Headmaster perked up. "Yes?"

"Was the butt destroyed?"

"Remus?" he asked.

"No."

"Well then, what kind was it?"

"How should I know? But I have it right here in my pocket."

The Headmaster, I thought, was as tired of Remus as I was. "Let's have a look, Francis," he said.

Under pressure from the Headmaster, Remus slowly extracted a tired plastic baggie and set it on the Headmaster's desk. It contained the crumpled remains of two cigarette butts.

"There are two," said the Headmaster.

Remus seemed reluctant to give up details. "One was in the trashcan by the door, and the other was on the piano."

"This one by the trashcan is hardly smoked," I ventured. "Tell you what, why don't you see if those are the same kind that Chickie—Ciccariello—smokes."

"Mr. Ciccariello?" said the Headmaster.

"He's known to be good for a cigarette once in a while, sir. I don't smoke, but that's what I've heard."

"You're saying if it were his brand—"

I wanted to say, 'obviously,' but I could not afford to be too much of a smart ass. "That was my idea," I said, finally. "If it's his brand, then talk to him. Maybe someone bummed a cigarette or two recently. Maybe he knows who that someone is."

"Anything else?" said Remus.

I was really beginning to get a little chafed with the guy. "Yes. I heard a rumour that Julie was asking about cigarettes."

"WHAT?" I thought the big man's head might burst. "Who said that?"

"Oh please. This is a very tight-knit community. Things get around. And yes, maybe it's actually her who's starting to get around. What's a young girl doing running loose at an all-boy school?"

"I don't like what you are insinuating!"

I thought Remus was about to shit himself. However, the fact was, looking at the butts, I was pretty sure one of them had some lipstick on it. The stain had turned brown where formerly it had probably been red. But you could see it, even from where I was sitting.

The Headmaster and I made eye contact then, and I was pretty sure he saw what I saw. He now stepped in. "Francis, I think we've got some useful intelligence from Robbie, and I am grateful for his frankness and cooperation. He's a little insubordinate, but I've learned that's part of his nature. Let's park this for now and I will talk to Albert myself. I'll keep this evidence for now, if you don't mind."

***

I knew I had to have a word with Cadogan immediately, but it wasn't going to be an easy task. Within about an hour, word got round that the Headmaster had been over to the smoking area and probably Chickie had told all. Things happened quickly, and soon we could see Masters gathering near the High House on the west side.

"It's a Discipline Committee meeting!" said Fish. "Somebody's getting busted!" We were over at the dining hall. If even Fish knew the outlines then yes, the shit was about to hit the fan.

I went round to Spanish 201 looking for Cadogan, and I could see him in class through the window but couldn't get his attention. I was about to tap on the glass when I heard someone behind me.

"Hello, Mister Gray."

It was Charlie, old Clint himself, Dean Stacks. "Looking for someone?" His eye was twitching and his smile was like that of a jack-in-the-box.

Christian liked to call him 'Clint' on account of his similar facial features to Clint Eastwood (and marked propensity towards gunning down errant students). And this moniker fit too well. I myself had the pet project to spread it far and wide.

"Are you trying to have a word with our mutual friend?"

"No," I said. "Just passing by."

"Better be on your way then." Stacks moved forward like a freight train and pounded on the door of the classroom but immediately passed in. In a moment I could see him escorting Cadogan out the far side through the other entrance, his arm on Cadogan's shoulder. I couldn't see Cadogan's face, but it was clear he was looking at his feet. He may have been crying.

***

So the Discipline Committee was on, and I had no way of knowing how that would go. DCs were uncommon and much feared; those meetings were how kids got expelled, and there was no appeal process; you were just gone. And of course, the school provided no tuition refunds and tuition for the year was paid in advance.

I didn't hold out much hope for Cadogan, but just by chance, I walked past and almost ran into William J. Brennan. "Oh! Hello, William."

"So what's the word?" he said.

"Well, Cadogan's in a DC. It's happening now."

"Interesting. Hmm."

I looked at William and he seemed to be considering.

"Yes?" I said.

He still paused, as if considering. Finally he said, "Come with me, there's something I want to show you."

We went up to William's room, which was physically more or less over the Headmaster's Office. "Come on in," he said. "Now, Sutra, you can't say anything about what I am about to show you. Scout's honor?"

"Honor among thieves?"

"Sure. OK then. I will hold you to that." He locked his door, and I figured he wanted to smoke a bowl or do whatever it was that William was into—I mean, everyone was into something—and I had no idea in his case, the guy was a quixotic specimen if ever there was one—but no, he put his finger to his lips as if to signal quiet was required. And then opened his closet and started taking out his shoes and other objects piled there.

I sat on the bed watching. I grew impatient and started to speak, but he stopped me with a look. After he had made space in the closet, he carefully lifted up some of the boards. I could begin to see what looked like a void. Yes, this was news! It seemed there was a crawl space between the floors. My face erupted in a grin. He smiled too in a way I had not seen before. Then he motioned for me to come close. "This building is old," he said in a whisper. "It was one of the first constructions on the Mesa."

I nodded. 'Holy crap,' I thought.

William went to his desk and opened the bottom drawer and took out a stethoscope, the kind of thing a doctor would wear around his neck. And indeed I realized that William had 'doctor' written all over him. Quietly, he handed the instrument to me. "Go down into the attic crawlspace. It's about 2 1/2 feet deep and three feet wide. Be very careful not to make any sound. Then put the stethoscope on the floor."

I understood the plan immediately. I slowly lowered myself down, feet first, but as my butt touched the flooring—I supposed it to be the ceiling of the lower floor—William turned on his cassette tape player—the song was "*Are We Not Men*," by DEVO. Then he began banging his shoes on his own floor. I looked at him from floor level in terror. But he just motioned me on. I realized he was making noise to cover what I was doing. Probably the Headmaster and others who used the office were used to the noise of the dorms above.

'William is a fucking genius,' I thought, even though he had almost given me a heart attack. 'Must be all that D & D role playing and imagination coming into use. Holy Hell. So it *is* actually good for something.' Those were the kind of thoughts going through my head.

I was in the crawlspace now, and William slowed his clomping but left the music on. However, using the stethoscope, I could clearly hear conversations below; the medical instrument worked to block outside sounds as well as amplifying those below. It seemed that the meeting was just getting started.

***

"Thank you all for coming on short notice. We need to consider the sad situation of Mr. West."

"But I—"

"Don't speak, Cadogan," said the Headmaster. "You will have a chance to respond in a few minutes if you choose. But I advise you not to dig your own grave any deeper.

"I spoke with Alberto Ciccariello this morning and he said Mr. West came to him a few days ago and asked for a cigarette, and Ciccariello, being a generous man, gave him two. Mr. Ciccariello smokes Marlboro Lights. You can clearly see these butts are of that brand."

"I knew it!" shouted another voice. I was pretty sure it was Francis Remus.

"However," the Headmaster continued. "You can also see that on one of these, are the marks of lipstick."

"Lipstick?" I did not recognize this voice immediately but the accent suggested it was Heine Henler.

"Yes, Heinrich. Lipstick. I don't think it can be anything else."

"And what do you infer from that?" growled Remus.

"Please calm down, Francis." This seemed to be from the Headmaster. "I apologize, but I've had to take this to Elantra."

"My wife?" Remus seemed amazed.

"Yes," he continued. "We learned this morning about a rumour that Julie was interested in smoking. I wanted to know if Elantra thought that was possible."

"But you should have spoken to me! I'm her father."

"I'm sorry, Remus. Elantra says Julie is going through a phase, a rebellious phase. Especially towards male authority figures. I won't repeat here all that she told me, but—"

"You're trying to say my daughter went to the music room in the middle of the night, with this boy, and lit my piano on fire?"

"Cadogan," said the Headmaster. "You need to be frank. Did you take cigarettes from Mr. Ciccariello?"

Cadogan seemed to mumble.

"What was that, please?"

"Yes," he said.

"And did you give those to Julie?"

"No."

"No?" The Headmaster was surprised.

"She wanted me to teach her. To do it in the music room. She said it would piss off her father."

"So you met her there?"

"Yes. I propped open the door earlier that day with a stick so we could get in that night."

"And you smoked cigarettes?"

"I just had a puff. As I always say, it's about the first puff. The rest is all downhill from there."

Someone chuckled at this, but it was indistinct and I could not tell who it was.

The Headmaster said, "Please, people, this is serious." After a moment he continued. "So you taught Julie how to smoke?"

"Yes."

"And did Julie leave her cigarette on the piano?"

Here Cadogan could not immediately answer, because Remus began to complain about the process. "This is unacceptable, Scott!"

"Please wait, Francis," said the Headmaster. "Cadogan, please answer the question."

"I don't actually know what she did with it," he said. "I don't remember her doing that. But she must have. I stubbed mine out and put it in the trash can."

"Which one," said Remus.

"The one over by the door."

"Well, Remus?" said a new voice. It was Charlie Stacks. "You collected the evidence. Did one of those come from the trash? Which one of those butts was on the piano?"

This question was not immediately answered. I heard the abrupt scrape of a chair being pushed back; in my imagination the big man had leapt to his feet. "Are you insinuating my daughter burned the piano?"

"Will you answer the question, please, Francis?"

"No! No, I will not."

I could then hear what I thought was the stomping of size 13 feet, and a door slammed.

It was quiet for a while. I tried to keep very still.

"Well," said the Headmaster. "It sounds like Francis wants to discuss this with his daughter. And he should."

"It's a family matter," said Heine. "We must be respectful of the Remus family and allow them to work out their own concerns. It is not for us any longer."

"I agree," said the Dean. "But what should we do with Cadogan?"

Here it sounded like Cadogan did something I thought was a little uncharacteristic for him: he sobbed. "Please don't expel me. Please, I won't smoke out of bounds anymore."

The group seemed to now be taking a straw poll. "How many in favour of expulsion. Heinrich?"

"No. By no means."

"Charlie?"

"Yes."

"Martin?"

I was surprised to learn that Martin was present. He had not spoken until now. But he said, "No. It was just a piano."

The Headmaster sighed. "If Remus were here, he would have a vote, but he has clearly decided to exit the Disciplinary Committee process, and so I will mark his vote as abstained. For myself, I think expulsion is not necessary. Cadogan is obviously distraught about this and remorseful. Right, Cadogan?"

"Yes, sir."

"But that doesn't seem good enough," said Stacks. "Shouldn't we make an example of him?"

I heard a cry from Cadogan, and felt a stab of anger enter my chest. 'You're definitely on my shit list now, Stacks,' I thought.

"No," said the Headmaster, "My anger is actually directed elsewhere."

"Oh? Surely not the girl? You mean the gardener?" said Heinrich.

"I think the smoking area needs to be closed down for a while. And I'll have to talk to Glen about Alberto's contract," the Headmaster continued. "Perhaps we need a change there."

At that moment, it seemed that Old Kickshaw burst into the meeting. "What's all this?" he muttered. "The gruesome unsolved murder of the piano—is this the culprit?"

"It's all right, Dr. Kickshaw," said the Headmaster. "Everything is under control...."

***

I'd heard enough—it seemed Old Kickshaw would need several minutes of redundant explanations, and my leg was starting to cramp. I took the stethoscope out of my ears; I tried to rise very slowly. William, to his credit, had paid attention and turned up the music and began stomping around then. I extracted myself from the crawlspace with some difficulty—I had become stiff from holding one position. But then William gently helped me out of the crawlspace and we soon returned his closet to its original configuration.

Finally I handed him the stethoscope. I had been wearing it around my neck. "These are really handy."

"Ah yes, always keep a stethoscope around, I say. You never know when you might need to check your own vitals."

"You mean, to see if you're not dead?"

"Exactly."

PART TEN — Kumbh Mela Mayhem

There once was a Desi young thing,
Who sat on the top of a spring,
And though it pushed hard,
On the top of her card,
She never did feel a ga-zing.

"I don't know, Robbie," said William. "I want to get a degree in ancient languages—probably Sanskrit. I want to be an academic. So for me, going to University is the only logical thing to do."

"William J. Brennan, PhD. Right," I said. "But, for philosophy—not Western philosophy, what about Eastern philosophy? Religion?"

"These days the study of philosophy or religion of any kind is an academic exercise. It's rather pathetic."

I was deflated by this because I could see the truth of it. "Yes. Fair enough."

William and I were talking about the future. I suppose he was the one person at Kickshaw I felt I could truly open up to.

"Why are you so down on college?" he asked.

"I don't know." I thought about it. "I just want to work with fundamentals. I want to laugh and cry."

"Yeah, I get that."

"Counting is for machines, not men. I also have a sense of disquiet about, well, about everything."

"Certainly the basic idea of economic growth—endless growth—as a necessary condition for the economy is unsustainable. As a matter of fact, from the biological point of view, endless uncontrolled growth has a name: cancer."

"Right! Exactly."

"There are also other things, have you read Marshall McLuhan?"

"No."

"Well, you might look into him. He just died last year, unfortunately. But his work is all about Media."

"The medium is the message? That him?"

"Yep. Cultural critique. I mean, that's what academics do, a lot of them. So you are clearly an academic, Robbie. Maybe you just can't see that yet."

"But—what if I want to do more than write clever things about society? What if I want to change it? Fuck it up or tear it down?"

"Yes. Of course. You are quite right. That's more of, you know, an inner journey first."

"Exactly."

***

"I just fucking hate it, William."

"It's a phase you are passing through. You will come out the other side."

There was a glimmer of light, I thought—*Star Trek* showed the way, although with significant inner contradictions— the Enterprise was both a science vessel intended to explore, and a brutal warship—a weapon of violence. The red shirts were killed in every episode; it was unavoidable to shed blood. That was a contradiction that over time became more obvious and led to the limitations of science fiction. That was a hard blow.

Kung Fu, also, with its Eastern philosophy, spoke of a different way. I loved *Kung Fu*. William had never seen *Kung Fu*, but to his credit, when I told him about it, over the break he made a point to watch. He was soon obsessed with the show. He talked about it for weeks. But even that, we agreed, was merely entertainment. Not a political philosophy. One cannot just wander around doing interventions.

But how did I become corrupted to the ideals of higher education? Where did I go wrong? That was my dominant thought. And then I remembered.

I told William, "I think I was poisoned at a young age by that television commercial for the College Entrance Exams, the one promoting the idea of college credit for existing knowledge. Do you remember that commercial?"

"No, I wasn't much of a television kid."

"Well, in it, an adult Abraham Lincoln joins a second-year college history course. The teacher observes Lincoln is a first-year student and wonders aloud if he can manage. But Lincoln explains he knows quite a bit about American History already, and proceeds to prove it to the astounded class.

"I liked that commercial, but it always struck me that in reality, Lincoln never did go to college, and never did need a degree. He was an auto-didact. So why do I need a degree? Why can't I be like Lincoln?"

"That's a good point," was all William would say.

Now in my third year at Kickshaw, certainly the blinders were off and some of the shine had worn from the gilded walls of the cage. And yet it was a beautiful place and I could imagine how University would be just as good; the lovely campus, the lovely girls, the lovely books and libraries filled with knowledge. Perhaps Berkeley, I thought, the glories of San Francisco, could open to me like a woman as it had for so many of the Beats. But then the darkness would settle on me. Wasn't it all a rosy picture of bong hits and babes and grandiose ideas expounded in sun domes not unlike those described by Ray Bradbury in *The Illustrated Man*? Sun and fun while the world drowned in a drenching rain of capitalist, war-mongering shit? William was right, the biology of it was cancer. Sickness.

However my vague feelings of distrust and unease took time to blossom into action. Months even. I was lazy. I knew that, but it didn't make me any less lazy to know. I needed a catalyst.

***

Ideas 201 was an extension of Ideas 101 and the attendees were all Ram's hardened fans and acolytes. We loved him. It was a few weeks into the new year.

"I have an announcement to make," he said. "A very special guest speaker will be coming to visit next week. It's Malcolm Walters. He's a Kickshaw graduate from the class of '76. Some of you may know him or at least have heard of him."

"I know his father was a Senator," said Cadogan.

"Oh is that so," said Ram. "Well, well. I had no idea. Such a distinguished gentleman."

Of course, Ram knew very well his protégé was from a well-to-do family.

"But regardless of his family and connections, Malcolm is quite special in other ways. His interest in spirituality led him to forgo University for a time and head to India in search of a living Guru."

"A guru?" I said. "Are there real gurus?"

"Yes, of course, Sutra," he said. "Some call their holy book their guru. That's the case in the religion I was born into, Sikhism. They believe the Adi Granth is their guru. But other traditions are intent on a living master, a living spiritual teacher. At any rate, Malcolm and I have been corresponding via the mail and he is back from Pune and would like to give us a report about his experiences."

"Did he find a Guru?" I asked.

"It seems so. But let's wait and hear from Malcolm directly."

The man himself appeared on the following Tuesday morning. He was late and missed our usual class period. We were expecting someone to pull up in a nice ride or perhaps a

Taxi. But it eventuated that Malcolm had taken the Grey-hound bus from LAX. He hitch-hiked up to the Mesa, which explained his tardiness. Ram greeted him warmly and suggested we all meet at the lunch hour. "We'll have some food out on the grass. It will be a regular satsang!"

"What's that?" I said.

"It's just an Indian word," William said. "It means spiritual gathering."

Ram and Malcolm went off to chat and we all met up in the dining hall a little after 11:30 a.m. We took our cafeteria trays out into the forecourt; there was a grassy area with part-sun and part-shade that seemed good for sitting. We didn't have chairs, it was Indian style, on the ground.

Ram did the introductions. "Everyone, this is Malcolm Walters, as I promised. So, Malcolm. Maybe you can tell us a bit about your India adventure."

"Of course," he said. "I remember a few of your faces."

"I was a freshman when you were a sophomore," said William.

"Yes, William, hello. Your face has filled out quite a lot," a statement that brought laughter from the assembled group. "Well, let me start by saying that after graduation I wasn't sure what to do, education-wise. And I really needed a year away. That 'year away' turned into two and then three. But I'm back in the United States now for the time being."

"What will you do?" I said. "What about college?"

"Oh, I'll go to college eventually, I think. But right now I'm more interested in helping the Bhagwan get established here."

"Bhagwan?" I said.

"Yes, the Bhagwan Shri Rajneesh. He's a Guru I met when I was in Pune."

"So you did find a guru!" said William.

"I think so, yes. But I am jumping ahead! Let me go back to the beginning. First of all, we flew into Delhi. It's in

Northwest India, up by the Punjab. My traveling companion was Rob Standish, he's the son of the school nurse, you may know her."

For some reason this produced laughter, and Malcolm could not discern why.

"Rob is one of my other Ideas students," said Ram, in order to move things along (and perhaps save me embarrassment.)

"So Rob and I flew into Delhi with the general plan of visiting the Ganges. It is also fairly far to the north; the holy river is fed off the melt water of the Himalayas. That whole journey was by train, and it was by turns shocking and maddening and beautiful."

"So you bathed in the Ganges?" Ram said.

"We did, although it was across from a power plant. There was new and old India in contrast everywhere. And it was far from spiritual. But then we travelled up-river for a while and met some yogis. They told us about the Maha Kumbh Mela."

"It's a Hindu river festival that attracts millions," said Ram. "Millions and millions of pilgrims."

"Sounds like complete mayhem," I said.

"Well, sure." Malcolm said. "And unbeknown to us, the great festival was soon to start. That year the festival was in Allahabad, which was not that far off, maybe 100 kilometers as the crow flies. But this was India! It could take a long time to get over there. Still, we started walking."

"You walked?" I said.

"Sure. We hitch-hiked a bit also. The festival—I'm not sure there are words for it. But every twelve years they do a big one. And this one was big."

"Millions of Hindu pilgrims come from all over India," said Ram. "And most especially Sadhus and different holy men. All different practices, ideas, philosophies."

"Just the crowds were kind of hard to fathom. Millions of people. One day we were down at the Ganges. I saw a human skull in the sand; and nearby, someone had made their toilet, and a human turd pile lay there. The entire extremity of the human condition seemed to be posited by those two artifacts."

William could not help giving a chuckle at this. "India is not all roses, is it?"

"It's true. India, modern India, is one of the harshest places in the world. Especially for a Westerner, for an American. The pollution in the cities, the trash, the raw sewage. I remember being in Delhi and smelling hamburger. I've been a vegetarian for years, but you know how it is, you smell something and it smells good. But this wasn't hamburger. Anyone want to guess what it was?"

Ram was smiling. "I know but I won't say."

"OK, you got us, what was it?" I said.

"Dead bodies. There are burning ghats on top of buildings all across the city. The smell of human fat burning from the bodies permeates the city at night."

"Ugh," I said. "That's pretty hard core."

"It is," said Malcolm.

"But tell us about the Kumba Mela," said William.

"The first day into Allahabad I thought it was crowded. I was wrong. The festival had not even started. Soon there were Sadhus and mysterious figures, half-naked, loin-clothed holy men everywhere. They were pouring in like rain. Pilgrims gathered around these figures, worshiping and giving alms, in packs and hordes. We were swept up in the religious fervour of the pilgrims, many of whom spoke English. And of course, we were strangers there, strangers in a strange land, and so pilgrims approached us too, wanting sometimes to teach us, or help us, to explain things, but also, occasionally, to see if we were possibly spiritual beings, clothed in the garb of Americans, come to deliver a message. It seemed every Sadhu had a message, every holy man had something to say. And I guess to them we were no exception."

"And what did you tell them?" I said in awe.

"Mainly I tried to channel Ram here—" he said, which made Ram laugh. "I talked about the ideas class. Pilgrims and even some Sadhus listened and looked on in wonder. 'Does such a thing really happen in the United States?' said one Sadhu. "I swear it's true," I said. 'We learnt about the Bhagavad Gita in class,' and I repeated something from that book, but of course translated into English. The Sadhu was stunned. 'This is amazing,' he said. 'You are Devas come down to show us something.' But my attitude was, remember to be humble, we should leave. We moved on before too much of a commotion ensued."

"The next day we made our way slowly down to the river—the Ganges. We had bathed in it already, but this was the day of the festival, it was a holy day to do it. We made our way down to the water's edge. Rob went in, but before I could do that, A Sadhu on the bank took hold of my hand. He said, 'After you bathe, come and see me, I have a message for you.' I didn't know what he meant exactly, and I was afraid I would never be able to find my way back to this man, who was covered in ash with uncut hair that looked like one big rats-nest.

"But, we had to keep moving. I went into the Ganges and submerged my head, as Rob had done, and then I took hold of him by the hand and led him back to the bank. But the Sadhu was gone. I looked for him for a long time—probably hours. The day became cloudy and my brain was lacking calories. I was exhausted both mentally and physically. In the end I had to give up, and we went slowly back into the city to try and find something to eat. But just as I had given hope, there he was, suddenly, in front of us. 'Ah!' He said. 'I was hoping I would run into you. I am one of the *Maha-nirvani*, we worship Lord Siva. Last night I dreamed I would meet a Westerner. Lord Siva appeared in my dream—it is a very auspicious thing; also very frightening. But in the dream the Lord told me of your coming. I am to instruct you that your master is not here, he lives in the far West of India, in Poona.' 'And did the Lord tell you the name of this Master?' I said. He shook his head. 'No, I am sorry. But I suggest you leave immediately and travel West. I must go now. Good luck.'"

"And without another word, he left us. I wasn't sure if we should listen to him, but Rob was convinced. 'It's clearly a message, perhaps The Message, we have been waiting for!' So we slowly made our way out of the festival. It took a few weeks to get to Poone, or Pune as it had just been renamed."

"I've never been to Pune," said Ram. "What is it like?"

"It's warm and lush, very green. Tropical feeling. It's a cultural center, and much more Westernized than the surrounding countryside."

"So what did you do?" I said. "It sounds an impossible task to find someone in a huge city. I can hardly find my way around Carpinteria."

Malcolm laughed. "Yes, we had an impossible puzzle. But Rob and I were both committed to stay as long as it took. I should say by this point, we looked and smelled pretty funky. Rob and I both had beards going and were wearing Indian clothing, for the most part. We were turning into street people, by Western standards. We found a cheap place on the outskirts of town—basically in a slum, there are many of those—and suffered for weeks. Some places in India people speak a lot of English; but for whatever reason, in Pune that wasn't true. The people we encountered spoke a number of different languages but English was not usually one of them. It was a lonely time."

"Finally, after a few weeks, we met a college professor, an educated man. His name was Sundar Singh, and Rob literally ran into him by accident on the street. We started to have a conversation and he became curious. 'What are two young Americans doing here?' 'It's sort of a long story,' I said, 'but if you're interested, I'd love to tell it.' 'Yes, of course. Let's get some tea.'

"I told Sundar about the 'message' from the Sadhu, which he found quite interesting and took seriously. 'That is most important,' he said. 'I know a lot of spiritual figures here in Poona, he gave no name?'

'None,' I said. 'Just that we should immediately go West.'

'What that makes me think of is that we do have a young guru here in Poona who is starting to collect a lot of Western disciples. His name is Rajneesh. I wonder...'

"He scratched his chin, then, and both Rob and I jumped at the idea, that perhaps this was what the Sadhu meant. 'Where is this Rajneesh? Who is he?'"

"In truth I don't know much about him...he is a bit controversial...seems to be mixing traditions...but he may fit the description."

"We thanked Sundar profusely and began looking for this Rajneesh. He wasn't that hard to find, Sundar was right, he was gathering students. We went as soon as we could to a public discourse, a satsang, as they call it."

"What is he like?" Asked Ram.

"Kind of hard to describe. He speaks very slowly and you must address him; he never speaks first. He is calm and gives off a sense of divinity. He's different, in that he's not opposed to sexuality...and he is mixing different traditions. He's creating what he calls a 'neo-sannyasin,' a new kind of follower."

"A sannyasin is a renunciate," said Ram. "That means leaving the world behind—even women."

But Malcolm was undeterred. "Rajneesh proposes that we be renunciates, but also that we embrace energy, activity, and being a part of the world to do good. He's not opposed to money. He has big plans. Someday he may even come to America!"

***

The next Ideas class we discussed Malcolm's visit and I can't say I was that interested in Malcolm's guru—but I was starting to formulate my own plan. He was a seeker. I could relate to that. And India sounded magical.

"I see your eyes shining, Sutra. What are you thinking?" said Ram.

"I'm just considering if maybe I should follow Malcolm's example and go to India. Of course, I would need a traveling companion," and I looked over at William. But he just smiled and shook his head. "I'm no good to you, Sutra, in that way. I'm a bookworm. I'd never last a day without my creature comforts."

"The journey to India is no small investment in time and energy," said Ram. "And it's not all roses there, obviously. Keep thinking about it, Sutra. Perhaps the way will open for you."

Ram's eyes were downcast. "Meanwhile," he said, "I must inform you all that the Headmaster has asked that Malcolm not visit anymore and we are to discontinue discussions on this topic."

"Why?" I said.

"Apparently there have been some concerns raised by Dr. Kickshaw. He saw Malcolm on campus the other day and inquired about it. He said he is afraid students might follow Malcolm's example and take up with a 'crazy Indian Guru.' That's how he put it."

"That's so lame!" I cried.

"No, Sutra. No, no. Do not push back. Accept. We were able to meet with Malcolm after all, isn't that so? It was a form of grace. Always be grateful for what comes."

"But Ram!" I continued.

"No Robbie," he said sadly. "Listen to me. We must consider our time together on this earth as a form of grace. No one knows how long they have got. Always be grateful."

But I was flaming about it for days.

And then we got word that Ideas classes were abruptly cancelled. The whole thing, just done.

"We're reconsidering the value of that program of study," was all the Headmaster would say.

"But what about Ram?"

"That's not your concern, Mister Gray. Please go about your business."

"You guys suck!" I said.

I wish I had bleated out something more profound, obviously. But that was the best I could do between tears. It was truly the Kumbh Mela Mayhem and only ranked slightly below the '68 My Lai Massacre. At least in my estimation.

Meanwhile my relationship with my dad, who I idolized with a man-crush from day one, was also changing. I was long past the whole "uh-oh, he's gay" thing. Looking back it seemed sad that I didn't understand sooner. My dad was just doing what made him happy, and I was good with that and I wished he could get back with Larry, who had been such a positive force in his life. I missed Larry; he made things work. I even missed Conchita.

But a detente seemed unlikely now. And my dad was busy showing me a different side of himself.

The situation with the "rent strike" at *Rancho Bravos* had escalated to the stage where my father had got the courts involved. Once he had a civil judgment against a particular tenant, he systematically moved to crush them. He explained with glee how the Santa Barbara County Sheriff was especially useful. "As soon as I get a judgment, I garnish their wages. And if they don't have regular work—some don't—then I move to have them tossed out."

It was called eviction, and Conchita was one of the first to go. I wasn't sorry to see her *hombre* out on the street, but it certainly seemed ungrateful to bin Conchita like a piece of week-old pizza. I thought of her almost like family.

I wanted to make a joke, something like "can't you let her slide after the job she's done for you?" or "couldn't she just give us both a hand?" but it seemed in poor taste.

PART ELEVEN — Rope-a-dope at the Senior Prom

There once was a beautiful jade,
Who wanted to learn her a trade,
But she left with a guy,
Who kicked sand in my eye,
And pounded her poon in the shade.

Old Kickshaw caught me one day late in senior year. Not doing my private exploration in the woodwork, like a termite, or crawling the pipes underneath the dorms and classrooms, or haunting the trails, but just out and about. It was a glorious day and I was thinking about Senior Prom.

Kickshaw loved to roam the grounds and was the bane of many an escape plan for students trying to flee campus without liberty. But on this day, with the sun shining high in the sky, he caught me. "Young Master Gray, a minute of your time!"

"Uh, Hi there, Doctor Kickshaw."

He had crept up on me, or else I was asleep at the wheel in my daily constitutional, having smoked a secret hit or three in Christian's closet. My eyes were soaked in Visine, and a breath mint gave me the confidence to speak, but I was buzzing. "You startled me, sir."

"Daydreaming, were we? Very good, lad. Now, what about a quick chat?"

"Uh, well alright then, but can we walk? You see, this is my daily walk. I need the exercise. And it helps me to think and, you know, do better in my studies." I was starting up my full-on bullshit mode, running on auto-pilot, but Kickshaw was hard of hearing, so I was not sure it mattered. Still, some of my best ideas were the products of this quick thinking (as I liked to call it).

"Yes of course, lad. We shall walk, you and I. I love a good constitutional myself." Old Kickshaw was, like, 90 years old, and walked with a cane, so I slowed a bit, just out of courtesy. But we continued to slow, gradually, as he spoke. "I understand you did very well on the Advanced Placement." He said this with no context, and as far as I knew the results were not yet published.

"I don't know sir, I have not seen the results. But certainly I had a lot of confidence when I sat the exam."

"Let me be the first to congratulate you in that case, my boy. You sat a very respectable 780. Your AP Math skills were significantly lower, a mere 550, but that English score is enough to put you in the top of your class. I was most impressed."

"My goodness," I said. "Perhaps I had better stop reading, my head might explode."

"Yes," he mused. "Indeed. Indeed. A most respectable score."

We walked for a bit and then Kickshaw broke into his concept. "You see, Young Master Gray, our intention here at Kickshaw School for Boys is to help find the things that boys love, to develop their skills, their inner needs and wants by which I mean, for their career. For their future. It seems to me that you would make an excellent writer. Do you like writing?"

"Uh, yes. Yes sir, I do. I have been writing since I was a small child and was given my first Etch-a-sketch."

"Excellent. Now, as you may know, there is a gap in the team that will construct the 1981 yearbook. There is no currently configured or assigned Editor. Nor is there a writer. I may be able to find a Master to help with the editorial function, I would not pressure you that far. It is an awesome responsibility, the editorial function. But a staff writer..."

I saw where he was going now. He wanted to get me on the yearbook staff and help design the thing. The current staff consisted of James Goldstein, who I had noticed wandering around wasting a lot of film with his Canon AE-1,

and probably Mrs. Jones, the occasional wife of the Geom-
etry Master, who would help with the financial aspect of
"interfacing with the publisher."

"I don't know sir, I've got a lot on this semester...." I tried
my best to think of an excuse, but, still buzzed, I lacked the
strength. 'Damn this Thai Stick,' I thought. 'It's just too
stoney.'

"Nonsense," Old Kickshaw was saying. He had stopped
walking, his mission completed, and I took several steps
forward before I realized he had come to a halt and was no
longer at my side. I turned around and looked at him. He
looked old. Up close he was a bit younger, because when
you could see them, his eyes were often wide and wild.
Those eyes lay hidden beneath black round-framed rims
mounted on his dome-like bald head, and the eye-glass
frames acted like telescopic enclosures. But the corneas hidden beneath would flame into prominence when he was en-
livened with passion, like a feral cat's eyes suddenly per-
ceiving a Blue Jay. It was only through his bent frame and
the general dissolution of his corporeal form that his real
age manifested.

When I turned, he was already making his goodbyes and
had his hand in the air, perhaps in a haughty gesture of dis-
missal; or maybe he was just done and his hand-sign meant,
'I'm on to the next thing.' I did not know. But what he said
was, "I'll see Mrs. Jones is informed of your new role! Good
luck, my lad!" And he went on his way, setting off in an entirely different vector across the lawn, in the general direction of the dining hall.

I sighed a general sigh of relief that he had gone. I made
my way slowly towards Christian's room. He was again in
the Hermitage; he had settled in with his secret stash box
and invented a clever, fully functional way to disseminate
pot smoke. The contraption, which looked like a stove pipe,
worked beautifully, he said, as long as the wind was blowing the right direction. "It carries the smoke right out over
the edge of the Mesa, and then on out of the area."

"Ingenious!" I announced, not having the slightest faith in the device.

"Listen, Christian, Old Kickshaw caught me out on my walk and has assigned me to be on the Yearbook staff. Do you want to join me?"

"Nah. Well, maybe." I could see Christian had a concept. "My father loves to make scrapbooks. What he does is collect a lot of pictures and then cut them up and organize them into collages."

"That sounds cool," I said.

"I wonder if we could do the yearbook as a big collage?"

"I don't know," I said. "Sounds pretty rad."

"Yeah, totally!"

Christian seemed pretty excited, so when I had my first meeting with Fish and Mrs. Jones, I convinced them to let Christian do the yearbook design. "He's really into design," I told them. "What do you think?"

"I guess," said Fish.

"You give him your photos—take tons—and he's going to organize them into yearbook pages." I didn't say too much about the collaging, I figured that 'artistic' aspect was something that was better left unsaid. Of course, I reasoned, the designer of the yearbook layout would have some latitude, and creativity was the price of admission. Fish was unaware, but he did like the idea he could take all the pictures he wanted.

"Sure, I guess," he said. "The more the merrier. Just keep taking pictures."

"I don't know, Robbie," said Mrs. Jones.

"Give him a chance, won't you?" I said.

"All right then. I'll inform the Headmaster of our plans. Christian will do layout."

And Christian got happy. For my part, the senior yearbook task was simply to write funny things about different people, perhaps a limerick or two, that could be used to decorate a page or work as the caption for a disarming photo.

That's how I thought about it. Old Kickshaw had said almost nothing useful about the task, and I was of no mind to seek clarification; I decided just to do what I wanted. I was the staff writer now, he said; well, fine. I had a few things to say. We had a nice picture of Charlie Stacks in a hallway, and I thought Christian might work a collage of him with these words to go with it:

The dean with a squint, cold and scary,
Stalked down halls like a Harry.
With a glare like a fiend,
And a mind that's machine,
"Said, are you feelin' lucky, ya' fairy?"

For Dr. Kickshaw, I wrote,

The king of old Kickshaw did fight,
Tried to keep his head feeling aright.
He banned all the bongs,
And luxurious dongs,
But dreamed of just loosening his tight.

For Remus, I considered,

A teacher's young daughter named Claire,
Smoked like a devil-may-care.
One flick, and oh no—
The grand piano!
Went up like a blaze of her hair.

***

I have not said much here about Susan. She moved into a downstairs Hermitage single for Senior year so she was just down the hall from Christian. Susan and I used to interact

in Aikido class, but as a senior, I no longer had a requirement to take sport, and our interests seemed to be different;
I rarely saw her except sometimes at assembly, where we
would make eye contact. She always smiled her shy,
friendly girl smile and I would nod my head. Her advisor
was still Martin, but I didn't sit with them.

For Susan, I had several limericks, but I didn't think we
could actually use any of them:

A boy with a soul dressed in pearl,
Deep down was yet always a girl.
She loved an old friend,
Who swore love must end—
But his heart was forever to hurl.

and

A boy with a heart soft and wide,
Knew she had pussy inside.
She fell for a guy,
With a skeptical eye—
But he left for a much tighter bride.

However I expected these were too personal and revealing
to be used.

Sometimes I'd see her in the hallway over at the Hermitage when I was visiting Christian; and sometimes she
would ask about what I was reading. "I always remember
you giving me *Stranger in a Strange Land,*" she said. "I didn't
understand the book at first. But now I get it. You were so
kind to me that year." Or "How is your father? I hope he's
not been getting into any trouble?" She meant with the .45.
Our joking talk about guns that night we saw *Rocky Horror*
had stayed with her.

***

"Sorry dude, but I don't feel like being social."

"Alright, man. Sorry."

It seemed that Christian was going through some things, and even though the yearbook project was keeping his mind occupied, he had periods of darkness. Sometimes I'd knock and he'd not answer, and then after a while, he'd peek his head out and just look miserable.

It got so that I started to worry about him.

Of course, others could say the same about me—not because I was sad, but because I seemed to care less and less about the future. I talked openly about giving away my possessions, and when I tried to do this, Martin came and asked me not to. "It's too crazy, Robbie."

"But it's what I want," I said. "I don't need all this stuff."

"But what about college?"

"Yeah? What about it?"

"Robbie," he said, "don't mind me asking, but why aren't you talking to the guidance counselor about school selection? They want to know."

It was Martin, so I gave him a serious answer. "I'm not entirely sure I'm going."

"But Robbie, this is a prep school. Of course you're going."

"I don't know, man. I mean, what if what I want in life is just to experience life? What if it doesn't matter what kind of job I have or what kind of house, or what kind of car?"

"But you like culture. University is where all the interesting people are, all the women you want to meet."

"Perhaps. But maybe I don't really care about what other people say. Maybe I have to figure out what matters."

"Even if it's the hard way?"

"Well, that does sound like me, doesn't it?"

"Yeah," he said. But he wasn't smiling.

"I have to get more experience, not more education. I'm tired of the fake. I'm tired of practicing. When does the real thing start?"

He looked at me. "Be careful what you ask for. In my case reality set in by force. I had to go to war. We shot at people and sometimes the bullets hit. I didn't want to do that, I was drafted, made into a soldier, and I hated it. It did change me and I did learn important things about life and all that. But then I went to UC Berkeley. It was like heaven. I went from hell into heaven in the span of just a few years."

"Maybe I have to fight my own war, make my own path."

"Sure. But I'll tell you honestly, all the things you're interested in, that life experience, a day will come when you wish you had got college credit for that."

Sadly, I wasn't convinced. I didn't listen. Probably I should have.

***

Our work on the yearbook was progressing nicely (in my way of thinking), and while I did have some qualms about subverting it—a sense of anxiety, but also the joy of schadenfreude—Old Kickshaw was going to get what he asked for, and then some, I thought—still, everyone seemed so pleased we were doing it. Even the Headmaster chimed in.

"You and Christian are doing a wonderful service. I can't wait to see what a great yearbook the class of '81 will have."

"Thank-you, sir. Yes, I'm sure it's going to be memorable." That's all I would really say: "It's going to be memorable." And that was not bullshit. That was a true fact.

Time passed, and Christian thought he was done collaging; either that or he just burned out. I wrote one last limerick about Clint's wife, who we had heard only the day before, quite clearly, complaining to her husband, the Dean. Just by chance Christian and I were on our way to the Dragon's Den, and went past Longhouse.

"What am I supposed to do up here, Charlie? What is there for me?" It was poor Angela Stacks. They were having an argument.

Christian smirked, but I felt a bit sorry for her. She was beautiful, and quite young, perhaps in her late 20's, and stuck at a boy's school with a bunch of leering clods and feckless old men and a preppie husband who everyone hated. Cadogan bragged he had managed to get close to her, but I was pretty sure that was bullshit.

***

I thought Mrs. Jones would be involved in the proofing process for the Yearbook, but she made it clear she was only doing the ordering. It seemed there was a missing role in the team—an actual adult editor. But she was unconcerned. "If you think it's good enough, then let's get the order in. It looks like Class of 1980 bought 300 copies. Do you think that's enough?"

"Oh, no, at least 400, I would say. This is going to be memorable, very memorable. I'm sure some people will want two copies!" I was shining her on, like a complete shit, but she took every drop of it.

"Fine," she said. "I'll get that order sent out next week." I didn't realize her lack of interest was also a lack of responsibility. She put it all on me and Christian. Lazy old bag.

***

"Hey, Sutra!" Fish said. "I found this really cool place on the trails. It's got a couch!"

"Really?" I said. "That's very interesting." My heart sank. It was interesting all right, but for all the wrong reasons: if Fish had been to the Dragon's Den, then word was getting around, and it wouldn't be long before the Grounds Crew heard about it. We knew there were a couple of spies running their mouths about students out of bounds, and other goings on. It had never really occurred to me that my behavior, my very presence, probably ticked certain people off. But it did. Maybe it was jealousy. But then I had a kind of asshole, 'screw you,' vibe sometimes that probably had something to with it. And we figured Clint was not above seeking and developing sources of information within the student body.

Spies.

Christian decided to go down and remove anything incriminating that morning. He came back holding his hand over his eye, which was swollen.

"What happened, man?" I said.

"I left a bottle of Welch's grape juice down there. I picked it up and the cap shot off and hit me in the eye."

"Dude!" I said. "We've got to get you to the infirmary."

"No, I can manage."

But I was convinced he needed medical attention. I thought his eyeball was going to pop out. Eventually he relented. It seemed that I was right, Mrs. Standish had him transported down to the Emergency Room immediately.

Very soon after, the Dragon's Den was destroyed by the Grounds Crew. The sad thing was you could see the debris and wreckage from afar, even as you approached the Mesa: there was the miraculous couch, smashed, the boards Christian had laboriously carried up there in the dark of night scattered on the hillside. It was horrendous.

"It's ruined, man!" He said. I thought he was going to cry.

"I know. I know...."

And then we had to endure another bug hunt in Assembly, as Clint tried to smoke out who had built it. "The Grounds Crew found paraphernalia down there. Whoever built that hideout is in serious trouble!"

***

There were good things that year, too, it wasn't all doom and gloom and idiots and test scores. It was May, and the prom was coming. With Larry gone so I had to make my own arrangements for a tuxedo. I ended up with an insane outfit—white tie, gloves, tails and all. But I thought I looked pretty debonair. Anyway, I was going for it.

Isabella was my prom date. She wasn't always approachable, and some days I yearned just to see a trace of her, a piece of paper with her handwriting, a scent on my jacket; besides school, which took up all her weekdays, her cop father was no pushover. I finally met him, not in the best of circumstances, but at a traffic stop. Christian and I were riding double, going down to Carp on his moped. The cop car pulled us over, siren and lights and everything.

Out stepped this guy who looked like he was from CHiPs—an aging Erik Estrada. "Where are you boys going?"

"To my dad's house, sir," I said. "I live here."

"Is that so? Do you have a license?" he said to Christian.

Without a word, Christian pulled out his wallet and handed his license over.

"And you?" he said to me.

"Well, I'm not driving, sir," I said. "But sure." I produced my driver's license for him.

We waited while the cop did his thing. When he returned, he seemed steeled. Two rich white kids. And one in particular.

"So, you're Robbie Gray?"

"That's what the license says, sir."

"Haven't I seen you in a tan VW microbus?"

"That's possible sir."

"Is that your bus?"

"Well, sir, yes. The title is in my father's name."

"And who is that?" he said.

"Richard Gray. He's a real estate agent."

The cop's face seemed to change. "Ah. Yes. We've heard of him around here. They call him Tricky Dick. He was on the local news."

"Something like that," I said, my face downcast.

"Well, maybe you know my daughter. Isabella."

Inwardly I blanched. 'Oh shit,' I thought.

Christian had listened to all this in silence but now couldn't help himself. "If you don't mind, I thought this was a traffic stop. We've been patient, but we have a place to be."

"Oh?" said the cop.

"There's a game on."

"You're confused. There's no football on today."

"It's called the Youth World Cup. We're hoping Robbie's dad can get it on the cable."

The cop seemed impressed. "I see. So you know about that?"

"I play forward, actually. It's just the youth finals. But it matters to me." Christian was a scrappy kid and he didn't take shit from anyone. Not even cops.

The cop couldn't help but smile. "*Bueno*. But listen. You aren't supposed to ride double, and your friend Robbie doesn't even have a helmet. You can go. Go watch your game. But get a helmet," he said to me.

"Yes, sir," I said.

"Adios Cabrón!" said Christian.

So that was how I met Isabella's dad. "What a ball breaker," I said under my breath.

"Sucks to be you," said Christian.

***

Still, the prom was the prom, ball breaker dad or no. I couldn't believe I had a date (something I never would have contemplated). And Isabella was a prize. All the guys thought so. I knew that, too, which was part of the amazement. I mean who was I? I wasn't cool. I wasn't Sinbad the fucking Sailor. I couldn't even surf.

I stood around waiting impatiently outside the prom venue, a Santa Barbara three-star restaurant with an inner terrace, an atrium, that was open to the sky like in a Roman villa.

Finally Isabella's father pulled up in their old Chrysler and Isabella jumped out. She was beautiful in her white prom dress. There were flowers in her hair. She spoke to her father through the rolled down window and I said "¡Hola!" to CHiPs Mr. Torres and waved and he scowled at me and drove off. But I didn't care, Isabella was radiant and laughing and we stood for a while admiring each other and the profoundly good circumstances we found ourselves in.

"I've got this thing for you," I said.

"What?"

"It's a flower. Or more flowers, I should say."

"Oh, you mean corsage."

"Sure." I haplessly tried to pin it to her left chest until I hit skin and then she stopped me and took a hand. Then I gave her mine, and she deftly pinned the boutonniere to my jacket like a pro.

"You're good at that," I said.

"Yeah, all of us Mexicans make great maidservants," she said, laughing.

"Mama Mia!" I laughed.

"That's Italian, you dolt."

We looked into each other's eyes and I rested my hands on her shoulders as she put hers on my waist. It was like a dance pose but we were just enjoying the moment of closeness. I could hear the others inside the venue and thought about going in, but it was hard to let go of the togetherness. I was like a greedy pig pretending to be a boy who was pretending to be a man.

Then something happened that if you put it in a book, the reader would say 'that's ridiculous, it's completely made up and fantastic, like a fairy tale.' And it's true, it's hard to convince people that something is possible if it has never happened to them personally. But in this case what happened was, while we watched, the clouds opened up and the sky changed color, not a rainbow exactly, but an atmospheric phenomenon of light, such that the sky and cloud looked pink and deep blue and purple, and then sparkled. It was like Walt Disney or aliens giving a blessing.

"Do you see that?" I said.

"Yeah! Whoa, that's incredible."

We stood there looking at the sky, and it was like a lightshow, the gods smiling on us, and then Isabella said, "Hey, we should tell people, shouldn't we?" And she started moving to go into the venue, because she was like that, and wanted us to share the experience, but I held onto her and said, "No. This is ours, Isa. They wouldn't believe it, or if we did go in, when we came back it would be gone."

"Yeah. You're probably right."

She let me kiss her then. It was a nice kiss, I wasn't too good at kissing quite yet in the scheme of things, but it was OK, I think. She tasted like brown maple syrup and lip gloss.

We eventually stopped doing that and finally did make our way into the venue. It was a restaurant and bar, and it was open and filled with people, so we walked through and then a hostess led us into the back, where the atrium was. It was marked off as a private party. The hostess departed and I could see various and sundry classmates transformed into their party clothes: there was Felix in tails with a very round date he had somehow corralled, there were various members of the Malibu Mafia with pretty, mostly blond girls wearing deep tanning-bed tans and frilly dresses. Christian had a date, apparently someone from Palo Alto he knew who flew down that afternoon, Shelly was her name; and Cadogan had come stag, but was already talking to one of the young servers.

I was thinking how I might get some champagne for Isabella when Joey O'Dell, who was already clearly drunk, pushed his way into my face.

"You can't bring your Beaner wetback in here, Sutra!"

"What's your problem, Joey. Back off." I was in no mood for the guy.

"No wetbacks!" His face was just way too close to mine, and then something happened that surprised me. I wanted to hit him, and basically I was gearing up to do that, but I felt Isabella pushing me aside.

"I'll handle this, Sutra." She took up a stance in front of Joey and without speaking to him, kicked, low and hard, directly at his balls. The blow landed and made a low crunching sound, like hitting a Hacky sack, probably not audible to anyone but Isabella and me (and him, obviously) and as he exhaled he groaned and his tongue seemed to pop out of his mouth. His eyes were bulging. She pushed back on him with her hand, then, a palm on his chest, and he just sort of crumpled and fell back. It was like a pratfall, and he went down gripping his privates, rolling on the floor in agony.

"I'm not a beaner, you piece of shit!" she shouted. She looked like she was going to kick him in the face.

A few of the Malibu Mafia took notice, but oddly, they didn't rush into his defense. I didn't understand that until I glanced back and noticed that Jonah and Christian were standing behind me and Isabella. They both looked like they meant business; and certainly Christian, who had been gaining bulk and filled out his rented tuxedo, so that his chest was bulging like a young Doc Savage, arms at his side in balled fists, made for an imposing figure. Jonah came forward then and stood Joey up and pulled him aside, and they had a quiet word over by the bar, the bar tender and servers suppressing smiles, and Joey still holding himself white-faced, groaning, and looking like he was going to puke.

"You don't have to defend me, Robbie," Isabella said. "I can take care of myself."

"I see that," I said. "Did your dad teach you that?"

"No, we have a girl's self-defense class up at Santa Anita."

"But I thought you disapproved of violence?"

"Nah, you're projecting. Kicking Nazis in the balls is a good idea just about any time."

"Joey's just a pig, try to ignore him," said Christian. "We all do, somehow."

"I don't like you, man!" yelled Joey at Christian, pointing at him from over at the bar.

"Likewise," he said.

I was genuinely surprised at Isabella. But the consensus in the room seemed to be in her favor and a lot of the guys were now laughing and smiling in our direction. If I had hit Joey, there would have been hell to pay, maybe even a police report. But Isa? No way. I don't know if Joey ever lived it down.

"Nice one, Isabella," said Felix, slapping her on the back as one would a boy. "You showed him."

"Yeah, that was well-placed," this from Fish, who had a slim, slip of girl beside him. She was wearing a chiffon floral gown and her hair had been done up beautifully, but her eyes were sallow. I thought she might have malaria. She looked a bit like Anne Frank in need of nourishment. Fish was holding her hand and she was smiling and funny and brave.

"You should have hit him harder, the damn Smurf Nazi," she said, and then they both laughed. I think they'd been into the champagne. The girl was very cute and perhaps more fishlike in the face than James but I never got her name.

It was cool to see James happy. His round glasses were shining and reflective in the sun that filtered down in the heavenly space of the atrium. For a moment, it seemed to me an angel sang. I realized I was glad we had spent time together working on the Yearbook, because James and I could have been good friends if I had tried to be one. He died of Tay-Sachs at only the age of 30.

Eventually Jonah came back with the now sorrowful Joey who said, "Sorry dudes!" and we shook hands and he said, mainly to Isabella, "Fine. We'll accept the beaners. But we don't. Want. The Irish!" Joey had quoted *Blazing Saddles* and everyone including Isabella laughed. I guess he wasn't so bad after all. Joey O'Dell was, you know, Irish.

We moved into the venue now and a server brought around flutes with tall stems and they had something bubbling inside and Isabella and I stood drinking from them and admiring the sunlight and the vines that grew on the walls, climbing up towards the sky like our spirits.

One of the guys, perhaps Jonah, now popped the cork on another bottle of bubbly and something happened that I could not have predicted, and was totally out of character for me and could only have occurred because I was now drunk: the Moet bottle's cork shot up high in my general direction from the other side of the atrium, and I reached out and caught it easily. The great circle of the cork's flight had been in contact with my Chi, my life-force. It was like a confirmation that things were meant to be. Everyone cheered.

But then Jonah made a toast. He said, "To all of us College-bound, and to Sutra, who is too good for it!" Everyone laughed, because I had been telling people for at least a month that I didn't want to go to University, that I wanted to learn from the Book of Life, I was too good to go to College, University was for suckers, etc., etc. I had gone all in on my plan, which was still secret, to go to India. But somehow I never managed to tell Isabella about it. She had been very busy, to be fair. But I didn't prepare her. She looked at me sharply for a minute and I had a sense of impending doom, like a kick to the balls was incoming.

I wasn't so far from wrong.

***

"What do you mean, you're not going to College?"

We were post-prom, and everything had more or less fallen apart. I never did figure out if Jonah had done his toast

entirely without malice, or if it had been carefully con-
ceived—premeditated murder, as it were—or if, maybe it
was just karma. Just fate. Probably the latter. It was impossible for me to impute Jonah with mean spirited behavior.
Sure, all is fair in love and war. But he was my friend.

"Are you going to answer me?" Isabella said.

"I'm sorry I didn't talk to you about this sooner."

"So that's it?"

"There's more. Are you willing to listen?"

It was about 10 p.m., and we should have been smooching
and I should have been copping a feel, at least, just like all
the rest of the guys were doing. But that was now totally
impossible. I knew Isabella.

"What happened was this," I said. "First of all, there's a
sense of the false in our lives. Don't you feel that?"

"I don't."

"Well, wait a while. Maybe you'll feel it. Anyway, I have
thought about this for a long time. It is not just a whimsical
lark. I need to do something other than schooling. I think
schooling is pretend. It's a game to make people fit into a
society that I don't even like. I don't belong. You know?
Kickshaw—I don't really belong there. I liked going and
all."

"And you enjoyed all the benefits!" she said.

"Yes. I did. I also started going to Ideas class."

"You've told me about it. About your precious Ram."

"Well, yeah, He's a good guy."

"And?"

"So Ram had one of his old students, Malcolm, come to
give a talk a few months back. Malcolm's father is a U.S.
Senator, Isa."

"Is that supposed to impress me? It's Privilege. You guys
are soaking in it like Palmolive."

"I think I taught you that expression, but fine. It's true.
Anyway, he gave up all that to go to India. He was looking
for a Master, a Guru, and eventually he found one."

"And you are going to take up with this guru? Is that it?"

"No. I don't think so. Not that one. But I want to find one. I want to go to India. India, Isa!"

"India," she smirked. "You are such an idiot."

"I know," I said. "It's true. I am an idiot. I'm not worthy of you."

For a minute she seemed mollified. But then she lashed out again. "If you think that's going to get you laid tonight, you're wrong. If you think I'll let you touch these," she said, hefting her breasts, "you're wrong."

"You sure have a mean streak. You get that from old Papa Erik Estrada?"

"You bastard."

We sat for a while, I think both of us trying to figure out how everything had suddenly collapsed. It was going so well.

"So tell me one thing, Isabella." I used her full name, which she didn't like much, but it was her true name. "Tell me one thing. Why is it so wrong for me to not go to University? I mean, what if it's just a year off or two? What does that matter?"

"The thing you don't understand, Robbie Sutra, the thing none of you Kickshaw bastards understand, is what it's like to be poor. What it's like to struggle. It all comes so fucking easy for you. But for someone like me. Just think of the strikes against me, the things I have to deal with: I'm a woman, that's strike one. I'm not white, I'm a beaner they say, that's strike two. And finally, I'm poor, my Dad is raising me alone, and he doesn't make enough to send me to college. I have to try and get a scholarship, I have to work my ass off, just to get to where you guys are with zero effort. It's not fair."

I didn't say anything.

"You seem to think that it's nothing, that it's worthless. This education thing. But you don't understand what it means to people like me. It's the difference between being a maid and having a decent career, a life."

"You're right," I said.

"It's not possible for you to understand."

"No, it's not."

We sat in silence for a while. I thought vaguely of Conchita, her big tits flopping in my dad's face, and how she said she laughed when Larry caught my dad with her. But maybe my dad had done that to himself. Maybe he had been a complete idiot. And I was the idiot's son.

We were outside the prom venue, there was a park a few blocks down, and more than one pair of Kickshaw couples were in that park. I had a sense of their amorous energies wafting through the night air. Thinking briefly of Conchita connected somehow to Isabella, who was in a whole different league but now claimed to be disadvantaged. I agreed with everything she said, but I didn't understand how it applied to me. I wanted to be free of the world that she said held her down, the world that we agreed punished her unfairly. Couldn't she see that? I was with her. I was on her side. But she wasn't on mine.

"We could have done it, tonight Robbie," she said. Her eyes looked dull in the light of the streetlamp. "I was ready. My dad doesn't like you, but I didn't care. I started taking the pill for this night, you bastard."

I didn't say anything to that. Inwardly I had a lot to say, but I didn't think any of it was good. And then I did something really stupid.

"So—I guess you'd better go find Jonah."

She looked at me. "What?"

"I've seen the polaroid. You and he together. When was that?"

"Oh, boy, Robbie, you sure are on a runaway train tonight."

"Come on, then, out with it."

"No."

"No? No talk? Fine." I did the unthinkable then, of course, as I am prone to do. I got up and started walking. I don't think Isabella expected that.

"Robbie? Where are you—where are you going!"

But I just kept walking.

"How do I get home?"

"Ask Jonah!" I yelled. I think the whole park could hear me.

***

So prom was a bust from my point of view. Christian seemed happy that night, but it was short-lived. I have not said much about Susan. Yes, Susan did go to the prom. She went stag, but she went. I saw her out of the corner of my eye drinking from a fluted glass. She was allowing herself a little bit of champagne, and I thought that was healthy. Everyone needs to let their hair down once in a while.

But I couldn't help noticing her eyes kept going to Christian. I did not think about this until a day or two later. I was drowning in my own emotions; it seemed like things were over with Isa. I had been a total asshole, a jerk of the highest order. Should I call her? Apologize? What? So that took up most of my attention. But a small part of me, the clinical part, the logical part, must have been working on it in my unconscious mind. I put a few things together in my head: the fact that Susan had decided to live in the Hermitage, which was where Christian was; the fact that she had met him early on in Lido; the showering she did, which everyone knew was happening in the middle of the night because she wanted privacy. She would have been alone and no one would have considered intruding. And then I remembered that when John Lennon died, she seemed touched, and not because she knew anything about John Lennon (she knew nothing), but because Christian seemed so sad. She asked me then about Lennon, even wanted to listen to *Imagine*, which I thought unusual. Christian was the connecting link. That night when we got drunk, the whisky, and then the shower running and running.

"Oh crap," I thought.

***

I didn't say anything to Christian. And there was no reason to think the year would end with their secret coming out. But Christian had his own troubles. He didn't get into his first or second choice schools, we learned. Emotionally, that would have been a strain.

"I guess it's Chico State for me!" he laughed. But I could see he was crushed. He "settled" for UC Santa Cruz, which was not exactly dog food, as far as I knew, and I told him so, but he didn't think his dad would be satisfied. And certainly not impressed.

And then there came a day when you could feel something was up. I went into the morning assembly and could hear a lot of noise, a lot of talk, and Master's shushing people, and the Headmaster came up to the front. "Let me have your attention, please. I'm sorry to say something happened last night that is a grave source of concern. There's a Discipline Committee meeting this morning, and I would appreciate it if everyone minded their own business. Please do not spread rumours. This is sensitive stuff."

"But what's happened?" This was a general question and not from any particular direction.

The Headmaster was grim. "A student has been caught having relations with another student."

There was an audible gasp.

"That's all I'm going to say about it. Everyone is to mind their own affairs, as I have said."

***

I hoped against hope it wasn't Christian, but when I went to check his room, he wasn't there. I knocked on Susan's door down the hall and got no answer either.

But then a funny thing happened. There was a knock on my door. Clint—Dean Charlie Stacks himself—stood framed in the doorway.

"Holy shit," I said in surprise. "You startled me."

"That's not very nice, Mister Gray. Come with me. You're needed to give testimony at the Discipline Committee."

***

"Mr. Gray, we have a report that boys have been meeting in the shower late at night in the Hermitage. Do you know something about that?" The Headmaster was asking the questions and I knew I had to be very careful. Christian was red-eyed, as if he had been crying. And Susan looked terrible. There were more Masters present, it seemed, than for Cadogan's DC—at least ten around the table. I couldn't believe they were doing this.

And Old Kickshaw was there, which I thought was concerning. I suspected he was dangerously befuddled.

"Well?" said the Headmaster.

"I do know something about that," I said.

There was considerable movement around the table.

"Go on," the Headmaster said.

"I would like to explain a few things. First of all, these are my friends. Are you really stupid enough to think I would say anything that would hurt them?"

"That is highly insubordinate, Mr. Gray," said Stacks.

"But also very commendable," replied Heinrich.

'Good old Heine,' I thought.

"I would like to not be interrupted, please. Thank-you. Now, secondly, some of you may or may not know, but Calvin, here, I realized early on, when we were Sophomores, that he was actually a she. Calvin is a boy on the outside, but a girl on the inside. I don't know how that is possible but I can only surmise it is the result of natural genetic variation in the brain. Brains are funny things. As we know from ancient cultures—Master Bosworth over there can tell you—ancient peoples understood this mix-up was possible. They even have a term for it: hermaphrodite.

"Calvin told me that his inner name, his true name, was Susan, and I've called her Susan for so long that I can't think of her in any other way. So I will do that.

"Susan is a Catholic. She is very devout. The one thing I know about her for sure, is that she would never do anything sinful or go against her religion. She and I got to be friends, of a sort, and I wanted to help her.

"And how did you 'help,' Mr. Gray?" said the Dean.

"Well, I thought she would benefit from reading *Stranger in a Strange Land*. It's about a human being who is raised by aliens and then has to go and live on earth. Everything is very difficult for him. I thought Susan might feel that way being the only black person on Campus.

"I also took her to see *Rocky Horror Picture Show*."

"Oh?" Said the Headmaster. "I didn't know that. When was this? Were you both on liberty?"

"You can check up on that yourself, sir. Dean Stacks keeps those records I'm sure. Or you can call my dad. He drove us and stayed and watched the film. He thought it was fantastic. So yes, of course we were on liberty."

"Why did you take Calvin—Susan—to see Rocky Horror?" said Martin quietly.

"Because I thought maybe if she saw transexuals, she would feel less alone. I thought, maybe, that she was a transexual. I was trying to help her find herself."

"And what happened?" said the Headmaster.

"Well, you can ask Susan yourself. But I think she hated it. As a good Catholic, Susan is opposed to extra-marital sex. Isn't that right, Susan?"

"Bless you, Robbie," she said.

"But he showers late at night!" exclaimed Old Kickshaw. "What is he hiding? What are you saying?"

"Susan wants privacy," I said. "Why is that so hard for you? If you were a girl at an all-boy's school, wouldn't you want some privacy for God's sake?"

This was too much for Old Kickshaw, who seemed to lose it. He was on his feet now. "I've heard enough!" he shouted. His hands opened and closed convulsively. I thought he might have an epileptic fit.

"Doctor Kickshaw, please," said the Headmaster. "Sit down."

Old Kickshaw's round head bobbed up and down furiously. "You think you can make fools of us all? Is that it? You think you can make a fool out of me?" He seemed to be directing his ire entirely at Susan.

She was cowering now, bent over with her thin arms raised to head height as if to fend off blows. "No, no sir, never!"

"You can't get away with behavior like this at Kickshaw! I will not allow my school to be turned into a—a den of homosexuals!" He sputtered and could not seem to find the right word to describe what he wanted to say. "Or whatever you are!"

The Headmaster now had come to his senses and intervened. "Please Doctor Kickshaw, stop. This must stop. You are badgering her. Besides, I am in charge of the Disciplinary Committee meetings."

"But I am still the school founder!" he exclaimed. "In extraordinary circumstances I can still make decisions. And this situation is intolerable." He pointed now at Susan. "He is not a she! Stop encouraging her—him—it!"

"Please, Harold," said Master Henler.

But Kickshaw was becoming more and more obstinate as he became more upset. "I will say what needs to be said. And I pay you, Scott, to look after the business-end of things. What goes on in the school, who goes to my school—is entirely my decision."

The Headmaster sighed. "Yes, Howard. But this is a very sensitive matter, a lot is at stake. The world is changing. America is changing. The school has to change with it."

"No!" Old Kickshaw was adamant. "I want this problem solved." He pointed now at Susan. "And we are going to settle this once and for all. You are going to undergo an examination. You will report to the Nurse, Mrs. Standish, at the infirmary at two o'clock today. Two o'clock. Sharp. If it is determined that you are in fact a girl, something I very much doubt, but if it is true, then you will be suspended and sent home. According to the school rules, Kickshaw Boarding School for Boys only accepts male students. And we will sincerely apologize to your parents for any confusion. But if the nurse determines you are a boy, well, then, you will have to be punished severely for trying to make fools of us. The Discipline Committee will reconvene tonight and decide what to do about you. You may be expelled anyway."

"You didn't let me finish," I said. But by then it didn't matter.

Susan left the Headmaster's Office in tears. I trailed after her. "Susan," I said. "Wait up."

"Robbie! I don't want to undergo an 'inspection.'"

"I know," I said. "Sit down for a minute."

We sat by the chapel, ironically, on the cold concrete step, and she looked cold and drained of life, like a leaden statue. "I wonder if this is how it feels to be dead," she said.

"Don't give up, Susan. Say your rosary, why don't you."

"You're right Robbie. I, I need to go to confession."

"Right. I wonder..."

I thought Martin Quinn might have an idea about that, and he answered his door when I knocked. "You are quite right, Robbie. And I even know the right person. Let me make a call."

***

Nurse Standish was very gentle when Susan opened the infirmary door. The little bell jingled. "Come in, my dear," she said. "Robbie, what are you doing here?"

"I'm just a friend, Mrs. Standish. I'll wait outside."

"No, Robbie can be here," Susan said. "I want him to be here with me."

"Hm," said the nurse. "You can sit out here, Robbie, or out by the smoking area, there are chairs out there, but you can't go in the exam room. Understood?"

"Of course," I said. "I'm just here for moral support."

"They made me come," Susan said. Her small hands were shaking. "The Headmaster and Doctor Kickshaw."

"I know, dear. Don't worry. Why don't we talk a little." She gestured and Susan sat down in a chair near the nurse's desk. "I understand you like to be called Susan?"

"Yes."

"That's all right. My name is Sarah Standish. I'm a registered nurse. You can call me Sarah."

"Yes, ma'am. Sarah."

"That's a very nice Saint Christopher's medal you have there."

"Thank-you."

"Are you a Catholic, Susan?"

"Yes, ma'am."

"Well, so am I. So we have that in common. The Headmaster was saying that you keep the Hours, is that true?"

"Yes, I always do."

"He says you also rise very early. So you even keep the vigil?"

"I like to keep myself in prayer in the night hours. It's a very quiet time, very good for meditation."

"And do you have a rosary?" asked the nurse.

"Of course. But I only use it in private. I don't want people to think I am vain, to have such a thing. It would look very pretentious here. No one else has one."

"Hmm. Yes. Susan, do you also get up early in the morning so you don't have to be seen bathing by the boys?"

Susan seemed a bit sheepish. "It's true."

"Is that because you are a girl?"

"It is not proper."

"Right. Well, I agree. A girl should not be bathing or showering with the boys. Susan, you understand what the Headmaster asked me to do?"

"Not exactly."

"Well, he asked me to give you a physical. I'm not a doctor, but I can certainly take a look at you and see if there is anything wrong that might be concerning. I also want to tell you that Doctor Kickshaw's ideas are very old-fashioned and absurd. If you don't want to do this, then we don't have to proceed. He has asked me to report on your physical health."

"I—I am healthy. I'm sure of it."

"Well, it is true that you are quite thin."

"Yes, ma'am."

"Do you fast? Are you fasting regularly?"

Susan didn't respond immediately. "Sometimes."

"Right." The nurse got her stethoscope and a blood pressure cuff. "Do you think I could take your blood pressure?"

"OK."

"Hmm...100 over 60. That's low. What have you eaten today?"

"Well, I had some toast. And a little juice."

"Nothing else all day?"

"No."

"Why don't we have some juice right now. Would you like that? Or perhaps some hot tea?"

"Juice, please."

The nurse went off to get some nourishment and it seemed that after Susan had consumed some orange juice and some crackers that she was in better spirits.

"Well, Susan. Now is the time to decide if you want to let me examine you."

"But what will you tell Doctor Kickshaw?" she said. "What will happen to me?"

"The reason I think you should let me examine you is I am sympathetic to your situation. But I have to tell Doctor Kickshaw and the Headmaster the truth."

"But what is the truth?"

"That is what I want to know."

"Sarah. Listen. I have the parts of a boy. On the outside I am a boy. But on the inside, in my innermost self, I am a girl. I know I am a girl. Robbie knows that; I told him a long time ago about it. It has always been like that. Even when I was very young, I knew my body was not right for me. God has made me different. Not in my body so much, but he has put a girl in a boy's body."

The nurse thought about that for a minute. "So you think a mistake has been made?"

"I used to. But I realized that I am supposed to be like this. I'm not sure if it is a punishment, or a blessing. But it is my cross to bear. I bear it every day, every hour."

"Yes, I understand. Let's go into the exam room."

After a while they came out.

"Don't worry, Susan," said the nurse. "Everything will work out. Do you know how I know that?"

"How?" said Susan.

"Because you are a Catholic. God will take care of us. You believe that don't you?"

"Yes ma'am." She seemed resigned to disaster.

"Robbie, would you please see that Susan lies down and has a rest in her room? Make sure she gets there."

"Of course," I said.

***

I was not invited to the evening session of the Disciplinary Committee, but I had my way of listening in on it.

"William," I said. "You are indeed a saint."

He smiled. "I'll get the David Bowie going."

***

"Nurse Standish," said the Headmaster, "before we have the accused students come into the meeting, can you please give us the results of your examination?"

"Yes Headmaster. Susan, as she likes to be called—"

Here Old Kickshaw interrupted. "Do you really have to use that name?"

"Yes, Doctor Kickshaw. I choose to do so. The student in question is about 17 or 18 years of age, very under-developed physically, with male sexual characteristics and male genitalia—"

"As I expected!" cried Kickshaw triumphantly.

"—But with clear evidence of malnourishment, apparently from fasting. The student also admitted to keeping the hours. For those who do not know, that is a series of prayer vigils throughout the day and deep into the night. She is mentally under great self-inflicted stress."

"What are you saying, Nurse Standish?" asked the Headmaster.

"I am saying that Susan, or Calvin if you wish, is beatific. In case you have not noticed, she has a stigmata on her right hand."

This produced considerable discussion around the table. The Headmaster let this go on for a while. "Let's stay on target here. Doctor Kickshaw, do you understand what the Nurse just said?"

"What, what, what?" said Kickshaw.

"The nurse just said the student is a very religious person, a devout Catholic, and possibly a saint. Are you really willing to delve into this area?"

"But what do you mean? Are you trying to say she didn't do anything wrong? I was told she was caught having sexual relations with a student in the shower. That doesn't sound like a religious devotee to me!"

"All right then. I think we need to talk as a group how to proceed with this and we need to proceed very carefully, very delicately. The reputation of the school is at stake."

I could hear Stacks clear his throat. "It's obvious to me," said the Dean, "that they both need to be expelled immediately. We need to quash homosexual activity. That's all there is to it."

"I would like to point out," said Martin, "that I have been in contact with Susan's—"

"—Calvin's," interrupted Old Kickshaw.

"With Calvin's Confessor. Father Ferapont. He helped identify the student in question as a remarkable person, someone who would grace this school."

"Hmph," grunted Kickshaw.

"—And he's coming to the school today."

"What?" said Kickshaw.

"That is correct, Harold," said the Headmaster. "I have approved his presence."

"But what is his purpose?" shouted Kickshaw.

"He is visiting in his religious capacity. I thought it would calm the student in question. And he may be able to help us avoid a terrible outcome to this—situation."

Kickshaw seemed skeptical. "Well, Let us hope so."

"We must now return to the problem at hand," said the Headmaster. "Are we agreed, if inappropriate sexual behavior has occurred, what we will do about it?"

"Has there been an enumeration of the facts? Or is this merely to be a decision based on hearsay? What is the evidence?" Asked Nurse Standish.

"We have the report of Mister Joseph O'Dell, who asserts he saw Calvin and Christian in the shower together. He asserts this has happened repeatedly, but he only now has come forward."

"And did he say what they were doing? It is a group shower. Perhaps they were simply bathing?" asked Master Henler. Martin seemed to chuckle at this.

"According to Mr. O'Dell, they were mutually masturbating. He claims he has witnessed other acts but does not want to go into detail."

"But is this really a matter for the Disciplinary Committee?" asked Master Henler. "Perhaps the right first step is for the advisors of those students to work with them on the expected behavior in the dorms. Why has this risen to the level of expulsion?"

"Because it must!" demanded Old Kickshaw.

"And why is that, Harold," asked Nurse Standish.

"Because—because it is homosexual!"

"Homosexuality," said Martin, "is not a crime in the State of California, Doctor Kickshaw. It became legal in 1976."

"But surely the school rules forbid it!"

"I'm not so sure, Harold," said the Headmaster. "I warned you this course of action might lead to trouble. There are technical legal issues here, things for the board of trustees to consider, and we do not need a lawsuit. There is nothing specific in the school charter, or in the rule book, that bans two boys being in love. We do not need to become a *cause célèbre*. We do not need the publicity."

"Well, I for one will not have it."

It seemed Kickshaw was not willing to change his mind. I had a sense he was an obstinate old fool. I wondered if any of the other Masters shared my opinion.

The headmaster sighed. "If that is so, then let the consequences be on your head."

"It is my school, after all," Old Kickshaw asserted. "Bring in the boys! We will ask them directly. There is no other way."

"I want to go on the record, that this is wrong, Harold," said the nurse. "It may impact the mental well-being of one or both students."

"Bring them in!" demanded Kickshaw.

***

"I don't know if I can listen to any more of this, William," I said.

"Is it not going well?"

"It's not. I feel like throwing a Molotov cocktail into the meeting."

But William was wise, smarter than I was. "Try to record some of the more egregious statements. We can complain."

"To whom?" I said.

"To the press, of course. I'm sure Kickshaw would hate bad press—it could potentially ruin the school."

And so I began to make some notes.

***

"Mister Benoit, we have a report that you were caught engaging in lewd sexual activity in the shower. Do you deny it?"

Christian did not answer for a time. "What is the definition of lewd?"

"Oh come now," said the Headmaster. "Surely we don't need a dictionary."

"I disagree," said Master Henler. "If you are going to use a word, the student has a right to know the precise meaning. I myself do not know the meaning of this word. I know, when I was young, that the Nazis said many things about the Jews, and also artists and malcontents, and among those was the statement that they were lewd. Tell us the definition of this word."

It seemed that the Headmaster was taken aback by the ferocity of the Physics Master's statement. But in a moment he said, "Fine. That is reasonable. I have the Oxford English Dictionary here. Let me see. *Lewd. An adjective that means referring to or involving sex in a rude or offensive way.*"

"Well then I can answer that question and say I have never done anything involving sex that was rude or offensive. Never."

'Good for you, Christian,' I thought.

"But did you have sex in that shower at 2 a.m. or not!" Old Kickshaw had become belligerent. I imagined he was probably starting to sunset. "Answer me, young man!"

"I, I cannot lie. I touched Susan—I touched her."

"And did she touch you? Did she?"

"Yes." Christian seemed to be weeping.

"You see!" shouted Kickshaw, as if he had won a prize.

"And what about you, Susan, or Calvin, or whatever you wish to be called? Did you touch this fine young man? Did you instigate this? Are you the source of all this trouble?"

Susan seemed terrified. She did not answer.

"Answer me!" shouted Kickshaw.

"I did not do anything except give love and receive love. We are human beings and you have decided to insert yourself into something private, something personal, between—between two young people. Two people who care about each other. That is wrong."

"But what you did, what you did in the shower, in the middle of the night—that is a mortal sin in your religion, is it not?"

"I, I think that is a matter for my confessor and not for you," Susan said quietly.

"This cannot go on any further," said Master Henler. "I will not allow it."

"There is no need to go further," said Stacks. "It is obvious we must now vote. The two students should wait outside for our result."

I heard chairs move as Susan and Christian departed. Christian was clearly still crying. Susan seemed strangely composed.

There was silence for a while, as the room seemed to move into a phase of contemplation, perhaps even regret. Finally the Headmaster spoke. "We will now vote on whether Christian Benoit and Calvin Tyrone Gay—that is his legal name—are to be expelled from Kickshaw School for Boys. Because I suspect this is likely to be the subject of a lawsuit, I will be recording the vote. On the subject of ex-pulsion, do you recommend expulsion? Dean Stacks?"

"Yes."

"For both boys?"

"Yes."

"Master Henler, do you recommend expulsion?"

"No."

"Master Quinn, do you recommend expulsion?"

"No."

"Master Remus?"

"Yes."

"For both boys?"

"Yes."

And so on down the room. The Headmaster duly wrote down the responses.

"Very well, the result is as follows—"

Kickshaw let out a shrill cry. "But what about me?"

"You are not a voting member of the Disciplinary Com-mittee."

"Oh," said Kickshaw. "Well, I won't argue that now. Go on. What is the result?"

The headmaster was making meticulous tick marks. "Let me re-count this. Yes, it seems to be a tie, there are seven votes for expulsion, and seven against. I am the tie-breaker. And I vote for—"

At that moment, there was a knock, and the door opened. It was Christian.

"Mr. Benoit, we are not yet completed in our delibera-tions!" shouted Kickshaw.

"What is it, Christian?" said the Headmaster.

"I think you should know that Susan has left. I think you should know that I am concerned. I think you should know that she is capable of doing self-harm. It has happened be-fore. If you had taken the time to ask the right questions, you would know it."

At that moment, several things happened at once. I could hear multiple chairs screeching, and voices all talking at once. But Christian kept on speaking. His voice sounded hollow, almost mechanical. "I think you should know that you have treated one of your students very poorly, without regard to mental health. You have done something criminal here...you are monsters...!"

But the masters were already now up and moving, and they pushed past him. Eventually it seemed no one remained except Christian and Old Kickshaw himself in the room. It was silent. The old man seemed confused.

"Mister Benoit? What did you say? What happened? I did not quite—"

I could not tell for sure, but it seemed Christian turned around and walked out without answering.

PART TWELVE, SAINT SUSAN — *(Backstory)*

A god made a man out of clay,
And told him to work hard all day,
But along came a tease,
And suggested he ease,
His struggles and worries her way.

Father Ferapont hefted the heavy wooden cross that was his regular burden on Sundays after Mass. It made him look a bit like a madman to wander the streets of Watts, in South Central Los Angeles, carrying and sometimes even dragging this huge cross; but this did not bother him. In fact, when people drove by and laughed, or shouted obscenities, or threw bottles and trash, he would smile with pleasure. The Penitence Walk, as he called it, often included parishioners from Saint Bartholomew's, his church. Sometimes someone might walk behind him in prayer, or sometimes they would ask to shoulder the cross for a stretch as he walked with them. For Ferapont, the cross was a way to bring a certain amount of drama and immediacy to his mission, and the community often responded well once they understood that he was there for all, black and white and brown, with no distinction or prejudice.

Ferapont was a Capuchin, which means, in essence, that he was a Catholic Priest in an order similar to the Franciscans (those who follow the teachings of Saint Francis). Except Ferapont's order was more extreme, an order intent on poverty, service, connection to nature and worship through God's creatures; austerity, and absolute renunciation, all in pursuit of Christ. To this end Ferapont wore a plain brown tunic the color of coffee mixed with cream, bound by a single cord of rope rather than a belt, and sandals. The sandals were, perhaps, a kind of acceptance of life in California and his connection to place. Most of the contemporary Capuchins wore shoes; but here sandals struck the right chord.

On this morning he dragged the heavy wooden cross of polished Oak using his shoulders to heft it and slowly walked South in the direction of the Watts Towers, the wonderful, inexplicable craft of Simon Rodia that stood visible from afar. Those towers were in truth called *Nuestro Pueblo* (the name given by Rodia), which in Spanish means "Our Town," and Ferapont was grateful that his mission always benefited by being able to explain, even to the most hardened gang-banger, that Watts was "our town," a town for everyone. "Simon Rodia said so. Everyone in Watts is together, my friends," he liked to say. "We are brothers and sisters, black and brown and white. And here we all are in the thick of things. We have to make the best of it, together."

Watts was a tough gig. Ferapont defied police there on several occasions when tensions and even gunfire broke out in years past; he was respected by Black and Latino alike for his courage in taking up the struggle for peace and justice against the LAPD. He was a young man, a Vietnam Vet, and this usually did mean something to the cops. The infamous riots of 1965 were before his time; but the stain of the riots and the daily brutality of the LAPD, visible to all in the form of blood and bullet holes, were most certainly not. Sometimes it did not matter that he was white or a priest or a veteran. Sometimes the cops mistreated everyone more or less equally. It was their own kind of equality.

At this moment he was also walking the streets with a distinct purpose: he was looking for someone who needed him. He was not sure who he was looking for, exactly, but there was a message from a parishioner, and a description: a boy, very thin and fragile looking, perhaps 13 or 14 years of age. "He's been kicked out of the house by his father, apparently," reported a neighbour and parishioner. "I don't think he will last too long on the street; he looks like a leaf blown by the wind."

Ferapont thought perhaps the child would gravitate towards the towers—many people in distress did, just naturally. The towers were like a spiritual magnet or perhaps an invitation to carnival, depending on personality type. Of course, those who lived nearby rapidly forgot the marvel in their midst or even despised it. That was how human nature worked, he knew.

'There,' he said to himself. He saw a recumbent figure loitering, thrashing almost in agony, under some cardboard boxes near a dumpster. Ferapont leaned the heavy cross against the fence of the Watts Towers enclosure and stretched his arms and back for a moment to rest. Then he approached, his arms raised, hands open and lifted, and he made sure that he smiled. 'It is important to always smile when encountering the poor and wretched. Not the fool's smile, but a smile of calm, of peace, and friendship.' Thus he had been taught.

"Hello, little friend," he said. "Are you OK under there?"

The boy peeked out unseeing from behind the cardboard. He looked weak. "I'm thirsty," the boy said.

The priest gasped. He could see the teen's bloody right hand. There was a ten-penny nail driven through the palm. "You're hurt!" he cried out.

The boy did not answer immediately. Ferapont pulled back the cardboard and began to cry.

"He couldn't have done it himself," the ER doctor was saying.

"So it was a crime," said Ferapont.

"I'd say. A horrific one. But the kid isn't talking."

"May I see him?"

"He's on IV fluids. He was dehydrated. It's probably OK. Just a few minutes, then? The PD will be down pretty soon."

"Yes, thank you, Doctor."

Ferapont went over to the gurney where the boy was resting. "Hello again."

The boy gave him a weak smile.

"Feel like talking at all? No? Well, they're going to need to at least know your name and who to contact."

"I'd rather not say."

"I think the police aren't going to take no for an answer. They'll want to know how that happened." Ferapont gestured to the boy's hand. "I'd kind of like to know myself."

"I—I did it to myself."

"I see." Ferapont paused and then spoke more quietly. "The doctor thinks that would be very difficult."

The boy didn't say anything. "It—it was."

"Are you Catholic?"

"Yes."

"Hmm. Would you like me to hear your confession?"

The boy seemed incredulous. "What, you mean right here?"

"I can close this drape." Ferapont pulled the curtain that stood near so that they had slightly more privacy. "Do not be shy. I have given absolution many times in a war zone, in Vietnam, and here, also, in the war zone that is Watts. ...There we are. You know I'm a priest, right? I am ready to hear your confession."

"Bless me Father, for I have sinned. It has been a few weeks since my last confession. I drove a nail into my hand because I wanted to feel Christ's agony. I am sure that is a sin somehow. Also, I spoke back to my father and will not obey him."

"Oh? What did he ask of you?"

"He wanted me to give a blow job to one of his customers. He's a pimp, you see, my father. He says I'm old enough to work. It's summertime, after all."

"I don't see any sin in refusing to perform a sexual act."

At that moment a cop peeked in through the curtain. He saw the priest, then, and closed the curtain as Ferapont gestured him to step back.

But the boy was now spooked. "You won't tell the cop, will you? About my dad?"

"They cannot compel me to tell anything. But it may be in your interest if I do. What's your name?"

"Calvin Tyrone Gay," the boy said, slowly.

"Calvin, have you any other sins to confess?"

"I refused to do what my father told me. That must be a sin, isn't it?"

"You did not Honor your father. I can see how that disturbs you. Very well, say Five Our Fathers and Five Hail Mary's."

"Yes, Father. I—I cannot move my arm to cross myself."

"I will do it for you, then. There. Now give thanks to the Lord, for he is good."

"He is good."

"Now rest, Calvin. I absolve you. I absolve you in the name of our Lord, Jesus Christ."

"Thank you, Father."

Ferapont paused for a moment, thinking.

"Calvin?"

The boy opened his eyes. He had closed them and now seemed afraid of a new burden. "Yes, Father?"

"Please do not carry out any penance, such as you have done with the nail, without consulting me first. I am your confessor now; I want to guide you. Do you accept me as your spiritual guide and counselor, in His Name?"

"Yes Father. That is kind of you. I understand everything now. He has sent you."

"It is kind of you to accept. And yes, I am to service all God's children if I can. When you are better, I want you to come to Saint Bartholomew's. We will talk more."

"It is clear to me you bring a message. I hear and I obey. It is His Will."

Ferapont did not think much about this statement at the time. Outside he spoke with the waiting cop. "His name is

Calvin Gay. He says his father asked him to prostitute him-self and he did not do it but then punished himself for not obeying."

"Sounds like a nut job."

"Don't be hard on him, please."

"I'll have to speak to him."

"Be gentle. This is a very fragile soul. I have an idea how to help him. And by the way, I'm 100% sure he would never implicate his father or bring charges."

"One of those, huh?"

"Yes. One of those."

Later that day Ferapont made a phone call to a friend up the coast. A brother in arms.

"...So you see, Martin, he might be a good candidate for Kickshaw. He's small in stature, I thought he might be only 13 or 14, but according to the PD he's completed 9th grade. He could go in as a Sophomore."

"It will be hard-sell to Old Kickshaw. But he likes me. I'll talk to Terry Hawk in Admissions. You remember him?"

"I remember him answering his door with a bottle of Vodka in his hand and taking a big swig when I needed Ge-ometry help."

"That's about right. But he's back together now with the Missus. And everyone says he's good at raising money."

"Yes, money. We had our moment in the sun up there, didn't we?"

"And raised plenty of hell. But I suppose that's no longer in your line."

"Well, Watts is not exactly a heaven on earth. But we do what we can."

"Peace be with you, Father."

"And with you, dear friend."

FINALE — 'A Very Memorable Yearbook'

The end of the day is all gloom,
With a boy and a girl in a room,
But after the rain,
There's a dull, aching pain,
And there's nothing to eat but the poon.

I figured Susan would go to the Chapel to pray. The wide-arched building full of stained glass was unlocked, but it was dark inside. I pulled on one of the big wooden doors and it opened wide.

"Susan?" I called out.

But there was no answer.

As I was coming out, I saw Martin running towards me. With him was another man who seemed to be wearing a dress.

"Robbie?"

"I thought she might be here," I said.

"That was a good guess. But no luck?"

"No."

"Robbie, this is Father Ferapont. He's a friend of mine; we fought together in Vietnam. He knows Susan."

"Hello," I said. "I think I've heard her speak of you. We need to find her quickly, Martin."

"I know," he said. Martin did not seem surprised that I knew Susan was missing, nor did he ask how I had got my information. "Where do you think we should look next?"

"Well, who else is looking?"

"We have teachers going through the dorms and the grounds. Father Ferapont and I were just in the Hermitage. Christian is in his room, but not Susan."

"Do you have an idea?" said Ferapont.

"I have," I said. "Come with me."

We hurried across campus to the Rayburn Theater. "Master Henler would have been through here, Robbie," said Martin.

"Not where we're going," I said. We walked across the big open space where we had morning assembly, and I led them up the stairs on the side, and then across a catwalk. Suddenly I heard a cry of pain. It started out low but gained in force, as if someone were tearing themselves apart.

"Something's happening, Robbie!" shouted Martin. "But where is she?"

We reached the top floor of the theater, the area where the lights and curtains hung, and I pointed to the crawl space where the false door was hidden. "Stay here for a minute," I said. I crawled into the void and found the hidden panel by feel. I called out, but quietly. "Susan?" I said. "It's Robbie. Can I come in?"

After a while I heard a small voice. "Come in, Robbie."

I opened the panel and set it to one side. Inside the hidden room, I could see candlelight glimmer. "I'm coming in," I said. It was always tough to get into that space; I never knew how Christian got a mattress in there. I plopped down through the hole a few feet onto the padding of the mattress and let out a startled cry. She was holding herself in a posture of anguish, like something out of a horror movie.

"Susan?" I said.

"Don't look, Robbie."

"Are you alright?"

"Don't look. I, I did something."

"We heard a scream."

"Is Christian alright?" she said. "What happened with the DC? Did he get expelled?"

"I don't know, Susan." I could see blood on the mattress. "Are you bleeding?" I said.

"Don't look."

"I have to." Then I realized what she had done. Christian had left some tools up in the space—he was always working on it, secure in the knowledge no one knew about the hidden access—and she had found a hammer and some large nails. There was a nail projecting through her left palm, and blood on the hammer, on her hands, and on her face.

"Susan, did you do that to yourself?"

"I had to, Robbie. Dr. Kickshaw was right. I sinned. Christian, it was all my fault. My vanity, to shower at night..."

She was gulping for air now, obviously in pain. She looked about to pass out. "Kickshaw...gave me a message, as cruel as it was. I had to accept it."

"I heard what he said. It really pissed me off."

"You heard?"

"Yes. I was listening."

"But how? Oh—yes, you are my angel... My sweet friend— the only one who tried to be my friend...somehow you knew..."

Martin's head now projected into the room through the small entrance. "Susan?" He said.

"I'm sorry, Martin, don't look."

"Father Ferapont is here, Susan."

"Father Ferapont?" she said. Her voice rose. I interpreted that as a sign of hope.

"I'm here, Susan," he said. "It will be alright. Please, let us get you out."

***

I didn't understand why Susan had decided to drive a tenpenny nail into her palm, but I supposed it had something to do with Jesus, with suffering, and with the need to punish herself for doing whatever it was she had been doing with Christian, night after night, in the dark. But Father Ferapont disagreed.

"She is beatific, Robbie. That means she feels such a close connection to our Lord Jesus Christ, that she experiences his pain, and must also relive his wounds. When she does that, she feels a closer connection to God."

"But, well, that sounds crazy."

"Perhaps," he said. "Perhaps not. Sometimes life is a mystery. It's not always for us to solve. I'm going with her in the ambulance down to the hospital. Do you want to come too?"

"No," I said. "I think you have things under control. You can do, you know, do your stuff."

He smiled. "Yes. Don't worry, I will do my stuff."

"I need to find Christian," I said. "He would want to know what happened."

"That's a good idea. With all this focus on Susan, Christian is probably suffering terribly. I will speak to the school on his behalf; ask for mercy."

***

I went down to the Hermitage and stopped to wash my hands in the shared bathroom. I looked over at the shower room, now dark and cold, and apparently harmless. I was not sure I could ever shower in there again.

I knocked gently on Christian's door. "Christian?" I said. "It's me, Robbie." But there was no answer. I thought maybe he was sleeping. I went to my room and sat on the bed, but there was a note on my dresser. My heart sank. 'Oh no,' I thought. I reached over and picked up the paper, which was labelled 'Robbie.' The note read:

Hey dude,

Sorry about things. It's a good idea not to go into my room right now. I've put my stash and a few incriminating items under your bed. I hope you don't mind. I guess I won't be needing them, so, consider them yours.

In my room, there is a note to my father. I don't think I could face him after this, which is why I am checking out of Hotel California. There is also a note to the headmaster. I take responsibility for what happened. Susan did not instigate things. I did. She is not to blame. She is definitely a girl; she just has boy equipment. So I'm not gay. At least I don't think so. We did not do anything weird or gross. It was all very loving.

You are a good friend, Robbie. I love you like a brother. Please tell everyone that I said goodbye.

Your friend,
Christian Benoit.

I jumped up and ran to his room. The door was locked. I ran down the hall and up the stairs, and pounded on Franklin Bright's door, but there was no answer. I ran, then, towards the offices. The first person I saw was the Headmaster. He was talking to Nurse Standish.

"Headmaster!" I yelled. "It's Christian! Get his room key!" He seemed to understand. I slumped down to my knees and sobbed. I had a pretty good idea what Christian had done but I thought he might still be alive.

It took what seemed like an hour, but eventually Stacks emerged from his office along with the headmaster. Stacks may have thought I was joking, he did not seem very serious; but the Headmaster understood. They hurried past me towards the dorm. Meanwhile Nurse Standish had come over and slumped down beside me on the grass.

"What's happened, Robbie?"

"I think Christian has killed himself. He left a note." I took Christian's note out of my pocket. It was already a crumpled ball; it seemed so small in my hand.

"Oh no," she said. She scanned the note quickly. "Oh my God!"

***

So that was how things turned out. I had to talk to police and there were some grisly details. Christian's father came to the school; there were angry renunciations and yelling from the distant office rooms that I had so recently been in. And there was a funeral somewhere but I wasn't invited, I think they took his body back to Palo Alto. I didn't want to know. I was only interested in the living Christian, who was always so filled with life and caring and vitality. His remains were of no consequence to me. I imagined he would be quickly reincarnated, perhaps as a whale or a lion or a cobra. He was a champion and a demigod as far as I was concerned, that never wavered.

It was about two weeks before the end of the school year, and you might figure they would end the school year early or something humane, but they didn't. And that left time for a few 'final outcomes,' as they say.

There were big changes at the school eventually. The very next year, in the Fall of 1982, girls flowered on campus. Kickshaw became co-ed. It was just a few at first, but more came later. That change, people said, was long overdue. But I guess no one sees that until something bad happens. Then it all seems obvious.

One positive was that I was able to read Christian's note aloud in the morning assembly. I wanted to make sure everyone knew the truth, and not some bullshit cooked up by the school. Christian had been hounded to death by the Discipline Committee. The headmaster didn't want me reading the note, but Martin stood up for me.

"He needs to read it, Headmaster. I have seen the note. There is nothing in it but the truth."

Another positive was that Father Ferapont reported Susan was going to be alright. She would not be returning to the school, but he was going to make sure she found the support she needed.

"I have heard her confession, and she has been absolved."

"That's pretty cool. I wish that worked for everything."

"Well, Robbie, it does. Maybe you should try it."

I laughed. "You guys, always proselytizing."

However, my progress on recovery from the shock of losing Christian was shattered when the yearbook boxes were finally opened. It was about two weeks later, a day or two before graduation.

The first inkling of something explosive about the yearbook was the laughter and derision of the various students who received their copy. A line had formed outside the Alumni Office (they were handling the distribution) but it soon became clear that something was wrong. I didn't know about the commotion until lunch.

"Sutra you pud! You're in for it now, my man!" said Cadogan.

"What?"

"This yearbook!"

"What about it?"

"Well, it's crazy. I mean, it's art and all, but the whole thing is a big collage. Page after page of crazy mashups. And then the limericks..."

"Yeah," I said, smiling. "I wrote those. Funny, huh?"

"They're funny as hell, but something tells me they aren't going to go over too well with you-know-who."

I thought Cadogan was exaggerating, that most of the guys would love what we had done. But actually, the general response was pretty bad. In fact, a crowd soon gathered around me to complain. The only person who seemed receptive was William.

"This is great man, I love it! My page is hilarious! But, well, you may need to keep your head down."

Then we heard shouting over the intercom. "Mr. Gray! Mr. Robert Gray! Report to Dean Stacks' Office immediately."

I didn't feel like 'reporting to the Dean's Office,' so I walked the opposite direction. 'Bastard,' I thought. I went to my room and decided I was done. Done with the whole place. Just done. 'Fuck 'em.'

I took out Christian's bong from its hiding place and filled the bowl. Lit up right in my room. Ah, it felt good! I thought about my friend, and how I was the survivor. That seemed kind of bogus. Christian, I thought, was the much better man. I thought about Obie Blackmore and how he had floundered into disaster once his partner in crime was gone.

"Suicide!" I thought. Well, I wasn't quite that brave. But I was feeling self-destructive.

"Fuck'em," I said again as I hit the bong hard. It was the Dragon bong, and I could never look at it without thinking of our Den on the hillside. The base was cracked. Christian had tearfully recovered it from the wreckage. Now he was gone.

There was a knock at the door that sounded a bit like Fate; you know, the "da-da-da-DA". And I opened it. "Ugh," I said. It was Dean Stacks. Old Clint Eastwood himself, in the flesh, with the twitch and the branded smile burned even harder in place than usual. I blew smoke at him.

"Mister Gray," he said. "Well, well, well. It is as I suspected. Let's have a little talk, shall we?"

"Your place or mine?"

"Get moving!"

***

I was sitting slumped over in his office a few minutes later. I was flat-out busted and we both knew it. He basically dragged me by the collar. He was enjoying himself immensely.

"Mister Gray, it seems to me you don't want to be at Kickshaw anymore. You don't want to follow the rules, you never did. But now, seeing how things are, you're just over it."

"You have summed things up admirably, Dean Stacks."

He was smiling again, but his left eye was twitching. I'd seen that before. "Let me make a suggestion. I can give you your diploma right now, and you are done. Really done. But you can't go to the graduation ceremony. You take this piece of paper—" and yes, it seemed to be my actual high school diploma, he held it up. "You take this now, and be out of here and off campus by tomorrow morning."

"Or?" I said.

"Or, we have to go through the motions of another Disciplinary Committee Hearing. This time, just for you. You've never had the pleasure, have you?"

"Oh, but I have a good idea what goes on."

"It's not much fun."

"No, I don't imagine it would be."

Stacks looked at me, his left eye almost closed. "What's your decision?"

"I'll take the diploma of course. I could care less about your bullshit graduation ceremony."

I could see his teeth now. "That's good. Very good. Well then. Here you are," and he handed over the precious piece of paper. Presumably he had it ready and had planned out this whole scene. But I didn't care.

"Thanks for making the right decision," he said. "You never did belong here, did you? Well, we won't have to see you or your fag father on this campus ever again."

My mouth dropped open. "You sure have found yourself a home, Clint. I bet you love all this. But what does the wife think about it?"

"Get out!" he shouted.

***

I was pretty much in hiding, due to the yearbook thing, and I passed a restless night with the shades drawn on the windows to my room. I dreamed of Christian with nails through both of his hands, and Susan turned into a real girl with big breasts and a vagina. But the vagina was in the wrong place. She looked a bit like Conchita, but younger. Gradually she changed into a version of Isabella yelling at me, and I woke up feeling miserable and just a little sorry for myself.

The truth, I realized, was that I was peeved with Christian: after all my work with Susan, after everything I did, Susan chose Christian over me. I never got any hand jobs or late-night showers or hide-away kisses. Hell, I didn't even get the much-lauded prom pussy from a Bonafide girl, which should have been *de rigueur*. No. Me? I had lost out to another jock, maybe two if you included Jonah. But at least I was free. It was done. No one was saved, apparently, like in *Eleanor Rigby*, except maybe Susan, but she was gone, too.

So fuck it, I decided I'd smoke a celebratory joint, right out on my room's back deck. I mean, what could they do to me now? I had graduated. I had my diploma. There it was, laying on my desk, the Headmaster's tidy signature in black ink and everything. I was free of their rules, their bullshit.

No joint ever tasted so good. I wasn't much for joints; they were really only for sharing. But I thought, I'm sharing this one with Christian. And Susan. We had never gotten high, the three of us, I wondered how she would react. Probably she would giggle. 'This joint is for you, Saint Susan, and all your kind. May it soothe your spirits, may it soothe your mind.'

I thought about Christian's father, who was now revealed as nothing more than a talking asshole. And in fact he reminded me of the talking asshole from *The Wall*. That had been pretty hard to take on acid (the acid had been Christian's idea) but the reality of Benoit senior was not much better.

"I knew he would never amount to much," he rasped. "He was too much like his mother. He couldn't even get into a decent school. And it looks like you and some others helped him to crash and burn."

"You've been listening to the school, I guess."

"You're that Robbie kid, right? The Dean doesn't rate you very highly."

I laughed. "I guess that feeling is mutual."

"And who is this Ghetto girl? This transvestite?"

I just shook my head at him.

"Get a haircut, kid!"

We had nothing more to say to each other, and he waved his hand dismissively and drove away. I watched the dust settle as his Cadillac roared off down Paradise Alley, temple now of broken dreams. The trees didn't seem offended by his exhaust. But I was.

"Who was that?" said William.

"A jerk," I said. "Christian would have been alive except for that old fart and his master's from Harvard Business School. Expectations."

So yeah, parents just really sucked sometimes. And then I thought about his mother, who I tried to talk to on the phone a few days after Christian died, but she didn't seem too interested.

"How did you get this number?" she said.

"I looked it up in the phone book."

"Well, don't call here. Talk to his father. I haven't seen Christian or his brother in ten years." What a bitch.

So I sat and basked in the sun blowing smoke like a boss. A free man. Someone, a freshman, I think, walked by gawking. It was late May and the summer was coming on strong. And it was still California. It was fucking glorious. And I was good and stoned. In a little while I'd pack up the van with my meagre possessions and drive off into the sunset.

I wasn't too sure about the immediate future, to be honest. My dad was not exactly happy with me. He had changed the locks, I found, the last time I tried to go 'home.' It was a bit of a shock and I was even angry for a while. But then he was pretty torched about the whole 'India' thing. Probably that was fair. He just needed a few hand jobs from Conchita and he'd calm down, I figured. I found myself wishing I had stolen his Rolex. The thought had never oc-curred to me that he would cut me off.

Then I saw what I thought at first was an apparition.

"Robbie?"

"Mom?" I said. "Mom? Is that you?" I got up out of my lawn chair and fell backwards. I was still pretty high. I guess I wasn't certain if this was a dream. "What are you doing here?"

She had come up the narrow path behind the Hermitage to the back door of my now mostly empty room. "They said to come this way."

"But is it really you?"

"I came to see my son's graduation, of course. You didn't think I was going to miss that, did you?"

I felt kind of defeated. "Hi, Mom," I finally said.

She reached out and gave me a hug.

"Son, you smell a bit like wacky weed. And you need a haircut."

"Yeah," I said.

"Are you all right? They said your friend killed himself."

"He did."

"I'm so sorry, Robbie."

"It's a long story, Ma." It felt really good to see her, I was overwhelmed now. We had a minute. I didn't realize how much I missed her. "I kind of screwed up," I said.

She looked into my room and saw the last of my bags. "You're leaving already?"

"Yeah, mom. I got kicked out of school, more or less."

"But today is graduation day. How could you get kicked out?"

"It's a long story, but basically the Dean told me I could leave—he gave me my diploma." I went into my room and brought it out for her to see. "See? But he said I couldn't go to the Ceremony if I took the diploma. He said I wasn't wanted. That I should leave before it starts. I'm done."

"But what did you do?"

"Oh, a lot of things."

"Hm." She wasn't too convinced. "I think I need to have a talk with this Dean. Where is he?"

"It's not going to do any good, Ma."

"Oh? Well, we'll just see about that! Come on."

I didn't exactly look forward to meeting up with Clint at that moment, but my mother had appeared out of nowhere like a Deva and suddenly we were walking on air. It was like entering the spirit realm or taking Ayahuasca. Something out of Carlos Castaneda. "So, where's Sam and the kids?" I asked casually. I thought more ghosts from my past might materialize at any minute.

"It's just me, Robbie."

"I see."

It was a short walk to the Dean's Office; as I have described, it was in that lower section of the High House/Lido complex where so much of my early days at Kickshaw had been spent. It seemed like such a long time ago and in a galaxy far, far away.

I tentatively opened the door to the Dean's Office and said, "hello?" and my mother pushed by me. I could see Clint at his desk in the office around the corner from reception squinting. By chance, Old Kickshaw was there, his back to us, apparently having a chat with Clint. "Dean Stacks?" I said.

The two men stopped talking, and Old Kickshaw swiveled around. "Mister Gray," he said, and then he noticed my mother behind me. His face changed.

"I'm Robbie's mother," she announced.

"A very good morning, ma'am," said Kickshaw.

Stacks was smiling too, at least initially.

"Not from where I'm standing," she said. "I understand this man—she pointed at Stacks—has barred my son from attending the Graduation Ceremony. I came all the way from Florida to see him graduate. What on earth are you playing at?" My mother directed herself mainly at Kickshaw, who was somewhat at a loss. Possibly he did not even know the situation. It was Stacks who answered.

353 DAVID R. SMITH

"Your son has shown a unique unwillingness to follow the rules, uh, Missus—"

"What kind of unwillingness? He's here, isn't he?" she said, ignoring his attempt at civility.

"I'm sure he wasn't really—" began Kickshaw, but Stacks had the temerity to interrupt him.

"He was caught smoking pot," said Stacks. "I walked right in on him"

"Smoking pot? Well, all the young people are doing that these days, aren't they?" she said. "What, didn't you smoke a cigarette or two in high school?"

"Perhaps, Mrs. Gray, but that's not the kind of thing we allow here."

"And was this the first time he was caught?"

"There have been many times when Robbie's behavior was insubordinate. His best friend was to be expelled for something truly horrible—"

"I'm not interested in his friend's behavior, or your ideas about insubordination. My son has just been through a terrible trauma. A friend has died. You would think an intelligent response would be to cut him some slack. My son is also free spirit, and very intelligent. I suppose you have seen his test scores?"

Here Kickshaw connected. "Yes ma'am, of course we have. He is a model student in, well, in some ways."

"He has always needed more intellectual stimulation than we could provide back in Florida. This school was supposed to challenge him and motivate him."

"That's as may be—" said Stacks.

Kickshaw was listening to this exchange across him and not necessarily understanding, but he probably began to realize I was the editor of the disastrous school yearbook. "But Mrs. Gray—ma'am, I am sorry to inform you that Robbie, your son, and the dead boy, together they have managed to cause a catastrophe with the school yearbook!"

"The school yearbook?" my mother repeated. The way her body language changed, as her arms crossed over her chest and her eyebrow arched, caused me to smile. Meanwhile Stacks rolled his eyes. He probably knew what was coming.

"Yes, the Kickshaw 1981 Yearbook. Young Master Gray was supposed to write glowing stories about the school and his memories of his time here, but instead, he wrote limericks—nasty limericks—you could not imagine the kind of thing he wanted to put in there! And now we have piles and piles of these yearbooks, which are completely unacceptable..." Kickshaw then proceeded to find and open a copy—perhaps he had brought a box in with him, it may have been the subject of his earlier conversation with the Dean, I did not know. But he began there and then, to show my mother the now banned yearbook. "Look at this!" he said. "And this!"

"It looks very modern," my mother said. "Who did all that wonderful collage work?" she said, looking in my direction.

"My friend Christian, mom," I said. "They expelled him, too. Before they killed him."

"What?"

"Your son is making a hideous joke, but not entirely wrong," said Stacks in his oily way. "The boy he mentioned was caught having homosexual relations."

"With *my* son?" she said.

"No, of course not, dear lady," said Kickshaw. "With a tragic case from the Ghetto that we funded to add color to the student body. For diversity's sake. A very strange boy who claimed he was a girl. But the nurse proved this to be a lie. Although we never quite got to the bottom of the whole affair, the two young men involved—"

"This is an all-boy's school," my mother said with finality. "Not a girl in sight. What do you two idiots think would happen in that situation? Of course boys will be boys!"

Yes, my mother had just called the Dean and the school's namesake "idiots." My jaw dropped.

"You two sound like Anita Bryant," she went on.. "If that is how things are run around here, the kind of prejudice we should really only see in the ignorant, then I am not sure what all my ex-husband's money was spent on for Robbie's tuition. But as for this yearbook!" My mother looked at it and flipped through a few pages. "Robbie, did you write these poems?"

"Yes, ma'am," I said.

"All of them?"

"Of course, ma'am. They're only limericks."

"They look like poems to me," she said. "And what is this about Clint Eastwood?"

"We sometimes call the Dean here, Dean Stacks, *Clint.*"

"Hm," she said. "Robbie, that is not very nice."

"No ma'am," I said, lowering my head.

"Not nice. But it is funny." She was laughing now, almost deriding him to his face. "Look at this one about his wife..." she tried to contain herself. "Sorry," she said, looking at Dean Stacks, who was now clearly angry. She snapped the yearbook shut and put it under arm and then turned her attention to the two men.

"I want my son to attend the Graduation Ceremony today. Do you understand?" she said, pointedly, looking at Old Kickshaw. She spoke in a loud voice, perhaps because she perceived Kickshaw was hard of hearing. "I want him to attend," she repeated, pointing with her index finger at his weak chest, until Kickshaw seemed to grasp the solution to the current difficult alumni situation.

"Of course, Madam," he said. "Of course he can attend. We are very sorry to have troubled you. This was all a grave mistake."

Stacks was hardly satisfied with that answer and began to interrupt, but at that moment the Headmaster came into the office and then much of the previous conversations had to be reiterated. My mother was blistering in her criticism. The Headmaster's attitude towards the situation, however, was markedly different from his Dean. He quickly moved to mollify what, for all he knew, was a prospective future Alumni Fund donor.

"Please forgive the inconvenience, Mrs. Gray," the Head-master said, repeating the mistake of Old Kickshaw, but my mother let that slide. She was winning.

We stepped outside the office and I pulled the door closed; the door made a satisfying click. It felt good. Inside, through the glass panes of the door, darkly, I could see Stacks speaking in muffled tones to the Headmaster, as Kickshaw sadly looked on, shaking his head.

I smiled.

***

"Robbie, let's go sit down somewhere. Can we?"

"Sure, Mom. Let's go to the dining hall. We can probably get you some coffee. I think it's still even possible to get breakfast."

"That's good, I did not get much this morning, just a bite at the airport."

We walked over to the dining hall and I could see some coffee being set up for the visiting parents by none other than Mrs. Sauvage.

"Mrs. Sauvage," I said, "Hello, it's Robbie Gray. I have the honor to present my mother."

The old woman had turned around to face me, and then looked at my mother. Her face changed into a warm smile of welcome. I thought she looked like an old, dried apple core. "Very nice to meet you," said the apple core face. "So Robbie made it to graduation after all. To be honest, I didn't think he'd make it."

"Yes," my mother said. "It was probably touch and go."

"A mother always knows....would you like some coffee, dear?"

"Yes please," said my mother. "I'm famished."

"I will arrange to have some toast brought out for you."

"Thank you so much!"

We sat down in the dining hall—I suppose it was still early; there were only a few people milling around—I saw Fish in the corner with his parents—and I enjoyed the fact that the sun was streaming into the hall. We didn't say anything, my mother and I, for a few minutes, as I was enjoying the light and she the coffee.

Finally, she looked over at me and said, "I see you drink coffee now. Is that black?"

"Yes, it started when Christian and I went down to see a concert in LA—it was The Who. God it was great, but Pete Townshend had his arm in a cast. And afterwards, I was driving back and it was late, I almost fell asleep at the wheel."

She looked at me in that way, her way, and then I said, "Well, yes, OK, I actually did fall asleep at the wheel twice, before I finally decided it would be a good idea to pull over. So we went into a Denny's and ordered coffee. I had never liked the taste, you know, but that night it sounded good, and it tasted good, too. It was just cheap restaurant coffee, but it did the trick, and then I could drive."

"And then suddenly you liked it." She seemed very steady and "present," like old Treebeard in the Two Towers when he wanted to discuss current events.

"Yes, exactly, Mom. I love coffee now."

"This Christian, is he graduating today?"

"No Mom. Christian was the boy who died."

"Oh. I'm sorry. Robbie." She sat for a minute and then she said, "Sam and I, we're splitting up. We're getting a divorce."

"What?"

"We're getting a divorce," she repeated.

"But, but—" I couldn't seem to grok it.

"He moved out a few months ago."

"But why?"

"Well, I guess he wasn't happy."

I looked at my mother somewhat in the same manner she had looked at me, when I said I 'almost' fell asleep at the wheel. She smiled. She was a little sheepish about what came out next.

"He found another woman."

"WHAT?"

"Robbie, not so loud," she said, looking around. "He found another woman. Sam has been having some man troubles. He thought I was to blame."

"Man troubles," I said.

"Some troubles in the bedroom."

"Ah, I see. Limp dick syndrome."

"Robbie!" She scolded me. "Please don't say things like that to me. I am your mother."

"OK, Mom. But I know what you mean."

"Yes. Fine. Anyway, he was having problems. I thought it might have to do with the amount of Vodka he was consuming in the evenings; he would conk right out after he got home. Sam is getting older. But he thought it was me. I wasn't exciting enough for him, I guess. Maybe I wouldn't do what he wanted. I'm a very traditional person, Robbie. You know that I guess. So, anyway, he found someone with bigger boobs."

I had never heard my mother say 'boob' before and I was surprised at her. "I see." It almost sounded like she was discussing her sex life.

"I guess he thought that was the problem. I'm an A-cup. He wanted more. He had always complained about that. But about a month later, after he had been with this woman, and they were talking about marriage, she called me. He was having the same problem with her, and she wanted to know what was going on."

I laughed. "Oh sweet revenge. I'll bet that was a good call."

"Now Robbie."

"OK, Mom, I'm sorry."

"Anyway, we're not together anymore."

"But what about the kids?"

"Usually in a divorce, the mother gets custody. But we'll have to see what happens. Maybe the judge will give us joint custody. I don't see how he would, though. Sam left. He's a home wrecker. And he'll be paying alimony and child support to me for a long, long time."

"I see." I sat digesting this.

"Robbie," she said, "I was wondering if you wanted to come home."

I had a visceral response to this. "Mom. You know very well I hate Florida. Kwai-Chang was killed by a snake there, remember?"

"Yes. I know."

"I'm sorry, but I'm not going back to Florida. Not now, not ever."

"I know. But, well, what about this. What about if I moved out here?"

I was incredulous. "You would move to California?"

"I've talked to your dad a few times lately, Robbie. I know you're not going to College. Your dad was outraged."

"Yeah. That was kind of hard. He's not doing that great lately, I don't know how much of his situation you were told—"

"I know quite a bit, actually. Your father and I were married a long time, seven years. And I knew him in high school; he was my first real boyfriend. So he's no great mystery to me. I can read between the lines."

"Hm." I didn't know how to take that. "But did you know—about Larry—"

"That your father says he's gay? Yes, I knew that."

"What, you don't believe it?"

"He's not gay, exactly, he just watched too much gay porn as a boy. He still likes women, too. Your dad, well, he's kind of naughty."

I laughed. "Now you sound like Anita Bryant."

"*Breakfast without Florida Orange Juice is like a day without sunshine*," she said. "I know."

"But Mom," I said. "Why did you two split up? Why did you get divorced, if not because Dad is gay?"

"It's a little embarrassing, Robbie."

"OK," I said. I was disappointed. Perhaps she could see that, because she said, "The truth is, Robbie, your dad and I just didn't like each other very much. We got married so young, and then I was pregnant with you. That was an accident."

"WHAT?"

"These things happen, Robbie. We didn't know much. We did what we were supposed to do in those days, which was get married if there was a child coming. But the truth was, we had very little in common. You dad is a bit of a weirdo."

"Hey!" I said.

"I know. But he's not my type. I am pretty straight-laced, as you know. I go to church. I needed someone more responsible, more normal. So we just weren't right for each other. We stayed together for your sake for a long time, longer than some people would have, but eventually I met Sam. And Sam took me away to Florida, which was pretty great, at least in the beginning."

I was not sure if this explanation really satisfied me, but I didn't want to push my luck. "Thanks for explaining, Mom."

"Anyway, Robbie, your father says you want to go to India. He's not going to give you any more money I don't think, if you do that. He's a rich man, by the look of things. You might want to consider that. He said he gave you a car, and some money."

"He did. And then he changed the locks on his place."

"He mentioned that. But if you went and explained, talked to him, and gave him a better plan, maybe things would change."

"I know. But I don't need him or his money. I'll work. I can save money. I know how to economize. Like in *Siddhartha*, he says, 'I can think, I can fast, I can wait!'"

She looked at me. "Robbie, I'm glad you had time with your dad. I'm glad you came here. But I need you. I'm the one who needs you now. I really do. I have the kids, and I have to figure out how to work, at least eventually."

"But Mom!"

She continued to look at me and I caved pretty quickly. This was my mother, after all. "OK, fine." I said.

"We can live together here in California; it will be like a new start."

"But where in California? Here in Santa Barbara?"

"If you want."

"You mean," I said cautiously, "you'd let me pick where we live?"

"Sure," she said. "Where do you want to live, son?" She looked at her coffee cup, because the toast had come. "Think about it while I get more coffee." She got up and walked back to the kitchen.

My imagination stretched out. 'Holy hell!' I thought. She seemed to be serious. A whole world was out there. My mother was blowing my mind one minute at a time. Finally she returned and I felt timid and shy, suddenly.

"So have you thought about it?" she said.

"Well, could we live in San Francisco?"

"Sure."

I just gawked at her. "What about Berkeley?"

"Sure. I've never been to Berkeley. You think that's a good place? Maybe thinking about the University? Is that it?"

"Oh, Mom."

"Eventually, I mean. Eventually."

"Yeah. Eventually." Actually I was thinking about Martin Quinn. "This cool teacher here, he went there...and maybe that's where I would want to go, if I had to really go to University. But I need time. Time to do what matters to me for a while."

"OK, son. That's fine. So we'll spend some time together here in California, in Berkeley, before you go off into the unknown parts of India. Or University. Or whatever you want to do. We'll be a family, of sorts."

"Sure, Mom! Wow! This is going to be great!" I was thinking about Buddhism, and maybe Ram would be at the Graduation—I missed Ram a lot—and maybe my Mom would like to meet Isabella, despite the fact that she dumped me for Jonah. Yes, I had confirmed as much. Jonah was playing dumb, but I was pretty sure Isabella would be at the graduation ceremony. I smiled thinking how I would scare the hell out of both of them by giving Isabella a big kiss and introducing my mother to her. 'Ah, life!' I thought. I couldn't wait to get to San Francisco.

"You know, Mom, even the 6th Patriarch, before he went off to find his master, made arrangements for the maintenance of his mother. And that was how Zen Buddhism was born."

"I don't know what that means, but I'll take it," she said.

END

The Chicken's Head

David R. Smith is an American expat. He currently lives somewhere in the mysterious bushland continent of Australia. He is happily married and has four adult children.

His pen names include *David Apricot* and *Mia Sandalwood*. He has four previous novels and a number of translations.

There is a website:

https://www.metamadbooks.com/

Inquiries to the author may be directed to:

metamadbooks@gmail.com